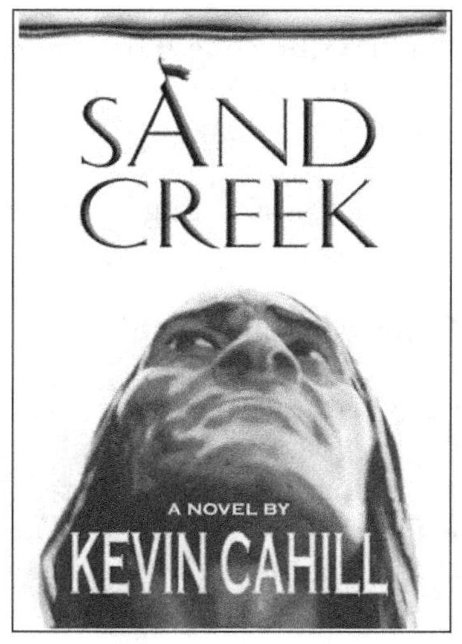

"Brilliantly written and thoroughly researched historical detail comes to life with novelistic flair in Kevin Cahill's Sand Creek. Informative without being boring or dry, this novel is remarkably unbiased in its presenting of the story of the Sand Creek Massacre, revealing in detail how fear, misunderstanding, and a few violent men on both sides led to so many lives being lost."

- Colorado Country Life Magazine

1864 . . .

The Civil War had swallowed a nation whole in a struggle over power and providence, splitting the country's heart, and slaughtering the white sons of America's founding fathers.

But on the plains of Bleeding Kansas, America's true natives are embroiled in a life or death struggle, indifferent to the political collision between blue and gray. The inevitable war between ancient native culture and Anglican progress in the New World is about to explode on the dark and frigid banks of a Colorado river that the Cheyennes call *Ponoeohe.*

Kevin Cahill dramatically assembles the labyrinth of power, politics and controversy that surrounded one of the most notorious events in the history of the American West. His remarkably insightful resurrection of the true-life Indians, soldiers and settlers involved in the Sand Creek Massacre provides a poignant look at the monumental struggle for life on the Plains.

WHAT AMAZON.COM REVIEWERS ARE SAYING:

"I applaud Mr. Cahill for his research and writing about the events that lead up to the Sand Creek Massacre. This book should be a required reading on College campuses everywhere."

"Kevin Cahill certainly catches the mood in this amazing historical novel."

"This book will hold your attention from beginning to end."

"This rendition brings it all together in a very thoroughly researched way. It also quotes many of the original documents (I've checked their accuracy) in between chapters of fictionalized dialogue. This book was the only one that cleared a lot of the confusion for me over what happened in the months preceding and the original day."

"Although Sand Creek is a dramatic interpretation, Cahill's novel takes readers to this sad chapter in America's history with a strong effort to remain true to the historical record. Some events are condensed or combined with fictional augmentation to enhance the novel's plot, but the essence of this remarkable true story remains solidly intact."

"SAND CREEK spends a relatively small and mercifully tasteful amount of time on the Sand Creek carnage itself, focusing rather on why this despicable event ever occurred in the first place, and what happened to the soldiers and Indians in its bloody wake."

"For those interested in the historical significance of the massacre, SAND CREEK provides a lively and accurate dramatic portrayal. If you simply want to read a ripping wild-west saga about those tragic days on the Colorado prairie, this book also adequately fits the bill."

"Cahill's novel paints in broader strokes, illustrating the complexity of two vastly diverse cultures that collided during an acrimonious and wildly uncivilized period in the American West."

SAND CREEK is available at Amazon.com and other online stores.
Available in paperback, hardback, Kindle and Audible.

Novels by Kevin Cahill

Sand Creek

Letters to a Rose

The Last Café

Knights of Harvest

Simon Sez

Available in paperback, hardback,Kindle, and Audible formats at Amazon.com

More information at
www.kclonewolf.com

Author contact
mailto: admin@kclonewolf.com

Letters to a Rose

KEVIN CAHILL

LoneWolf

ISBN-13: 978-0-9969544-9-5
This second edition published by KC LoneWolf,
Colorado Springs, CO USA, 12.20.2020
admin@kclonewolf.com

Paperback first edition published by Author House
Bloomington, Indiana USA 03.11.05
ISBN-13: 978-14208-3111-5
Library of Congress Control Number: 2-0059-0232-0

My sincere thanks to James Taylor and David Crosby for permission to include lyrics from the following:

For more information, visit www.kclonewolf.com
Author contact information:admin@KClonewolf.com

A special thank you to Vance Huddleston for upon numerous occasions taking me to the jungle and back without ever having to leave the safety of the Bear.

A second thank you to all who bravely served in Southeast Asia. Gratitude from your nation is in short supply, but there are many of our generation who will never forget your sacrifice and your dedication to honor and duty.

For my friend Ruthie
and all our fellow travelers

1

Metamorphosis

1962

May 8, 1962

Dear Diary,

And the final "Dear Diary" it shall be, Diary, for today I have become a man. Today I am sixteen, and as I depart my childhood, you, Diary, must change with me. "Diary" is too frivolous - too sissy. When a writer matures, so must his work. I have no alternative but to rename you.

And so, from this important milestone, I shall no longer write a daily message to my Diary, but will pen an entry into my "Journal." Indeed, Journal, it is a special day for us. Good-bye childhood. Good-bye trucks and sandboxes. Good-bye snakes and grimy jeans. Good-bye frogs and ponds. Farewell childhood.

Hello acne...

Let the celebration begin!

For the occasion, I obtained at no small risk of life and limb a six-pack of Hamm's - the beer from sky blue waters - a pack of Chesterfields, and one shot of Jack Daniels whiskey, carefully siphoned from Dad's stock. How, you may ask, did I manage to pull this off? It is due in part to the assistance of the only boy I know at school who has reached the age of eighteen without turning into a horse's patoot.

He is Michael Golightly, the strangest human being at school. More on him in a moment.

Ah, this beer, Journal. At first taste I admit a rather interesting reaction. To be perfectly honest, my bunger tightened. My first thought is how in the world has this vile-tasting swill become common man's most honored beverage? It dominates hours of social interaction, quenches the thirst of sports heroes, and lines the pockets of innkeepers the world round. As I drink a second and a third time, I suspect that beer becomes an acquired taste. In fact, the very effect of the alcohol cleverly disguised within seems to deaden the rancid tang. And numbing the taste buds is but one effect this beer has. My tongue is beginning to slumber.

I know this to be true, for when I just moments ago felt a sudden urge to rush to the bathroom, I quickly stood and became dizzy, and I accidentally bumped into a wall. When

Mother called from upstairs to question the racket, my lazy tongue said: "No problem, I thlipped." How odd to hear a properly formed word in the brain squirt out like that.

More important facts lie ahead, Journal, as I must report the events of this day. I shall save the best for later and first tell of the extraordinary trouble encountered while trying to prepare this party for Me. The ordeal of smuggling beer and cigarettes into my den borders on an Ian Fleming novel and deserves your attention. Mother has mandated many house rules, some equitable, some not so, but those with which I cannot argue include the prohibition of liquor and cigarettes for the minor members of the family. Of course, Dad is exempted from this rule, and if I were to wager (which is another of Mother's house sins), my money would be on Dad allowing this one-time indulgence; but when it comes to the household canons, Dad is truly a man without a country. Although he enforces them, he does not establish laws in this house.

It is this fact, Journal, that puts my life at great risk, and I would rather imagine if I am detected with my contraband at any point in this evening, Mother may snuff out my life like the burning stubble of the Chesterfield I smoke. You may ask why I chose to become a man in the confinement of my writing room rather than out in the world where a man is entitled to stake claim of his domain.

Two simple reasons: Tonight is a school night, and I do not have a driver's license.

So, I sit with you, Journal, celebrating my sixteenth, and bidding farewell to childhood alone. To date, the family has always respected my privacy here in the basement den. I pray the walls remain closed. And, as I reflect upon the clandestine operation that created this small but important journey from cursed puberty, I must declare my appreciation to the aforementioned Mike Golightly, without whose assistance I would never have been able to buy cigarettes and beer for this party.

And now, the smuggling incident:

I gave Mike five dollars to wait for me after school outside Miller's Grocery Store. It was adequate pay for a simple task; however, Mike demanded another five for a "Hazardous Duty Bonus."

"Had to fake like I was sick," he said in his grunting, sandpaper voice, "so's I could get outta my violin lesson."

He had to lie to his overweight mother, Journal, thus risking her wrath if she found out he was not, in fact, going to the dime store for Pepto-Bismol. If not for the lateness of hour and the bleak prospect of reaching manhood without cigarettes and beer, I might have questioned Mike's suspect ability to play the violin, for it is common knowledge Mike is supremely challenged by such tasks as correctly spelling his name. However, I could ill-afford losing my partner in crime at that point.

I suppose I might have asked Uncle Vern for this favor, but there required a guarantee of success, and although Vern is not of the same parental notions as Mother and Dad, I could not take any chances. Consequently, I agreed to Mike's demand and was off to the liquor store with this unlikely human.

A bit of background: Mike, although considered to be normal enough to attend a public school, is a most unusual fellow. His huge forehead enters the room before the rest of him. It dramatically slopes to a nose that resembles a Washington apple. Mike's eyes are very close together, and he wears a pair of thick horned-rim glasses. When wearing these binoculars, Mike looks Japanese. Another distinction is Mike's crooked chin, which looks as if Vern Gagne put the sleeper hold on him when he was very young. And, after Mike talks for any length of time, there appear white globs of spittle at each corner of his mouth. His breath reminds me of bad cheese, and there is an unmistakable odor of sweat on and around him, especially when he wears his woolen sweater on a summer day (go figure). Mike's voice reminds me of fingernails scratching across a blackboard, and when he laughs, I think of the sound one's foot makes when it is pulled from deep mud: Sluyuck, yuck yuck.

This, Journal, was my partner in crime. Is there any wonder why I had misgivings about success?

We forged across Colfax Avenue and down two blocks to 'Land of Liquor,' an establishment rumored to sell beer to people under the legal drinking age of twenty-one. For insurance, I chose Mike to assist me because, although he is only eighteen, he looks forty-six. And, all things being equal, we might have pulled off our folly if it had not been for a police officer who, when taking note of Mike entering the liquor store, burst into Land of Liquor with his gun drawn. He ordered Mike to hit the deck and put his hands over his head. Mike, not a candidate for the GE College Bowl, got the orders confused and hit the deck with his head. He sustained a bloody nose and a deep bruise on his right cheek.

Meanwhile, I awaited outside, peering in the window and hoping Mike would not betray my involvement. The police officer had mistaken Mike for a wanted liquor store robber, but realized the moment Mike started bleeding that this wasn't his man. Embarrassed at his faux pas, the officer bid a hasty apology and bolted before checking any identification at all. Moments later, Mike Golightly emerged from Land of Liquor with my Hamm's and Chesterfields neatly packed in a brown paper bag and a tissue stuffed in his nose.

"I'm sorry you had to go through that," I said to Mike.

"Go through what?"

I attempted no explanation. Telling Mike to keep the change, I quickly left Land of Liquor and the bloody-nosed Mike Golightly. I crumpled the bag under my arm and began my long journey home. Oh, what paranoia! It seemed as if the whole neighborhood was watching me as I crept the back roads and alleys like a bandit on the lam with my treasure tucked next to my pounding heart. Journal, in all of my fifteen years, never, never once have I taken these back roads and encountered a police car. But on this day, I counted three! When I finally caught sight of home, I felt much older than sixteen.

However, I was not yet out of the woods.

I now faced several obstacles between me and the downstairs den. I decided to carefully plan every step. The primary objective was to slip in without arousing suspicion. This would not be easy, for the house is always brimming with life at the dinner hour. I decided my best chance would be entry through the kitchen where I would find Mother waist-deep in pots and pans. My route would take me down the back hallway, past Lyla's room, Mary's room, and into my bedroom where I could stop and collect my bearings. Once there, I would plan the final assault to the back stairway, which would lead me to the promised land. It was a logical plan, and a darned good one at that. Time was on my side since Dad would still be out driving his bus. Mother wouldn't notice a smuggled elephant if it was not your wish for her to see it. Lyla holes up in her room every afternoon and sees nothing that isn't reflected in her bureau mirror. Mary sees only the television she incessantly watches, and baby Jonathan, although he sees everything, has not yet learned to talk.

Alas, all details of a plan, if one expects success, should be practiced before any attempt at execution. Who knows? Dad might have come home early and could be lurking about; perhaps Lyla's mirror was broken; maybe Mary was tired of TV for the day.

I hid the beer and cigarettes under a stout evergreen in the yard and entered the house to check things out. Inside, all was secure. Mother barely saw me through the steam rising from her pots. Lyla was brushing her hair, and Mary was preoccupied with Howdy Doody. Dad was gone, and Baby Jonathan, saints be praised, was snoozing face-first in his stewed peas. Who could have asked for a better situation? No one even noticed me walking back outside.

Arriving at the evergreen, however, I was dismayed to find Bob, our neighbor's 125-pound Doberman Pinscher, with jaws firmly clutched around my brown bag. Bob is the neighborhood beast. When our eyes met, he growled through the bag and dared me to take my property from him. I have never liked Bob and have never hidden my distaste for him, and now I was certain he was about to avenge all the years I tossed stones at him. Not that I don't care for dogs, Journal. On the contrary, I loved our old Cocker Spaniel, Edsel, and I shed many tears when he went to sleep one night and never woke up. In fact, I like all animals with the exception of Bob The Dog.

Bob leaves potty on our lawn. He piddles on any upright structure. Bob barks at three a.m.; he chases other dogs, eats cats and squirrels, bites mailmen, and generally gets sadistic pleasure from harassing all living things. I have resorted to climbing a tree to escape Bob as many as a dozen times in my life. Now it appeared I would not only be up a tree again, but I would lose my beer and cigarettes as well.

We faced off, eye-to-eye, Bob still clutching my bag and bearing his yellow teeth. His growl buzzed through the wet, brown paper. I first tried diplomacy. "Hi, Bob," I said.

Bob's eyes widened. I know he was disarmed by my charm because I've never had a civil word for him. He was clearly confused, and so, I continued this approach.

"Nice Bob," I said. "How ya doing, big fella?" I slowly reached with my hand clenched in a fist so I would not expose any tasty little fingers. The last things I wanted them to be were Bob's party hors d'oeuvres. As I approached, Bob growled and let out a blood-boiling bark that dropped like an ice cube down my spine. When he barked, the bag fell from his mouth, and we now stood, frozen, staring at the bag on the ground and awaiting the other to make a move for it.

"Nice Bobby," I said, slowly reaching for the bag and mindful of those yellow teeth. When I touched the bag, Bob put his right paw on it and blankly stared at me. I moved my hand back, and Bob moved his paw back. We did this three times. I then looked across the street and said, "Look, Bob, a big, juicy cat!"

No sale.

Bob refused to budge. After another tense moment of confrontation, Bob sniffed the bag, and it was only at that moment I realized Bob had not a clue what was in it. He was simply enjoying his moment in the sun and could not care less about the contents of the bag. He dug his wet nose inside it and snuffed about. He picked it up and shook it to and fro. The bag tore, and a dozen or more Chesterfields scattered across the lawn. I grew angry at Bob's disrespect and was about to muster the courage to fight this beast when he suddenly lost interest. If the bag had contained twenty or thirty pounds of raw human flesh, Bob would have been long gone with it, but Bob apparently had no interest in cigarettes and beer.

He simply gave me a bad look and walked away.

I was relieved, but suddenly chilled with paranoia. Someone might have watched this showdown! I hastily gathered the cigarettes and plugged them into my pockets after wiping Bob's spit off them. I wrapped the beer in what was left of the wet bag and stashed it under my arm. Miraculously, I wasn't seen, and my presence here with one beer downed and a Chesterfield suavely hanging from my lips is evidence of my success at contraband smuggling.

I do, however, wish to note one warning for future reference: when one opens a can of beer that has been shaken in the jaws of a 125-pound Doberman Pinscher, it is wise to turn the can away from the face.

This beer is slowly becoming all it was cracked up to be. Previously I mentioned my initial distaste, but the flavor has improved now that my taste buds are entirely numb. With numb buds, I'm understanding what all the to-do is about.

I'm a man, that's why.

Men swill beer and guzzle Scotch. We spit in the street. We don't have time for milk. We grunt and scratch our crotches. Gosh, I'm giggling. I'm a man. Men are king; we take our women and drag them to our caves; and we win the bacon...and the eggs and ham and eggs.

I feel odd.

Happy birthday to Me, happy birthday to Me, happy birthday, dear Meeeeee. Happy birthdayyyyy. Tooooooooo Meeeeeeeeeee!

I'm all alone. It's my birthday. Oh, to share it with someone special. Okay, Mother did serve my favorite meal, followed by a chocolate cake with sixteen candles. From Mother, I got a cool pair of blue jeans and the great news that

I can get a driver's license. Lyla gave me a forty-five of "If I Had a Hammer," and Mary gave me a Red Cross button.

But, nobody gave me what I want most. I wish I had a girlfriend.

Today, I saw the most extraordinary girl at school. She's who I want for my birthday. That's the most important part of today's entry, Journal. Someday when I'm a famous writer, there will be scholarly gentlemen who will peruse my journals to see what it was that made me tick. I know my chance confrontation with Bob The Dog won't expose a pivotal moment in my literary life, but I have a feeling my first perception of this beautiful girl will be most important when literature students read about me.

To describe what is in my heart is impossible because I have encountered a most unusual awakening in my soul. Today, a girl crossed my path, and at that moment I felt a grand calling inside that was both white-hot and icy cold. My heart raced in my chest, and to be a might explicit, my loins felt a tingle unlike anything I have ever felt.

God, she was cool!

How Hemingway could capture moments like these, but I need to do this in my own words. It was nearing the end of the day when I joined my pals, Marc and Steven, in the lobby to partake in our daily arm slugfest and 'Dozens' game, otherwise known as 'Your Mother Insult Festival.'

To wit:

"It's time for The Dozens
well, The Dozens is a place
where it's hard to kiss your mother
when she's sitting on my face..."

Although I stayed up practically all night thinking up that one, Steven hit me in the arm so hard that I still have a numbness in my fingers.

It was during this moment of Great Literature when my eyes fell upon Her. How, during this entire first year of high school, I never managed to see her until today is beyond comprehension, but there she sat on a bench with her friends, laughing, talking - glowing. She stood out in the crowd with maturity and grace unlike any girl I've seen. As the afternoon sun gently peeked through the window behind her, I swear there was a golden halo, evanescent, dancing around her head like a light-footed angel. Her hair, caramel brown with a touch of gold, fell over her soft shoulders, and even at the safe distance from where I secretly watched, I saw gentleness in her pretty eyes that drove me mad:

"She walks in beauty, like the night
Of cloudless climes and starry skies;
And all that's best of dark and bright
Meet in her aspect and her eyes..."

God, how much in love Lord Byron must have been to write that. I've often read Byron and wondered how a man could be so moved by the countenance of but another human being, but now I read those words and curse for not having written them myself. Perhaps, if Byron notices, he won't care if I use them. I'll respect his copyright.

Happy brrrrthdyyy. Toooooooo. Meeeeeeeeee.

May 9, 1962

God, am I sick.

I'll be brief, Journal. This was the longest day of my life. I am mortified, and God, am I in trouble. I'm drained, ill, and very pukey. I feel like I ate six pounds of molasses and sauerkraut. My bulging head feels like it's in the Twilight Zone.

I will never drink alcohol again, Journal. God, I swear if you'll just let me live through the night, I'll never do it again - even if it means giving up my newfound manhood. What happened to me last night I would not wish upon Bob The Dog. I only wish I had let him take my beer and cigarettes when I had the chance.

Unfortunately, the events of last evening are, and shall forever remain, a cloudy memory. I can only report to you what was reported to me by Dad, who is the only person in the family speaking to me. Jonathan gives me an occasional "goo," but even he's a bit testy. Mother, the leader of Troop Hysteria, has declared my existence null and void. She's branded me a modern-day Hester. She claims she is going to write to several military schools and look into my eligibility for immediate enrollment.

It is painfully evident, although I'm relying upon Dad's report and my aching head, that I imbibed a little too much last night - so much that I showered with my clothes on. At first appearance, this might have easily been explained by one of sober head. I had no sober head.

"I didn't want to catch cold," I might have said, or some other quick-draw solvent. However, being short on thought and long on drunkenness, I was helpless. In the shower, I sang: "Maria, I just met a girl named Maria..."

All of this might have been forgivable if it hadn't been for the fact that Lyla was in the shower when I came in.

Dad tells me I tried to reassure Lyla that siblings often bathe together. Perhaps at age sixteen and eighteen is a bit of a stretch, but...

Lyla was not amused. I do recall her screaming, "I'll kill him!" And I also recall that she tried.

I must admit Lyla's body has changed quite a bit from what I remember of childhood baths together, although her breasts haven't changed much. Now, it is during this shower incident that I do remember some things. I recall trying to salve Lyla's wounded pride as Dad dragged me out. "Don't worry," I said, "what I did see didn't amount to much..."

Although on paper these words seem innocent enough, apparently somewhere in my inflection did she misinterpret my meaning. She's lobbying for me to be shot through the head at close range, but I think Dad is going to go to bat for me. He guided me to my room where I ralphed on my new blue jeans. I believe he felt pity - somehow, the ill draw sympathy - and Dad, too, has been there more times than I can count. In fact, he was pretty blotto himself at the time.

"It's one of those things," Dad said to Mom this morning.

"The boy's going to have his first drunk sooner or later. Mine was at sixteen, too. Better he does it here than out in the streets somewhere."

Mother didn't buy it. Privately, she scolded me until my ears were raw. "You aren't going to be like your father," she said. "I forbid it." She has a way of saying "forbid" that sounds like she's crushing stones with her teeth.

Nevertheless, I'm doomed. My punishment is: an indefinite suspension from taking my driver's license test; the assignment of all Lyla's household chores in addition to mine for the next month; and I am grounded until the year 1987.

I'm sure Dad will eventually lessen the sentence once Mother has had some time to think about the consequences of having me around the house until I'm forty-one, but I seriously wonder if the damage done to poor Lyla's psyche is reparable. Only time will tell, I suppose.

Manhood isn't as easy as I thought it would be.

Need to go, Journal; must vomit…

May 10, 1962

Such a sense of loss.

I'm depressed over my birthday. It was so long coming - so greatly anticipated; and now it's over. What a letdown. At least I recovered from my first bout of what Dad calls 'The Jack Daniels Flu.'

Ah, but to remember, Journal. The pretty girl at school, Mike Golightly lying spread-eagle on the floor, Bob The Dog spitting on my Chesterfields, and Lyla's ittybitty breasts. These are the things of which legends are made. If only the memory wasn't so hazy.

A thought: On the subject of breasts, what is it that so possesses a woman to wish for large ones? I'm the first to admit a fascination with large hooters, but it certainly isn't a prerequisite of femininity. I don't worry about such perversions as an attraction to my sister, but I do remember a tingle for which I cannot account upon the perception of Lyla's naked body. Small breasts are beautiful; so are medium breasts. Poky breasts are just as exciting as big, spready breasts. Playboy magazine doesn't discriminate.

But, whenever I overhear girls speaking about their breasts (it's tricky, but I manage), they never seem satisfied with what they have. They don't realize it isn't so important the size of the wave, but the motion of the ocean.

As I said previously, it was just a thought.

Back to Lyla's breasts: Hers are not ugly just because they are small. I must say I've seen fat boys in the locker room with bigger breasts than Lyla's. Of course, I would never tell her that. In fact, I'm overwhelmed with guilt over the shower incident.

Odd...

I can remember Lyla and me bathing together when we were little. I recall splish-splashing in the tub, with Mother and her movie camera in hand, and Dad with his sleeves rolled up, laughing and doing with us what seems so perfectly natural. Mother and Dad never covered their bodies until we started getting older. We seem to cover up more with each passing year; covering up what should be considered perfectly natural. Here I sit, embarrassed to have seen my own sister's natural, and very beautiful body.

What a stupid world.

May 11, 1962

It's an unbelievable day! It has happened again, Journal! My eyes have fallen on Her again, and when they did, my heart leaped with joy! God, what is it about this girl that makes me feel like this? Although the last few days have been trying in recovery from my first bout with manhood, my mind has been entirely upon Her, and now, I saw Her again! Such eyes I have never seen, and her smile lights up the room. And, the smell! That gentle fragrance of her hair pierces my mind like the sparkle of a diamond.

From the top, Journal: I must gather myself. I have only fourteen days before the end of school to find out who is this incredible girl; and then to meet and marry her.

But what, please, God, no, if she is a graduating senior? What if she is an older girl who will be off into life without the man who would cherish her toes for eternity? Who is this stunning creature? Why do I feel my stomach turn into knots at the mere thought of her beautiful eyes and her lovely brown hair?

And why, Journal, am I asking you?

I must get a grip on myself.

It was in the school gymnasium where I saw her. She sat directly in front of me, almost within my reach. I need a plan. I curse the fates for not letting me see her earlier this year - not just scant days before the long summer vacation. Surely she is a senior. That is why I haven't seen her. Senior girls hate sophomore boys. We're "cute," but not of eligible dating stock - not even for the ugly senior girls. It is a major setback for a senior girl to even be approached by a sophomore boy.

But, I'm a man now. I'll have a driver's license just as soon as Dad convinces Mother to commute my 25-year sentence. I'm sixteen, and I have a hint of a moustache. I could be good enough for her if she would just wait until I outgrow showering with my sister and ralphing on my jeans.

God, I'm doomed!

But, Journal, I detected a smile.

I must recall every bit of information. We walked into the gym for some sort of school assembly, its subject I don't recall since my brain went blank when I saw Her. At first glance, I forgot everything, including the step over which I tripped and fell to the appreciative applause of the crowd. Steven Joel and Marc Komac, my best friends, were with me. When we sat, I prayed she might come near, and behold, she did! She sat directly in front of me, but first gave me the slightest hint of a smile before turning to sit. I felt in my heart a warm rain like the soothing feeling of a nice hot shower trickling over me.

During the course of the assembly, I took notice of a rather homely girl sitting next to Her who appeared to be a good friend. I remember this girl from one of my fall classes. Perhaps she holds the key to the mystery of Her. If I play my cards right, I might find the homely girl and inquire as to whom her incredible friend is.

Her hair, Journal, flowing down her slim back, had that halo again, and the slightest hint of her most compelling perfume wafted up and made me drunk, not like on my birthday, but drunk with infatuation. I can smell it even now as if it were pouring over me. I believe it is a smell I will remember all of my life. One time, she leaned back and accidentally brushed against my knee, launching an avalanche of icicles down my back. It was all I could do to keep from reaching out and touching Her shoulder.

That would have been my literal death!

I've shared my secret with Marc and Steven, and they were not unaware of my situation at that moment. My ribs are sore from the nudges they gave me. To bolster my standing with Her, Steven aloud said: "Are you going to take Senior Calculus next year since you're so far ahead of everybody else?"

"Yes," I said, not having any idea of what Senior Calculus is.

I'm not sure she overheard us, but I appreciate Steven's loyalty.

Wait!

That's it! Senior Calculus! Steven mentioned it because that was the reason for the school assembly! It was a registration assembly for next year's classes!

Journal, she would not have been at the assembly if she is graduating this spring!

There is a God!

She'll be returning next year, and what's better, I still have time before summer vacation to meet her! What a prospect! Hot summer days followed by cool Colorado summer evenings, just Her and Me under the summer moon. Swimming, horseback riding (if only I had a horse), boating (if only I had a boat), dancing (if only I could dance), moonlight drives (damn, no license)...

And yet, what a summer this could be!

Another plan: I shall find her tomorrow; I promise. If it takes every fiber of my body, every ounce of my intellect, I shall somehow find a way into Her heart. First, I'll seek out the ugly friend to find out Her name. Tomorrow, Journal, I vow to find Her. I'm on a mission. I'm on a quest.

Oh, Christ! I'm doomed!

Tomorrow is Saturday!

There is no God!

May 12, 1962

Didn't sleep a wink last night. I tossed and turned, fantasizing my play for Her, practicing speeches and declarations, and generally schmoozing at the thought of this incredible girl. I haven't eaten all day. I'm not hungry. Mother suspects I'm drunk again. She should direct her suspicion toward Dad, for he's happily drunk in the family room and watching television with Uncle Vern, who's smashed, too.

Today, Lyla uttered the first words she has spoken to me since our shower the other night. In fact, I confessed to her why I am so gloomy today, and she offered me some sound advice on finding out whom this girl is.

I wanted to apologize to Lyla for getting drunk and seeing her naked, but the words didn't come. Because of the tension created by Dad on weekends, she must understand what booze does to one's inhibitions. I think we'll be friends again. Her graduation is next week, and next fall she will leave for Harvard.

Imagine, Harvard.

I don't recall the last time Lyla ever received anything less than an 'A' in school, and now she has a scholarship to Harvard. She plans to study law. Someday, when she sits on the Supreme Court, I'll be able to say: "I used to shower with Justice Hill. Big brains, little breasts."

God, I hate Saturdays. Dad begins drinking the moment he gets out of bed. It's a two-day-long binge every weekend. He's impossible when drunk. It comes over him like a veil of darkness, and I can instantly tell when he crosses the line by the strange, vacant look that marks the passage of his senses. With beers one through five, he is a happy man. After beers six and seven, the eyes glaze. From beer eight and on, hold onto your hat because Dad's over the edge. If shots of whiskey are intermingled, the moment may come at any time. He grows abusive and ill-tempered.

I envy Lyla. Soon, she'll love Saturdays.

Look at the clock, Journal. Five twenty-two.

Who is that girl? What is her name? For more than an hour this afternoon I pretended she was downstairs here with me. It was glorious. We talked about ourselves, our dreams, our love. I told her of my dream to be a playwright, and I pretended she was going to study art in Paris. We planned a rendezvous on the bank of the Seine where we would live forever on love, she with her brush, and I with my pen. We laid around and ate a lot of grapes, too. I pretended my pillow was she, and I kissed it. It only produced a mouthful of lint. Kissing pillows is fine for a boy, but not for a man. I need real lips. I need Her lips, pink and moist.

Five twenty-nine. I'm not going to survive until Monday.

May 13, 1962

Everything remains the same. Never a change. I don't recall when I have been so depressed. I hate Saturdays, and Sundays are worse. Dad is slowing. He's nodding off on the sofa now that two o'clock has come and gone. He'll be in bed around five as Sunday dinner, as always, proceeds without him. By tomorrow around nine or ten he'll be transformed back into a human being again. One thing I do admire is his consistency. How can a relatively normal man, dedicated to family and work, turn into such a cruel, inhuman sot? Is his life truly that shallow?

Dad grew up on the dust-swept plains of northern Colorado, one of two sons of a railroad man. I recall the endless tales of the depression years when beans were daily fare, and ice cream a once-a-year delicacy - usually on the 4th of July. Gramps, who died in 1952, is but an enigmatic shadow in my memory. I remember a big man with a hardy laugh who would thrill Lyla and me with stories of the big trains and the fierce northern Colorado winters when the winds liked to rip a man's skin from his face. Gramps died of a heart attack, or so I'm told, but I hold an uneasy suspicion there might have been more to blame for his relatively youthful death. He was only fifty-seven.

Dad's binges strike an uneasy chord in my mind when I remember Gramps. There is something familiar about his blackened glaze, the sour smell of whiskey, the strange behavior, and the loud, chesty explosions of temper when Mother or Dad would suddenly pull me away from Gramps.

Dad is a good man. He'd die for any one of us, but inside of him is an inherent weakness that hangs over this family like a gray shroud. I often fear when I look into his black eyes that I am looking into a mirror.

Links in a chain, that is family.

Could it be I'm simply the continuance of the dogma that man is here to survive, pad his cave, perpetuate his flesh, and pass at the end of the cycle without so much as a whimper of declaration that he was here? Do we all enter and exit through the same door?

I'm depressed, Journal.

What is that girl's name?

The spring sunshine outdoors ushers in a cold wind today. The wind reminds me that winter is not yet finished with her rage. It is the strange habit of nature to grow ambivalent during the season's change. Tomorrow, Journal. Tomorrow, I'll learn Her secret. There is such a vast emptiness inside that can only be filled with such knowledge. I smell her hair in my mind, and I feel her warmth in my heart. How can such a warm, wonderful feeling at the same time feel so cold?

May 14, 1962

The deed is done, Journal. At last. For the first time, I shall write Her name: Marie Rose Robbins.

But, you might suspect from my tempered tone, the victory is hollow. Life has thrown a blow that would deck Floyd Patterson. As if it isn't enough that my entry into manhood has been wreaked with drunken havoc and utter hormonal disarray, I now spend an entire day in search of a quest that chose to spit upon me when I found it. Her name, colored with love and beauty, is an empty bounty. It is a name, and nothing more.

God, if You're home, answer me this: Why? Why me?

Here it is, Journal, for what little good it has done me: My plan, under sound advice from Lyla, was to find Her with the bold intent of a direct introduction, a confession of my interest, and a suggestion we might sit together at lunch to become better acquainted. It seemed simple enough; an honest declaration. The worst thing that could happen was rejection and my subsequent suicide - the best, I'd get a chance reserve a spot next to this girl all summer. I was resolved - all, or none.

Instead, I get all of none.

Why, Lord? Why me?

And so I proceeded, honesty my hallmark. Lyla said most girls rarely encounter an honest boy at school and they are smitten by the shy element like Me. We of the shadows rarely step forward, but rather, we stew in the corners of our recessive box, never to come out in any public display of interest in the opposite sex. This leaves girls the prey of the bolder athletic type; those Neanderthals, Lyla said, of the jock itch set who conclude the best approach to romance a bottle of Port Wine in hand, and a Trojan rubber in pocket.

Lyla's been around, boy.

Thanks to her advice, I had my plan - a direct play for Marie Rose Robbins' attention by exuding my charm, wit and most importantly, honesty. I would best display my genuine intentions and not imply I regard her as a leg of lamb. This I planned for the better part of five hours, including lunch period, as I searched halls, classrooms, nooks and crannies in search of this, my Holy Grail. During my quest, I received two admonitions for tardiness to classes, a detention for being caught glancing in a girls rest room, a sprained ankle from running to one of the classes where I received the tardiness admonition, and a bloody nose inflicted by one of the girls at whom I glanced in the girls rest room.

Mortification was my reward for searching for the most beautiful girl I have ever seen.

The day mercilessly slipped by with no sight of Her. Panic iced my veins, for I promised myself, Journal, to find and meet Her. Frigid desperation chilled me as I sat in my sixth period study hall, the clock relentlessly ticking like a bomb about to explode in my lap. Pondering my misfortune, I sat, watching two football players stuffing a member of the Glee Club in the trash dumpster, one of the more productive activities that occur during study hall.

Then, I felt like a convict in the electric chair (I think it was James Cagney), awaiting instant death, but instead seeing the Governor (I think it was Gregory Peck) at the door. It was not Her, or Peck, sitting several tables away, but the ugly girl with whom She sat at the registration assembly the other day. My heart jumped at my reprieve. At least, I thought, if I could not find Her all day, perhaps the ugly girl would unlock the secret of Her whereabouts; perhaps a name; an introduction! Salvation! I thought.

Subtlety. That was foremost in my mind. Honesty. That was there somewhere, too. I stood and nonchalantly walked past the dumpster stuffing incident, wandering to a water fountain near the ugly girl's seat at the table. I then stood by her and disgustedly shook my head as the bullies laughed at the poor, stuffed baritone.

"Morons," I said convincingly, but careful to be certain they didn't overhear. I am a Boys Chorus member, I reminded myself.

The ugly girl looked at me and nodded. "Creeps," she said.

A reaction! This was good. "I can never study in here," I said. (I never study in there, Journal. I rarely study.) "I wonder," I continued, "I hate to be a bother, but I would also hate to be trashed in my prime. Would you mind if I sat here until those fellows go on their way?"

Oh, this was good, Journal. She smiled and laughed. "Sure," she said.

When I sat and drew close, I came to realize this poor girl was uglier than I had first imagined. Her face looked like the moon, all pocked with craters, and her teeth were bound in steel. I suspected this was the first time in her life any boy had spoken to her. This was good. An unfortunate fact of life at school is that one is never measured by intellect or character; rather, those who are most popular are pretty. A beautiful face, although perhaps masking potty for brains, will nonetheless gain more attention than a face full of moon craters.

But, I had no time to worry about this. I had to find out who was the most beautiful girl on earth. I had to know!

"Say," I said, "you look familiar. You sat in front of my friends and me at the assembly last Friday."

"I did?" she said.

"Yes," I said. Then, Journal, I, a man who plans a lifetime devoted to words, could think of nothing else to say. It felt like a plug had opened at the base of my skull and my brains gushed from it. Despite a drink from the water fountain moments earlier, my mouth had become an arid desert, and if at that moment the ugly girl had asked my name, I would have been hard-pressed to come up with an answer. I fumbled and groped for words and then said. "I wonder, are you taking Senior Calculus next year?"

"Yes," she said.

Now I was in trouble. In my ever-growing stupidity, I had forgotten to research what Senior Calculus is. A recurring dream of mine suddenly popped into my head: I'm lying in the road, paralyzed, and there's a 1958 Cadillac speeding at me. I labored to regain control of my mouth, otherwise I was going to babble my way right to the end of the period without even a feeble attempt to discover the identity of the ugly girl's gorgeous companion.

Then, it hit me (an idea, not the Cadillac). My plan! Of course! If honesty with Her would work, why not be honest with the ugly girl? Be honest! Tell the girl about your obsession with her friend. Suggest she be, in the tradition of John Alden, who told Priscilla of Miles Standish's undying love for her, my romantic liaison. Of course, Miles blew that one since he sent a more handsome person than himself to bespeak his love, but how could I lose with the ugly girl? Honesty was the key, however, and I determined to use it.

"Say," I said, "who was the girl with you?"

There came unexpected ire in the ugly girl's eyes. "Which one?" she said.

Which one? Which one? My God, Journal, is there any other? Again, my mind was an echo chamber. "Ummm," I eloquently said, "the one sitting next to you - in front of me - beside you - the one with the perfumed hair."

She looked at me as if I had just killed her cat. "Rosie," she said with a long sigh.

My heart stopped! "Yes, Rosie!" I said. "That's her name, Rosie. I knew that was who - that was - who was with -"

"Marie Rose," the girl said, now with certain fire in her eyes.

"Yes," I said. "That was who - that was who was - that was -"

"Marie Rose," the girl again said as she packed her books, obviously planning a quick exit. She looked furious.

"Yes," I said, now believing that if I looked over my shoulder I would see the 1958 Cadillac revving up. "I know that. I know her. I mean, I thought that I know her, but not exactly know her, although I know who she is, and that was her." God, Journal, if someone had a gun they should have shot me. "What I mean is, I know who she is, and thought that was her. Marie Rose. Yes, that was her." Then, Journal, my mind had a brilliant flash. "You see, her father, that would be Mr. Rose, was my little league baseball coach. I thought that was his daughter, and that was her - who was who I thought was..."

"Stop it!" the ugly girl said, standing. "Robbins."

"Robbins?"

"Her name is Marie Rose Robbins. Her father's name is Mr. Robbins, and he doesn't coach baseball."

"I knew that!" I said. "I knew it was Robbins, not Rose, but that was - who was that..."

"I call her 'Rosie,'" the girl said.

"Yes," I said, paddling for my life. "We all call her 'Rosie,' I know that..."

"I call her 'Rosie.' I'm the only one around here who calls her Rosie. Mr. Robbins also calls her Rosie. Rosie and I call Mr. Robbins 'Dad.'"

Slam! The Cadillac went right over me.

I squirmed and shuffled as if I had bugs crawling in my pants. I cleared my throat and let out a breathy squeak, a sound a dying person might make just before expiring. "I'm sorry," I said. "I have to tell you the truth. The fact is I have heard Marie Rose is particularly adept at Senior Calculus, and -"

"Stop it," Marie Rose Robbins' ugly sister said. "What you want is a date with her, that's what you want."

"Okay, yes! I'm sorry I lied to you, but I had to find out who she is. I haven't been able to stop thinking about her since I first saw her. Please, would you help me meet her?"

"Wait in line," she said as the bell rang, ending both the school day and my life.

It pains me to continue this dialogue, Journal. It sickens me. It is apparent that Angela Robbins, Marie Rose's older and ugly sister, has been asked several thousand times to impersonate John Alden. Marie Rose, although she is a sophomore, has her pick of hundreds of boys, which accounts for her ugly sister's jealousy. Yes, I suppose the entire damned school has asked Marie Rose for a date at one time or another. However, all attempts have been in vain.

"Rosie has a boyfriend," Angela said. I detected sadistic delight in her revelation of this bleak news.

Rosie dates, get this, Journal, a tennis player...a tennis player!

Journal, a person who extracts some value from life by chasing a fuzzy ball in his underwear is holding the hand of the girl with whom I will spend an eternity. But, that isn't all.

"He's a senior, and he's going to junior college next year," Angela said, as if she expected me to fall over dead. She seemed to think I should be impressed that my competitor isn't smart enough to attend a real university!

Oh, but he's attending on a tennis scholarship. Please, Angela, stop. I'm going to faint dead away. She acted as if she was deflating my plan to meet Marie Rose. She thought she was destroying my determination.

I was darned mad!

However, Angela Robbins did strike one severe blow.

"She went to Arizona last Saturday," Angela Robbins smugly said. "She's gone for the summer to a tennis camp. If you knew anything, you would also know she's the best tennis player on the girls team."

If I knew anything, she said. If I knew anything?

I know this, Journal: Life can sometimes be unbearable in its cruelty. I know this, too: I have no intention of allowing some tennis player to stand in my way of meeting Marie Rose Robbins, the girl I plan to love forever. The only salvation from my early setback is that this junior college-bound tennis ball did not go to Arizona with her. He wouldn't have the time to follow her. No, I would wager he'll have to study day and night to prepare himself for the rigors of junior college!

Alas, Journal, as you may see for now my victory is hollow. I am humbled, and temporarily defeated. While my Marie Rose spends her summer in training for some larger purpose, I'll be back here employing strange people to buy me liquor and cigarettes so I can get blitzed and shower with my sister.

Manhood. Fie! Is this what life holds for me as I ascend into my adult years? Anticipation blown into broken dreams of romantic summer nights?

Crap...

May 15, 1962

Dear Marie Rose,

This will be the first of many letters I shall write to you.

I hope you do not find this absurd, for you do not yet know me and will not until school starts next year. Please bear with me. I'm compelled to write anyway. Don't let it confuse you, for I have no intention of ever mailing this letter.

You see, I have spent many painful hours over the last week because you walked into and then out of my life, captivating me with your sweet smile and marvelous eyes. Seeing you has turned my night to day and made it seem as if my heart is newly born. Although you are not here, I see you everywhere. When my eyes close at night, you are there, and when morning comes, you rise with the sun. I am hopelessly, helplessly in love with you, and not to declare this at least on paper would be to seal my madness.

I declare this now and forever: I cannot accept this fate.

I shall be before you upon your return, and my heart will be as it is today, devoted to you. Until then, I'll be lost, longing for you to fill my life with your sunshine. I will endure this summer without you, but never again will we be apart. Not for the rest of our years. Although we have never touched; never shared a laugh or a tear, it is my promise that I will, with every fiber of my being, win your love.

And besides that, I am very cute.

As Always,
Me

June 4, 1962

It is the first day of my freedom from the boredom of high school; however, that freedom is inhibited by my summer job that started today at Central Drugstore. I've moved from mediocre student to common shelf-stocker in one fell swoop. Freedom is a relative term. I do trust that this job, familiar to me because I had it last summer as well, will help placate my troubled mind and occupy my thoughts for several hours daily so I might rest from the rigors of thinking about Marie Rose Robbins.

I envy Marc, who has taken to Vermont for a month's vacation with family to visit relatives. A change of scenery would do me well. Marc tells me of his three cousins, all around our age, who have access to a '59 Buick in which they have planned much merriment and mischief.

Please, God, let me see Marc alive again.

Steven is as unlucky as me. He is shackled to summer employment at his regular position at the country club as a golf caddy. An outdoor job like that would be invigorating, not to mention the tan, but I am not certain I would be disposed to following doctors and fat women around a golf course all day. I like my job, despite its monotony. It gives me ample time to dream. Mr. Lloyd, my boss, is of an even temper, and he feels I hung the moon. I, too, admit a certain liking for him and therefore am confident my summer employment will be as it was last year; uneventful and without disaster.

The job itself has enticements. Mr. Lloyd trusts me to indulge in an occasional Mr. Whizzy Bar without paying for it, I may work at my own pace, and I often have a moment - when Mr. Lloyd isn't looking - to wander off to the back room and scan the current issue of Playboy magazine.

It seems, Journal, that I am lately preoccupied with naked women. It makes me wonder if I am not beginning to undergo a deformation of character, leading me to some unspeakable perversion. Even now, when I write about Playboy magazine, my mind wanders to those enticing pages, which causes me to have a sudden boner.

Sometimes, I get a boner even when I'm not thinking of naked women.

I might be reading Milton. I might be reading Whitman. Perhaps I'm reading an Archie comic book, and whoop, a boner. It's annoying, sometimes painful, and always embarrassing. I have pondered the idea of never again wearing loose fitting trousers, for, when this phenomenon occurs, I've found only blue jeans an adequate disguise because of their inherent tightness. But, I cannot wear blue jeans all the time, Journal. How would it look on my first date with Marie Rose Robbins? Her father would have me put out on the street if I showed up at his door dressed like James Dean. I must find a way to prevent these indiscriminate boners, but there appears no line of communication between a man's mind and his gizmo. An apparatus that so loyally served a single purpose for fifteen years is now running amuck, and I do not know how to deal with it.

It is foremost that I find the secret of gizmo control before my anticipated encounter with Marie Rose Robbins. I would die a thousand deaths if this disrespectful organ chose to make its presence known in full view of my beloved. It's occurred to me to make a few test runs this summer with the girls available in the area. The city swimming pool comes to mind as a good place for my experiments. In years past, I never experienced unannounced boners in the presence of girls in bathing suits, but I suspect this strange diversion that has taken place of late might create a problem this year. Should it happen at the pool, I would have the safety of the water in which I could jump to hide this embarrassment. It will be risky, but I must practice self-control so I can master this potentially mortifying intrusion into my life.

I must admit, the pool has dogged my mind since the weather has grown hot. In years past, I looked forward to swimming, but this year it seems my priorities are changing. I can't wait to see the girls! They all seem to be growing rounder and softer than they have been in the past.

Oh, damn. Another boner.

God, why?

Marie Rose cannot see me struggle with this. I would kill myself! This whole thing about what's happening to my gizmo is dominating my mind. Things were normal for so long, and suddenly, everything is going haywire.

As I mentioned a million times, Journal, Marie Rose Robbins is subject of my obsession, not only during wakefulness, but in dreams as well. On two separate occasions my dreams were interrupted by my wetting the sheets. Here I am a man, and I'm reverting to my childhood. But, it's an unusual thing - difficult to explain. It doesn't seem like wetting the bed as baby Jonathan does. His is a river, but mine is as if there could be something physically wrong. God, it might be a disease. Cancer, or something. Maybe a mental disease.

Why me?

And, whatever it is, I can't help but be embarrassed. I tried to hide this indignation by bundling my wet bed sheets and mixing them with other laundry in the washroom, but

Mother must notice the sheets showing up days before their scheduled wash. She may be not only checking out military schools for me, but psychiatric hospitals as well. Certainly, if this was some normal change in my body, Mother and Dad would have forewarned me, but their obvious silence on such matters confirms I might be in trouble. Of course, boners and naked women aren't on the agenda of normal suppertime conversation. In fact, I am not sure I have ever heard the word 'sex' ever spoken in the house.

My biology teacher implied a marked contrast on the subject with what Playboy magazine suggests. In biology class I have learned there's a purely benign approach to human reproduction. But, I ask, how can the introduction of life be without this incredible heat I'm feeling? Perhaps I am the only male who gets the shakes at the sight of a naked woman.

That can't be. Playboy magazine has a huge circulation.

Biology class doesn't mention boners. In fact, it doesn't mention naked women, but its explanation of reproduction must involve some form of nudeness and enhanced passion that I'm feeling when I see boobs. But, in my wildest imaginative mood, I cannot fathom my birth is a result of Playboy magazine passion. Mother grows red just standing under the mistletoe at Christmas. No, I'm certain my parents gave me life through osmosis.

What a stupid world.

"Andy, our only crime is that we're attractive to women."

- Barney Fife

June 30, 1962

Motion sickness is all in the mind, Journal. That fact I was able to prove yesterday when the 'Tiltaloop' ride I boarded with Steven challenged my considerably strong stomach. Steven, however, is of a lesser command of his stomach, and he ralphed on both of us while we were suspended upside-down.

I believe his decision to eat a three-scoop chocolate ice cream cone prior to the ride was the root of his upheaval. Steven's purge made him feel much better, but I'll admit I was woozy as the summer sun baked Steven's sludge on my clothes. We made a quick escape to Sloan Lake where a quick dip cleaned us up nicely.

What a terrific summer this has been so far!

Right now, Steven's parents are away for a week, and his younger brother, Chris, went with them. Why, I asked Steven, should you spend the week alone? You need a companion to help pass the time. This was the reasoning Steven presented to his parents, and they agreed I should stay with him so he might have a partner for checkers, card games, television watching, and the like.

It is beyond me, Journal, how parents grow more naive with each passing year!

We went back to Steven's for a quick change before heading for the city in his parents' Olds. Our first destination was 16th Street, where guys cruise, show off, engage in odd behavior, and try to pick up girls. The last item is more a figurative term, Journal, as most cruising encounters with the opposite sex are comprised mainly of trading whistles and catcalls at stoplights. There is much talk of 'making out,' but I suspect those tales are more fiction than fact. The female of our species is unpredictable, and appears more enthralled by the chase than the catch.

Our next thoughts turned to beer. Because I am quite experienced in this area, I instructed Steven to head west to Land of Liquor, where we stood our best chance of obtaining contraband. Upon our arrival, we noticed a man in the parking lot who resembled Broderick Crawford. This person, thought I, would be an ideal choice.

"Excuse me, sir," I said, approaching him with a ten-dollar bill in my hand.

He glared at me with his Crawford eyes and grunted.

"Do you think you might take this ten and buy some beer for my friend and me? Seems we both forgot our IDs tonight."

"Yeah, right," Broderick said. He took the money and walked into Land of Liquor, emerging a moment later with a six-pack of beer under his arm. Steven and I congratulated each other for the ease with which we were able to get our contraband until Broderick got into his car and drove away with our beer and change.

Plan B: Steven, of a bit more manly build than myself, mustered his courage and proceeded to undertake the deed himself. He threw his chest out and cleared his throat. With startling self-confidence, he swaggered into Land of Liquor, looking more like he was sixteen and one-half than sixteen and two months. I peered in from outside and experienced deja-vu as I expected at any moment to see Steven spread-eagle on the floor. But, the counter clerk simply sneered, cautiously checked the window, and then bagged a six-pack. He took Steven's money and told him to get lost.

We headed for the foothills west of Denver where we'd heard there was a party taking place atop Table Mesa, aptly named because of its enormous flattened top. This hill is traditionally a most popular area for kids, for its difficult access and virtual invisibility from below makes an ideal spot for parties or private encounters. Steven and I deemed this location suitable for our summer night reverie, because, if the party rumor was false, we could still commune with nature, guzzle beer, and talk about things guys talk about.

As we made the long hike up the mountain, we drew closer and closer to the sounds of music, laughter, and the glow of a fire. Gathered were hoards of people, some familiar and some not, but most of them from our school. The party was a celebration for two spring graduates who were toasting their induction into the army. They attracted much attention as they stood with their chests expanded, discussing such noble subjects as honor, fighting, nobility, and blood. Yeeks! I can just vaguely remember Dad's return from the Korean War, and although he was proud to have served his country, the thing that sticks out in my mind was his nervous tremor and enhanced desire to get drunk. However, up on the hill, the girls were aptly impressed with these guys.

And, Journal, there was an ample supply of other girls to offset those who were helplessly lost in the nobility ruse. Case in point: One very pretty girl, a cousin of someone from school, found me attractive, or so she claimed, and she struck up a conversation. She had a six-pack of her very own, and we sipped and chatted in the moonlight near the warmth of the campfire. I've lost my initial distaste for beer. Its effect on my tongue was instantly agreeable, and I found talking with this stranger easy. Because Marie Rose Robbins remained foremost in my mind, I saw this encounter a perfect opportunity to merely practice my social skills with girls. The beer gave me courage to ask the girl if she cared to take a stroll in the moonlight, and she agreed. Initially, everything went well as we gently stepped across the darkened mountain top, my mind freely flowing over subject after subject, and my confidence bloating from the input of compliments I received.

What I was not prepared for was what happened once we rounded the bend. It brings to mind the tragedy of Pearl Harbor.

She suddenly stopped, wrapped her arms around me, and kissed me flush on the mouth. My head exploded, brains everywhere, and a volcano began to rumble deep in my loins. My arms must have been blown off my body, for I saw them flapping somewhere above my head as the girl kept kissing me for what seemed like forever. Finally, she stopped and looked at me with confused eyes. "Is something wrong? Don't you like me?" she asked.

"No," I said with a pitiful squeak. "I mean - yes!" What else could I say, Journal - 'No, I don't like you; I'm a homo?'

She sat on the ground and pulled me down. God, I'm in the company of an experienced woman, I thought, I'm about to make out. The mere thought of those words caused my body to tremble, and I prayed the girl would not detect the sheer, icy terror in my frame. My heart pounded so violently I could actually see my pulse quaking in my wrist, and if dynamite had been attached to my hands and detonated, I don't believe it would have loosened my grip on this girl. We kissed harder and harder as she flattened her breasts against my pounding chest.

And then, Journal, if you'll pardon the pun, a problem arose.

To digress a moment: When Steven ralphed on me earlier that day, my blue jeans inherited a rather pungent odor. We tossed the jeans into the wash at Steven's house, and he gave me a pair of his pants. Because he is bigger than me, the trousers fit loosely...

Back to the nightmare: As the girl pressed close, I could feel my damned gizmo rub against the inside of the girl's leg. I instinctively pulled back, but she did a peculiar thing. She moved her leg up against it as if she might at any minute slam her knee into me and equalize my newfound manhood with that of a smashed turnip. For some reason, Achilles came to mind. But my ruin was not her intent. Her leg remained closely pressed against my boner, but she never moved. My brain had felt a similar sensation earlier on the 'Tiltaloop' (before Steven ralphed, of course). We continued kissing, and I noticed that her body, too, was trembling. Then, a most remarkable thing: As we kissed, she suddenly poked her tongue into my mouth. God, what a bizarre thing! I've heard about this French kissing, but I was under the impression it was something people only did in Paris. It made me feel rather continental. For the most part, my first making out was going along splendidly, and I wasn't at the time all that concerned that I was kissing a complete stranger. Then, in the rear-view mirror, a 1958 Cadillac. Unauthorized, and acting blatantly upon its own, my right hand grabbed her breast. I might have been hit by lightning with less vengeance.

"Stop!" she said, grabbing my hand and throwing it back so hard it nearly dislocated my shoulder. "I don't go all the way!" She clumsily stood, looking at me as if I were a convicted murderer - a leper - scum - and she ran away, leaving me on the ground to stare at my traitorous hand.

Why? I asked myself. Why? I asked my hand.

All the way? Journal, I don't understand what she meant by that. All the way to where?

But, wherever 'all the way' is, it was the last of my concerns at that moment. If my crime of breast-grabbing wasn't enough to humiliate me for the remainder of my life, I became aware of a wet spot somewhere in the vicinity of my loose fitting pants. I looked in the direction of my Benedict Arnold Gizmo, which was still standing at attention and saluting everything, and discovered the bastard had taken another step in its relentless effort to drive me insane with worry. It seems, during the passion of my first making out, the damned thing drooled just enough to spot my trousers.

Life as a man, I am finding out, sucks.

If not for Steven, my best friend on the planet, I might still be curled up in a little ball under a bush on Table Mesa. There I sat, determined to either stay in the darkness for the rest of my life or to commit suicide. Steven soon came looking for me.

"Over here," I said.

"What are you doing?" he said. "I saw that girl come back without you."

"I'm finished as a man," I said.

"Did you make out?" Steven said.

"I'm through," I said.

Steven looked at me curiously, beginning to understand why I looked like a fetus. "Did you get to first base?"

I looked at him, helplessly lost and wondering what in the world did baseball have to do with humiliating myself? "I touched her...you know," I said.

Steven's eyes widened. "Wow! Titty?"

"I didn't mean to."

"Man, a stand-up double on your first at-bat. What, did she knee you?"

"No," I said, hunching my knees closer to my chest. "She

just ran off, saying she wasn't going to go anywhere with me, that's all. Now, leave me alone and let me die."

Then, Journal, a most remarkable thing. Steven looked at me with knowing eyes. He began to laugh.

"I'm glad you're amused," I said.

"What'd you do," Steven said, "cream your jeans?"

"What?" I said, glaring at my friend.

"You know," Steven giggled, "oozed your blues? She got you hot and you leaked! S'matter? This the first time?"

I was hit with sudden realization, a most blinding light. As if a ten-ton boulder had been removed from my back, I discovered this affliction I thought was either a perversion, or cancer, was in fact universal! Creamed my jeans?

"Actually," I said, "I creamed *your* jeans!"

Steven hooted, and I broke down with him. I confessed, not from guilt, but with relief. Afterwards, I told him about all the strange things that had been happening to my body lately, and he reassured me. "I thought I had cancer, too," he said. "But my uncle is a doctor. I told him about it. He said not to worry. It's just a natural thing and it would get better with experience. It's called maturity."

Maturity!

Did you hear that, Journal? Maturity. Why didn't I think of that? Why didn't somebody tell me about this maturity business?

Jesus, somebody ought to write this stuff down for us.

July 2, 1962

A wager. A simple dare.

Last night we sat by the campfire on the hill where lately it seems every night someone finds a reason for a gathering. A handful of us were enjoying the summer night, for it's easy to make friends around a campfire. The night seems to close you in the earth's womb as you share a laugh and talk about how things will someday be.

Talking about girls is fun, too.

But, last night, we broached the unusual subject of death. What is it like to be dead? Are you with God? Are you nothing? Do you travel around in the cosmos until you are born again?

"Have you ever seen a dead body?" asked one of the more colorful fellows I've met on the hill, Roy Perkins.

"I saw my dead grandfather," I said.

"I saw a dead guy in a car wreck," Steven said. "Woah, road pizza, man! His head was all mashed..."

"Hey, we're going for pizza later. Do you mind?" I said.

"Once, me and my uncle dug up a dead body in a graveyard," Roy Perkins said. He was instantly greeted with catcalls. "We did! Was a bunch of guys, just like us now, sitting around and drinkin' beer, and one of 'em bet me and my uncle we didn't have the guts to dig it up. Them guys put up fifty bucks, and we went to the graveyard. We dug up this fresh grave, busted open the casket, and sat the stiff up so's he'd greet the caretaker the next morning!"

"Bullcrap!" Steven said.

"Bet me," Roy said.

Steven looked at me. I shrugged. "I'm broke."

"You're just chicken," Roy said. "You wouldn't have no guts to do it."

"I'd do it for fifty bucks," Steven said.

"Yeah?" Roy said. "How 'bout it, guys? You wanna put up some money?"

Roy's friends all agreed and began pooling their money.

Steven, at first nervously surprised, mustered his courage and looked at me. "You help me."

"Me?" I said.

"C'mon," he said, "fifty bucks."

"I don't want to dig up dead people," I said. But, when the final tally reached ninety-eight dollars, I had a change of heart.

"This has got to be different," Roy said. "Since there's a hundred bucks here, you gotta do something tougher. How about we go to Mason's Funeral Home and you guys put a couple of stiffs in bed together!"

"Woah," I said. "Funeral home? Stiffs?"

"S'matter, bookworm," Roy said, "you chicken?"

"We'll do it," Steven said.

"In bed together?" I said...

Despite my protests, the group unanimously agreed this was an appropriate dare for the price. Although the notion of fiddling with dead people had no appeal to me, I figured to down several large swallows of beer on the way to the funeral home to bolster my courage. And, too, I could use the money.

We went to the mortuary; Steven was driving. He pulled the car into a dark alley down the street so we might not arouse suspicion. Roy told us the best way to get in was the back where we might find a window to jimmy. Having no experience at breaking and entering, Steven and I followed Roy's lead. We crept along the street and rounded the corner, and we began messing with doors and windows. To my surprise, I found one door slightly ajar.

Roy nudged Steven. "Go on," he said. "And it has to be good. You gotta make the Crime Reporter."

The Crime Reporter is an article in the neighborhood paper that reports the week's larceny. Pulling off a stunt that makes the Crime Reporter turns you into a sort of celebrity around school.

I was the first to enter. Steven followed closely as we groped through the darkness, leaving at the back door our companions to watch for trouble. We were in a long hallway, and there was a faint light coming from a window at the far end.

"I feel like I'm in Hell," I said.

"Shut up," Steven said. "You're always so dramatic."

"Do you hear the silence?" I whispered. "It's the sound of the dead."

"Would you shut up?" Steven said.

"The dead have eyes..."

"Shut up, or I swear..."

But, Journal, the silence was indeed dead. It was a silence with eyes.

The end of the hall introduced us to an open doorway. We went through it into a larger room that was bathed in soft light. It was the lobby of the dead. The moonlight gave hints to other passageways, and we explored about, knowing not exactly where we might find the bodies. We passed down a second long hallway and entered another room, this one much smaller.

There was a sudden burst of white light that made my heart seize my throat. "Jesus-to-hell!" I gasped, turning to find Steven had found a light switch.

"Welcome to the hall of the dead," Steven said in a bad impersonation of Boris Karloff.

"Now who's being dramatic?" I asked.

We looked around and discovered this room to be a large foyer with doors on each of four walls.

"I'll bet there's stiffs in those rooms," Steven said, the Boris impersonation trailing off.

At that moment, I began to flash back to a time when I was a little boy. Mother, Dad, Lyla and I stood in a room similar to this. Dad was devastated by his father's passing and behaved strangely. Mother took my hand and told me we were going in to say farewell to Gramps, and although the concept of death was too complex for my little mind, I knew when I saw Gramps that he was gone forever. He was in a bed, bloated and unfamiliar, his skin like yellow wax and very cold. It is a sight as clear to me now as it was that night I saw him, and I'm certain it is a sight that will forever haunt me. For five endless nights of horror after I saw Gramps' dead body, I lay awake, fearing if I closed my eyes I would see him...

"Go on," Steven said, nudging me from my dream. I approached the first door but found it locked. The second door creaked open.

After a moment of terrified giggling, we entered.

Inside, it was cool. The room reeked of flowers. The smell brought forth in my mind the image of Gramps' waxy face. It is a smell I always associate with death, that of flowers. How odd.

I clicked on the light, and we found ourselves looking across the room at a dead woman. My heart was doing 120 miles per hour as we cocked our heads and slowly walked up to her. She was ancient, her face drawn with gray hair neatly combed back off her pale forehead. Her eyes were closed on a dreamless sleep. I know Steven shared my morbid fascination with the corpse, as we'd look first at it, and back at each other.

"Boo!" Steve suddenly screamed, clutching my arm and making me nearly piss my pants.

"You bastard!" I said, slugging his arm with all of my strength.

Then, we both laughed. "Looks like your mother," Steven said.

"Up yours."

"Eat me!"

I suppose it was for comic relief that we broke into The Dozens, but the corpse was not in a laughing mood.

"Okay," I said, "pick her up and..."

"Bullcrap!" Steven protested. "I ain't touching her. This was your idea, you carry her."

"My idea?" I said. "You were the one..."

"We'll both carry her. How's that?"

"Wait," I said, "we might not find another open room. Perhaps we should find her mate first before we go to the trouble of dragging her out."

"Right," Steven said. "Go look."

"Me? Why not you?"

"Okay, you wuss," Steven said, "we'll both go look."

I hesitated before we left. "You know," I said, "if they're going to be, you know, making out, they're going to have to be naked."

On Steven's face was the look he had the day he ralphed at the amusement park. "This is getting gross," he said.

Without a word, we fled back into the foyer. I wanted to make some excuse to bail out of this situation as I halfheartedly tried the knob on the next door, secretly hoping it would be locked. No luck, it was open. We entered the room, turned on the light, and found a dead man lying in a bed.

When Gramps died, finding his body in a place like the

funeral home seemed to confirm that he was really gone. It has something to do with the rituals surrounding the death. But, what a sad and empty gesture to place a corpse on display, and then bury it in the cold ground with nothing but a stone to mark what was once a life. How strong the human body, but at the same time it is so frail as proven by the instantaneous deterioration once life's energy is lost. It's a mystery to me how we are judged less by the essence of that life's energy and more by physical merit. Religion teaches eternal life, yet, when life ceases, we create a monument to the empty shell.

Perhaps that is why I am driven to write. A writer is eternal; a writer is immortal. One needs only to open a book, and the writer lives on. Of course, these were not my random thoughts while standing illegally in the bedroom of a corpse last night, but it does give me reason to ponder.

I felt the birth of a coward somewhere near my anus as we gazed upon the dead man in this room, which, according to a plaque on the door outside was called a 'Slumber Chamber.' "Webster defines slumber as: 'to be sleeping lightly,'" I said to Steven, my eyes never leaving the cadaver. "If he's sleeping lightly, I'm Zsa Zsa Gabor."

"Jeez, shut up," Steven said, walking to the corpse and motioning for me to join him.

Again, we nervously stared at the stiff. This poor devil was young and not as waxy as the old lady. His hands were folded over his chest and he was dressed in a coat and tie.

"Why is he in bed with a suit on?" I rhetorically asked.

"How the hell do I know?" Steven said. "Go get the old lady and strip her down while I get him ready."

"Me?" I said. "You strip her down."

"I'm bigger than you," Steven said. "This guy's at least two hundred pounds. Besides, I think I'd ralph if I saw the old broad naked."

"I don't know," I said. "This isn't right. God really gets people for doing things like this."

"Look, there's fifty bucks in it for both of us, so shut up and go strip her down," Steven said.

I was riddled with guilt now, but I slowly turned and walked to the door.

"By the way," Steven said, "don't get a boner."

Steven is my best friend in the world, Journal, but sometimes he can be a real oink.

I stopped at the door, watching Steven clumsily try to position himself over the body. He first rubbed his hands together, took several deep breaths, then circled the bed like he was preparing to wrestle Vern Gagne. He pulled back the thin blanket, indeed finding the corpse fully clothed, right down to a pair of white high-top Keds sneakers.

This, I thought, was curious; very curious, but Steven didn't notice the shoes. He bent over and pulled the body upright. Suddenly, the corpse's eyes popped open.

"Yeeeeeeahhhh!" the corpse screamed, wrapping its arms around Steven.

I went blind with fear. It was that damned 1958 Cadillac roaring at me. There is a place where mind and matter, fantasy and reality, and the subconscious and conscious mind all collide in the face of terror, and I was somewhere in the middle of all this cosmic disarray.

"Gaaaaaaaaaaa!" the corpse screamed.

"Eeeeeeeyyyyaaaaaa!" Steven screamed.

"IIIIIeeeeeeeeee!" I screamed. I tripped over a small table and hit the lamp, dropping us into cold darkness.

"Aaaaaaggggggghhhhh!" Steven screamed.

I helplessly flailed about in the dark, my feet entangled in the lamp cord. My nose was wet with terror as I heard coming from the darkness a potpourri of screams, hollers, and what sounded like unlikely laughter. I quickly pulled myself to my feet when a bright light suddenly flooded the room. Steven still screamed in the clutches of the corpse, who indeed was laughing. He was laughing, and Roy Perkins and his friends were laughing. Everyone was laughing except for Steven and me.

We were had.

The room began to return to its rightful place on the earth, the stars back to Heaven, and my dinner back to my stomach as Roy and the boys came in, yuck yucking. The corpse released Steven, who leaped from the bed.

"Fuck you!" Steven cried at Roy. He stumbled back. "Fuck you!" he said to the corpse. "Fuck you!" he said to me.

I couldn't help it, Journal. I was laughing, too.

I'm not traditionally given to such impish humor, Journal, but as practical jokes go, this was of Olympian proportion. After Steven regained his wits, he, too, admitted to being suckered. The corpse, it turns out, is Roy Perkins' Uncle Tod. Tod is the night watchman at the funeral home. We were not the first to be bamboozled by this prank. A side note: Tod works at the mortuary to pay for his education in law school, which explains why Tod is a degenerate.

We didn't make the hundred dollars, but Roy bought pizza to atone for his sin. The whole affair was immature and abominable. It was childish, irreligious, and completely abhorrent.

I can't wait until next weekend, however, for Roy promises we can be in on the next funeral home scheme he's planning!

July 5, 1962

I find it hard to write today. I am compelled to express some thoughts, however. Yesterday was the most difficult of days. I don't know when I have experienced such horror. What was to be a day of fun and good cheer abruptly ended in tragedy.

Yesterday I watched Roy Perkins die.

July 7, 1962

I'm still at a loss. Most of my spare time I spend in my room.

Roy's funeral is Monday.

I sat on the couch with Mary for some time this evening. Mary is only a child, but I believe she understands. She is my sweet little girl. Her attention was not on the television, but rather upon me. She kissed me and put her head on my lap.

"Don't be sad," she said.

July 9, 1962

They buried Roy today. God, the service was at Mason's Funeral Home.

July 11, 1962

It was Independence Day, July 4, 1962; the day Roy Perkins died - a day I'll never forget. Dying was his fault, and yet, I feel guilty.

The 4th was different for me this year. In years past, the holiday has been a family affair. We usually picnic in the park and watch the fireworks display over Berkeley Lake. However, this year we broke tradition. Mother and Dad, with Mary and the baby, attended a picnic with the employees from the bus station. Uncle Vern and Aunt Millie went to Las Vegas, and I attended a party at the reservoir with Steven, Lyla, and her boyfriend, Nick.

There were hundreds of people at the party. Steven and I partook in a large supply of beer and wine, joining Roy, his Uncle Tod, and others we've encountered this summer on the hill. It is the liquor I blame for Roy's death. He and Tod drank more than the rest of us, and they were clearly out of control.

We celebrated in a large cove surrounded by towering rocks from which we were jumping or diving into the water below. Leaping into the water was fun, but most of us retained enough sense to know how high was high enough. Roy and Tod, however, made a contest of it. All afternoon they dared to climb higher until Roy finally scaled the top of the highest point some fifty feet above the water. I think many of us knew a jump from there could be lethal, but none of us spoke up. Roy bellowed and blindly jumped, twisting and flipping all the way down until he crashed into the water with a huge splash. Clouded by the alcohol, we cried out our approval, unaware that Roy was in trouble.

When Roy surfaced, it took too long for us to realize the gravity of the situation as we dumbly stood and cheered on the shore. In my mind, the terrible realization hit me like white-hot lightning when Roy disappeared back under the water. A single cry arose, and panicked screams followed as we ran to the water, Tod leading the pack. Perhaps if anyone had his wits about him, Roy might have been saved, but because of our hesitation, he was gone. It took hours for a rescue crew to finally recover him. All I recall of that moment was his limp, blue body lying still in the sand.

The autopsy report was clear. Roy's neck was broken, but his death was by drowning.

The liquor betrayed us. It's left me with a dark sense of guilt that cannot be filled with light. I know Steven shares my guilt. We spoke briefly at the funeral, the first words we've exchanged since that day. Roy was not a close friend, but my emotions run high through this tragedy. We are responsible for our actions - Roy, too - but his foolishness does not excuse the rest of us from shouldering some of the blame. Life simply is not as easy as I imagined. Death, on the other hand, is swift and final. It circumvents all.

As Roy lay there in his casket placed in the very lobby where we had laughed at death, I could not help but believe he would come back; he would pop his eyes open and say 'the joke's on you.'

But this time it wasn't a joke. Roy is dead forever, and forever is a long time.

I'm so troubled by this.

Steven is of no help because his guilt mirrors mine, his questions the same. Lyla is upset by the tragedy, but when Roy is mentioned, she shrugs it off and changes the subject. Mother expressed concern and thanked God I hadn't been so irresponsible, but she provides no empathy. Dad offered this sage wisdom: "Damned idiot should've known better than to hang off a cliff when he was drunk."

Hang off, indeed. For some reason I expect that from Dad. Coming from someone whose entire life has teetered on the edge of a black, watery hole, I suppose it's sound advice.

This tragedy makes me think more than ever about Marie Rose Robbins. I wonder if her thoughts ever find me, for I can't help an uncanny belief that our eyes met that day last spring on some kind of psychic plane. Okay, Journal, call me insane, or some metaphysical Kerouac or Walden disciple, but I believe some people mentally bond to one another without even knowing at first. Steven and I often catch ourselves with the same thought, or one will call just when the other is thinking about calling. Even my little sister Mary and I seem to connect this way when Lyla and I might as well be on separate planets.

I believe Marie Rose and I share this connection even though we have not met. When she looked at me last spring, her smile and her eyes spoke volumes to me. As I sit here in shock at Roy's death, the thought of her gives me comfort, and I cannot discount that feeling. What depth of love I might feel if only Marie Rose Robbins held me in her arms right now and said: "Don't be sad."

"To live in the hearts we leave behind is not to die."

- Thomas Campbell

July 20, 1962

Happy to hear from Marc, who returned from Vermont yesterday in one piece. Steven, Marc, and I plan an evening together tonight. Marc promised a large supply of beer on hand, and that troubles me. I have had no desire to drink since the tragedy on the 4th. My existence has been to work in the day, and come home at night to catch up on writing and some interesting reading. When Roy Perkins died, I was overwhelmed, but I was not certain if my grief was for him, or me. I'm reading one of my favorite books, The Prophet, by Kahlil Gibran.

Gibran, on pain: *"Pain is the breaking of the shell of understanding."*

I am abandoned by understanding. I fear a short lifetime is hardly enough for a human to grasp life's opaque purpose. When someone dies, the pain seems caused more by the mystery of mortality than the grief for physical loss. So many questions are unanswered.

Gibran: *"Much of your pain is self-chosen. It is the bitter potion by which the physician within you heals your sick self. Therefore, trust the physician, and drink his remedy in silence and tranquility."*

July 21, 1962

I have good friends, Journal. They will always be my friends, no matter where our lives lead. Last night was memorable not so much by action, but more in the unspoken gesture of good friendship. Marc is distanced from the guilt Steven and I share because he did not know Roy Perkins. His detachment, however, coupled with his understanding of Steven and me provided some useful insight.

"It wasn't your fault," Marc said. "Nobody made him jump from that rock; nobody wanted him to die. He pushed himself."

The simple sense of Marc's conclusion is comforting. I know Steven and I have said the same thing, but I suppose I feel validated when I hear it from an outsider. It is good to have Marc back for the rest of this slow-moving summer.

And, he taught us a swift trick!

Marc told me to drive Dad's Ford to the north part of the city near the train yards. He said he wanted to show us something he learned in Vermont. He took the wheel on a deserted stretch of road that was intersected by a train crossing, and he drove the Ford up onto the tracks. The car's wheel base, to my surprise, matched the width of the rails. By letting a little air out of the tires we were able to drive down the tracks to the next crossing.

Marc says this little game can be spiced with riding the rails toward an approaching train. He and his cousins experienced considerable exhilaration at the sight of the bright train engine light coming at them before they jumped their car off the tracks. Although Steven wanted to challenge a train last night, Marc said once was enough for him, and I was hesitant, but I cannot help but be drawn to such notions of recklessness. Perhaps I understand in a strange way what it was Roy Perkins died for.

To challenge and beat death could be man's most fulfilling victory.

August 4, 1962

God, this summer drags on! The pit of boredom grows deeper with every passing day. Today has been eternal.

But, as I sit in the stillness of this den, I am confronted by yet another question about sex, spurned on by something that happened today. The experience raises in my mind a question: What is morality? I internally struggle with these notions of what is immoral, and what is simply by all appearances human pleasure. I, myself, haven't gone 'all the way,' which, incidentally, was explained to me by Marc, who went there with a girl in the back seat of his cousin's Buick. He described it, not in these words, as 'pleasurable.' Immorality should not be pleasurable, should it, Journal? Amoral, perhaps, but not a full-blown sin in the way - let's say - Catholics describe it. Considering how many children they have, I can't imagine there isn't some fun involved.

Granted, I haven't been 'all the way,' but from the way

Marc described it, I look forward to going there some day.

And so, considering this question of pleasure versus morality, I wonder this: If I murdered someone, a blatant immoral act, I would not derive pleasure from it; so, why is it implied that pleasure and sex are equally immoral with murder? In fact, adults always talk freely about who was shot in a holdup, but it seems this journey to 'all the way' will get you hit with lightning if you even broach the subject with them. If you ask me, I think humans, not God, select these confusing rules to bind man to limitations of just how much pleasure he can have.

It's very confusing.

What so frustrates me is the lack of input. I find no books on the subject of pleasure versus morality. When I broached the subject with Mother, she told me to ask Dad, and Dad just mumbled something about manhood and wearing a raincoat.

What the heck does a raincoat have to do with it? He just said that I'd find out soon enough, and to quit bothering him.

On this puzzling question of pleasure, if it wasn't for Steven, I might still think I have cancer. Although I'm learning more about the pleasurable biological purpose of my gizmo, it still seems I should only acknowledge a single purpose of relieving my bladder. Society leads me to believe any thought of using it for other reasons is not the kind of thing a good boy should be thinking about; but lately, it's the only thing I think about. Conversely, my biology teacher says it is an important device in procreation, but it's immoral if I think about it before I get married.

I cannot help it if my gizmo is an immoral pig. Am I responsible for an organ that has a mind of its own? God help me if it were to kill someone.

This double standard casts me adrift in this moral morass.

If this isn't enough, love injects a third confusing factor. When I experienced my first kiss, I was excited; extremely aroused, but I wasn't in love with that wild girl. Society says the natural progression is: two people fall in love, marry, and then go to this 'all the way' place, and somewhere between pleasure and guilt a baby is born. However, when I was attacked, I wasn't thinking about procreation, biology or love - in fact, my gizmo took over my entire thought process.

The moral thinking is this arousal before marriage is wrong, but how can two human beings engage in this biological act without there being some emotional intensity involved? And, how can you wait all those years to get married when all you think about is feeling good right now?

Why, Journal, is something so natural the cause of such problems?

Even on Mary's blasted television people are murdered, but Rob and Laura Petrie sleep in separate beds. Joe Friday can shoot somebody and be a hero, but Rob can't give Laura any more than a little peck on the cheek. Why?

It's a stupid world.

I only bring this up, Journal, because of an odd occurrence yesterday afternoon that served as a light of revelation to me: Sex simply can't be immoral. Unfortunately, this light was cast at the expense of my poor sister Lyla again.

Lyla is an odd creature. I believe she is possessed of multiple personalities. One moment she can be serenely contented and civil, and the next she behaves like a paranoid lunatic. This summer has greatly enhanced her neurosis as she nervously anticipates her upcoming departure for Harvard, and I seem to be a primary source of irritation. I'm not sure exactly what I do that makes her warm and caring one moment and homicidal the next. Uncle Vern says that's just the way women are, and I had better get used to it.

This afternoon, I happened upon Lyla and Nick, who were kissing on the sofa. (By the way, Nick was wearing tight blue jeans.) They didn't know I was there as I curiously watched their emotional and sensuous embrace. When I was discovered, the clench was broken, and Lyla nearly jumped out the window. I quickly fled to the basement believing I would be killed, but to my surprise Lyla didn't follow me with a cleaver in her hand.

Tonight, after Nick went home, Lyla shared a curious moment with me. It began innocently at the supper table where I sat, lingering over some tasteless peas. Everyone else had quickly eaten and moved on, but I was contented to simply sit and hover over my plate, lost in thought. Lyla came back and sat across from me, apparently wishing to take advantage of the privacy. I feared she was going to threaten me like she usually does after I've upset her, but she was strangely docile.

"Are you going to tell Mother about me and Nick?" she asked.

The question took me back. I was embarrassed for intruding. "Why would I tell?" I said. "I'm sorry I looked. I didn't mean to."

"Mother said I can't have Nick in the house when she and Dad aren't home," Lyla said. "But I'm leaving soon, and I'm going to miss him."

"I understand," I said. "Mother won't make rules for you when you're gone. You'll have to make your own."

Lyla was touched by my respect. "Thanks," she said. "I don't let Nick do certain things. I don't go all the way."

"That's your business, not mine," I said. Although I sounded quite mature, I was confused again at this notion of sex having something to do with travel. Perhaps I'm just dense, but I do understand that Lyla must love Nick. Their affectionate embrace on the couch showed she has a genuine feeling for him. It's not immoral for her to care.

Lyla left the table, but she did a curious thing. She touched me on the shoulder, and she said, "I'm going to miss you, too..."

Lyla has never shown me much affection, so this gesture comes as a surprise. She's never touched me with anything but her fists the last three years. It makes me realize that, although Lyla and I have been at odds for a long time now, I will no doubt miss her, too. I never thought of this before, but I think this has something to do with growing up.

Some things, once lost, may never be retrieved.

August 24, 1962

Such a terrible turn for the worse.

Dad was involved in a serious accident this afternoon while driving his bus. He isn't hurt, but six passengers are hospitalized with various injuries, one critically with neck and spinal damage. The initial prognosis for this girl, only twenty-two, is she may be paralyzed. Nobody tells me anything, but from what I've heard and seen on the television news, I think Dad was at fault. He uttered not a word when we picked him up at the hospital, and his attitude was fierce. His defiant demeanor, almost as if he denies any responsibility, is transparent.

As I sit here alone, I fight off a dreadful suspicion. There is an ominous ring to Dad's behavior. He is not very lucid, something he attributes to a doctor's sedative after the fact, but I fear he was drunk when he had the accident. God, I pray I am wrong. I cannot fathom him willfully risking his passengers' lives by drinking on the job. It has always been his habit to drink off duty, but now I am not so sure. Because Dad is such a private man, I am not sure of anything anymore. One thing of which I am certain, I could not respect him if my wildest fears are true.

A huge river of misunderstanding flows between my father and me. I have never measured up to his expectations - never reflected his image in even the little things like sports, in which I never excelled, much to his dismay. Although we share enthusiasm for watching baseball, I was always the last kid to be chosen for a team, and I know Dad watched in frustration as I'd clumsily strike out every time. I'm the one who missed the important basketball shot, or the one who fumbled the football. I died a thousand deaths when I failed at sports, but now I'm certain my mortification was due more to embarrassment for my father than for me, for after each of my unsuccessful attempts to please him, he'd skulk home, get drunk, and become verbally abusive at my folly. How many times I cannot count when he'd accuse me of trying to embarrass him by "throwing like a sissy," or "blubbering like a girl."

The chasm between us is not restricted just to sports either. Although my desire to write is tolerated, Dad berates my dreams of someday writing for a living.

"Faggots write," Dad says. "They're lazy beatniks who panhandle and hang around street corners. Try to pick up a paycheck for making up stories – see where it gets you..."

Dad once scolded me when my report card showed a 'C' in Metal Shop, and an 'A' in English. When I suggested in the sixth grade that I'd like to try my hand at learning a musical instrument, you might think I told Dad I was interested in joining the Hitler Youth. Dad and I are so different, but I know somewhere deep inside of him he cares for me - for the entire family. He just never says so...

The house is so silent. How might any of us forgive Dad if a woman lies paralyzed for life as a result of his drinking? I'm in my den tonight. I may sleep here. Lyla hides in her room, and Mary has sacrificed her television watching in favor of her bed. There was considerable yelling going on in Mother and Dad's bedroom, which is directly above me, but now, there is total silence. Dad must be in bed, and Mother, in the kitchen.

Whenever there is a family crisis, Mother cooks.

August 25, 1962

Dad was home this afternoon when I arrived from the drugstore. He is suspended from work until the accident investigation is complete.

He's on a holy tear. I imagine he's been drinking all day, and Mother is climbing the walls. They're fighting right now as I write.

Giving it considerable thought, I'm certain he was drunk when he had the accident. The news reports suggest it, and Dad's attitude confirms; he would not be in such a rage if he was innocent.

It makes me want to hate him.

He'll lose his job, his pension, and he's exposed this family to financial ruin in light of the possible lawsuits. If that paralyzed girl were Lyla or Mary, I would want swift action against the man who did such a thing, but on this side of the situation I cannot help a selfish fear for all of us. Dad is an uneducated man. He's driven a bus all of his adult life and knows nothing else. At his age, how can he possibly start over? Driving is his life, but with this black scar on his record, how will he ever secure any job? I mean no disrespect to the poor woman who has paid for Dad's atrocity, but my foremost concern is what will happen to this family.

I've such an empty feeling inside.

I must ponder this carefully, for I am faced with the reality that I may have to support this family. Mother has never worked, and she will need help. God, the money I earn at the drugstore is attractive to a teenager without household bills, but for it to support an entire family is a ludicrous notion.

The future has become so uncertain, Journal. I never realized growing up would be like this.

I'm on the brink of a dream I've pondered all summer - meeting Marie Rose Robbins - but all of this has clogged the way.

God, I feel alone.

September 3, 1962

At long last, school began today, and with it, my great expectations. Although this day was tainted with uncertainty in the family due to Dad's escapade, I still must allow myself this:

Oh my God! I met her! Journal, I met her!

So many months have passed since I first laid eyes on Marie Rose Robbins, and I now find she is even more beautiful than I remember! And, could Eros have better planned what happened? Marie Rose Robbins sits next to me in my third hour poetry class!

There is a God!

Imagine, Journal, for the next nine weeks while in the company of Keats and Whitman, I will share the world's sonnets with Marie Rose Robbins. But, this isn't the best, Journal, not by any stretch of my whirling imagination.

It went like this:

I arrived early to class as I do at the beginning of every new semester because I want to get a good seat for something like poetry. There I sat, minding my own affairs, when in She walked. My heart leaped from my chest, spewing blood everywhere. Marie Rose Robbins perused the dozens of empty desks in the classroom while I pensively watched, stunned at the sight of her marvelous brown tan. Wave to her, my heart screams, offer the seat next to you; crawl; beg! She looked around, hesitated, then looked at me. God, can it be, Journal, that Marie Rose Robbins might have been sharing my apprehension? Could her ugly sister Angela have told Her of me? She approached as I tried to clean up the blood and put my heart back in my chest.

Then, she smiled at me - at me! There was no one else near. That smile was for me! And, after shyly looking around the room, she took the desk next to me. Next to me!

"Hi," she said as she sat. My God, what a voice she has!

"Hwuff," I said. I am such a master of the spoken word. My hands were icy and my knees so weak that I prayed there wouldn't be a fire drill. I would have to be carried out.

Marie Rose Robbins looked at her notebook while I tried not to stare. I just couldn't help it. "This is Poetry 200, isn't it?" she asked.

God, her voice is that of an angel. "Ung huh," I succinctly said.

Tomorrow, Journal, I vow to experiment with a conversation in English!

It was a miracle, Journal. I know somewhere inside of her is a spark. She didn't have to sit next to me, she didn't have to smile, she didn't have to speak. God, she is so beautiful with her Arizona tan, and that hair, so soft, cascading over her shoulders like waves of starlight.

The spell was broken by our teacher. "Poetry," she said, "is life. It is art. It is expression." Not bad for openers, I thought. "What is the motivation of verse?" she continued.

The room was silent, save the rattling of my heart. I looked around the room and then turned to Marie Rose Robbins when I spoke. "It's love," I said.

The teacher looked at me. "That's good," she said. "What else?"

Marie Rose, I believe just a bit startled, gazed at me and shyly smiled.

"In some cases," I said, "there is nothing else."

God, I was good! Tomorrow, Journal, I have a plan. Oh, this will be perfect!

September 4, 1962

The deed is done. It has been a long day, but what anticipation I have for this year. Journal, you would be proud of me.

Third period. I entered the classroom early, thinking I might have a chance to do my work prior to class in order to gauge Marie Rose's reaction. It could serve to make for an uncomfortable hour, I thought, but on the other hand, it could be perfect.

No luck. Marie Rose was almost late for class as she scurried in at the bell. Again, it cannot be my imagination. In her haste, she dropped her books while sitting. I moved like a Bengal Tiger and picked them up for her, and when she settled, I swear her tanned face was the slightest red. Her smile warmed me again!

But, I had work to do. I planned my move all period, knowing this would either shoot off a romantic cannon or kill me, but I could not last any longer without trying my best to win Marie Rose Robbins.

The bell ended class, and as we gathered our things to depart for 4th period, I carefully pulled out a piece of paper upon which I had written something last spring - the day I first saw her. I approached, and without a word, handed her the paper and walked away:

Marie Rose,

"She walks in beauty, like the night
of cloudless climes and starry skies;
And all that's best of dark and bright
Meet in her aspect and her eyes..."

- Lord Byron, my John Alden

December 18, 1962

Dear Marie Rose,

I am aware a Christmas card's purpose is to deliver a brief and cheery message to the receiver during the Yuletide season. But, when the intended is someone for whom I care so deeply, Frosty the Snowman doesn't cut it. Therefore, I offer this letter.

It's our first Christmas! As you know, I bruise easily, but I still need an occasional pinch to verify that I'm not dreaming. I've confessed to you the endless summer endured thinking about you; thinking about loving you, and praying you might feel the same. Even though those dreams came true, and Angela's plan to let you know what a jerk I was actually backfired, I still fear I will wake up soon in a hot August sweat and realize a terrible tragedy. I pray the snow falling on my window is as real as my feeling for you, Rosie.

Tell me this is true. Tell me I'm not going to awaken and find this is all a dream. Tell me the thirty dollars I popped for Homecoming wasn't wasted! Tell me the first taste of your kiss on that magical night will remain on my mouth forever.

Merry Christmas, Rosie! Thank you for caring for me and putting the sun in the sky. Thank you for being my girlfriend. Thank you for not dropping me on our first date when I flipped that hot pizza on your leg.

Most importantly, thank your parents for me. I'm so happy they didn't stop after they had Angela.

I love you.

As Always,
Me

1963

February 14, 1963
Dear Marie Rose,
Re: Saint Valentine's day:

Roses are red, Firetrucks, too;
Peaches are pink, Oceans, they're blue;
Grasses are green, Sunsets are orange;
Now I'm in trouble, No word rhymes with orange;
This poem I write, for you must make due;
I must break our date, Since I have the flu.

Burma Shave

As Always,
Me

P.S. Please find enclosed rain check, redeemable when I'm not nauseated.

May 21, 1963
Dear Marie Rose,

Please don't tear up this letter before reading it. Please don't twist it into a little ball, ignite it with flame, and stomp upon its ashes until you at least give it your patient consideration. I would hope the months we've spent together will warrant the opportunity for me to apologize for initiating last night's spat. If, after reading it, you then decide to burn it or me, so be it. If you do choose the latter, please grant my last request that you put my ashes in a nice urn and present them to my mother. At least she will have something to remember her slug of a son, who selfishly accused you of wanting to leave me for the entire summer so you can chase a fuzzy ball around an Arizona tennis court. I realize the tennis camp is important, and I will accept my fate of spending another endless summer without you.

My apology also covers the fuss I made about the sweater you knitted for my birthday, specifically my crack about one arm being longer than the other. I promise, since Bob The Dog often trees me from time to time, I'll hang from the shorter arm in order to ensure a perfect fit.

Rosie, I'm jealous of anyone, or anything that might keep you away from me; that is why I became snotty. For that I am sorry, and I assure you that I remain your biggest fan and understand the importance of increasing your skills so you might someday realize your dream of becoming a professional. Please allow me my blues at the prospect of not seeing you until next fall.

Don't allow this ugly moment to stand in the way of the last few weeks we have together. Will you put this behind us? Please? Pretty please?

As Always,
Me

P.S. Don't worry, the Dr. Pepper you
hurled at me didn't stain my suit.

June 6, 1963

Gad, Journal, this summer is going to drag on forever! The touch of Rosie is still fresh on me, but it feels as if she's been gone for eternity. I'm lonely. My life is grinding down to dust. She's been gone eight days, nineteen hours and fifty-three minutes. I've written nine letters to her three. Already, she is beginning to forget me. She spends her summer training herself for a bright future, and I spend it stacking Jujy Fruits and sneaking a peek at Miss June whenever Mr. Lloyd is looking the other way.

I've purchased several tennis magazines, and have spent some time in the library boning up on the finer points of the game so I might dazzle Rosie with my expertise. I have not yet gone so far, however, as to take lessons, for I made the mistake of trying to play her once this spring. Lovers should never compete on the gaming field, particularly in Rosie's case since she seemed to derive such a competitive pleasure out of dismantling me. She was a fire-breathing princess; "Gorgo," I call her.

Forgive me, Journal, if my entries shorten for the summer as I am saving most of my creative energy for letters. You understand.

June 11, 1963

Dear Marie Rose,

Thought I'd 'lob' one your way as I have been thinking of you the last minute. I feel fifteen hours is an adequate dearth between letters. No special news, just playing life at 'deuce.' Having stolen my heart, you must know by being away that my life is 'advantage, Miss Robbins.' Please do not 'volley' with said heart, for, if you do, it shall certainly be 'set, point, match, Miss Robbins.'

I send greetings from Marc and Steven, who miss you, too. Steven is dragging golf clubs around the country club, and Marc fries hamburgers at the McDonald's near school. We misbehave on Friday nights, and while they date on Saturdays, I stay home and pout.

Things at home are strained, as usual. Dad's grown more agitated lately and is driving Mother mad since he has virtually ceased all effort to find any kind of employment. We hoped this seemingly endless depression of his would soon turn for the better, but I don't think he cares one way or the other if he ever works again. Mother is working nights at the drugstore, days at J.C. Penney, and takes in sewing on weekends. I don't know how long she can hold up under the strain, but I'm doing what I can. I managed to pick up a morning paper route to supplement the income I give her from my job at the drugstore.

It all simply sucks, Rosie, if you'll pardon the expression.

But, enough blubbering. You're on my mind, did I tell you that? I hate snuggling pillows, but they provide some company when I pretend they are you. I also walk in the park several times each week and sit on 'our' bench when it isn't occupied by a bum, goose, or a guy who's bigger than me. I hope tennis is 'serving' you well. Perhaps you'll show me some new moves you learned while away. Hubba hubba. Going for now. 'Love' you.

As Always,
Me

June 30, 1963

Dear Marie Rose,

I'm sorry I have been slow to write. I promise you are never off my mind, but hard times have grown worse. Dad is unbearable, and a recent incident has thrown the household into turmoil.

I believe much of Dad's behavior was spurred by the news last week that the lawsuits against him, although settled out of court, left the city with no alternative but to indeed rescind Dad's pension. His criminal court appeals were denied, but the judge spared him time in jail in deference to probation. That is some compensation, but his twenty-year career is a complete wash.

Shortly after my last letter, Dad came home at three a.m., dead drunk and with lipstick on his collar. Mother, of course, was livid, and this produced a most terrible fight involving them, Lyla, and me. The incident began with Mother's suspicious questioning of what I would imagine was no more than Dad getting a kiss from some other slobbering drunk in the bar, but it escalated into a brawl right in the sanctity of our house. Dad screamed at Mother, blaming her for not giving him enough attention at home. Then he raved about her holding her weekly paycheck over his head when he wants to go out, and Mother returned the hysteria, calling Dad a worthless drunk who not only takes the household money and wastes it on booze, but on women as well.

Dad suddenly hit Mother with his closed fist and split her brow. Lyla witnessed this, and she attacked Dad just as I came running in. Dad threw Lyla to the floor, and he began pounding her. I lost all of my self-restraint, Rosie, and God forgive me, I attacked him with a blind rage inside of me. I hit him again and again, breaking his cheekbone and jaw and knocking him out, and I dare say I might have killed him if it had not been for Lyla and Mother, who dragged me away.

God, Rosie, I wanted to kill him - my own father - I wanted to kill him so we would be free of his tyranny and the damned self-pity shrouding the house. I wanted him dead for that poor woman who still lies paralyzed in a hospital. I wanted him dead for throwing our family into a ring of shame.

My God, Rosie, what has become of me to feel this?

The storm quelled, leaving the family in a helpless mass on the floor. Everyone was crying and bleeding. Dad was so drunk that I believe he was more dazed by the liquor than by the injuries. It seems hollow to say that everyone is now patched and recovering; the wounds run so deep. Dad withdrew into his darkened hole all the more, but Mother insists upon staying with him, and that is something I cannot fathom. In fact, Dad ordered me out of the house for beating him so badly, and Mother didn't come to my defense. She simply told me to give the incident time to fade. Meanwhile, I stayed with Steven and his family. I was thrown out of my home for defending my mother and sister, Rosie, while the tyrant remained.

Indeed, Mother was right, for Dad relented after a few days and told me to come back. It was more an order than a request, but the drunken Caesar absolved me by saying it was right for me to come to their defense. The bastard made me feel like I'm the criminal.

Rosie, I am watching my father degenerate in a sea of booze, and there is nothing I can do to stop it. I increasingly find my thoughts wandering to this terrible wish that he would just die and leave intact what little sanctity is left of my family. Lyla departed for Boston the next day, months before she was to return to school. She had little to say to me other than a weak apology for leaving me to fend for the family because she couldn't endure Dad's rage anymore. Her departure was greeted with Dad's typical indifference.

"Let her go," he said. "She's better than any of us, anyway, with her big-time Harvard scholarship."

I cannot believe he would say this about his own daughter. My father is gone, Rosie, and in his place is a pile of stinking, booze-ridden flesh. Why, while feeling such hatred for him, do I also feel pity? They stripped him of everything, and it has destroyed the whole family. I've read that this is a disease, but why does he not stop and look at what he is doing to us?

Rosie, I'm sorry to unload all of this at your expense, but you are my lifeline. You're the only person with whom I feel comfortable in sharing this. When I know you're there, it's as if there is nothing too formidable in its horror that can stop me. Thank you for understanding. I love you.

As Always,
Me

July 12, 1963

Dear Marie Rose,

Your letter has brightened this rainy day! I am so very proud of you! Congratulations on your tournament victory!

Also, news of the opportunity for you to teach there next summer is exciting, but it gives me the old familiar twinge knowing you'll be gone again. What a critical time in our lives we are embarking upon as fall draws near. It's so hard to imagine we will be graduating in less than a year, but the thought of it imparts the need for important decisions to be made as the months pass. I hope you feel similar comfort in knowing we will have each other to consult during this important time.

You mentioned some difficulty with thoughts regarding the direction you will go. Indeed, your instructors down there would have influence in securing an athletic scholarship, but if what they tell you is true, you may be ready to turn professional and have to set college aside for the time.

That prospect is very exciting! You ask for my advice, and all I can say is you should not jump to any hasty conclusions until you see what the school year brings. Be true to your feelings and I would bet you'll know the answer come next spring.

As for your needing a big kiss, hold on, for I am pucker practicing every day!

You ask how I am getting along with the ogre. First, I must again thank you for phoning after you received my rather desperate letter - you made me feel better. Regarding the house, everything has been strangely quiet as of late. Dad still drinks constantly, but he's generally happy to lie around his room. His all-night binges on the town have all but ceased.

As for me, I am confused. The future appears clouded. Oddly, this whole exercise in horror has borne inside of me an idea for a play that I am now drafting. It is entitled: Strange Potions. I believe it a psychological exercise for me to rid the demons that haunt me by writing about this thing that possesses Dad, and how it tears into the fabric of everything he touches.

But, back to plans: As you know, I struggle with the idea of attending college. Mathematics, history, and clothes-washing seem unimportant areas for the devotion of my time when I might better take advantage of my interests by packing up and moving to New York, where my interest in theater could be served. I haven't discussed these thoughts with my parents because the upheaval caused by Dad's antics has precluded any serious discussion of my future. At the rate we're going, I may have no other choice but to continue stacking shelves at the drugstore to help Mother support the family. Dad's last visit to the liquor store drained the last penny from their savings account, something they had been building for twenty years before his bus crash.

Mother cashes her weekly paycheck the day she receives it and takes the money directly to the grocery store because Dad immediately demands any leftover cash when she arrives home. Mother and I plan to secretly open a savings account together, where we can deposit our earnings and Dad can't touch it.

Just one happy family...

Mother hasn't said it, but I have a terrible suspicion she is struggling with the mortgage payments. I asked Uncle Vern for help, and as usual, he came through, but I must secretly accept since Mother's pride prevents her from taking his money. It so confuses me how Uncle Vern, possibly as free with the drink as Dad, always appears under control.

"Somehow," Vern says, "the devil missed me."

I'm not sure I know what he means by that. Vern tried to suggest that Dad attend an A.A. meeting, but Dad went into a screaming rage.

"I don't need any damned Bible-thumpers to whine to me about their problems," Dad said. "It's the city's fault I can't work - it's my worthless wife and kid's fault they don't bring in enough money for me to get a good suit so I can go find a job..."

Rosie, he always blames Mother and me. Other times he blames Lyla - sometimes it's Vern. But none of us were driving that bus, drunk as a damned shriner.

Vern is the most easygoing man on earth, but at times I see something solid beneath his eccentricities. He took me aside and said, "To straighten out, your old man has to want it to happen, but he doesn't want anything. He thinks beating up his family is easier than beating on himself."

Vern's a kook, but he almost frightens me with his latent insight. Whenever he says something, I think he's really saying something else...

But, so much for cheery news from home, Rosie. You don't deserve to hear it considering the wonderful turn your life is taking. Be assured, I am proud of you. By the way, I had dinner with your parents yesterday evening. I'm refreshed when I see a family possessed by so much love. Even Angela seems to be able to stomach me now, for I caught her secretly smiling at my incredibly witty conversation. Your father invited me to go with him next week to the country club golf tournament. He tells me he knows Arnold Palmer, and I will have the chance to meet him. Since you and I met, a whole new world has opened to me! Your parents expose me to a social and political world I didn't know existed, and they have an astonishing repertoire of well-known acquaintances.

I'm beginning to ooze with class!

I love you, Rosie, and I count the days to your return. Keep me current, and pucker practice every day! Bash those opponents; I am pulling for you!

As Always,
Me

September 4, 1963

School started today, Journal. I do not care for having to go straight from school to the drugstore, but it is something to which I will have to grow accustomed. Thank God Mother was given another raise at Penney's. I was beginning to believe I might have to work five nights and weekend days, but the boost has given me some reprieve. It sounds selfish, but this is my last year of school and I want to enjoy as much of it as possible.

Dad disappeared for two days. God, I hate him. It seems his feelings were hurt when Mother couldn't contain her excitement for the raise. Poor dad had to go wash away his blues.

"Got time for your writing and your girlfriend," he said to me just before he went off into the shadows, "but you got no balls to get a raise like your old lady did. You're as worthless as me."

Why did he say that? God, I hate him.

October 20, 1963

I have never been fond of Sundays, Journal. They are so neutral. They have no character, particularly during the fall and winter. Last night, Rosie and I attended the Homecoming dinner and dance. Of course, Rosie was radiant, even more than she was last year. There is a strange aura about her;

about me. Something has changed in our relationship, and it depresses me. Rosie so looked like a woman last night, and I felt so much like a man. The whole school affair seemed as if it was at a distance from us, perhaps as if we have outgrown high school dances.

Of course, my depression is understandable because I felt so badly all week due to my lack of funds for an expensive dinner. I couldn't rent a tuxedo like I did last year, nor could I ride up with Rosie in a rented Cadillac like a few of the fellows did with their dates. I guess it's all rather silly, but I felt badly that I couldn't show off. No, my money goes to Dad's social engagements at the Lakeside Tavern.

But that is not the whole reason for my feeling so low today. Since Rosie returned from Arizona, I've felt a change come about. I long for the spark that ignited into a passionate flame when I first saw her. Could it be we've grown too comfortable? Or, is love beginning to stagnate? I look at my home and my bleak future, and then I look at Rosie's and her wonderful family, and I ask myself if it is not inconsiderate of me to burden her endless potential with my dead-end existence.

I'm really beginning to feel I am only now starting to grow up.

God, I'm depressed. Home stinks, school stinks; my family life is comparable to quartering at the state prison. Dad has completely given up, and he is drinking himself to death. I'm looking at the beginning of my lifetime, and yet, I'm lost in a maze of worry for what this family has become. June is as dark to me now as it has ever been.

I hate Sundays.

November 12, 1963

Heard some terrible news today, Journal. I overheard a teacher speaking with the principal about my strange friend, Mike Golightly. I lost touch with him after he graduated in 1962.

The news is that Mike is dead.

He was killed in some place called Vietnam. I was stunned, and I had to ask the principal for more information.

The news was not detailed, but Mike joined the army shortly after he graduated, and he later went to this Vietnam sometime in the last year. I have heard news about some kind of war over there, but I did not realize there were Americans actually involved in the fighting. If asked to find Vietnam on a map, I'm embarrassed to say I would have no idea where to begin my search. Recent times have seen the growing unrest with Russia - we're always doing those inane 'duck and cover' drills - and there was the botched invasion of Cuba and the news about missiles there last year; but now this Vietnam issue has claimed the life of a boy I knew.

I must learn more about this thing. There recently was an assembly for the senior boys regarding our registering for draft into the armed services, but I must admit a foolhardy lack of concern on my part. I guess I haven't thought much about what will happen after I graduate next spring. Suddenly, this news makes me realize I had better start.

Mike is dead. I feel sad for him. I felt sad for him when he was alive. God, I can still see him lying on the liquor store floor on my sixteenth birthday, behaving as if he was accustomed to being treated so badly. And now, he is dead. Poor Mike.

Mike Golightly is dead...

"Safe upon the solid rock
the ugly houses stand:
come and see my shining palace
built upon the sand!"

- Edna St. Vincent Millay

November 22, 1963

This is a black day. The clouds over this house have grown thicker. It is very late. There remains the quiet babble of the television set upstairs. It has been on all day. The noise is telling the world how things have drastically changed.

President Kennedy was assassinated today.

I cannot comprehend the magnitude of what I have just written. Kennedy is dead. Unbelievable.

I shall try to organize my thoughts. Today started out as every other day. It is Friday, my favorite day. The air was full of Friday excitement, accentuated by the prospect of a football game tonight. There were plans for a rally outside the school, followed by a large car caravan to the stadium. Mother let me borrow the car so Steven and Paula, Marc and Karen, and Rosie and I could drive there together. We'd watch the game, and then go out for pizza, making for a grand night. It wasn't supposed to change as it did.

But, it did change. Shortly before lunchtime, Rosie met me in the lobby, and we walked together to the cafeteria. On the way, the school intercom blared on with the announcement: "Attention students. The school is closing for the day. All faculty members are instructed to go to the library; all students are ordered to clear the building and immediately proceed home."

We stopped and looked at each other in confusion as the announcement was repeated. Everyone in the cafeteria was silent. Some of the kids first let out a cheer, but they quieted at the eerie bluntness of the principal's voice coming out of the speakers. Perhaps stemming from my paranoia lately, I suddenly thought maybe after all these years of adults warning us about the Russians, this time it was no drill - maybe the A-bomb was falling on us right now.

The principal made the announcement again as Mr. Franks, my history teacher, wandered out of his room, his face ashen and tears streaming from his eyes.

"Hey, Mr. Franks," one boy hollered, "what gives?"

"Somebody shot Kennedy," he said. "Kennedy was shot..."

He walked away like a zombie as the intercom crackled - the principal had put the microphone to a television in his office. Walter Cronkite's voice related the shocking details: President Kennedy had just been wheeled into Parkland Hospital in Dallas with a gunshot wound to the head. Mrs. Kennedy, with the president's bloodstains on her dress, followed close behind...

"My God," I whispered. "I can't believe it."

"I have to get home," Rosie said.

She was terribly shaken. Her father had once met President Kennedy - in fact, he knew Attorney General Robert Kennedy well. Her family, as does mine, loved the president.

I took Rosie home and rushed to my house to find Dad sitting in the living room, staring blankly at the television. Dad, himself immersed in his own disease, sat stunned as the television spewed out its venomous bile, while Mother sat alone in the kitchen, her face in her hands as she listened to the radio accounts.

At that moment, Walter Cronkite's trembling voice echoed through the house: "President Kennedy died at one p.m. - some thirty-eight minutes ago..."

How can this be happening? What is going on? The president is shot down on a Texas street. The Russians could kill us with the push of a button. Negro people are being beaten and strung up in trees. Mike Golightly is killed in Vietnam. It seems as if the world is going mad.

The television upstairs is silent now. I hear footsteps. From the clumsiness of step, it must be Dad. Mother went to bed hours ago with both Mary and Jonathan snuggled next to her. Dad was strangely quiet tonight. He was glued to the television set all evening. I rarely even speak to him anymore, but tonight I sat with him for a time, trying to find words. Oddly, he was the one to finally speak.

He turned from the TV and looked at me with hollow eyes. "It's the end of everything, son - everything."

I couldn't answer. I got up and left, amazed at his sincerity, but frightened by the black emotion oozing from him. He may have cried, although his grieving was private and away from our eyes. Before this, he has always been of but a single emotion - rage.

He is wandering about in their bedroom now. I hear him.

I called Rosie just a moment ago. Her father answered and he cried when we discussed this tragedy. He is openly devastated and unashamed to share it with me. Rosie, too, cried, and when we said goodnight, she said, "I love you."

Utter emotional exhaustion grips me, but to sleep tonight will be of the most profound difficulty. The house is so silent.

Dad is still wandering. He is at the stairs, and is coming down here. I hear footfalls on the steps...

2

Insurrection

1964

"Where peace
And rest can never dwell,
hope never comes
That comes to all."

- John Milton

May 8, 1964

Happy birthday, Me. Happy birthday, Journal, I've missed you. I've proposed to emerge from this self-imposed exile to begin writing again. Mourning for Dad has ended. The crying lamp is out.

Eighteen years old today, gloriosky. Upon review, I see my last entry was on the day Kennedy, and Dad, died. How ironic were my last words written that night just seconds before what was not only Dad's death, but my rebirth as well. How I instantly changed is remarkable; God, I was such a child before.

I promise, Journal, I will do better and neglect you never again. I'm grown up, and I will act accordingly, for that is what is required of a man. A child would never survive what lies ahead, and I am prepared. Yes, Journal, I am a man.

Eighteen today. Reality. I hate it. I'll need you, Journal. You'll need me. This begins tonight when I discover pain.

God, how I hate inevitability.

May 9, 1964

Dear Marie Rose,

This is the most painfully difficult task I have ever faced. I am a coward, Rosie. This letter must be my messenger since I could not find the courage to face you with this last night. Please understand, I am not a man of verbal demonstrations; the written words can only suffice as my tool of communicating truest thoughts. Anything less would be an injustice.

We cannot continue our relationship. I am so terribly sorry for my bluntness, but I intend for my lifetime to never break my vow of honesty with you. Our superficial happiness of the last few months cannot screen the inexorable approach of graduation, and the disconnection from childhood. We must move on, and for me to expect your devotion and love would be an act of selfishness.

I know you have suspected this. You have often mentioned that I no longer respond in the ways of the past, and you are correct - I have changed. Something happened to me the night Dad committed suicide. He may have physically killed himself, but in me, he killed my idealism and the blind belief that the world can be of my choosing. I watched my childhood die with Dad's last breath. He successfully left me with his guilt. How many nights I prayed for him to die, that my hatred would be satiated by his passing, and how stunned I am now to learn how prayers, when sent from the heart, are answered. I am guilty, Rosie, guilty of Dad's death. No decent son would ever want his father to die. I, too, am guilty of wanting more for my family, myself, and for you, than what we all have.

Rosie, I have changed.

I feel like Kafka's Samsa: A metamorphosis without choice. What is more disturbing is that I do not know what I've become, and these troubled times are forcing me to travel the only road I can search. Destiny is pushing us apart, Rosie, and for me to insist we try to hold what we had is unfair to you. I suspect what I will find down the road is my father's son, and to be honest, you deserve better than that. I hate my father. He is a coward.

To you, I am grateful for your compassion for not only me, but my family during our darkest days. How we would have survived without you and your wonderful parents cannot be measured. Thank you for loving me, holding me, crying with me, and enduring my disdainful rage following Dad's crime. But understand: I cannot contain my rage, and I will just vent it upon you, the best friend I will ever have on earth. Because you will leave this fall for college in California, I refuse to drag upon you during this, a critical time of your life. I have made another decision, Rosie, one that is unavoidable. I cannot attend college. It is not attractive to me, and even if it was, it is financially out of the question.

And so, Rosie, I decided to enlist in the army to save America the trouble of drafting me. Mother needs the income the service will provide me, and I cannot turn my back on my country.

My dreams of New York are over.

The days ahead are uncertain. It appears my destiny to face them alone. I will not be without my wonderful memories of you, and I am certain the essence of your life will remain with me forever. It is impossible for me to feel for anyone else the intensity of my love for you, and I pray at least a small part of me will remain with you. We are growing up in a terrible time and place; a world over which we have no control. Life's cruel reality is that happiness, at best, is but a fleeting breeze that goes as quickly as it comes. It is only good fortune that it ever comes at all.

I am crying as I write this, Rosie. Perhaps this letter will not be my last, but for now, we must travel separate roads. Please search your heart to forgive me for breaking this way. I, in turn, pray you find a happiness that will never blow away.

As Always,
Me

May 9, 1964

I am sick, Journal. My heart is broken.

"I love you," Rosie tearfully said.

We shared a kiss and cried together.

"Always," she said, "and forever." Then, she ran from me. I hate this world. We're all so alone..

"But war's a game which
were their subjects wise
Kings would not play at."

- William Cowper

September 24, 1964

So much to catch up on, Journal. Have been remiss in my writing duties, both in writing to you, and writing letters home. Frankly, boot camp has been so excruciatingly taxing on my skinny body that I find time for little else than sleep during free time.

But, I feel guilty, Journal, for not writing to you, Mother, Lyla, and most importantly, Marie Rose, whose letter surprised me two weeks ago. I felt an inexplicable surge of love in my heart, but it was accompanied by my old friend, Guilt. How I hurt her when I broke off our relationship, but I still feel it was the proper thing to do. I still feel my life is fragmented, and it is simply wrong for me to expect her to wait.

But her letter, Journal, her words lightened my heart, and I cannot resist the temptation of her suggestion that we remain at least the closest of friends; to let love fend for itself so we can remain in touch while I am gone.

It is like her to be so rational!

And, I must admit my ill-found romantic interests here at camp, i.e. the local barflies, do not at all resemble my fancy for the memory of Marie Rose.

In fact, I miss the shit out of her!

Please note, Journal: Boot camp has taught me a new and colorful vocabulary.

Rosie wrote: "I don't intend to ever let our friendship die, no matter where our lives lead. If we end up together, so be it, but if we live apart, my feelings won't change. But one thing you better get through your thick skull, I don't lose, and I'm not losing you!"

I'm constantly reminded why I fell for Rosie in the first place. Losing her would border upon insanity.

And, speaking of insanity, Journal, let me tell you about boot camp: Someone once said, "You're in the army now," but I have never quite grasped the gravity of the thought until I signed on. My first six weeks were something out of Poe. The drill instructors were heartless, their incessant harassment and brutality of the most unbelievable order. I was at first appalled at their obsession with the notion of taking human lives. Rejecting them, I was ready to demand my rights and all the other stupid things a boot thinks he is entitled to. But I eventually saw the light. It reminds me of something Dad once said about his basic training: "It's like driving on an icy road. You're not in control. Turn with the skid and you'll do fine, but turn against it and you'll end up with a bumper in your forehead."

It was one of the few things Dad ever said that made any sense. The moment I started turning with the skid around here, the heat subsided and I became a good boot.

I must admit, I am in the best physical condition of my life, thanks to the relentless pounding by the drill instructors. I first believed I would be off to learn how to jump out of airplanes without vomiting on myself, but my D.I. took me aside one day and said he recommended me for the experimental 11th Air Assault Division. He finally took a liking to me - in a sadistic sort of way - and said he was impressed with both my attitude and my skills with a rifle. I'm blessed with perfect eyesight (blessed, I think), and Sarge recommended that I be trained as a gunner on a helicopter.

Imagine that, Journal, I've finally discovered a talent I inherited from Dad; I can shoot straight. I don't, however, plan to aim at my head.

In the 11th AAD, I've learned more about the army and Vietnam, for I finally got some purposeful training. What I've learned doesn't exactly set my mind at ease. Since the Korean War, the army has been intrigued with the application of rotary wing aviation to combat. Helicopters in Korea were used primarily for medical evacuation, but technology has produced faster, bigger and more powerful choppers. The army envisions the use of helicopters in what they call 'Airmobile Warfare.'

Presently, American advisers are training South Vietnamese soldiers how to defend themselves. Advisers lead them into battle against Communist guerrillas via double-rotor Shawnee transport helicopters with UH-1 "Huey" helicopter gunships providing escort and cover. The mobility allows them to descend on the guerrillas with remarkable speed, eliminating the problem of moving troops on foot across difficult terrain. It gives the South Vietnamese Army an edge in combating the guerrillas in the jungle. However, the army's idea of airmobile warfare far surpasses current procedures, giving rise to the 11th AAD test last year. The army is now training pilot crews and ground troops in all-out airmobile assault, using the swift hueys as both troop transports and covering gunships. Since its inception, the test has grown from a few thousand men to an additional two brigades of infantry and artillery units, and they're recruiting Warrant Officer candidates for helicopter school in Texas.

Riding in a huey is a head-swirling experience. They rise at breakneck speed, and pitch forward as if shot out of a cannon. On my first trip, my stomach was left somewhere on the ground, but it didn't take me long to grow accustomed to it. I'm training on a gunship rather than a huey troop carrying 'slick,' but I'm told I could be assigned either way. My sergeant tells me crewing on a chopper is preferable to the prospect of soldiering on the ground. The only drawback, he says, is door gunners are the first to get shot at.

What bothers me is this confusing history of Vietnam and America's 'advisory' participation versus the extensive combat training that I'm undergoing along with thousands of other men. I've learned from the old adage of 'Ask me no questions, I'll tell you no lies' that a good boot should keep his mouth shut. But I at least can ask you, Journal: If we are only serving in a limited advisory capacity in South Vietnam, why is this division so intensively training American ground troops in airmobile warfare?

The quiet talk around here concerns both Kennedy and Lyndon Johnson. They say Kennedy, who on one hand implied he was going to start withdrawing Americans from Vietnam and cut his losses, quietly on the other hand continued to approve of Marines training the South Vietnamese in counterguerrilla warfare. Then Johnson comes along. As a senator, Johnson fought against President Eisenhower, who briefly considered a nuclear strike against North Vietnam in 1954. But now that he's in the hot seat, Johnson appears to be equally hawkish by expanding the Kennedy policy of aggressive preparation for war. With the prospect of facing Barry Goldwater at the polls, it looks like Johnson can't afford to appear soft on Communism.

There is no doubt around here that we are being trained for combat. What annoys me is all of this appears not so much a military decision, but rather a political hot potato being tossed around in Washington D.C.

God, how this all looms before me like a black pall. It is so hard to imagine only months ago I was just a teenager without a rudder. Now, all of my thinking is done for me, and in return, I may be called to participate in the Vietnam War. I hear stories of leech-infested jungles, village massacres and torture, and guerrilla combat; all tales that set the hair on end.

Indeed, it's frightening, but at the same time, terribly exciting. Soldiers over the millennium have marched off to war, which has been the noble and rather romantic obsession of writers over the centuries. I've seen death on two separate occasions in my short eighteen years. I know in my heart I'm prepared for this journey, and I'm prepared to die for my country, if in fact its true purpose is to liberate the South Vietnamese from the threat of Communism.

Don't summon a doctor, Journal, for I am not implying a death wish. It remains deep in my heart to survive and live to be bald, but all of this holds a mystical calling to which I must answer. I'm simply turning with the skid.

Through study, I'm learning more about this war in Indochina and all of its consequences. Communism is spreading like a cancer, deriving its power from the previous wars in Europe and Japan. At the end of World War II, Stalin did not share Truman and Churchill's vision of sovereignty for all nations. The Russians have since devoured Eastern Europe and set their sights on expansion throughout Asia and Indochina. Although Vietnam is a seemingly worthless piece of land occupied by simple third world rice farmers, it strategically sits on the outer edge of Asia where seaports open the door to the West. Despite Communist denials, it's suspected that North Vietnamese guerrillas are empowered by arms and advisers from China and Russia to conduct a reign of terrorism and genocide in order to split South Vietnam in half and break down its government.

The United States and its UN allies have attempted to protect the south through military assistance, but the South Vietnamese Army is woefully weak, and its civilian population is resentful of outsiders who, in order to protect western interests, are in essence fueling a civil war. They say if we win their hearts, their minds will follow, for President Eisenhower once said if Vietnam falls - all of Southeast Asia would tumble like a house of cards. It appears today's politicians are looking to deal. It's a game of high stakes, Journal.

October 2, 1964

Dear Marie Rose,

I am scum. I am so humbled by your letter, and am overcome with a sense of worthlessness by not replying sooner. I hope you understand. How you could hold enough regard for me to write your well wishes is indicative of your forgiving nature, particularly after my cowardly retreat from you last spring. This summer away from all I have known has served as a wonderful growing experience for me, and I may be viewing life in a different light.

As you have asked how I am getting along at Fort Hernia, I shall do my best, but would be remiss if I did not first mention my pride in your successes on the tennis court this summer. I am glad, however, you are still comfortable with your decision to attend Cal Berkeley and continue your amateur career for the time being. If you do not think you're ready to turn professional, the time spent obtaining your education will combine well with your participation on the tennis team there.

As for me, I completed basic training and lived to tell it despite the army's attempts to kill me. The drill instructors make John Wayne look like a sissy. I was subsequently put into a helicopter for extensive training where I first believed I was going to stay for at least another six months. However,

I hesitate to say I have some ominous news.

I just received orders for Vietnam. It seems the army is very fond of me. In fact, they love me so much that they need my deft skills with an M-60 machine gun over there. How is it, Rosie, that after eighteen years of trying to find something I'm good at, it has to be this?

I have been attached to the 121st Army Aviation Company, and my duty is to replace a 'door gunner' on a helicopter that travels the speed of light over treetops and rice paddies. I am to ship out in three weeks to a base in the southern region of South Vietnam near the Mekong Delta called Soc Trang.

It is all very unnerving, Rosie. I have no concrete impression of what lies ahead, but I fear there may be no amount of training a boy from Colorado can receive that might prepare him for the Asian jungles. I will fly in a UH1-B helicopter called a 'Huey,' which is a small, high-speed gunship designed to escort the large troop transport helicopters into battle zones. We protect the deployment of the South Vietnamese soldiers into areas where Viet Cong guerrillas have infiltrated. After they deploy, we go back to the base and a warm meal, which is certainly more attractive than sleeping in mud.

Boot camp has been awful. Georgia is a tropical nightmare, but I'm told it's nothing compared to where I'm going. I have made some friends here, many boys of many backgrounds and colors, which serves to broaden my personal experience. What a marvelous orchard of characters there is here. I'm certain I will use it to my advantage in future writing projects.

On that subject, Strange Potions moves slowly. I have very little time to work on it, but I'm told there can be endless hours of free time in Soc Trang, so perhaps I'll be able to work more often. I remain dedicated to my journal entries, and I'll write millions of letters. The play, however, will piece together slowly, which might be just as well since it still reflects my anger with Dad.

At home, Mother has taken the news of my orders with

her inherent strong will. She has no preconceived notions of how life shall turn out, but I know she is ravaged with worry for my safety. She has finally resigned herself to Uncle Vern, who gives her a monthly check to help out the family. It is so like him to share even though he has very little himself. His money along with my earnings is at long last giving the family a life of more stability. However, despite the fact Mother's life has finally turned an important corner, I will provide many sleepless nights during my tour.

Again, Rosie, I cannot tell you how much your letter meant, and I hope you will write often. I have never been terribly adept at formal declarations of love as you well know, but I can say no matter where our lives lead, or what may happen, I shall always love you. There need be no other words accompanying this, as there has always been our understanding more of what goes unsaid.

As Always,
Me

October 27, 1964

Airborne.

Have completed first leg of the long journey. Vietnam lies ahead. I flew by commercial jet to San Francisco, and am now on board an old DC-7, strictly military, no stewardesses. We're an hour over the Pacific. A cold sense of loss came over me when the American shore disappeared behind us. Perhaps it was a similar feeling John Glenn felt when he left the earth. I resolve to write to Marie Rose religiously. We've fanned a rekindled spark into a flame. It could be a mistake, for now I feel so lost and lonely.

Could I possibly be flying to my ultimate death? I may never return the same man. I pray I'll be in one piece. So strange how visions of Hemingway and Crane are fading while the sudden reality of what lies ahead glares through the airplane window.

We are marching off to war, Journal...

October 29, 1964

Home.

That is not a word I'll use here often. Soc Trang will never be home. Never. I'm fatigued from the long journey. They say you learn how to avoid fatigue here because sleep and rest can go hand-in-hand with death. This place is not what I envisioned.

We landed in Saigon after a long and torturous journey over the ocean. Saigon is surprisingly modern and not unlike an American city, but with an Eastern flavor. In place of cars and busses are little Vespas and Lambrettas scooting in and out of traffic like flies around honey. It looks like a modern city; however, there are ever-present reminders of Viet Cong terrorism - a bombed-out building here, smoky rubble there...

The air is hot and thick, and everywhere is the odor of mold. I'm told it does not matter the weather, rain or shine, it is always hot. Our stay in Saigon was brief as I was directed to a big C-123 air transport in which we embarked on the short flight to Soc Trang. On each plane I boarded, I took another step back in time. I am so far away from what the men call 'The World,' or, Home. The C-123 is a huge beast designed to lift up to fifteen tons of freight with its two titanic turbo props. I boarded with eight others, five Americans and three South Vietnamese Army officers, destined for Soc Trang. A big man who called himself Russo, the crew chief, barked out orders as we quickly strapped ourselves into makeshift canvas seats that lined the cargo compartments. I've come from a commercial jet with stewardesses serving beers, to being just another piece of cargo strapped next to weapons and supplies destined for the dreaded Delta, where rumor has it the bush war is healthy and hot.

Russo instructed us on emergency procedures as we strapped on parachutes. "Sit your ass on your helmet and crouch in a ball if we take any rounds," he said. "If we go down, tuck your head to your knees and watch for flying debris."

This seems ridiculous. As far as I'm concerned, tucking my knees in a crash would only make it easier to identify my body, but Russo said there's always a chance of hitting the jungle trees, which might make the crash survivable.

Although landing at Soc Trang is the last thing I want to do, I felt a deep sense of relief when we touched down and our journey finally ended.

Back on the flight to Saigon, I met a most interesting man who is a correspondent for Newsweek magazine on assignment and based in Soc Trang to report on the latest offensives in the Delta.

"It's the asshole of the world, kid," said the man, Douglas Winslow. His friends call him 'Duke.'

"Thanks for the encouragement," I said.

Duke laughed through his pipe smoke. It smelled like sage. Duke has written about the wars in Europe, Japan and Korea. "This is a new ball game," he said. "The politicians are running this one, and they don't know squat about the Asians and their resolve to die. Plus, we're fighting with a whole new world of deadly technology. World War II was a slow war. Soldiers shipped out on boats, and they covered battle on foot. They fought face-to-face, hand-to-hand. But this place, kid, our boys furlough in Hong Kong and hours later are hanging out of a huey doing 120 knots."

I felt naive as Duke gave me a new perspective, nonmilitary, of what is going on here.

"This is guerrilla warfare," he said. "They fight in jungles and on mountains. The enemy is never easy to distinguish. They may be a variety of Asiatic, but it's a civil war, and you can't trust any of them, north or south. Americans have been here to advise and train the Arvins how to protect themselves and their hamlets, but the commies have Russian, French, Bulgarian, and Romanian infiltrators who disguise themselves as American defectors."

"It sounds like one can never trust anybody," I said.

"Choose American buddies and trust them, kid," Duke said. "You just might make it out. You watch, with the Kennedys out of the way and Johnson a sure thing in November, the stage is set for this thing to escalate like you won't believe. Problem is, the commies think America lost its nerve at the Bay of Pigs, and nobody around here is all that sure it isn't true, either."

I believe Duke could see the growing fear in my eyes as he spoke. He might as well have been speaking Greek to me.

"You're with the best, kiddo," he said, patting me on the knee. "Don't you forget it. I've rubbernecked a hundred missions with the 121st, and I'll tell you, they're good. When you're up in a huey, there are no politics." He blew out that wonderful smoke. "Woo boy, I could tell you some stories that'd pinch your crack, but you'll find out soon enough. Chopper pilots have some kind of stones on them."

Wonderful, I thought. "Duke," I said, "my crack needs no more pinching."

Duke laughed and slapped me on the back. We talked for hours on the journey, and he took a shine to my love for writing. I shared my experiences leading to Strange Potions, something I thought I'd never do with a stranger, but his interest was genuine. He wants to read what I've done so far. In return, he honored me with a request to read some of his war memoirs. He has one book on World War II published, and plans another on Vietnam. He promised me my remark about my crack had a place in his book.

I hope I live to read it.

I can scarcely hold my eyes open now, Journal, as I sit on my bunk among strangers. The other men have hardly acknowledged me, as they appear to be sizing me up. Duke's advice on finding buddies comes to mind. I know I must earn the respect of the fellows before I can call any one of them a buddy. Trust is surely a commodity most rare in this terrible place...

October 30, 1964

Had very little time to acclimatize as I was thrust into three separate missions today. My every fiber is drained, my nerve endings burned. I went to Hell today, Journal. I'm not sure I can make it if it is going to be like this all the time. In all of my extensive training at Ft. Benning when I hung from speeding choppers and pretended I was a soldier, I never experienced what I did today.

This is war.

There are no trumpets blaring, no heroic charges up a hill on horseback. There certainly is the rocket's red glare, but it is nothing about which I would write a song. Instead, it is a cold, terrifying experience. I am scared and confused, and my hands are still shaking even though the action ended hours ago. On top of all this, I am sick as a dog. My stomach is ripped by something my crew chief calls the Vietnam Virus. Duke Winslow calls it Drippy Tummy. I call it Anal Hell. My stomach is cramping, and I have a dreadful case of the runs and heaves. Perhaps it is nerves, but I hate to have my body betray me when I most need my wits about me. I wonder if I just curled up in a little ball, maybe the army might mistake me for dead and ship me home.

The missions can only be described as a sort of organized pandemonium. I'm the 4th of a crew on a gunship aptly nicknamed 'Rage.' Everything around here has a nickname, including the platoon – known as the Vikings. These hueys are treated with incredible care until airborne; then, they are pushed to the edge.

My crew chief is a sandy-haired fellow named Charlie Hayman. He is from Mississippi, and he has a drawl as thick as sand. He served his first tour here, and after a short furlough home, he signed on for a second tour here as a Crew Chief so he can draw better benefits for his family back home. His disposition is like a caged tiger. He introduced himself, and then said:

"That's the last time you hear the name, Charlie, understand? You can call me Hayman, or Dutch, or The Dutchman. You can call me Asshole, but if you call me Charlie, I'll bust your head, hear?"

It took me a moment to understand, Journal, but I suddenly realized Hayman doesn't want to be associated with the nickname most often given the enemy.

Hayman's twenty-two; he stands about five-ten, and weighs close to two hundred pounds. He's mean and foulmouthed, and he barked at me all day through a cheap, unlit stogie. In all, I thought him a rather unpleasant Asshole. But, when we strapped into our gunner saddles and dove into antiaircraft fire, I found Hayman knows his stuff. He gave me some sense of security amidst the madness as he deftly ran the mechanics of the chopper, never flinching under fire. I was treated like a child on this first mission, but looking back, I understand why.

Hayman sympathized with my Vietnam Virus and my virtual lack of indoctrination before flying into what he admitted was a very hairy trio of missions. Something about his treatment of me today gave me confidence even though I felt like a school child.

Hayman's vocabulary would barely fill a page of note paper, the majority of those words obscene. Every noun is preceded with 'fuckin,' 'motherfuckin,' or, one I've never heard before now, 'shitsuckin.' He calls the enemy 'slopes,' 'dinks,' 'gooks,' 'zipperheads,' 'VC,' - I suppose 'Charlie' is the most common term I've heard from others, but Hayman used the racial slurs more often than not. I wish the army would print a dictionary.

The pilots on our crew are both officers, unlike most choppers that are piloted by Chief Warrant Officers. Major Jack Putnam is in the right seat. He's called 'Fury,' like the stallion, because he is in army jargon a 'mustang,' which is an officer who has come up through the ranks. He's a veteran of the Korean War with calm manners, and his orders have a touch of 'please' in them. From San Diego, Major Putnam is forty, and he's married with two children.

Although both pilots are experienced in combat flying, Rage is commanded under no uncertain terms by Colonel Eddie Strauss, an old west-type character full of immodesty and pomp.

He owns a ranch in South Dakota where he plans to retire someday. They call him 'Cowboy.' His handle is painted on the left nose of Rage under his real name. Strauss hasn't said a word to me yet, and he doesn't appear pleased to have me on his crew. Strauss is smallish, but I imagine if you looked under his uniform you would find petrified bone held together by a grisly mesh of barbed wire.

Strauss packs a .45 with abalone handles in a handcrafted leather holster. He wears his bandoleer everywhere he goes. His head is shaved, which emphasizes a horrid zigzagging scar across the top of his skull. Dutch says the colonel always ties a purple kerchief around his neck just before we take off. Cowboy (I call him 'Colonel,' or Colonel, Sir) wears a beautiful pair of snakeskin boots, hardly army issue, but I doubt any officer here at "Soc Trang International" has any objections, for he is the battalion commander. The colonel flew fixed wing aircraft in Korea, and he has earned the Distinguished Flying Cross with ten, count them, ten oak leaf clusters. He is the senior officer among all the pilots, even though he is not much older than Putnam, and I can tell he is a proven leader by listening to him run the show.

I wonder if I am up to the task of serving with such a highly experienced crew. All three men have obviously been here for a long time, and I am fearful I may foul up. Judging from today's performance and the way Colonel Strauss leered at me, I think I may be better suited digging latrines.

Today's mission saw us escort the Shawnee troop carriers into a VC stronghold near a village called Rack Gia. The South Vietnamese rangers, ARVN (Army of Vietnam - or, 'Arvin'), planned to overrun the VC in three waves. They had to secure the LZ first, then pursue VC 'recruiters' and knock out a radio jamming station operating in the area. The huey gunship is agile and capable of providing an arsenal of cover for the big, slow-moving Shawnees. They respond to enemy fire with lightning quickness, armed at the nose with 7.62mm machine guns and 48 rockets, operated by the pilots, and two M-60s on the doors, manned by Hayman and me. Our landing zone was a rice paddy - which looked more like a muddy swamp to me - but this one was lined by a thick forest full of VC snipers. They call this a Hot LZ - a landing zone held by Charlie.

In training, I grew accustomed to the sights and sounds of the huey; the incredible roar of its engines, the heart-stopping dives and dips, the thumping of the chopper rotors, and the sizzle of rocket fire. But today, everything was exaggerated when icy reality hit me. I abruptly awoke to a world of beasts with a real M-60 in my hands. I'm no longer shooting at inanimate targets, and our rockets rain fire upon human beings now. I learned a new sound I've never known before; that of enemy fire hitting the aircraft. I felt I was hiding in an oil drum upon which someone was outside pounding with a metal hammer - like the Grim Reaper knocking. It's that nightmarish 1958 Cadillac all over again, but this one had explosives in it.

On the first two missions, everything was relatively ordered and without incident other than one moment when a sniper fired at us from the trees. We responded by pitching down and rattling the forest with gunfire to make Charlie burrow deep or run away.

It was the third mission when all hell broke loose. By that time, the Arvins had engaged the VC, causing heavy casualties for the enemy. We were bringing in ammunition and general supplies to secure the LZ. As we descended, the VC made a final stand directed at the choppers.

A barrage of small arms and rocket fire hit the Shawnees from a grove behind the LZ. Strauss responded at the point, followed by the choppers, Tracer, Eagle, Hawk, and Mercury. With all the concentration I could muster, I fired rounds into the trees as the rockets flared out below my feet. My weary stomach granted me a moment's reprieve during this time, thank God, as we pitched nose-first toward the forest. My heart pounded with adrenaline, shoving blood through my brain and giving me the most remarkable sensation as we blindly blew past the trees, which erupted in a huge orange-gray ball of flame. Random voices popped over my headset, speaking in frenzied, but deliberate tones.

It was Strauss' voice I remember most: "Tracer, bank right! - Mercury! Hawk! Skid the tree line! Too low, Eagle! Pitch up and grease that flank! Good kills! Good kills, gentlemen!"

Circling the forest of fire like angry wasps, the hueys searched for movement while we listened for further gunfire.

Strauss brought us about and my sharp eyes suddenly caught a human emerging from the smoky trees. He was dressed in black pajamas and a heavy metal helmet, what I've learned is a sure sign of a full-time Viet Cong guerrilla. He drunkenly ran, unarmed, with wisps of smoke and fire trailing from his clothes.

Dutch Hayman saw him at the same time. His voice barked over the headset: "Hard hat, Colonel, bank left!"

"Got him," Strauss said. "Coming up on your side, Dutchman. It's early Christmas - grease him!"

Hayman let out a whoop and swung about in his saddle, fixing his M-60 in position to fire. "Watch this, Newboy," he said to me.

The huey pitched low and approached the staggering VC. Hayman cut loose with the 60, tracing a very short line on the ground right up to the man. He burst into pieces when Hayman hit him, his entrails falling into the mud in a puff of steam. Hayman let out a terrible yowl.

"That's my crew chief!" Strauss called. "Little windage, Dutch, good economy. The taxpayers save a bundle when my chief spends ammo!"

"Thanks for the bone, Colonel!" Hayman said as he turned and gave me an insane grin. "Ibiddy-ibiddy-at's all folks!..."

My swirling head holds the fading memory of some laughter and more battle cries as we headed back to base.

It's war, Journal.

The ferocity of the moment kept my lunch in my stomach, but when the burning forest became a small dot of smoke on the horizon, I badly wanted to purge my guts on myself. The image of that VC fragmenting into the mud squirmed in my head. The base came into view, and in moments we flared up and landed on the tarmac. Hayman was still laughing and slapping me on the back as we jumped from the chopper. We met other emerging crews, everyone shaking their fists and reaching for handshakes. My legs wobbled when my feet touched the earth. I tried to move away from the celebration, feeling I'd hit the deck any second. Suddenly, I felt the strong hands of Major Putnam take my collar.

"You OK, kid?" Putnam asked.

I nodded and tried to steady myself. "I'm fine, sir."

"Right," Putnam said with obvious sarcasm. He dragged me to the other side of the chopper, where we were out of the view of the others. My eyes by now were rolling to the back of my head and my stomach tumbled. My lunch exploded from me as my knees buckled. Putnam reached around my waist and held me out of the mess while I did my thing.

The purge cleared my head, and I was embarrassed. Putnam let go of me and patted my shoulder. "There. Good as new."

"Jesus, Major," I half whispered, shaking my head. "I don't know what happened. The minute I touched the ground..."

"It's a reminder from God," Putnam said, half smiling.

"Sir?"

"My first kill made me puke in my lap," he said. "I think God keeps you together up there, and then he twists your gut after you're out of harm's way to remind you this isn't something you should ever want to do for a living."

"I...I don't know if I'm going to keep from ralphing every time, sir," I said, still choking back the bile.

"Call me Maje," he said. "All my friends do." His smile made me feel better. "You'll get used to it. You don't have a choice. Just don't learn to like it and you'll be okay."

Putnam left me to regain myself. I took a deep breath and wandered back into the celebration. As we walked toward the base, a medical evac chopper came in and landed in front of us. The medics unloaded an Arvin soldier and carried him past Hayman and me. The ranger's pants were torn away, exposing a shredded, bloody leg.

"Check it out, Newboy," Hayman said, nudging me.

"Jesus, what -"

"Punji stakes," Hayman said. "The gooks dig holes and crisscross bamboo spears in 'em. Step in one and that's what happens. I seen one pierce an Arvin's heel and go halfway up his leg. Some stakes go clear to their balls. This guy must have tried to pull his leg out and got fish-hooked."

I watched the ranger as he passed. He was full of morphine, but was still obviously in excruciating pain. He let out not a sound, but his body trembled and his eyes clenched shut.

"That old boy's gonna have a stump," Hayman said, still calmly chewing on his stogie. "The gooks wipe human shit on the punjis to increase the chance of infection." We took a few more steps and Hayman grabbed my arm. "That's why nobody calls me Charlie over here. Forget anything you ever learned about human decency in The World, Newboy; throw it all out, because nobody thinks like us over here. The gooks are fuckin' animals. When I cut that VC in half back at the LZ, I saw a look in your eyes I didn't like. That hard hat was probably wiping his ass with a punji with my name on it just a few minutes before I wasted him." He pulled the stogie from his mouth and pointed it in my face. "Don't ever look at me like that again, or I'll dot your eye, hear?"

"Yes, sir," I sheepishly said. "I won't let you down, sir."

"Fuck that 'sir' shit," Hayman said. "They call my daddy 'sir.' I already told you your options."

"Anything but Charlie," I said.

Hayman smiled and slapped the back of my head. "You're okay, boy. I'm gonna make a Viking outta ya. Ain't never seen a newboy shoot like that on his first run. You must be a shootin' stud like they say. Let's go have a beer."

We had four. I wish beer could cure the runs.

Upon reflection, I wonder how I can possibly survive this. Despite what Hayman said, never in all my training did I expect the real war would make me feel like this. I believed I was ready for anything, but I was wrong...

Hayman just came by and gave me some 'No-go pills.'

"These'll dry you up," he said. He sat on my bunk and lit a smelly cigar. He offered me a puff, but I think that would put me over the edge. "You done good out there today, Newboy," he said. "I was hoping my new crew wouldn't be a dickhead."

"Hope I didn't disappoint you," I said.

"Shit, no," Hayman said. "You held up good. You didn't blow cookies until we were done. You made three missions without messing the cabin."

I know my face was crimson. "I prefer to be sick alone."

"Don't worry about it. Everybody does it. Hell, the guy you replaced blew lunch before we got to his first hot LZ."

"Where is he now?"

Hayman mindlessly puffed his cigar. "Dead."

"Sorry."

He waved me off. "Didn't know him too well, but he was gonna be a good gunner. He was only on Rage for three weeks. A goddam round bounced through the cabin and caught him square in the neck - he bled to death before we could get him back. It was a damned freak hit, the poor guy. Let that be a lesson to you - we all got a bull's-eye painted on us. You and me are gonna get closer than two peas in a pod, so I don't want to watch you suck your last breath in my arms. Whether you're in the clouds, on that bunk, or in the middle of the shit, remember that fuckin' lead can find you anytime, anywhere. Charlie loves to kill Arvins, but he hates us more for crashing his party. Fact is, ain't no Newboy should be assigned to our chopper. The flight leader needs a tested crew."

"Jesus," I whispered. "Why me?"

He puffed and smiled, the smoke pushing through his yellow teeth. "Just lucky, I guess. I don't know if you know this or not, but they tell me you can not only pick a fly's wings off at a hundred yards, you got steel balls, too. I expected a pissed-off kill junkie, but you don't look it. You got something to prove, or do you just got an attitude?"

"I have the runs," I complained.

Hayman laughed and pulled from his shirt pocket a photo of a very lovely woman. "There's the prettiest girl in Biloxi."

"She's beautiful."

"She's too fuckin' good for me, but I ain't gonna bitch. She made me a daddy last month. You got any pictures from home?"

"Sure." I pulled out a few snapshots of my clan, the first, of course, a picture of Marie Rose.

"Woo boy!" Hayman said. "You're too ugly to have a woman like that, Newboy. I guess you and me are lucky stiffs."

"Lucky?" I said with a sigh. "Look at your wife. Look at Rosie. Now look where we're sitting, Dutch."

"Hey, boy," Hayman said. "This ain't so bad. You got ten or twelve seconds of dangerous shit on most missions during deployment. We had combat only one out of three today. That's acceptable. If you do have an attitude, lose it now. Follow my fuckin' rules, and make up your mind there ain't nothin' here worth getting wasted for. As long as you listen to me, you'll kiss that pretty girl again, hear?"

I nodded. Somehow in all of this insanity I feel comfort in Hayman's advice. I guess I've made my first buddy, thank God. We talked a little more, and I learned Hayman is on his second tour. He plans to go home after this one. I told him of my passion for writing and my plans to someday write a successful play. As lights out approached, Hayman told me it was time to give me a real nickname.

"'Newboy' don't suit you since you proved yourself out there," he said. He thought for a moment. "Shakes," he said. "That fits."

"Christ, Hayman," I said. "That's all I need. Why not just call me 'Chicken?'"

"No," Hayman said. "Shakes...short for Shakespeare. You and him, you got something in common. I loved reading 'ol Bill in high school."

And then, Journal, my stogie-chewing, foul-mouthed crew chief floored me as he rubbed his stubble chin and looked off into the night, quoting:

> "In peace there's nothing so becomes a man
> As modest stillness and humility;
> But when the blast of war blows in our ears
> Then imitate the action of the tiger:
> Stiffen the sinews, summon up the blood."

I sat, silently stunned. He grinned and gave me a gentle slap on the face. "Bet you thought I was just a dickhead," he said as he dropped to his bunk.

'Shakes.' Shakespeare. When I think about it, I guess I could do worse.

"I feel within me
A peace above all earthly dignities,
A still and quiet conscience..."

- 'ol Bill

November 1, 1964

Dear Marie Rose,

Greetings from paradise! What fun so far!

God, what a liar!

Sorry it has taken so long to write, but this is the first day the shaking of my hands has subsided enough for me to pick up a pen! So, here I am, wherever that is. Vietnam. Although I have sometimes questioned the existence of God, I am certain if He does exist, then He is not perfect. Vietnam proves even God can make a mistake.

I hope this letter will not simply be an inventory of complaints, but I find it difficult to observe anything good about this place. The life of helicopter crews is similar to living life on a perpetual roller coaster. One moment, I am sitting comfortably in the shade of our huey, involved perhaps in a good book or conversation, and the next, we're suddenly diving into gunfire in a blaze of roaring terror.

Vietnam is a mysterious painting of stark and unusual colors. Modern Saigon lies in contrast with the primitive outlying hamlets. But, wherever I go, I feel I reside in the ancient past. The solid comfort of home, just scant weeks behind me, feels as if it never existed. I already long for such menial luxuries so taken for granted at home, like a hot bath, a double bed, or, most importantly, your touch. I've finally conquered a most distasteful bout of what every new man gets here, namely the Vietnam Virus, i.e. the runs. Thank God my stomach has adjusted.

The South Vietnamese soldiers (we call them 'Arvins') are gallant at times, but they are often hesitant to fight. We're supposed to be helping them defend their country, but I rarely have any contact with them at the base. They fear our western 'decadence' can be contaminating.

You're welcome, Arvin.

Admittedly, I did expect them to be rather like savages, giving fuel to the obvious gap that separates our cultures. But, they are simple people, compelled to protect their homeland from the Communists who infiltrate the villages and recruit soldiers by hog-tying them and throwing them into the back of a truck. At least when I enlisted, I was given time to pack my underwear.

These villagers are the Communists' most valuable resource, and it is the army's task to insert trained South Vietnamese troops into vulnerable areas to flush out the Viet Cong. The Marine Corps goes through the agonizingly long process of educating able-bodied villagers in martial arts and antiterrorist tactics. This is difficult, since many villagers have little or no idea what Communism is until they're overrun and their freedom is taken. Freedom is difficult to define over here. Our role is enigmatic. We are in a war, but the government is very precise with its semantics. They impose a strict directive of firing only if fired upon, a somewhat confusing idea in the face of battle.

I have much to learn about politics, Rosie, politics and war.

I have several good friends here. My favorite is Duke Winslow, a war correspondent from Newsweek. We share an intense love for writing and spend hours discussing it. Another friend is Dutch Hayman, my crew chief. Hayman looks like a Mississippi hillbilly turned warmonger, but privately, he fawns over pictures of his new baby, and he can recite Shakespeare sonnets by heart. My newest friend is a Negro door gunner named Jimmy Moon. His nickname is 'Blackjack,' which at first might sound insulting, but the handle was given him because of his prowess at cards. His brother is a Chief Warrant Officer stationed in Da Nang, and his father is a retired drill instructor who fought the Battle of the Bulge in World War II.

Jimmy says his father's pocket watch once saved his life when it deflected a bullet. Indeed, the watch has a dent in its back. I'm not sure I'd want to earn a lucky charm that way. My new pal's other lucky trinket is a Yankees baseball cap. He always wears it either backwards or sideways when we're off duty, and once in awhile he lets me wear it when we're playing ball. He has a baseball signed by Mickey Mantle for which I offered him a million dollars, but he declined.

"You'll have to take this off my dead body, Shakes," Jimmy said.

Oh yes, I'm known as 'Shakes,' Rosie. Everybody has a nickname. Mine is short for Shakespeare, but I think it really designates a characteristic trait I've developed since coming here.

I miss you, Rosie, and I love you.

I was going to try to avoid too much emotion, for it brings on pain. Now that it has been said, I will stop bleeding. Enclosed is the address to which you can write me, and with it, a plea for your letters. The thought of you will help to get me out of this place alive. I hope college is going well and will not consume all of your time for writing, and I also hope you have plenty of envelopes and stamps.

As Always,
Me

November 24, 1964

Slow day today. Duke is in from Da Nang, and we had lunch together at the mess. His timing was perfect, for the weather grounded us for the duration and he was dying for a drink. He brought rice wine and three cases of beer, all of which we smuggled back to the barracks for the enlisted men. The officers have an endless supply of booze, so forget them.

I'm drunk.

The whole fucking world is drunk as far as I can see.

Duke likes my play, what there is of it, and he made some suggestions I hope I can remember tomorrow.

Although I've been here just a month, I feel my home is long gone, replaced by this shithole of a country. It is Hell. We're all no more than animals on the hunt, except animals don't kill for enjoyment like we do.

Duke went out on long-range recon for fifteen days into deep jungles with the Green Berets and some Arvin rangers.

"We found a village the VC took just days earlier," Duke said. "The young men were gone and everyone else were dead. Old men, old women, children - all executed. We pursued the VC and caught up with them two days later as they were taking another hamlet.

"It took fifteen hours to retake the village. When the smoke cleared, there was nothing left but carnage. There were hundreds of bodies and body parts everywhere, Shakes. Many of them were mutilated from torture. We found the mayor, his wife, and five other town elders strapped to trees with their throats cut. The Berets dug holes and piled up the bodies with a ton of lime, called in the press for some propaganda shots, and then torched the whole place. Be damned if the VC will ever terrorize that village again."

Through crossed eyes, I tried to grasp the scene. I simply can't. "The Green Berets," I said, "what are they all about?"

Duke gave a breathy smirk. "Special Forces - the subversive arm of the army. Their agenda differs with Congress. They take their orders from the CIA; and the CIA runs the war. You see, kiddo, over here it's no different than in America; shit rolls downhill in this hemisphere, too."

"I guess I don't understand," I said. "They keep telling us this is Arvin's war."

Duke laughed and then just put his hand on my shoulder. "You got a lot to learn, kiddo. Who's flying your huey? Who's shooting your M-60? Who's laying slim odds of getting out of here alive? Son, let me give you advice: When things get hot, nobody's keeping score. Your colonel worries about you more than Arvin, so don't wait for the VC to shoot first, okay?" Duke was overpowered by booze, but I don't think he was talking out of his head...

November 26, 1964

Thanksgiving. Just came back from the mess, where I had a surprisingly good turkey dinner and a cold beer to wash it down. The mood was light, but the air was thick with longing for home and family. Even class clown Jimmy Moon wasn't his usual high-spirited self, something I've come to count on. In all of this bleakness, Jimmy usually finds a way to make me laugh.

There is not a damned thing to be thankful for except a little gratitude for a hot meal and a roof over my head. Thanksgiving is always a feast at home. Last year, of course, we had no Thanksgiving because of Dad's little trick in my den, but what a happy time we've had on past holidays. Mother is the greatest cook alive. It seems many of my fondest memories of her revolve around the kitchen. Oh, Thanksgiving: Turkey stuffed with wonderful dressing, fresh cranberries mashed in honey and sugar, mashed potatoes with creamy white gravy, corn, beans baked in mushroom sauce, fresh biscuits with whipped butter and orange marmalade, wine, coffee, iced beer, cashew nuts, ripe olives, homemade ice cream, pumpkin pie...

Damn, I'm hungry again.

To show the VC how thankful we are to be here, we flew two missions in the Delta today before dinner. I saw something that would surely have ruined my appetite three weeks ago, but I have learned to create a proper set of priorities in my life, and I pass this off as par for this rugged course.

I had my first close-up look at a VC today. We met during our second deployment of Arvins to a village rumored for a VC attack. As the Shawnees were putting down, we received a call from one of the pilots. He was taking rounds from a lone Charlie in the bush. Arvins wounded the sniper in the leg and dragged him to the LZ where we landed to pick him up. Having no taste for any further combat, the VC threw his hands in the air and pleaded in his gibberish for mercy. We searched him and took him back to the chopper.

Before we left, an Arvin officer by the name of Ngu ran up, demanding to ride back with us so he could interrogate the prisoner. At the time, I didn't understand when Hayman said: "Watch this. Colonel Ngu's interrogations go something like, 'if you no talk, you fly.'"

I curiously looked at Hayman, and he raised his brows, telling me to be a good boy and follow Strauss' orders - just ignore Ngu. Ngu is a stolid little man, very serious. He has the appearance of many Arvin officers - cold and every bit as ruthless as the enemy. We took off and Ngu moved in on the POW, ripping away his black pajama top to expose bright white clothing. Incensed by the sight, Ngu began beating the POW in the face until blood flowed from his nose and mouth. He then stomped on the man's wounded leg several times while the prisoner bellowed in agony.

Ngu looked at me and wickedly smiled, pointing at the POW. "Spy," Ngu said. "He spy. He not know who he is."

"Uh-oh," Hayman said.

I leaned over. "What?"

Hayman shushed me and listened as Ngu screamed at the POW over the roar of the huey. The prisoner screamed back in a pitiful pleading tone. Hayman nudged me. "The VC always wear black, but this chump had white clothes on under the black pajamas. Some of them make a quick change of clothes, depending on who's looking at them at the time."

Christ, Journal, I look at Ngu and the POW, and I can't tell the difference; they're all Vietnamese as far as I know. Hayman listened to some more of the gibberish. "I ain't all that good at gook talk," he said, "but this here boy's SDC."

"SDC?" I said.

"Self Defense Corps," Hayman said. "They're local freedom fighters. They ain't recognized by the Arvins, because there's so many of 'em working both sides of the fence. You don't know if he's gonna shoot the gooks or slit your throat. These Arvins don't mind an SDC who's sincere about fighting Charlie, but when they find a dirty one, he's as good as red meat."

Ngu continued hollering at the POW, and once he took him to the door and made him look straight down while screaming in the crying boy's ear. I thought Ngu would shove him out the door, but he didn't. He finally threw the POW to the deck and stood over him until we put down at Soc Trang. I thought the boy was going to be taken to a POW camp, but Ngu dragged him to the tarmac and sat on his chest, resuming his frantic screams. He pulled out his .45 and put the barrel in the POW's mouth.

I stood next to Hayman, frozen. Putnam and Strauss joined us, but they said nothing. Ngu ripped at the POW's hair, still hollering, but with the gun in his mouth, the boy could only gag and cry.

Suddenly, the .45 exploded in the boy's mouth. At first, he didn't realize he was dead, but then his eyes rolled as a gob of red and gray goo spread out below his head. We all stood in fixed terror as Ngu calmly stood and holstered his weapon.

He turned to us and nodded with red murder still in his eyes. "Now he know who he is."

I did not shudder, nor was I sickened. I was frightened, but more of Ngu than what it was that so enraged him. Major Putnam walked off without speaking as Hayman, Strauss, and I remained and stared at the lifeless POW. Colonel Strauss took a long breath as he fished in his pocket for some chewing tobacco. He shoved a pinch in his mouth and started to chew. He turned and headed for the officer's club, mumbling, "Hope God forgives us for all this, boys."

What has happened to Steven, Marc and me sitting on a peaceful mountainside? To Mother's love? To Marie Rose's tender touch? It's gone. Everywhere I go, there is someone who wants to kill me, and what's worse, they all look alike. Watching one die just enforced my courage in believing I have just one more tiny chance at going home alive. Now I understand the logic of it all: It's one less man here who can kill me.

I sat at the holiday table, visiting with Hayman and Jimmy Moon without a thought about what we had seen earlier, when Colonel Strauss came up and sat next to me. He has barely said a word to me since I got here, but suddenly, I felt his acceptance.

"Happy Thanksgiving, guys," Strauss said. We returned the salutation. He looked at me and nodded. "Ain't much fun over here, is it?" he said.

"Not really, Colonel," I said. "But, I'm getting used to it."

"You don't really get used to it, Shakes, you just tend to grow into it."

I felt an uneasy twirl in my head as he spoke, but at the same time, I felt good. He called me Shakes. I didn't think he knew I existed.

"I guess I learn the hard way," I said.

"We all do," Strauss said. "You're a good gunner, son. I'm proud to have you aboard." He handed me a black beret with a blue diamond on it (the badge of the Viking). "Probation's up and the platoon's vote is unanimous. Like it or not, you're a Viking – for life. Let's hope it's a lengthy association."

"Thank you, sir," I said as the fellows gave congratulations.

"Duke Winslow tells me you're a writer."

"I suppose," I said.

"Maybe someday you can tell the world about what goes on around here."

"Perhaps," I said.

"Just do one thing, son," he said over his shoulder as he stood and walked away. "Tell the truth."

Happy Thanksgiving, Journal.

December 13, 1964

Dear Marie Rose,

This shall be brief as I feel I am without many words tonight. Your last letter touched me, and you should know I love you very much, too. I'm scared, Rosie. I'm more scared than I ever thought I could be. I'm scared when I'm awake. When I can sleep, I'm scared I won't wake up. There is no place around here where I feel secure. Tonight, we are on full alert, and some not-so distant shelling is making the ground shudder. Arvin's enemy is always out at night, and we sit between them with orders to wait until someone shoots first.

I am under a blanket with a small penlight in one hand because we are in blackout. There is, however, the faintest sound of music coming from Jimmy Moon's vicinity. It's the Beatles on his tape recorder: "A Hard Day's Night."

I love you, Rosie. I need your prayers. I need you.

As Always,
Me

December 21, 1964

A ghastly day, Journal. It has taken most of a bottle of Scotch to calm me tonight. I've been sharing it with Dutch, Jimmy Moon, and a couple other gunners in our barracks. They've been toking grass we got from some Marines yesterday, but my few experiences with Marijuana have made me feel even more paranoid than I already am. I stick with the booze. Thank God for the CARE packages Uncle Vern sends.

Colonel Strauss was seriously wounded today in the most horrifying combat I've seen to date. I am not overstating that it is a miracle we all didn't get killed.

The morning was bright and sunny, and there was only one mission scheduled. Recon reported VC activity in a small sector near the Song Gia River. We had to deploy a battalion of Arvin rangers on S&D (it's a nicer way of saying Search and Destroy, Journal). The reconnaissance report claimed the enemy was small in number. It reported they appeared armed only with homemade weapons.

I'm learning that Military Intelligence and weather forecasters are much the same; they guess. Not only did the supposedly mild weather deteriorate, the 'small buildup' was about three platoons of hard hats - not recruits, not a little band of part-timers, but hard-core VC guerrillas. The LZ was as hot as it gets. We landed in scattered rain showers, and we suddenly took rocket fire right in the teeth. We had only two hueys, ours to deploy supplies, and Eagle (Jimmy Moon's chopper) to cover the troop carrier.

There was no indication of resistance, so Strauss gave the order to go in before our L-19 observation planes had time to scout ahead to be certain of the LZ's status. It was a 'milk run.' We were complacent coming in, laughing, joking, and planning to drop our load and get back to the base for cocktails. To make things worse, Eagle touched down to help us unload before the troop carrier had landed. We simply were in too much of a hurry to get finished so we could go home.

Suddenly, the Shawnee was engulfed in a monsoon of rocket fire and made a hard belly landing into the muck. Strauss pulled pitch and tried to make a translational lift, because a heavily loaded chopper needs to reach maximum speed to gain altitude. It is a tricky maneuver even when you're not under fire. We scrambled to dump some weight as the huey raked the rice paddy, and bullets were popping around the cabin like firecrackers. Finally, we pulled up and out of the fire, swinging quickly and dropping snout for a direct tree line assault.

"Earn your pay, guys," Strauss calmly said, "we're going in."

I did not panic. I don't anymore. Grabbing my M-60 with confidence, I fired at movement in the trees. I could hear the ack-acking of Hayman's gun behind me. Our first pass was at treetop level to allow the huey's skids to rip through the tree branches. That, along with M-60 and rocket fire, generally enhances the horrible thunder of a huey attack for those on the other end of an assault. It often buys us a second of time to bank for a more accurate and deadly attack.

But we weren't dealing with untrained and unwilling village recruits who scatter at the first sight of a screaming bird of prey. These guys have a hard-core religious foundation based on the honor of dying in battle. We came about in a blazing dive, when a sudden lurch and bang shook the forward cabin. Rage made a violent bank to the right, and over my headset, I heard Colonel Strauss' muffled cry. He took a blast dead center, shattering both the left cockpit window and Strauss' head.

Putnam took over and brought the chopper under control, pulling us away from the trees and back behind Eagle for cover. Unbelievably, Strauss was still alive. He courageously barked orders to keep firing while he held his head together with one hand and fired rockets with the other. After two passes, Eagle and Rage laid waste to Charlie's nest, several of the rockets fired by Strauss blowing bodies and artillery into the air. Putnam brought us about and we put down near the disabled Shawnee, which was now on its side and sinking deep into thick mud. Arvin rangers were falling out of the dying bird, the uninjured or partially wounded forging through the mire toward the burning forest to kill off what was left of the VC. The other seriously wounded Arvins were lying in and around the Shawnee.

"Get the wounded out, Shakes! Worst cases, load 'em up - I'll call for a dust-off," Putnam said.

I jumped into the mess and joined Jimmy, who emerged from Eagle, while Hayman sprayed the trees with his 60. Several dead rangers were inside the downed chopper, but I found one Arvin boy alive, with serious burns on his legs. I wrestled him on my shoulders and made the arduous trek back to our huey. As each foot slucked in and out of the mud, I thanked God for those blasted drill instructors back in The World who beat me into shape. A sudden burst of gunfire zinged past our heads, but I continued, praying Hayman's cover fire would protect me.

Hayman helped me load the wounded. Putnam was behind Dutch, wrapping a T-shirt around Colonel Strauss' head. Beside Strauss was his shattered helmet.

"How many more?" Putnam said.

"Jimmy pulled two out!" I called. "There's four dead, and two walking."

"Medical choppers are en route for the dust-off," Putnam said. "We gotta get Cowboy out of here! Shakes, come here and hold this shirt to his head as tight as you can."

I complied and pulled Colonel Strauss close. Putnam spoke over the radio and then turned back to us as he climbed to the flight deck. "Hang on, Eddie, hang on!"

Rage screamed as we pitched. Hayman helped the injured Arvin stretch out behind us as I embraced Strauss to keep him as still as possible. Hayman joined me and helped hold the colonel's head. I barely caught a glimpse of his injury when I covered him, but knew it was severe. He had a jagged hole above his left brow and his eye was destroyed. He was semiconscious and somewhat coherent, although his speech was slurred and shocky. Luckily, he was struck by a glancing blow; otherwise, the back of his head would have been blown out.

This gives us hope for his survival.

God, Journal, how brave Strauss is. He must be fashioned from concrete. Breathing with clenched, bloody teeth, Strauss taunted death by uttering not a single cry of pain. His other eye rolled about, but it focused on Hayman and me.

"Hang on, Colonel!" Hayman said.

"Get me home, boys," Strauss shakily said. "Tell them we need some glue..."

Journal, I sit here, my mind clouded by Scotch, but I cannot remove from it the terrible sight of the colonel's head. It looked like someone had pried it open with a crowbar. What was left of his eye dangled from its socket, and a piece of skull flapped over like the top of a disemboweled tin can. I've seen worse sights here. In fact, the dead soldiers in the Shawnee were badly torn apart, but this is the first American - the first friend I've seen seriously injured.

Hayman, Jimmy, and the other two gunners from the Shawnee are now trying to sleep. As I wrote of today's events, Putnam came in to tell us he heard Strauss is now out of surgery at the hospital in Nha Trang.

"He's critical, but he did well in surgery," Putnam said.

"Is he gonna make it?" Jimmy asked.

Putnam just shrugged. "Too early to tell," he said.

Hayman took a long swallow of Scotch and offered the bottle to Putnam. "Need some oil, Maje?"

Putnam gratefully nodded and sat next to me on the bunk. "If anybody asks, I'm not doing this."

Unlike with Colonel Strauss, there are unspoken times when Major Putnam drops ranks - usually when he comes into the barracks. When he does, he becomes more like one of the guys, and we feel free to say what we please. But Putnam is still the Major, and we are certain the army knows we regard him as such.

He took a long drink from the bottle and let out a sigh. "Eddie is like a brother," he said. "We've pitched into the shit together more times than I want to know. If he dies, it would be like cutting my arm off." He leaned back and closed his eyes.

"You saw him wax that tree line with one goddam eye, Maje," Hayman said, lighting up his soggy cigar. "Colonel's too ornery to die."

I wish I could share Hayman's optimism.

With closed eyes, Putnam spoke. "You boys were good out there today; damn good. You reacted quickly, you risked a lot to pull in those rangers, and with some help from God, you may have saved Eddie's life. I recommended all of you for the Bronze Star. I'm proud of you."

A Bronze Star…

A little bronze medal is all that will symbolize what happened in that swamp today. The base commander, meeting us when we got Strauss loaded onto a medical chopper bound for Nha Trang, affectionately called us heroes. I appreciate his compliments, but frankly, heroism is routine around here. Those Arvins, some of them bleeding and dazed, thought nothing of running through the muck to secure the LZ. The one I carried onto Rage cursed us for not letting him join his platoon despite the fact he couldn't walk. I'm certain he would have crawled into the shit.

It is less heroism than it is simply survival.

I'm not going to die here, Journal. I refuse. This is a terrible place to die. I want to die an old man on a Colorado mountaintop, not in some stinking swamp. Death can bang at my door as much as it wants to. I am not going to answer. Not here. I will do anything I must to shut him out.

Anything...

December 23, 1964

Oh, the weather outside is frightful...

Some moron has been playing Christmas songs on this wet, muggy cave of a day. I'm sitting here, listening to Christmas carols squeak over the base PA and awaiting orders for a mission that probably won't come because of this swampy weather. I should be home trimming a damned tree; blowing a month's pay on presents for everybody!

I'm not sure what is worse, flying a mission, or sitting in endless boredom. I can't relax while wondering what may happen when and if the orders come.

Oh hell…

Sorry about the interruption, Journal. Jimmy Moon ran in and popped me right in the face with his orange snow cone.

"Merry Christmas, cracker!" he yelled as he ran out. Now there's permanent juice stains all over this page in my journal. Better than blood, I guess. He nailed Hayman with the juice, and Dutch is chasing him through the compound. God, those two fools could have fun at a Catholic funeral.

Let it snow, let it snow, let it snow...

God, how I miss home. Right about now, Denver is alive with the holiday season. It's cold, but not unbearable. Denver sits on a high plain at the foot of the Rockies. One winter day might see a blizzard, and the next, fifty degrees to melt the snow. At Christmas, neighborhoods have house lighting contests, and the city and county building downtown glows in a splendid display of lighting and pomp. In the heart of downtown is the May D&F store. The store has an elaborate Christmas window display that Rosie and I should be enjoying right about now. 16th Street is decorated from end to end with garlands and lighted bows at each intersection. All of downtown is alive with cars, buses, and taxi cabs full of Christmas shoppers.

The city has grown so...

Let it snow, dammit!

It's raining again. Jesus, it's raining again.

Well, Journal, good news. The word just came: My company may stand down. I'm off duty. Let the drinking lamp be lighted. Hayman and Jimmy made up and came in with a bottle of genuine Kentucky sippin' whiskey. It's homemade stuff Hayman's grandmother sent him. Go Granny go! Hayman doesn't sip sippin' whiskey, he gulps. Jimmy took a good one and passed it to me. It tastes like chopper fuel.

I'm delighted to see Duke Winslow, who blew in early this morning. He plans to stay at Soc Trang for Christmas. Duke went to II Corps near Pleiku where he spent some time with Montagnards in the central highlands. Seems the struggle with Charlie is hairy up there, which does not bode well for those of us here in the south.

Duke looks drawn and tired. I'm glad he'll spend Christmas with his friends. His eyes lit up at the sight of Hayman's mash, and I have one bottle of Scotch left from Uncle Vern's last CARE package that should go well this evening. Vern hinted in his last letter about a Christmas package to which I am looking forward. Perhaps we'll be able to drink enough to blot out Christmas entirely.

Before I lose control, Journal, I want to report that, even in Vietnam, there is a time now and again when news is not bad. Major Putnam heard that Colonel Strauss is expected to live! I can't imagine a better Christmas present than that. The colonel lost his eye, but there was only superficial brain damage. With therapy, he should recover completely. He'll be at Nha Trang for a few more days, then he'll go to the Philippines for therapy to regain some strength. His next stop is a stateside hospital for reconstructive surgery. In The World I'm sure they will have enough glue! Putnam says Strauss is already giving orders to doctors and nurses, and has requested his Skoal, cowboy boots, and his favorite Louis L'Amour novel.

Some men are simply born to war.

December 24, 1964

So depressed. Tomorrow is Christmas. Vern's package, as if sent on the wings of an angel, arrived today just in time. God, let the war rest for a day. Charlie doesn't believe in Christmas. He doesn't believe in God. There have been times when I didn't, but after coming here, God is the only thing to which most of us cling. I believe it was Edward Young who said: "By night an atheist half believes a God."

Christmas Eve. Mother is wrapping packages, splitting her time with the kitchen, which is full of delicious aromas. The kitchen is regimented into two separate divisions: Christmas Eve feast, and Christmas Day dinner. It's remarkable how she keeps them straight.

Lyla is home from Boston and will spend several days, perhaps a week, with the family. Mary will be sitting in front of the blasted television, but maybe she'll be watching 'White Christmas.'

Jonathan will be in front of the tree, inspecting the presents and thoroughly shaking each one, his eyes widening with each tantalizing rattle inside. Uncle Vern and Aunt Millie will show up around five with arms full of packages. Tonight's feast will be small in comparison to tomorrow's dinner, but everyone will commit to post-holiday diets after it's over. And then, the packages will be opened.

And, I won't be there.

Marie Rose and I had two wonderful Christmas holidays together. She came to our eve celebration, and I went to her home for their Christmas morning party. This year Mother invited Rosie for dinner. I'm glad she'll be with Mother tonight. It will make things easier. Mother's letters grew melancholy as the holidays approached. I miss her very much.

How my thoughts have been on Dad as of late. When he took his life before my eyes, I could not possibly have believed I would ever forgive him. But, now, I have much to ponder. I'm seeing things that might explain how a man perched on a precipice of despair might find life an unacceptable alternative.

I don't know, Journal, it will be a long journey to forgiveness if I choose to take it, but for the time, I wish Dad peace.

December 25, 1964

Dear Marie Rose,

What a most incredible lift to receive your letter on this of all days! Just as I manage to reach the pit of my unhappiness here, you provide for me a light of hope! I've been weepy on three separate occasions in just this last hour because your letter made me happy. I hope to finish this and mail it quickly because there is a distasteful rumor that something is brewing today and we might be called on a mission. All crews are on full alert.

Thank you for writing such a wonderful

1965

January 2, 1965

Dear Marie Rose,

I am well. Don't pay the undertaker. Don't sell my clothes!

I know how you have anxiously awaited news from here; news from me. I apologize for causing you such worry, and it's my hope this letter will serve as proof that I am only slightly damaged, ruffled, and woozy, but I am healthy. Honest.

Boy, did I ring in the new year.

The past week is but a cloud to me, and that is the reason it has taken me so long to write. It is only now I'm able to piece together what happened. To begin, I've enclosed a letter I was writing on Christmas day when the whole ugly affair began. As you can see, I was interrupted in mid-sentence. We had an emergency scramble just as I was writing, and all chopper crews ran to their aircraft.

Apparently, some Marines ran into a nasty ambush and were pinned down in an area near the village of Vinh Long.

We were ordered to assist the Marines and evacuate the wounded. It was a large operation involving the 57th Medical Detachment, our company, and a squadron of T-28 bombers. When we arrived, we found the Marines in deep trouble. The VC (that's short for 'the bad guys,' - Viet Cong) attacked as we came in. We returned fire into a thick covering of woods and jungle. It was a terrible battle, but our gunships were too much for the VC. We called for medical choppers and troop carriers to bring out the Marines and replace them with Arvin troops. Our chopper came down to stand cover for the evacuation.

Just as we touched down, we were hit by a volley of fire. A wounded Marine was limping to us, and when the fire began, I unstrapped myself so I could run to help him. What dumb luck I had. Just as I unstrapped, a bullet unbelievably exploded the heel of my boot. My foot wasn't hit, but the blast upended me, and I fell halfway out of the chopper. I was precariously clinging to my M-60 for balance, but awkwardly hanging out of the aircraft.

Then the fun began. Major Putnam, reacting to the attack, fired the rotors and pitched up, not knowing what happened to me. I was upside-down, hanging onto my M-60, and off we went at maximum boost. We must have ascended at least fifty feet before I could holler over my headset that I was in trouble. Dutch Hayman was shooting out his side, and he didn't realize what had happened until I cried out. He quickly came over, but he couldn't get any leverage to pull me up. Instead, he just grabbed my legs and held onto me as we kept pitching up.

God, Rosie, I never thought war could be this fun.

I was looking straight down at Vietnam with nothing between me and a head-first drop but Hayman's brute strength. I wrapped my hands around the muzzle of my machine gun, and I prayed.

It was at this point where reality and my reliance upon the reports of others must merge, because things grow a bit opaque from this juncture. Putnam came back down when he realized his gunner was riding in the cheap seats. We reached the ground, and Dutch let go and I splashed into the mud. Putnam started to lift off again, because they were too vulnerable to wait for me to get out of the mud. Instead of just burrowing in and keeping my head low until the hueys could blast whoever was ruining my day, I decided to make a run for some bushes where the wounded Marine had fled. As the huey lifted and turned, I jumped up to run and got hit by the rear stabilizer. Actually, it was more of a 'thud!'

Hayman tells me I was airborne for about ten feet. The impact knocked me cold even though I was wearing a helmet. It broke my nose, gave me a concussion, and stopped my watch. I still don't know what time it is. I imagine, too, the VC could no longer shoot at us because they were laughing too hard.

But I am okay, Rosie. I look like I was on the short end of

a fifteen-rounder with Cassius Clay, but I'm fine. But I do wish someone would answer the damned phone. Believe me, if I could find a way to keep my nose swollen the size of Rhode Island, I would. Hospital duty is the best I've drawn since coming here. I lie around all day and sleep or read. The doctors, graduates of the Attila The Hun Medical and Torture College, tell me I will be released in another day or two. Oh, boy. I only wish losing a few rounds with a huey warranted a return home, but I guess I'm lucky, considering what could have happened.

My only complaint in this hospital is the ominous sound of patients in surrounding wards. We see injured soldiers for a short time, but here, the pain and suffering is close and personal. I wonder if Lyndon Johnson hears those cries. Yesterday, a nurse wheeled me around the hospital. This place is something out of a cheap horror movie. This is a war of children, and women, and old men.

From the air, my perspective of the battles does not include faces, but rather, targets. Here, I see little kids without arms and legs, and old men with napalm burns. It is like walking through a human parts factory.

A bunkmate of mine told me an interesting story about a pilot who was here a week ago:

"He came in here for an emergency appendectomy," my bunkie said. "He told me he'd been on hundreds of napalm strikes."

Napalm, Rosie, is an incendiary jelly that spews from a bomb on impact. Watching a napalm strike literally sets your hair on end. Unlike most bombs that drop straight down, napalm canisters cartwheel, and when they hit, it looks like an ocean wave of fire. Hundreds of yards of jungle are consumed. The jelly sticks to the skin, making it twice as lethal, even if you aren't in the direct line of fire. Just getting a small spray of napalm can kill you because it keeps burning and burning. Because the enemy nests in the thick cover of the jungle, the napalm is used to clean out their hiding places. The problem with this is the VC hides among the women and children of a village. At very best, it is highly difficult to distinguish between the two sides of this war; therefore, napalm strikes are indiscriminate. I'm sure the government would never admit this, but the pilot told my bunkie that some strikes incinerate a huge faction of Communists, but take out many innocents or Arvins who happen to be in or around the kill zone. It's what they call "collateral damage," a chilling reference to what boils down to being in the wrong place at the wrong time.

My bunkie said, "I asked this guy what he thought about killing innocent villagers, and he said he never thinks of it in those terms. A pilot is ordered to a target, drops his load, and returns to base.

"But his eyes opened here in the hospital," my bunkie continued. "The other night he wandered around the hospital and saw some of the civilian burn cases. He was real quiet the rest of the night, and the next morning right after breakfast they found him in the latrine with his wrists cut by a shard of broken drinking glass..."

I don't know, Rosie. Seeing this suffering makes it all the more difficult to understand the position of America in this war. We don't call it a war, but it certainly looks like one. We're called advisers, but when we deploy Arvins into battle, there are American officers at the point. When an American plane goes down, there's an Arvin in the rear seat to keep diplomats happy, but it's an American pilot up front. We're providing window dressing to make it look like this is Arvin's war, but that was me hanging out of Rage. I don't know why they don't acknowledge it and get on with winning so we can go home. My God, Rosie, with a dozen divisions like the one I trained with at Ft. Benning, we could destroy the VC guerrillas in six months, but we just set jungles on fire and then retreat.

And, no one asked my opinion, either.

As I review this letter, I hope you aren't disturbed by my anger. I'm angry with the whole world for sending me here. Isolation is a dreadful thing, and nothing angers me more than ignorance cloaked in self-righteousness. I feel isolated because my opinion never gets out of this place; nobody's does.

Shortly before my accident, Soc Trang was visited by journalists from the foreign press. One of these so-called objective reporters, a pompous Frenchman, asked to go on a mission with the Arvins to see for himself what is going on here. His attitude was so typical of the stories I read in the western press (good old U.S.A. included). He wanted to expose the liberal far left cries of American political interest forcing its imperialism upon South Vietnam. The bastard geared up to spend a week in the bush with the Arvins, claiming he would objectively report his experience.

When the Shawnee pilots told me what happened, I could not believe it: They pitched to three thousand feet and he began to scream in terror. He then froze completely when they flared into the hot LZ. The bastard panicked and hugged the deck as the rangers stumbled over him to get out. He cowered in the chopper and begged the crew to take him back.

He immediately caught the next plane back to Saigon. I'm sure he's sitting somewhere, drinking rice wine and writing about the imperialist dog Americans and their Arvin puppets. Everyone wants to sit in judgement from a peaceful veranda and talk about the interventionists, but none of them have the guts to go into the bush and look at what the Communists are doing to innocent people. These Arvins are in a desperate struggle for their lives and homeland. I wish the journalists and the protesters could live just one day in the bush and watch the executions, the rape, and the unspeakable brutality. Let them exist where their lives are worth no more than the mud under their feet before they sit and write about American imperialist's puppets. Hell exists, Rosie, it's right here, but they only let us assist this woefully undermanned population perpetuate it rather than allowing us to stop it.

And, who asked me?

How easy I find preaching when all you wanted to know was, am I all right. I'm sorry. I am also sorry you had to first hear about my injuries from the army before I could get this letter to you.

Well, Duke Winslow just walked in with a bag of beef jerky and a bottle of Hayman's Kentucky mash. Hayman said to tell me the bottle is from Rage, who apologizes for punching me out. I forgive her.

Duke says to tell you hello, and that you should leave me for him. Don't do it. He's terribly old.

He is on assignment up north and stopped here in Nha Trang for the night to have a drink with me. He says it's time to get my loafing bottom back to my crew who misses me. God help me, I miss them.

But I miss you more than anything on earth, Rosie. I am sorry for bending your eyes with this letter, but I did blow off some steam. When I come home, I promise I will not be full of hatred and anger. For now, it seems to give me energy. I am still scared spitless, but fear can either save you or get you killed. Fear, mixed with anger and resolve, will keep me alive. There is no way I will leave this world with the sight of this terrible place in my eyes.

I'm angry that I do not see your face or the clear Colorado mountain sky; angry that I cannot taste Mother's cooking or hear Vern's big laugh. These are things of which I have had not enough in my lifetime. Don't ever take for granted those things you hold so dear, Rosie, for there is no greater blight on the soul to imagine them taken away and replaced by what is before me now. I live to hold you again.

As Always,
Me

January 12, 1965

God, my head hurts.

R&R - Rest and Relaxation, although it is more affectionately known to the troops as Rape and Ruin - and sometimes paraphrased as I&I, or, Intercourse and Intoxication...

I saw Hong Kong! I just got back to the base with a head the size of Utah. But, what a leave we had! I'm considering putting in for three more days R&R so I can recover from the last. I have eight hours before I go back on duty, Journal, but I must spend at least one of them with you.

I got the leave because Rage needed extended attention in the shop. While I was in Nha Trang, the crews have been at it day and night, and Major Putnam finally insisted his crew and the huey get some rest. The chopper wasn't safe anymore, Maje said, and neither was Hayman, who hasn't had any leave in ten months. Since Hong Kong, I've discovered Hayman isn't safe at any speed!

Eagle and two other hueys were in similar disrepair, so Jimmy Moon joined us, along with Duke, who arrived from Pleiku just in time.

The timing for this trip was perfect, for I have been shaky since returning to action. During two missions before the R&R orders came, I had trouble getting back in the saddle. The willies, to put it mildly. Not since my first day in country have I choked in the saddle, but I think the extra time with the guys has given me more confidence to get back up. I have to kill that fear, or it'll kill me...

We hitched a ride on an old C-47 to Saigon and caught a transport to Da Nang. Jimmy's brother, Doug, got a pass and joined us there. Doug is a carbon copy of Jimmy. Although three years older than Jimmy, he has the same unmistakable wit and charm. How I laughed when Doug rounded the corner at the Da Nang air base, strutting just like Jimmy and wearing a Yankees baseball cap turned backward. After a riotous reunion of slaps and hugs, Doug greeted us like long-lost brothers. A long wait for our transport connection was made more pleasant when Doug took us on a bar tour of Da Nang. They were stocked with booze and local girls, so we got well-oiled.

Hong Kong. What a city. They call it the Paris of Southeast Asia. Although I've never been to Paris, I dare say there is nothing I have ever seen to match the romance and excitement of this pearl of the orient. Perhaps my excitement was heightened from escaping the blight of war-torn Vietnam, but I felt like I took my first breath of vitality in some time when I stepped off that plane. It was as if I was suddenly transported back to Earth.

The excitement of our holiday mounted while still on the transport as we passed a bottle of Scotch and smoked American cigarettes. I even lost my virginity to a Havana cigar Hayman bought in Da Nang. Although I didn't tell Dutch, the stogie is the most vile and pugnacious thing I've ever smoked, but I was drunk and determined to continue this bizarre trek to manhood no matter how sick it made me.

When we arrived, we rode rickshaws to Duke's favorite hotel, The Clover, and checked in. Duke and I shared a room, Jimmy and Doug another, and Hayman shared one with a Marine we met on the flight. His name was Kyle Porter, on leave to recover from wounds he received in a firefight in the Delta. Kyle is from Georgia, and he and Hayman hit it off in a big way. In the room, I had to fight off an urge to sink into a hot tub and sleep for a day or two, but it was the shank of the evening and Hong Kong was calling.

We hit the city, Duke leading, since he is familiar with the better spots where we might find some mischief. Hayman, too, is a Hong Kong vet, but his memory only extended to falling off his first bar stool last time he was there. Hayman has an incredible capacity for alcohol, but more times than not, he gets himself into trouble when he's drunk. We spent much of Rape and Ruin keeping Hayman at a distance from the MPs.

Our first stop of the evening was The Golden Phoenix, which was wall-to-wall with American servicemen and beautiful girls. Duke, Jimmy and I were famished and unwilling to do any more damage to our livers until we had dinner. Our counterparts were more interested in the bar, so we parted and planned to reunite later. We went to the dining room, where I enjoyed a wonderful dinner. I was initially hesitant, remembering my early bout with Drippy Tummy when I first went to Hell, but I was so weary of army food that I decided to take a chance and 'go on the country.' Duke provided some reassurance, and he promised me I would not regret my decision. It would also be silly to come to Hong Kong and eat C-rats.

I made a good decision, for we were treated to a marvelous oriental meal. Of the eight or nine different dishes in which we indulged, I was most taken by a delicious soup.

"What is this?" I asked.

"Snake," Duke said.

There was a long silence as I looked back at my empty bowl. Jimmy snickered. "I thought it rattled when you ate it," he said.

I finally gave in, happy I didn't know before. "It's delicious," I said. "But when I think of snake, I think of being the eat-ee, not the eater."

"If you get the urge to crawl in some elephant grass, fight it, Shakes," Jimmy said.

Giving it more thought, I grew apprehensive. "Look, the army told me a million times to look out for rice snakes and Kraits, and now you're telling me I just ate one?"

"Shakes," Duke said, laughing with Jimmy, "you don't want to offend the management. They consider snake a delicacy over here. It's safe, kiddo."

After whining a little more, I relented and ordered another bowl. It was good! Snake has an unusual taste with the possible hint of chicken, but that might be what the slimy little bastard had just eaten before somebody turned him into soup.

Full of good food and rice wine, we joined Doug, Hayman, and Porter at the bar. They were in the company of three of the most beautiful Chinese women I have ever seen. Until then, I had found oriental girls rather plain and unappealing to my obviously western taste. I simply don't find the typical slim frame, jet-black hair, and nonexistent breasts to be particularly exciting. But these girls were different, and they had equally attractive friends who appeared out of the din the minute we joined the boys. Duke warned me about this. I quickly plugged my hands in my pockets, for these girls are interested more in American dollars than the boys to which the money is attached. As in Saigon and Da Nang, Duke said you'll find many of these girls in desperate straits.

"First of all," Duke said, "they got diseases jumping off

them. Second, many of them are Cambodian, Vietnamese, and northern refugees, all looking for a free ride to the states. Drunk boys fall in love because they're lonely. They keep a girl on the line; maybe make a baby, and when they get their DEROS (that's Date of Eligibility for Return from Overseas, Journal - yet another military acronym), they split and leave the girl worse than she started."

Journal, I could not in my wildest dreams find myself adding this to my list of mistakes since joining the army. This game of titty-go-round played by the others was not why I wanted to come to Hong Kong. More on that later.

Then, we got into a fight!

Since I arrived in Vietnam, one of my closest friends here in addition to Hayman and Duke is Jimmy Moon. I had never known a black person before I met him. One aside I must make: I always used the word 'Negro' before I met Jimmy because I always thought the word 'black' was insulting.

"Negroes are old men, Shakes," Jimmy once said. "They don't mind it because it beats hell outta 'nigger.' But we are black. I don't call you Caucasian, do I? Black is right, black is beautiful, else why would you white boys always lay out in the sun trying to look like us?"

He has a point.

Back to the fun: I never worried about racial differences, especially over here where my life is dependent on every soldier. Growing up in the north, I haven't seen bigotry like I read about in the south. We had an interesting discussion on that, too.

"No bigots in Denver, huh?" Jimmy said.

"We don't segregate busses," I said. "I've seen pictures of white-only bathrooms and water fountains down south, but you won't find that in Denver." There was a touch of pride in my voice.

"Yeah?" Jimmy said. "How about the country clubs? You seen any blacks in them?"

I had to remember back to the country club Rosie's dad took me to. "No," I said.

"Restaurants," Jimmy said, "you ever eat at a table near a

black family?"

God, Journal, Jimmy was right.

"I live in New York," Jimmy said. "It ain't the south, but I don't eat at white places in New York either."

Jimmy opened my eyes, but I didn't really understand him until the incident I'm about to describe. As we carried on in the bar, and I kept my hands on my money every time one of the girls rubbed against me, Doug Moon became very friendly with one of the girls. He gave her four dollars, the going rate, to hold her hand, and he bought her drinks. Near us was a group of drunk sailors, all white. One of them started making loud remarks about Doug being with 'a white girl.' I think the girls over here are referred to as 'yellow,' but that didn't matter to this obnoxious sailor.

After using words like 'boy' loud enough to make us all notice, he made his intentions crystal clear. "Nigger ought to find hisself some dark meat," he said.

That was it as far as I was concerned. I was full of wine, Scotch, beer, and snake meat, and I had the courage of a lion despite the fact this goon was at least twice my size. I began my approach to death, but Hayman's big hand caught my collar and brought me back down on my stool.

"I got it, Shakes," Hayman said, standing. Although from Mississippi, Hayman has only displayed bigotry toward the enemy. He treats Jimmy Moon like they were brothers. Dutch walked over to the sailors with a big grin on his face, flashing some southern charm to the oaf. "Sounds like you're from my neck 'o the woods," he said.

Disarmed, the sailor smiled back through his drunken haze. "Alabama, and shit proud of it," he said.

Hayman let out a whoop and slapped the creep on the back. "Shee-it, a reb!" You might think the Communists retreated the way Hayman and this crud carried on. Confused, I stood, wanting to slap Hayman and get killed by the sailor, but Jimmy nudged me.

"We gotta watch this," Jimmy said, pushing me back on my stool.

"Tell me something 'bout you bama boys," Hayman said,

putting his arm around the jerk.

The sailor downed a shot of something that looked like blood.

Hayman looked him in the eyes. "They say you boys love to suck cocks and sleep with hogs!"

I don't believe the sailor understood for a moment. His smile froze and then turned down.

Hayman suddenly locked his arm around the sailor and 'commenced' to flatten the good old boy's nose while the other sailors stepped back in disbelief. 'Bama' hit the floor with a thud. I cannot actually call it a fight since it ended as quickly as it began. The other sailors wanted no part of Hayman, and in fact, they cooled him down with a fresh beer and an apology to Doug and Jimmy Moon for their buddy's comments. They offered to buy all of us the next round, and before we knew it, we were partying with these four mariners while Bama slumbered at our feet.

It was an interesting crew: Briggs, a big man from California; Scooter, a freckle-faced kid from Houston; Chief, an older chap with a pot belly and a penchant for Hayman's Havana stogies - he's from Kentucky; and an Italian kid named Albert from the Bronx, who genuflected whenever Jimmy and Doug mentioned the Yankees. They were stationed aboard a cruiser that put into port for repairs. Most of their tour had been off the coast of Da Nang.

Bama finally came to and shook off the effects of Dutch's haymaker. He wandered off into the night without a word while we had fun with his pals. Porter, our Marine buddy, hooked up with some other Marines who invited us to go with them to their hotel to smoke some hashish. Hayman went with them, but Duke and I declined. Jimmy and Doug headed for the hotel to catch up on family talk.

Duke and I remained at the bar for another hour of beer and talk. Marie Rose came up during this conversation. I don't talk much about her when I'm drinking with the guys. Talk about women too often turns sour and insulting, and I wouldn't want to end up mad because of an unthinking comment made by a pal. But Duke is more like a father, and he understands my feelings about Rosie.

"You miss her, don't you?" he said.

"You don't know," I said. "She's my link to The World. She's the thread I cling to for salvation in this insanity."

Duke nodded. "She's home," he said. "There's not much around here that reminds us of home."

"This war is tearing me down, Duke," I said. "It's eating my soul. I focus on her, Mother and my family as a reason to survive, not just in the physical sense, but morally, too. Without them, I only think of the people I've killed."

"You were high school sweethearts?" he said.

"Classic," I said with a sigh. "But I have so much hatred for my father - and for this damned place - that I think I'm contaminating her with my anger. She was there through it all, and now she's here with me in spirit, always with a word of happiness from home to keep me plugging through every day."

"So someday there's wedding bells for you two?" Duke said.

"I don't know," I sighed. "It seems she always does all the giving. It's as if I'm some kind of emotional invalid who can't deal with my problems. Rosie's my best friend, but why the hell would someone like her want to marry me?"

"Oh, that's pitiful, Mr. Shakespeare," Duke said. "And what makes you so inferior?"

I shrugged. "She's got money, she's going to college, she has a father and mother who love her. Me? I'm stuck in Hell with nothing back home but an alcoholic father who hated me so much that he blew his brains all over my typewriter. What the hell would a woman like Rosie see in someone as sorry as me?"

"Jesus," Duke said, "with all that hatred and self-pity, when do you find the time to take the sights off yourself and shoot at the enemy?"

"Look, Duke," I said, luckily realizing the booze was starting to wake the dark half in me. "I hate my father, but I'm getting mad at you, so let's change the subject, okay?"

"Sure, no problem." Duke raised his hands in surrender

and then took a long swallow of his beer. "Let's go back to Rosie, where we left that boyish grin."

God, I felt so stupid. "I'm sorry, Duke. What the hell is wrong with me? I didn't mean to - "

"Cheers," Duke interrupted, clinking his glass to mine. "There's something about getting shot at that makes us all a little testy now and again. The problem for you, Shakes, is you don't vent the anger by doing what most horny, angry GI's do when they're in Hong Kong. That's why you're getting drunk with this old fart instead of chasing those ladies - or did my lecture about communicable diseases sink in?"

"Those women look pretty hard to me." I then felt embarrassed. God knows how after six million beers, but I was. "I'm a virgin," I whispered.

Duke smiled. "Don't be ashamed of that, kiddo."

I shrugged. "Rosie and I have kissed and all that, but we never, you know, did it." God, why did I suddenly feel like I was back in high school? "I don't know, Duke," I said, "I thought life in The World was confusing, but over here I scream around in choppers and kill human beings. Everywhere I look there's hatred and murder - so much immorality. Look at me - I'm a part of this sick existence, and yet, I haven't even been laid!"

Duke laughed until he cried.

"I guess those girls are pretty exciting," I continued, "but if I did it with one of them, it would be the only sick thing I haven't done since I got here. When I first arrived I was terrified of dying, but now I'm more afraid of living to remember what kind of evil I participated in. Rosie's decency connects me to the only hope I have that I'll someday be forgiven for what I'm doing here. Do you have any idea how many guys are getting Dear John letters from so-called girlfriends back in The World who think we're all a bunch of baby killers? I mean, what the fuck's up with that?"

Duke sighed and nodded.

"Rosie's loyalty reminds me I should at least try to salvage some self-respect in all this madness."

Duke put his hand on mine. "Such a man in a boy's

body," he said. He sadly looked away as if he was looking into the past. "In 1951, I was in Tokyo. I'd been shot through the hand in a firefight near Pusan, South Korea." He showed me the scar. "I was covering the war for the Boston Globe. That was the third time I'd been hit in a war. I got it twice in WW II, both were fairly minor wounds, but I was afraid my luck was wearing thin. Shakes, I never felt so alone. I was scared and I was sick of watching boys die.

"Then, I met this beautiful Japanese girl, her name was Dawn. She was a port in my storm of fear. I was in love with my wife, but she was a million miles away in Connecticut with my two sons. She was a world apart from me and my desperation." Duke looked at me with sad eyes. "I never told my wife about the affair with Dawn. It was over with as quickly as it had started, and I thought I'd simply take my secret to my grave."

"You were lonesome and afraid, Duke," I said. "Probably drunk, too..."

Duke smiled and sighed. "Then," he said, "Clare developed cancer. It was inoperable and had spread all over by the time we found out what it was. Before she died, she told me she knew I had been unfaithful while in Japan. She said she knew all along because I had changed when I came back to her. She had always been afraid my career would someday break us up because I was gone for so many long stretches, but when I came back from Tokyo, Clare said I had grown closer to her.

"She was right, Shakes. I loved her more after Tokyo, and my love grew to the day she died. She said the strengthening of our marriage was worth the sacrifice of what happened. Can you imagine that?"

"She must have been a very special woman, Duke," I said.

"Never been with another woman since," Duke said, draining his beer. "It's the guidance of the heart that determines the nature and strength of the soul, kiddo. You resist temptation for the same reason I didn't, but one thing is certain, Shakes - life is as fragile in The World as it is here. Be true to Rosie, and you'll be true to your heart..."

Duke's words roll in my head now as I remember them. I wish he had been my father.

We crawled back to The Clover, mindful of the conversation we'd had. Unfortunately, the alcoholic haze made me pay a dear price the next morning.

I awoke around noon with a head much too large for my bed. Duke, the best drinker I've ever known, had been up since eight. He'd already had breakfast, a shower, a morning walk, and was perusing the newspaper when I came to. On the other hand, I proceeded directly to the toilet and ralphed, and I feared I was destined to holler for Ralph the rest of the day. But Duke appeared at the door. I finally looked through swollen eyes and saw what appeared to be a glass of tomato juice. I hollered for Ralph again.

"OK, gunner," Duke said. "I've waited for you long enough. We've got places to do and things to go."

I waved him off. "Go them...do there...let me die..."

"I will not be the one to tell your mother you died in this war with your head in a toilet," Duke said. "Now you get back on the horse and drink this. It's a Bloody Mary."

I ralphed again. "Duke, kill me, please, but don't let me drink again. This horse kicked and peed on me."

"On your feet, soldier," Duke said. He pulled me to my wobbly legs. "You don't have much more R&R left. I'll be damned if you're going to spend it licking porcelain."

Duke wobbled me to a chair and demanded, under my violent protests, that I drink the cocktail. He said it would give me a second wind.

"Don't make a practice of it," he said as I finally choked the drink down. "But it's a sure-fire method to get you moving. We're going to the bath houses..."

Glory be, Journal, Duke was right. The Bloody Mary cleared my hangover. After a second cocktail, I felt human again and ready to go. We went downstairs and found Hayman at the bar, nursing a Bloody Mary. (I thought maybe Duke had a patent on the idea, but obviously not.) Hayman planned to join Jimmy and Doug, who were going on a shopping spree in the city. There are tremendous bargains on tape recorders, cameras, and tailored suits in Hong Kong. Jimmy and Doug have a friend in the states who pays a good price for them.

And so, Duke and I were off to an exquisite bathhouse which, Duke assured me, was operated by legitimate masseuses. They were wonderful, very beautiful, but indeed not working girls. In the hours we spent soaking and getting a rubdown, I thought perhaps I was in Heaven. I'm not, however, that stupid. We topped off the day with another great dinner at The Bayside, and then we sadly wandered back to catch the transport to Da Nang…

I'm weary, Journal, but I am rested. I think I can face it tomorrow. Welcome back to war.

I just got some news that made me happy. Major Putnam has a new permanent co-pilot, CWO James Clairborne. He just transferred in and is a decent sort. I also received a Purple Heart for my boxing match with Rage. The base commander came in to give it to me. I'll mail it to Mother first thing tomorrow. This is all a bit strange to me. I won a Bronze Star for our episode with Colonel Strauss' injury, and now a Purple Heart. It's not that I don't appreciate the army recognizing what we do over here, but I would just as soon receive no more hardware since one has to break his neck to get it. Right now, I'd trade them for a cheeseburger and my warm bed at home.

And there was more good news. The best. Colonel Strauss went stateside! Putnam said his recovery has been so swift that he was ready to get home far ahead of schedule. 'Cowboy' sent a letter to Putnam, who read it to us. The Colonel had a personal message for Hayman, Putnam, and me. Mine read: "To Shakes, you've a heart of a tiger. I am proud to know you, and more proud to have served with you. May God always fly with you, and please don't ever forget the Cowboy. I pray we meet again in peace. Remember, tell them the truth..."

God bless Colonel Strauss. I won't forget the Cowboy.

January 19, 1965

Dear Marie Rose,

Received your package today! The brownies were wonderful, and the sweater is proof of your improved knitting skills. It fits perfectly! It is, however, a little warm for this climate. I put it on and nearly died of heat exhaustion, so I shall keep it in a safe place for use upon my return to Colorado!

As for my physical condition, I am fully recovered with only a trace of bruises remaining under my eyes. The nose, although tender and a tad bent, is fine. I recently returned from Hong Kong on a three-day leave with Jimmy, his brother, Doug; Hayman, and Duke. I only wish the short respite had lasted longer. When I returned to the base, I was awarded the Purple Heart. They like to give you medals for doing stupid things around here. I'd prefer the Tin Star for hiding under my bunk for twelve months, but I don't think I could pull it off. Before I sent the Purple Heart home to Mother, I tried it on and stuck myself. Ironic, no?

The war continues. That is the only consistency in this insane asylum. Peace talk rumors persist, but from the temper of the battles, things just continue to heat up. I was shocked at the campus newspaper you sent. Thanks for first warning me you don't believe in all that tripe. That newspaper reporter doesn't have any idea what is really going on here. I am not slaughtering children. How do students justify throwing rocks at police and burning campus buildings while marching for peace? What a bunch of fucking hypocrites! How dare they claim that reports of Communist exterminations are merely American propaganda. It angers me, Rosie.

Here's some 'propaganda:' Two days ago we were ordered on a mission to help the 57th Medical Detachment. They went to a little Hamlet near the Mekong; one you wouldn't find on any map. The VC had embarked on a 'recruitment campaign' there, but the army more appropriately tagged the area a 'Kill Zone.' The Arvin defended the village in a bloody battle, and the aftermath was one of complete destruction. The total body count was one hundred and three villagers, fifty-nine Arvin rangers, six Marines, and one hundred sixty-eight VC. If not for American air support, the number of dead South Vietnamese would have been three times greater, and the VC losses negligible.

Our mission was custodial. We had to clean up the carnage. We made eight flights out of the area, five involved moving out dead and wounded soldiers, three involved the villagers. The dead soldiers were taken back for identification, and the dead villagers were taken to a mass grave site about three klicks - kilometers - up river. I personally carried more than fifteen women, children and elderly, who all had been cleanly shot once through the head (those who refuse or are unable to fight for the north are exterminated by the VC). Some of these college reporters ought to come here and smell the stench of the babies we buried. I wonder if they would cry like Hayman and I cried.

America is another planet, Rosie. We don't understand what it's like to live as these people do. These hairhead college kids point the blame at soldiers when the government should be blamed for its ambivalence. Nobody at home realizes the VC are prepared for a long battle, and they intend to fight to the death. For every one who is killed, two replace him. As long as we sit on our hands and watch this guerrilla war fester, we'll just be vulnerable custodians here to clean up the mess. And if Hanoi sends in its deadly army, this thing will go on for a very long time.

I want to come home, Rosie, but I don't know if I can come back with all of this on my conscience and still be the same naive kid I was. I love you.

As Always,
Me

February 9, 1965

It seemed, Journal, no matter the circumstances of the war, I would always feel relatively secure in the surroundings of the base. I fear that feeling will never return.

Last night, the VC attacked our base. We're in the army now.

The time: 22:30. I had a few moments alone to write a passage for Strange Potions. Most of the fellows were at the base theater watching the movie, El Cid, and I was enjoying the rare privacy. Tension was high because of a fierce VC terrorist attack on the American base at Pleiku the day before. In retaliation, US and South Vietnamese planes bombed targets in the north, and we had been on full alert all day. A thorough search for 'sappers' - VC infiltrators - was conducted, and the base was tightly secured. No one truly believed our security could be breached.

Suddenly, there was an incredible explosion nearby; a sound familiar to me in the field, but never this close to my cot. Mortar fire hit the end of the runway, and the roar literally knocked me to the floor.

The Communists had slipped in close enough to target the choppers, and if they had come close enough for their first shot to hit where it did, we were all in serious sewage. I bolted for the door, clumsily gathering my gear as I ran, and immediately headed for Rage, where I knew I'd find my crew. The boys in the theater poured out like water from a bursting dam, and other men were scrambling from the barracks, latrines, the mess hall...one fellow, so rattled by the initial explosion, burst from the showers stark naked on the run for his chopper.

We scampered across the tarmac, hitting the deck each time a mortar exploded and spewed hot shrapnel. Our priority was to boost the hueys out of harm's way. In seconds, I met the crew at Rage and we lifted off, circling the tree line where the fire was coming from. It was a nightmare, Journal. We were firing right into our own back yard. I felt like I had encountered a dangerous intruder in my own basement; right in the sanctity of my own home.

The Communists countered with artillery, erasing any doubt of their prime objective: Destroy the hueys. Luckily, an airborne gunship might as well be the face of death to Charlie. He obviously made the mistake of thinking the

'American Imperialists' were as unprepared for a sneak attack as the weak Arvin might be. He missed his best opportunity to destroy the choppers, for now the hueys were angry birds of prey. We defended ourselves with the furious vengeance of a mother eagle protecting her nest, for there were hundreds of American lives on the base depending upon us. We pounded Charlie again and again, fire and sparks blazing. The battle cast an eerie shadow of death on the black sky. In the distance we heard the ominous thump-thumping of more hueys. It was the 13th Army Aviation closing in from their base at Can Tho. God bless those birds of a feather.

Driven back by our assault, those Charlies who weren't already tits-up turned tail and ran as the 13th helped us grease those black-pajamas bastards, who only now are beginning to learn about American airmobile combat. It was over, a forty-five minute scourge of Hell thrust upon our own house.

We slept in the bush last night, the hueys taking cover off base as protection from a second offensive. We came back in at dawn to find the base remarkably intact, the damaged runways swarming with demolitions experts who combed every foot of ground for clues to Charlie's offensive strengths. Arvin rangers set off in search of our attackers as we met the weary faces of our friends still gathered in the terminal where they spent an anguished and sleepless night.

I never sleep soundly here. At best, I doze into a light, dreamful sleep, my mind fully alert to sounds and thoughts. Now I wonder if I can sleep at all. If the terrorists had destroyed enough hueys in their initial attack, we might all be dead right now. We aviators are sadly ill-equipped to defend ourselves on the ground. America is being sucked into this war, and the few of us here can only wonder how long we can survive until she responds. God, how I hate being here...

March 19, 1965

Dear Marie Rose,

I am sorry for the gap between letters. It is just that I am numb - engulfed in terrible, black grief.

Jimmy Moon is dead. Jimmy, my friend.

I'm sorry to write in this terrible state of mind, but I am devastated and have no one here to talk to. My friends are so wrought with grief that they offer little comfort. I hate to bring the war to you like this, but I need to sound my grief, for it is welling so deeply that I feel my heart might explode. The base chaplain suggested I write to someone close to me. Even Duke, my dearest friend here, learned of Jimmy's death only today, and he is badly shaken and unable to offer comfort. This morning, I sat with Hayman and Duke on Jimmy's cot. There was no trace of him but his deck of playing cards and his baseball cap. We all cried together...

On March 13, we embarked on the second of three missions that day. It was the largest trooplift I've seen since coming to the Delta. The second mission alone included fifteen new CH-47 Chinook troop carriers loaded with Arvins and Marines. We assaulted the VC-held landing zone in a blaze of combat. The VC is growing stronger with an increase of Soviet-made weapons, and this LZ was extremely hot.

Rosie, I have never faced my own mortality here, for I have never believed for one moment that I will die in this place, but my confidence was severely shaken on this day. Not even when I was hanging out of the huey last Christmas with rounds zipping by my ear did I ever believe I would be killed, but I have never known the true horror of war until now.

As we converged upon the LZ in a hail of artillery fire, the Chinook in front of us was hit by a missile and exploded in a ferocious ball of orange and black fire. It spun down, many soldiers falling out in flames, and fragmented when it hit the ground. We came about in a defensive formation and headed toward a grouping of VC hootches (makeshift huts) from which there came considerable fire in our direction. Around the hootches, there was pandemonium as farmers and villagers mixed among the VC were running and screaming. Some were taking up weapons and shooting at us while some shot at each other. As we circled, we pegged the main battery of fire while the ground troops emerging from the choppers moved in to flush out the VC. We came in and hit the hootches hard, forcing the enemy to scatter into the waiting fire. Although the fight was severe and surely the most violent of all I've seen, it quelled as we gained control.

The crashed Chinook, however, was still burning and the men inside were obviously doomed. Our huey and the huey Jimmy was on put down to help the incoming medical choppers search for survivors. Although the LZ was secure, random rounds from the surrounding bush hit the medical teams, so we set down in the line of fire and covered the medics.

Another troop carrier loaded with Marines came in about one hundred yards downrange from the evac site. I sprayed fire into the trees, but I quit shooting when I saw a hard hat - a black-clad VC soldier - emerge from the bush with a little boy in his arms. It's a common practice employed by the enemy to use civilians as a shield. I had no doubt in my mind who the man was, but I couldn't shoot because I would hit the child. The hard hat suddenly dropped the little boy and pointed him at the incoming Chinook. The kid then ran for the chopper. I first thought that perhaps the VC was trying to save the kid.

The little boy was slowed by waist-high mud, but he vigilantly trudged toward the incoming chopper, which was now setting down. Suddenly, Jimmy appeared on the flank, running as hard as he could toward the boy. I called to Hayman, and he looked out.

"Oh, Christ," he said.

"What's he doing?" I said.

"The kid may be rigged!"

The child's clothes were bulky, but we could not determine from that distance if there might be explosives planted on him. "Maje!" I cried over my headset.

"Baby sapper - three o'clock! Blackjack's on his tail!"

Hayman called.

"I see it," Putnam said. "They're on your side, Shakes. It's your ball. You're free to fire!"

"Jesus!" I cried. "I can't tell!"

"The kid's runnin' heavy, Shakes," Hayman said.

"He's trudging through mud!" I screamed.

"He looks loaded! If you grease him now, Jimmy might clear the frags. Make a fucking decision!"

God, Rosie. It was up to me to shoot that little boy. Jimmy was going to catch him, and if the boy was rigged, they'd both die. If not, I'd kill a child who was simply trying to run to safety.

I prayed to God for an answer.

My finger froze. I couldn't do it. I could not kill a baby. "It's not on me! I won't do it!" I finally cried out, and I let go of the trigger.

"Please, God," Hayman said, putting his hand on my shoulder as we watched Jimmy pounce on the kid.

The two of them burst into a blue-white ball of fire.

A cold numbness engulfed my body as the blue turned to orange and then black. I remember Hayman's guttural scream and Putnam's voice: "Oh, God dammit - Oh, my Christ - Jimmy...Jimmy..."

The smoke cleared, and through it, streams of Marines burst from the Chinook into the trees with savage vengeance; they knew they were alive because Jimmy and that child were not.

I barely remember jumping from the chopper with Hayman on my heels as we ran to where we had last seen Jimmy. Rosie, I cannot tell you what we found. It wasn't him. God, it just couldn't be my friend, my brother, Jimmy Moon.

I fell to my knees and heard myself scream as the red mud soaked into my pants. Hayman stood by me, his teeth clenched and his eyes closed. Putnam gave us the order to return to the chopper, but I felt as if I was frozen to the ground. I looked at what was left of Jimmy, and my eyes were attracted nearby to something glistening in the wet mud. It was the twisted back of a pocket watch Jimmy always carried with him; it had once saved his father's life when a bullet struck it, instead of him. There was nothing else left of the watch but just this piece. Nothing else left.

God, Rosie, I hate this place. I hate myself. I have tried hard to prevent this act of insurrection upon my soul, but I am losing. Since Jimmy's murder, I feel I am turning into something of which I am terrified. I boil with hatred. If it had not been for Putnam hollering at me in that killing field of mud and death, I would have run into the forest, armed with my pitiful .45. How can humanity possibly tolerate such savagery? Every night I sit in a cold rage, anxiously awaiting the sunrise and my next chance to kill as many of Charlie as I can. I'm sinking to his vile, murderous depth. I feel a flood of fresh hatred rush into me every time I pull the trigger. When I shoot, I'm blinded by passion like a shark with blood on its primitive brain. With every kill, both Hayman and I cry out in garish joy.

I'm losing my mind, Rosie. Murderous heat pulses through me with the need to avenge Jimmy's death. I turned to the chaplain to share these beastly urges, but he offers little solace:

"God understands," he said. "No matter what you might have done, or how you now feel, He forgives you because of these mitigating circumstances."

That's an answer I am sure he has pasted into his feeble mind like a yellowed military directive on a wall. How can God consider killing a child to save Jimmy mitigable? Duke, Putnam and Hayman all agree I did the right thing. We all would have done what Jimmy did, and we know he would not have approved my shooting the boy. Both Putnam and Hayman admit they would not have shot either, but their consolation serves no purpose. The point is, no one should ever be confronted with such a decision in the first place. None of this should be happening.

It seems we all have gone insane.

My Rosie. I fear that, upon my return home, you will not know me. How can I be anything but changed? Perhaps you should not wait for me...

Can I get back?

"As Gregor Samsa awoke one morning from uneasy dreams he found himself transformed in his bed into a gigantic insect."

\- Franz Kafka, The Metamorphosis

March 30, 1965

I just don't fucking know anymore...

I am no longer certain of my survival, Journal. I barely reach the half point of my tour, and I can scarcely breathe. Last night I awoke soaked in my own urine. This place has invaded what was formerly my only hiding spot, my dreams. They, too, have turned against me. I dreamed I was home. Everything was as I remember it, but I found Rosie lying dead before me. Her face melted away, her eyes falling from their sockets. She was screaming...

God, I'm going mad.

I lay on my bunk, afraid to stay awake in Hell, afraid to go to sleep. That hideous dream is still fresh in my mind. I've had a few shots of whiskey, something forbidden right now as there is an early mission just a few hours away, but I hope the booze will relax me enough to allow at least a few minutes of dreamless sleep.

The barracks is somber. Unlike in months before, there are more empty cots. No one rests well here. Hayman is tossing in his bunk. There is a new boy who came in today. He's in Jimmy's bunk. Around him are new pictures from The World, new gear, new trinkets from home...

His back is to me, but I'd wager his eyes are as wide open as mine were on my first night. He's no doubt frightened and lonely. I hope he is unburdened with the knowledge of whose bunk he occupies. We don't talk much about Jimmy now. I've said hello to the new boy, but I find myself treating him as I was first treated when I got here. Trust must be earned. It's our best chance for survival.

With each passing day, I find acceptance of Jimmy's death more concrete. I've seen so much death, but it had not touched me until I lost someone close. The tragedy of March 13 still ripples through the base since Jimmy was one of a large score of casualties - many of them American - that day. The pilots and crew of the downed Chinook were all killed as well as many Arvins. I still recoil at the image of that bloody rice paddy. How could it possibly be that we found ourselves standing knee-deep in the entrails of Jimmy Moon? How will

I ever be able to blot that from my memory?

And what of my fate? Until Jimmy died, I believed I would survive, but that blew into these winds of terror. How could I be so naive? Life has only the value put upon it by me and those I trust. Within this evil world, I have been slow to learn I must beware of reflections and delusions, for even the most familiar paths are often iced with treachery. There is nothing more sour than the decay of man's morality, but to survive this wickedness, I may be forced to make certain decisions with which I will have to live the remainder of my life. With a child again in my sights next time, will my finger unfreeze? And if I am in Jimmy's shoes, will I sacrifice myself?

God, Journal, I have to move away from this...

Uncle Vern...what a peach.

I've downed the last of his whiskey, but I have two more flasks tucked away. I wrote to Vern and asked for more, including some guilt money in appreciation. Vern's the one who will knock people down in a race for a dinner check, but I can't help but feel guilty for the endless supply of booze he sends. I believe Vern has taken it upon himself to adopt the whole family since Dad died. I love him very much.

This booze has become much the ally that Hayman, Putnam and Duke are. It quiets me and often allows me a dreamless sleep. I have smoked 'reefer,' but the effects disturb me. Marijuana has the quieting effect, but it has rebelled on the two times I've tried it, causing me sudden paranoia and some unpredictable sensations of emotional volatility. A lucid moment can quickly turn into irrational fear. Dutch has experimented with something he calls 'acid.' He used it our first night of R&R in Hong Kong and says it's a strong mind-altering drug that causes hallucinations. He's never used it on base, thank God, and he told me to be smart and never give it a try. Enough said. God knows I need no more hallucinations than the ones that surround me twenty-four hours a day.

Dear Dad, are you there? How ironic for my judgment of your character as you gave in to booze, and now I find we both worship the same deity.

I'm compelled to forgive him, Journal, so I can forgive myself. He gave in to his hell, but I am not ready to surrender to mine. Just writing these words helps me find the courage to regain my confidence. No, this booze is just my booster. I may dwell in Dad's bottle because it is my temporary refuge. There is no other safe place to hide. But it will not command me like it did him.

The new boy tosses in his sleep. What a dark journey lies before him. I'm only halfway along, but at least I'm not starting out like him. I resolve to not allow this boy to become too close to me, for I want no more friends in Vietnam. I have to live with the fear of losing Hayman, Putnam or Duke, and that is enough. If I had been smart, I would not have allowed myself to come to love those guys. I detest my callous attitude, but cold strength is the best defense here in Hell. Love is far too risky a proposition in war.

I am learning, Journal. I just pray God will forgive what I've learned.

April 12, 1965

Dear Marie Rose,

Received your letter. Jeez. I don't ever recall your use of the word 'fuck' in any letter or conversation. I believe college is corrupting you. What would your mother say?

I'm shocked.

You call me 'fucking inconsiderate.' I infer a certain amount of anger directed at me, but must you resort to vulgarity? You sound like my barracks companions.

I'm sorry for being 'fucking inconsiderate.' I'm fucking sorry, in fact. Please understand the frame of mind from which my last letter was written. I know that you care for me, that you are my best friend, and you have no intention of abandoning me. That you will wait for my safe return home is a comfort, Rosie, I assure you.

Fucking inconsiderate, indeed. You're fucking right.

I promise you, I'm dealing with my grief, and am far from my desperate attitude of the 19th when Jimmy's death was still fresh inside. I am sorry I've had to contaminate you with the horror of this place as this was not my intention when I first came here.

I'm coping as best I can, Rosie. I have to.

We've been called up. I must go. Thank you for setting me fucking straight. Jeez.

As Always,
Me

June 18, 1965

A strange coincidence today, Journal. I met a Green Beret in the mess hall who was passing through with a few minutes to kill. We discovered through conversations that we had a mutual acquaintance, Mike Golightly, who was killed here in '63. The Beret, Brad Adams, knew Mike well.

As I reflect upon Mike and remember the day when the news of his death came to our school, I'm saddened by my complete lack of awareness of what he was facing here. Even now, I'm embarrassed by my historical illiteracy.

Adams filled in some holes: Once under French rule, Vietnam, then French Indochina, struggled for independence in a bloody revolt. Their leader, Bao Dia, dubbed the 'French Puppet,' was overthrown by Ngo Dinh Diem in the mid-'50s, and the country split. Diem's south remained free, but the area north of the 17th parallel was controlled by the Russian-influenced Communists. This thing has been going on virtually since 1948 as both factions have struggled for control of the entire country. America made its first commitment to a limited Vietnam advisory role when Truman was president. Eisenhower expanded our presence in 1955 because of the growing suspicion of Communist eyes on strategic southern ports.

"By the early '60s," Adams said, "Kennedy had about ten thousand troops here. We was the MAAGs, the Military Assistance Advisory Group. We was supposed to advise the south on self-defense against the commies invading, but these gooks didn't know commies or Democracy any better'n their assholes."

I find, Journal, this continuous paradoxical notion of commitment to duty versus an inherent bigotry toward those we are supposed to be helping. I cannot help but be reminded of the VC who murdered Jimmy and that little boy. Back in the time of the MAAG, I'm sure even then the Green Berets fast learned of Vietnamese treachery, and were unsure if the very people they were helping might not turn on them.

But, regarding Mike Golightly: "Mikey was a Green Beret, too," Adams said. "Yeah, he was one mean mother - a little fugazi, you know, crazy. He'd picked up martial arts like he was born to it, and that boy didn't have an ounce of fear in him."

God bless him, Mike didn't have a brain, much less fear, but I didn't tell Adams this.

"Mikey was on a team assigned to a hamlet near the 17th," Adams said. "We was part of this 'Strategic Hamlet Program,' designed to fence in the southern villages and train the gook men and boys in counterguerrilla warfare. The hamlet Mikey was assigned to was overrun by the commies, and the MAAGs got taken prisoner. About a month later, we found them after we took the hamlet back.

"They was in a POW camp where the recruits was used as rice workers to supply the VC troops. I was in the platoon that rescued what was left of the MAAGs; fact is, only one was still alive, and he was in a little bamboo cage all covered with his own shit and weighing maybe a hundred pounds. We found one Beret tied to a tree with his balls stuffed in his mouth...guess he was a reminder for the gook prisoners to be sure to behave themselves. Mikey's body was in a hole with his commanding officer. His colonel was shot once through the head, but Mikey's body was in pieces."

I was appalled at the matter-of-factness in Adams' description. He continued to gulp down his lunch as he spoke, but I had lost my appetite.

"The boy who was in the cage is a ranking officer now," Adams said. "He got a Silver Star, too." Then, Adams gave me a hollow smile. "Don't fuck with the Green Berets, boy."

I simply shrugged. "I can't imagine living in a cage like that," I said.

"Part of it," Adams said. "Takes guts. If you ain't got 'em, you're greased for sure. Fact is, I kind of wish I'd been the one in the cage so I could show Charlie who's got the hardest stones. Mikey died a hero. I figure you die a hero, or you don't die at all."

Jesus Christ...

This soldier was a war machine, not a human being. He was nothing like the flying cowboys I live with - those who tremble every night in their cots. He had an air about him that could not be sliced with a saber. I don't think I could ever get that cold, no matter how long I survive this shit - which makes me even more fearful of my chances over here.

God, until meeting this Brad Adams I thought I had my priorities straight. I was certain I would not die. But now I see a fate worse than death. For me, a bamboo cage, or being emasculated while strapped to a tree is a far worse fate than a clean shot through the temple.

This war, or whatever the Pentagon is calling it, is tearing at my soul. Charlie kills Arvin, Arvin kills Charlie, and we're in the cross fire, unable to shoot until shot at. I'm nineteen, but I feel like I'm ninety. If I am at war, for God's sake why can't I be done with it? Christ, this is 1965, and we are the most powerful nation in the world. We finished World War I and II with decisive action, but here, we sit on our hands while all of these atrocities are going on. The Communists aren't trying to unify this country. They're exterminating it.

President Johnson keeps spewing propaganda about effective bombings of the north, and now he's committing Marine and Army ground troops in small doses, but all that does is strengthen the enemy's resolve. The Communists are fanatically obsessed with their objective, and they have enough fodder to fight until the last man is dead. Meanwhile, we get to enjoy this lovely countryside; this land of hook-worm and huey-sized mosquitoes; of flatworm, roundworm, sprue, malaria, black plague, tuberculosis and mold; this country where the heat is measured not by temperature, but by the gallon. It soaks you to your skivvies and scalds your lungs. Oh, the people are nice, too - these slant-eyed devils who plant explosives on children and dismember their enemy piece by piece.

Yes, this is paradise, this festered boil on the planet's ass.

Poor Mike Golightly. His biggest mistake came years ago on the day he bought beer and cigarettes for my 16th birthday. He should've gone for that cop's gun and let himself be shot dead. At least he would have died in one piece, and for a worthy cause. At least he would have taken his last breath in a place where savagery appears to be the exception and not the rule. I hate this place.

June 29, 1965

Dear Marie Rose,

A ray of pure, clean light that pierces my darkness; it is you. Your letter brought forth happiness as it does every time I hear from you. Just about the time your preceding letter becomes dog-eared with wear, a new one arrives! Thank you for sending the good luck charm. Imagine, a genuine stuffed Mickey Mouse from Disneyland! I've always been fond of that little rodent. My only regret is that he must spend the next four months here instead of California. It seems everyone is getting drafted these days. He and I will keep each other safe, I promise.

I'm sitting in the shade of Rage, awaiting the commencement of an anticipated mission. Hayman is snoring beside me. The day passes so slowly when we sit like this. Missions are dangerous, but they at least make the day go by swiftly. Boredom is so...boring.

For example, this morning simply flew by, no pun intended. We embarked on a dawn deploy and we encountered fire from a mountainous jungle nearby. Contacting the enemy in mountainous terrain can be tricky. If the skirmish gets hairy, a chopper pilot's skills can turn against him when he starts zipping around mountain trees. We requested air support to clear the bush. Shortly, five T-28 Tigers loaded with napalm appeared on the horizon. They dropped in out of the morning sun and prepared to turn the mountain into an ash tray. Suddenly, dozens of VC troops came out of the bush like rats from a sinking ship. You could see, even from our altitude, their panic-stricken realization of what was coming. The Tigers came in low and let Charlie have it with a napalm tidal wave that swept over the whole mountainside.

Like Hayman says: "Ibiddy-ibiddy-at's all folks!"

What happened epitomizes this whole war, Rosie. The enemy knows our superior strength, but they know, too, as long as we continue our ambivalence and persist in believing they think as we do, we cannot win. Tomorrow, that mountain will be full of Communist troops again, and the day after that, and the day after that. They will not only wear down the Arvins, but they'll wear down American ground forces, who trickle in here at a snail's pace. I wish someone could convince Johnson that this is a full-blown war over here.

So much for life at the office. Since I can't change things, I'll just seek contentment sitting here in the shade writing to you. Afterwards, I'll read your letter again...and again...

I must ask this of you, however. Indeed, we are living in the '60s, and I fancy myself a progressive person. I, too, realize you took a creative writing course last semester, but I would prefer you not practice your prose in the letters you send.

To wit: "I miss you desperately, and I live and die with each parcel of news from that terrible place. I long for your embrace; for the time your skin will touch mine and I may calm you so you will feel safe inside of me..."

I mean, Jesus Christ, Rosie! Do you have any idea what words like those do to a man reaching his sexual peak among a pack of unshaven, beer-swilling, cigar-chewing, frightened out of their skulls treetop flyers? It is like telling a dying man in the sweltering desert to think of anything but a cool glass of lemonade!

Jeez...

Reading this most wonderful passage endangers my mental health as much as taking rounds in the cabin of a huey blasting at 120 knots. You mustn't use words like skin when every night I sleep next to a fat guy from Mississippi whose idea of fun is going to a park to beat up queers! God help me, if I were to reach out for something warm in the middle of the night and I found the barrel of his M-16...

Now, please don't allow this minor criticism to dissuade your marvelous command of sensual prose, but let me suggest you hold off with this stuff until I'm a little closer than six thousand miles. By all means, continue thinking these thoughts, but please reserve them for when we can explore them in the flesh.

Oh, God, now I'm doing it!

Hayman is going to kill me.

On to cooler subjects. I love the picture of you and Angela at Disneyland! Those braids make you look like an Indian, but may I be candid and ask: Did you and Angela forget some underclothing? Gosh, things at home are changing.

Hayman just woke up. I showed him the photo and I think he sucked in a mosquito. He says hello, and 'va-va-va-voom!'

Can't say hello for Duke, for he's been gone quite a while. He's covering the bombings up north. Duke's helplessly addicted to adventure, and we can only sit with the prayer that no news is good news.

Thanks for calling Mother when you visited Denver on spring break. She went on for four pages about the shopping trip, and the dinner your family had for her and the kids. Then she went on for eight pages about how she'd break my neck if I ever let go of that 'sweet thing.'

On a more serious note, let me apologize for Vern pinching you on the bottom. Uncle Vern is a lecher, but he means well. He added a paragraph at the end of Mother's letter telling me he hoped we would forgive him. He sobered right up and regretted the whole thing. The ringing in his ears cleared right up the next morning, and he feels he deserved the slap, despite the fact you broke his glasses...

God, I miss home.

As for Lyla, I'll thank you for never reminding me of her again. I have only one sister, and that is my little angel, Mary. I recently declared this to Lyla after she wrote me a letter pleading that I lay down my arms and denounce my government's systematic extermination of the People's Republic of North Vietnam. The letter was accompanied by a newspaper clipping and a photo of her with her hairhead friends being carted off to jail from a Washington peace demonstration. She had peace signs painted on her face, and she held a sign in her hands saying: 'Baby killers.'

Lyla is a sow. Since being expelled from Harvard, it seems she's gone on some antiestablishment rampage, but this, to her own brother, is unforgivable. I wish I could rub her ugly face in the red mud of a rice paddy where I stood knee-deep in the guts of Jimmy Moon and that poor child. They gave Jimmy the Medal of Honor. He is a hero. I'm doing my best - we all are, so Lyla can go to hell with her precious People's Republic of North Vietnam. I hate her.

And, Rosie, I'm sorry for venting this at you. Damn, this place has made me bitter.

My love to you and your family. Are they still rich? Ha ha. October is not far off, My Rose. I'm beginning to think like a bona fide short-timer. I love you.

As Always,
Me

July 11, 1965

A quiet day, Journal. It's raining water buffaloes. The missions are scrubbed. I'm off duty.

I got a package from Uncle Vern today. Enough said.

Drunk.

Mother sent cookies, which were nothing but crumbs. Mary wrote a sweet message. "I love you," she wrote, "come home soon."

Damn, I wish she didn't have to know where I am.

Mother said Mary came home crying the other day because her best friend's brother was killed over here. I wrote her a long letter telling her she's my little girl, and I was going to see her soon. I told her I'd carry her letter with me wherever I go. I have that and that stupid stuffed Mickey Mouse doll Rosie sent. I feel like they are made filthy by being here. Sorry, Mick, you're not stupid. I'm stupid. I'm in the stupid, fucking army. My fault...

Hayman is asleep on the floor by his bunk. He sleeps with a picture of his son, the baby he has never seen, on his chest. He just got his DEROS: August 17. Sometime after then, he rotates home. I can't believe this is the end of his second tour. How did he survive two? Putnam informs me I'm going to be promoted and assigned as the new Crew Chief of Rage. He also said it's bait to get me to re-up for a second tour.

"Thanks, Maje, but no thanks," I said.

"Just thought you should know," Putnam said, "promotions have a hidden agenda. The brass thinks your skills are too good to let you slip away. I think they have designs on sending you to chopper school..."

That's why I'm depressed. Maybe I should stop being so good at what I do around here. So far it's created nothing but trouble, and now Putnam implies they want to turn me into a pilot. No thanks, Journal, that's what I'll say. I'll serve my tour and that's all. They sent me here earlier than most boots, so they'll just have to find a place for me back home for the rest of my hitch. All I have to do is keep my head low until I get an autumn DEROS....

Hayman and I got on the most absurd laughing jag late this afternoon. It all started when he talked me into sharing some reefer he had stashed. It was raining buckets all day. The wet tarmac is like a skating rink. Quite a few chopper crews took advantage of the break, the officers all crowding into the officer's club, and the grunts crowding into the barracks for cards, reefer, and beer. Hayman and I were shooting the bull when a pompous chopper pilot named Mackmull staggered out of the OC. We watched him run in the rain toward one of the Chinooks and take a sudden header. He picked himself up, tried to run again, and landed right on his butt.

We were hysterical.

Mackmull rolls around in the water, gets up, and slips again. He landed on his face and broke his nose.

By now, Hayman and I are delirious.

Mackmull finally gets up and makes it to the chopper, but he slips again and bangs his head on a wheel well. He laid there for ten minutes until somebody finally went out and got him.

I was in tears - Hayman's on the floor.

Mackmull will probably put in for a Purple Heart.

God, I hate this place.

July 26, 1965

It's very quiet tonight, Journal. I can't sleep. I'm bothered by a conversation I had tonight with CWO Clairborne while we waited for the movie to start at the base theater. I've been careful to avoid becoming too close to him, the reasons I have made clear before, but tonight, I'm concerned.

"You up for tomorrow?" he asked.

We have a series of missions in the morning, expected to be very hairy. But, they're all hairy. "Ready as ever, sir," I said.

Just as the lights went down, Clairborne's face appeared unlike anything I've ever seen. He was very pale, almost green.

"Are you feeling all right?" I asked.

"I'm not gonna make it out tomorrow, Shakes," he whispered, staring at the screen.

"Sir?" I said.

He kept on staring forward, his eyes way off somewhere. Shaking his head, he whispered, "Jesus..."

The movie blasted on, muffling my words. "Take it easy, sir," I said.

He suddenly touched my hand with his. It was cold; icy.

Then, he whispered something I did not hear and got up and walked out of the theater.

I can't sleep...

August 11, 1965

Dear Marie Rose,

I'm sure this is a letter you've been waiting for.

Probably the first time you've ever been visited from the grave. Sorry, bad joke, but I hope you're laughing instead of crying, as I'm sure you've done the last few weeks. Please laugh, Rosie. I'm alive. I'm well, relatively speaking - all parts still attached at least.

I'm not sure where to start. I'm told the army reported to Mother over ten days ago that I was missing in action. Now they say they informed Mother only yesterday that I'm safe despite the fact I've been here in the hospital for over a week. That means you all have spent at least two weeks thinking I was missing, in a POW camp, dead - or all of the above. They should call it the SNAFU Army. I don't have any idea how long it will take this letter to get to you, but I'm sure Mother was able to at least let you know I'm alive. I pray this letter finds you soon, for I'm sure you have gone through enormous agony in the waiting.

This letter should serve as proof that I'm not dead, although the army hasn't confirmed that either. I'm in the Nha Trang hospital again, and I go to Da Nang tomorrow for some surgery on my shoulder and knee. On that subject, let me inventory myself to reassure you I am not critically injured, although it will be some time before my sanity returns. In addition to a broken clavicle, my poor nose is again broken, I've four broken ribs, torn knee ligaments, a fractured jaw, I'm dehydrated and have six million scratches and mosquito bites, and this time I lost my watch. On the nerve side, I shake all day and wake up three times nightly in a cold sweat. Other than that, I am okay.

I think...

I'm sorry to joke, Rosie, but I know you're in tears right now; just help me thank God I'm alive with a good laugh. Ha ha...ouch!

So, I suppose you want to know where I've been and why I didn't call. Well, if you have the stomach for it, you'd be a marvelous help if you'd let me tell. (It's another one of those 'Nam Things' the psychiatrists insist I get off my chest so I won't be a fruitcake when I get back to The World.)

On the afternoon of the 27th, we embarked on a mission near the Seven Mountains. The mountains, four in South Vietnam and three in Cambodia, divide the two countries. Recon reported enemy troop movements there, and the Arvins were ordered to search and destroy. As it turned out, these Charlies were entrenched deep in the dense mountain rain forest. They were heavily armed North Vietnamese Army regulars - the hard-core elite Communist fighting force - whose presence in the central highlands and along the borders of Cambodia and Laos had until recently been the subject of speculation and rumors. The guerrilla VC are dangerous enough, but the NVA is better-equipped, better-trained, and less likely to lose 'recruits' in the face of battle. Our tactics had to be less saber-rattling and more aggression, which isn't the Arvins strong suit. Adding to our woes was a ludicrous directive forbidding pursuit of the enemy across the Cambodian border, which gave the NVA a back door. They could regroup and reload whenever they wanted without fear of being chased by an enemy that plays by rules. It's interesting how allied diplomats scream about Communist insurgence, and then send us to stop it with our hands tied behind our backs.

The preceding was an editorial comment that does not necessarily reflect the opinions of management or their sponsors...

Anywho, the mission was hot, and we held our own despite the obvious handicap, but our chopper was suddenly hit in the rudder by a missile. It damaged the entire tail rotor, which is essential to the guidance system. Thank God the missile didn't hit any farther forward or Rage would have exploded and finished us right there.

We spun out of control, but I was confident in Putnam's piloting skill. "Mayday! Mayday!" he called over the radio.

"I'm hit! We're going in!"

My heart was spinning with the chopper, Rosie, but the oddest sensation of excitement pumped through me. For some reason, I knew I was going to survive. I gritted my teeth and prayed, but Hayman, always in character, yowled and kept on shooting his M-60 as he chewed on his stogie. I preferred discussing the problem with God.

The chopper yawed to the right while Putnam fought the stick to keep our nose up. Rage was dying, but Putnam tried to keep her alive long enough for a survivable crash. The unfriendly mountainous jungle was our only hope for survival, for its thick foliage would cushion the fall. The downside? That jungle was thick with the enemy.

However, landing in Charlie's back yard was the last thing on Putnam's mind. Rage gave an awful groan as Putnam pitched us with a final burst of power that exaggerated the yaw. I suddenly found myself looking directly down through the open door at the mountains four hundred feet below. The mud and rice paddies flew by us as they drew ever closer. Putnam valiantly pulled Rage away from the battle.

Treetops crashed against our skids with a terrible bang as the higher branches slapped us as if we were a giant, pesky fly. I heard the familiar sound of gunfire below us, bullets rattling on Rage's skin. The rounds zinged past Hayman and me. A single, shattering crackle pierced the air as the rotors buzzed into the tree branches, and Rage flipped. I grabbed the door and hung on, still strapped in. The thick jungle swallowed us, and we flip-flopped through the trees. The bird finally dragged to a halt, entangled about thirty feet above the jungle floor. There was a raging fire in the craft's tail, and because of the angle at which the huey was perched, the fire was coming up toward the flight deck, the fuel, and the rockets. Our formerly friendly bird was now a ticking time bomb. This was not a good thing...

Putnam ordered us to jump as he struggled from his seat and helped Clairborne - the other pilot - unstrap. Hayman hopped from his door as I struggled to mine. I couldn't see anything through the thick smoke, but I was in a crapshoot and had no choice but to jump and hold my breath. A missile shot straight up into the air when I leaped, its spewing fire tickling my neck. I grabbed at anything that might slow me down as I tumbled into, over, and through the net-like verdure. I felt like I was being punched and kicked by the branches as I came down and finally hit the jungle floor with my face. Luckily the ground was soft and muddy, and my helmet kept me from being knocked out. The impact rattled me, but I remained aware of the danger overhead. As I dragged myself away, the chopper exploded and dropped most of her belly right where I hit only seconds earlier. Rage was dead.

My knee hurt, but I stumbled farther away from the burning hulk and fell into some thick brush. Hayman was nearby, his leg and arm broken, ribs cracked. He was cursing as only Hayman can curse. About that time, we spotted Putnam. His head was bleeding and his rib cage shattered, but he was alive. He staggered to us and we hid in the brush together, catching our breath and looking through the thick foliage for Clairborne.

"Do you see him?" Putnam said, squinting.

"Did he get out?" Hayman asked.

Putnam, still breathing hard, shook his head. "The cabin was full of smoke. I bailed out, but I couldn't see if he made it."

We searched while part of Rage continued to burn in the trees above, the other half still sputtering and exploding about forty yards away. Finally, Putnam and I managed to get to our feet. Hayman's broken femur had pierced through the skin and he was almost unconscious with pain. I did my best to straighten his leg and stop the bleeding while Putnam went to find Clairborne.

It did not take long before Putnam found him lying near the burned-out hulk of the chopper. He had severe burns on his back, and his neck was broken. Clairborne was dead.

Putnam dragged his body to some brush and hid him there. He came back and helped me wrap Hayman's leg with my flight jacket. Then we hunched together.

"I make us about four klicks up from the LZ," Putnam said.

Klicks are kilometers, Rosie. The army doesn't speak English. It meant we were about two and one-half miles north of where we were first hit.

Hayman's mind was clear despite his pain. "The NVA was huge, Maje. We took an ass-kicking at the LZ," he said.

I agreed. "A Chinook augered in when we got it."

"I saw it, too," Putnam said. "Tracer acknowledged my Mayday, but if they don't secure that LZ soon, Charlie will spread out and come looking for us." We sat silently for a time. The sound of the distant battle at the LZ was still raging, and it was beginning to get dark. Putnam nodded. "Boys, it looks like we're camping out tonight."

This was not a comfortable image, Rosie.

"We need some heat," Putnam said. He pulled out his .45 and checked to find he had four full clips. "You guys got your weapons?"

I nodded, but Hayman did not. "Lost mine," he said. "But I got Betsy." He pulled out a switchblade and snapped it open.

"Good, Dutch," I said. "What do you think this is, West Side Story?"

Putnam looked toward the burning chopper. "The huey M-60s are probably destroyed. I did throw out an M-16 before I jumped. Let's look for the rifle and Dutch's .45, and let's get Clairborne's pistol."

The major spent several minutes locating the M-16, but had no luck finding Hayman's .45. We came back and divided the weapons. Fortunately, Hayman's left arm was broken, so he could use his right to handle one of the pistols.

"You're the best shot, Shakes," Putnam said. "You take the M-16." I took the rifle, and Putnam kept his gun. We were armed, albeit pitifully.

"Did you hear some rounds when we fell in?" Putnam said.

"I did," Hayman said.

"It sounded like small-arms fire," I said.

"Somebody's close by, but they might just be locals," Putnam said.

"Or the fucking NVA," Hayman said.

"Let's not assume anything," Putnam said. "Whether they're NVA, or just freelancers, we'll have the dark on our side soon."

"The dinks love the dark, Maje," Hayman hollowly said. "That damned burning chopper is a compass point."

"So we'll dig in, Dutch," Putnam said, now irritated. "Jesus, how about some rhythm here?"

"Diddy bop," Hayman growled as he laid back in obvious pain. He grabbed a fresh stogie and plugged it in his mouth.

"They may think we didn't survive the crash," Putnam continued. "Either way, we have a new moon and I don't think anybody will come snooping until daylight."

"I just hope Eagle saw which way we went," Hayman said.

"Look, guys, the reality of this isn't anything you didn't learn in basic. There will be a rescue mission, but we may have to fight our way down to an LZ where we have a chance to be seen. No chopper is going to land up here," Putnam said.

"You mean hike out? You got any more good news?" Hayman growled.

"I'm out of beef jerky," Putnam said.

God, Rosie. I've never felt so alone in my life despite the fact these were the only two men with whom I'd want to be in that situation. We spent the last moments of light tearing Major Clairborne's trousers into bandages. We fixed a splint on Hayman's leg and arm. Putnam wrapped his broken ribs and tried to stabilize a fracture in his wrist. I wrapped my swelling knee, but had nothing to help my shoulder and jaw - or my nerves.

Night fell and the sounds of the battle at the LZ subsided. We burrowed in, far from the wrecked huey. Putnam is a tried combat veteran, and Hayman is too mean to die. I felt entirely capable, too, but cold terror iced my blood when the sun disappeared. The moonless night threw no shadows into the jungle, but the darkness ushered in an ominous feeling of doom.

I didn't sleep that night. I don't think anyone did. I wasn't really in much pain, because the anxiety of our precarious situation acted like morphine. My mind shifted entirely into a defensive posture, but pain was an occasional intruder as I lay on the hard ground. We laid feet-to-feet in a triangle so we could be alert to movement from any direction.

The jungle is every nightmare I've ever had, Rosie. Now I know how the ground troops feel with the prospect of an entire tour in the bush. Charlie may be the deadliest enemy in the jungle, but there are others. There are insects, spiders and poisonous snakes out there, and the night is full of bizarre sounds. I remember asking God how a boy from the peaceful climes of Colorado managed to get himself in this wicked place. Sleep was impossible, and when the sky felt the first breath of the sun, we roused and unsuccessfully tried to stretch away the aches.

"Let's make a plan to get the hell out of here," Putnam said.

"You gotta leave me behind," Hayman said.

His statement left me cold. "What are you talking about?" I said.

"You guys go get help. Lying here all night seized up my leg, and the pain's jacking me up. I'll just drag you down if you try to get me out."

"That's not a consideration," I said with finality.

"Then you're gonna fucking die, Shakes!" Hayman said.

"Shut up! You stay - I stay, and I'm not staying! I'm not leaving you behind!"

Before Hayman could speak, Putnam clamped on me. "Both of you shut up and calm down!"

It was the only moment during this ordeal when I felt real panic, Rosie. The last time I saw a friend offer himself up for sacrifice, he ended up in pieces, and I couldn't bear the thought of it happening again.

"No one stays behind," Putnam said. "We all go, but we go on my order."

"Shit," Hayman said, leaning back in obvious pain.

"No one else is going to die under my command, is that clear?" Putnam said.

Who were we to argue? Whatever happened, we agreed to survive or die together. We, too, agreed no one would surrender. Becoming a POW was unacceptable. It's difficult to fathom now, Rosie, but our pact included what under normal circumstances seemed unthinkable. I thank God we never faced the ultimate decisions to be made if we had encountered a losing firefight with Charlie…

The dawn put filtered light into the jungle. By then, I finally made friends with the darkness, feeling secure in its arms. Now, I was unnerved by the light - the sun was about to tell Charlie where we were.

My most vivid recollection of that dawn was finding Clairborne's body, which was lying so still under the brush; and Rage, which still kicked black smoke into the air. Although she could no longer protect us, she remained our loyal servant by sending a rescue signal into the cloudy sky. I prayed the signal was not reaching the wrong eyes.

"We'll lay low for a while," Putnam said, "and we'll see if there's any sign of the rescue team. If we're lucky, help is on the way and the choppers will scare off Charlie."

We waited, biding our time with small talk about home, who we miss, what we'd do when we got back. It was optimistic talk; talk which did not include the inevitable encounter we all knew was coming when hours passed without any sign of a rescue. And it happened, Rosie. As close as I could measure, around nine-thirty or ten, we began a long and horrible fight with my sister Lyla's beloved People's Republic of North Vietnam.

The first sign was ominous rustling in the bush. We moved to a position forty yards into the deep bush for cover near a big termite hill, where we had a decent view of the surrounding area. I was the first to spot them, recognizing movement in the distance. My heart almost exploded when I recognized these weren't locals, nor were they packing homemade weapons. These were NVA soldiers. They wore green uniforms, camouflage pith helmets, and carried soviet-made Kalashnikov AK-47 assault rifles. We counted five of them as they came onto the crash site and carefully sifted through the area. Clairborne's hidden body was discovered, giving away the fact we were alive since he was stripped to his skivvies.

The enemy gathered around the body, speaking in their rapid-fire gibberish. The Charlie in charge suddenly shot a burst of rounds into Clairborne's body while the others wickedly laughed. I don't suppose a quickly decaying corpse with bugs crawling all over it was proof enough that Clairborne was indeed dead. They wanted to make sure, just for fun.

Two more Charlies emerged from the bush, apparently drawn by the gunfire. They all snooped around the crash site like cockroaches around a garbage can. We strained to make out conversations, none of us with much command of the language, but we were able to make out that they planned to pan out and begin an extensive search. They knew there were three of us left.

"What's the play, Maje?" I whispered.

Putnam quickly perused the area. "We take them out now before they spread out, and we pray there isn't a division somewhere behind them. We do it swiftly. Shakes, you have the left flank. I'll take the right. Dutch, you're here on the point. We'll flush them into the middle and you pick them off."

"Fish in a barrel," Hayman said as he pulled his .45 and checked the clip.

"Shoot true and don't waste ammo, boys, we're packing popguns," Putnam said. "Play this right and we'll have those AK-47s. They could get us home."

We quickly maneuvered to an acute angle so as not to line up in a crossfire. We coordinated a fifty count so we would open up on them at the same time. I am so thankful, Rosie, that I've had some combat experience prior to this. If this would have happened to me early on, I might have never kept my composure under such dire circumstances.

Our attack was a surprise, and we caught them bunched together, forcing them to run right toward Hayman. Because I had the only formidable weapon, the burden was on me to do the most damage. I downed two instantly, and wounded a third. Putnam wounded another, but as I feared, Hayman's pain prevented him from shooting accurately. The survivors scattered into the bush, and I swallowed a ball of panic in my throat when everything grew deathly still.

I quickly took inventory and counted two kills. The two wounded were out of sight, which left the possibility of five still operating. As this thought raced through my mind, the air was pierced with a guttural scream in Hayman's direction. Hayman's voice is much deeper, but in this spot, under these conditions, I could not be sure the screamer wasn't him.

Again, the jungle was silent and remained that way for what seemed an eternity. The overcast sky and the thick green foliage created such a dim light that it was difficult to distinguish hard from soft shadows. I held my position and dug in, still mindful of the potential of more enemy support coming in behind us. I was aware these soldiers were trained for the jungle and we were not. My best option was to assume all five Charlies were still operating. I continued to sit and watch for movement.

The jungle had a disorienting effect on my mind as time slowly passed. The distances between Hayman and me, Putnam and all of the Charlies were meshing into a single blurred ball. There were hundreds of sounds, some natural, but some ominous. I first heard strange clicking noise I thought was the chirping of bugs, but there was a pattern to it. The NVA soldiers were tapping on their rifles in code. Then, a second deadly enemy appeared. About ten feet from me, a green, black-eyed snake slithered from the bushes.

The army warns of the deadly reptiles that inhabit the jungle, and there are popular stories about the infamous Johnny Two-Step, who bites you, and you fall down dead after two steps. I'm matching wits with the NVA, but a poisonous worm was scaring the hell out of me. Jimmy Moon would have laughed me out of Heaven if I showed up with a snake bite on my butt.

I slowly backed up on my haunches and slipped away, crouching as low as possible. My torn knee greatly inhibited my mobility, making me clumsy, and this drew the attention of the enemy. A burst of fire rattled over my head, and I hit the ground hard. I had no idea where the fire came from, and I didn't waste ammunition trying to find out. They had me pinned, but incredibly, the only thing frightening me was that damned snake somewhere behind me. What bizarre priorities! My body ached and my damn broken nose was now bleeding. I must have looked like something out of a Vincent Price movie. As I lay there in my pain and blood, desperately searching for enemy movement and squirming at the thought of a venomous snake lurking about, I couldn't help but curse Hemingway for making war sound like a romantic adventure.

Then, there was rustling in the bush. One of the wounded Charlies drunkenly sat up. He was in obvious pain as he tried to aim his weapon downrange. He didn't know I was just a short and lethal distance from him. I cut him down before he could get off a single round. Three dead now.

I looked in the direction Charlie had planned to shoot and I saw Hayman. He was burrowed in not more than thirty feet from me. I did my best to ignore the pain in my ribs and shoulder, and I crawled on my belly to the dead man and swiped his AK-47. I then crawled to Hayman, rolling into his refuge and landing on top of a dead Charlie, whose throat had been cut by Hayman. This was the screamer. Four dead now.

"Jesus," Hayman said, his voice soft and weak, "I thought you got wasted."

"A great exaggeration," I said. "Have you seen Putnam?"

Quite delirious, he clutched his switchblade and winced. "Don't you ever insult Betsy again."

"Come on, Dutch, where's Putnam?"

Hayman shook his weary head as his eyes rolled back.

"I'm losing it, Shakes," he said. "I think I'm bleeding inside...my head's swimming."

"Lay back," I told Hayman, "but try to stay alert. I may need you."

He nodded. "Stogie," he said. God, Rosie, Hayman was half dead, but he wanted me to fish a fresh cigar out of his pocket. I grabbed one, and he took it and began to chew.

We fell silent, Hayman slowly rolling the cigar in his mouth to try to keep himself conscious while I watched the bush. The dead Charlie was next to me, his cold black eyes staring at the trees. I'm certain the minutes turned to an hour, maybe two, and after watching the wounded Charlie I had shot earlier, I was gaining confidence by telling myself Charlie was just a human being, frightened, desperate; no different from me.

We were playing a macabre game, each one waiting for the other to make a fatal move. There were still three unaccounted for; one wounded and possibly dead. I lost my fear because the tedium of waiting numbed me. Life in The World is so soft and comfortable that we are impaled with a deep fear of losing it. But Charlie's survival means little more than eating another bowl of rice or keeping dry in a mud-floor hootch. We expect everyone to have the same morals and values, but that is simply impossible here in Hell. Hayman summed it up when he whispered as I looked at the man he had killed:

"Him or me, man," he said. "If I'd done that on the streets of Biloxi, I'd get the chair. Here, they'll pin a medal on me..."

A quick burst of gunfire roused us, followed by a single shot, obviously Putnam's .45. I squinted into the bush, my heart suddenly dropping at the sight of five fresh Charlies, who appeared from nowhere. They scurried into the trees. This game was only beginning...

We could only guess if Putnam was still alive. We sat at our position for close to another hour, and then the rain began to fall. We had been motionless for so long that my shoulder and knee begged for relief. I had to stretch them, and so I slowly began to move, my weapon still poised. I pulled up and tried to arch my back, using the bush for cover. I'll never know how, but my loyal eyes, as if suddenly solving some abstract puzzle, caught Charlie standing not more than five feet from me in the rainy bush. I pulled up my rifle just when his shocked eyes caught me. I cut him in half with a quick burst.

He shot into the air as he went down, and when he hit the ground, he looked incredulously at his ripped midsection. He then looked directly into my eyes, Rosie, and he whispered something before he died. I'll never know what he said.

More fire zinged past me, and I turned to find three more in full sight. I hit all three with the same burst, and they fell dead as I dove back down to Hayman.

"Easy, Dutch," I said. "I greased four more. We're winning."

Hayman's head swiveled, his eyes trying to focus. He grabbed my arm and gave it a reassuring squeeze. "Keep huntin,' Shakes."

Frantic Vietnamese chatter suddenly rattled behind me. I spun around and found myself looking down the muzzle of an AK-47. Charlie screamed, obviously ordering me to drop my weapon, but that was something I simply was not going to do, Rosie. I would not allow myself to be taken prisoner under any circumstances. Life cannot be so important that I would spend it living in torture and confinement.

Charlie screamed again. He wanted to capture a huey pilot alive. He had murder in his eyes, but there was something else there: insane fear. He was alone, his comrades all dead. I sensed I might have one second to surprise him by falling away and praying my shot would be true.

Before I tried, his eyes suddenly popped in surprise and his weapon fell away from my head as he staggered back. Charlie fell, blood streaming from his forehead. He was dead before he hit the ground.

I turned and looked out into the bush, finding Putnam, who was still aiming his .45 at the fallen man. I didn't even hear the shot. Maje gingerly walked up and stood over his prey.

My voice trembled. "Jesus, Maje," I whispered. I hugged that big pilot.

Putnam fell to his knees, exhausted, and he kept his hand on my shoulder. "Round one," he said. "Round one goes to the good guys..."

The fight had pushed the day to late afternoon. We dragged all of the dead Charlies to the crash site, laid them together, and took their weapons. Rage had long since given her final signal, and the heavy rains delayed the chance of a rescue mission. We couldn't stay put any longer, because Charlie surely had more troops heading our way. We were going to have to go down the mountain and quite probably fight through more Charlies who were on the way up. Putnam and I caught as much rain water as we could in a helmet and shared a drink with Hayman. He fought hard, and at times he was lucid, but we feared his broken bones might be festering and gangrenous. Shortly, the rain let up and we perked to an ominous sound beating on the cloudy sky. It's a sound I've come to recognize even in my sleep. For a grunt in the bush, it's the sound of music. For Charlie, it's a death march.

"Choppers," Putnam said, putting his ears to the sound of steady thumping in the air. We listened to the sound grow louder and perked when we heard the ack-acking of M-60s.

"Gunships!" Putnam said. "They've contacted Charlie."

"A rescue team?" I said.

Putnam nodded. "Hell, yes!" he said. "They're a few miles down, I'd say. We'd help them and ourselves if we try to meet them. Problem is, there's Charlie between us and home."

"Then we go home," I said with finality.

Putnam nodded. "You're officer material, Shakes."

"Fuck you, sir," I said. I meant that.

Through the jungle, two miles is more like two hundred. We hoped, however, the landing operation would be successful and a platoon of Arvins might meet us halfway up around dawn.

We packed up our Kalashnikovs and as much ammunition as we could carry. I tied Hayman's splints as tightly as I could. The chopper sounds gave him a second wind, so I fashioned a cane out of some bamboo and helped Hayman get to his feet.

For a moment, I believe all three of us shared the same thought as we looked back at Clairborne's body. Putnam drew a long and heavy sigh. "We all go, or none of us go."

"Absolutely, Maje," I said.

"Okay," Putnam said. "Dutch is alive, Clairborne's dead; which one do you want?"

I pointed at Putnam's wrist, which had grown to the size of a softball. "Your arm's gone. Dutch is a bigger load. I'll take him."

Putnam nodded. He went over and picked up Clairborne's body, draping it over his shoulder. I pulled Hayman up.

"You don't dance for shit," Hayman growled through his stogie as we hopped around. His leg burned with fever, but he refused to give an inch to the pain. Fortunately, it was my right shoulder and left knee that were injured. With a little luck, I knew I could carry Hayman if it came to that.

Finally, we were off. We regimented our pace as we slowly moved down the mountain, and we thanked God for the small favor of not having to travel uphill. We broke to rest every fifty yards to keep from exhausting ourselves, but by the third stop, it was apparent this was to be a grueling hike. Putnam virtually dropped Clairborne's poor body and fell to his knees, gasping for breath, and Hayman was obviously losing steam. His eyes were glazed, and his speech slurry.

After our fourth trek, Hayman couldn't even move his good leg, so I had to carry him. The sounds of battle at the LZ had died, and night was quickly closing in. Exhausted, Putnam and I could carry our friends no farther. We decided to burrow in for the night.

"Please, God," Putnam said, "don't let them forget us."

He slumped down after taking poor Clairborne downwind while I helped Hayman situate himself. Again, the rains came. We caught more water for Hayman, but it afforded us very little to drink. Our resting point was a thick growth of bush, where we literally disappeared into the dark. I was so spent and dehydrated that I dropped instantly to sleep without a thought of Charlie, snakes, bugs - anything.

That night was different from the first, for I imagine I was finally indoctrinated to the sounds of the moonless jungle. I didn't really sleep all that much. Hayman's lucidity came and went, and Putnam was as groggy as me, but we somehow got through the night.

We awoke shortly before dawn. Putnam was sitting up near me, his eyes vigilantly fixed on the bush. Dutch was conscious, but very out of it.

"Let's saddle up," Putnam said. "We got a chopper to catch."

My spirits were shallow. "You think the rescue team is still out there, Maje?"

"Bet on it."

"I don't know," I said. "We've been deeper in the shit than you thought."

"I knew where we were all the time, Shakes. But you don't go into the fourth quarter twenty points behind and say, 'we're screwed.'"

I tried to smile. I pulled Hayman to his feet, and Putnam picked up Clairborne, who was now getting overly ripe. I thanked God for my swollen nostrils, but Putnam, God bless him, hoisted his co-pilot on his shoulder without a complaint.

My God, Rosie, I doubt I'll ever witness the kind of bravery and resolve I saw in Putnam and Hayman.

We moved out, and again Hayman fought to take steps. He kept himself awake by reciting his favorite Shakespeare sonnets, but it didn't take long before his weight was falling on me. We finally had to shorten our hikes to twenty yards between breathers. I was numb and very dizzy, and I longed for a drink of water. The morning heat sapped my strength, and my bones were growing brittle, but something - I honestly believe it was my thought of you and my family - pushed my legs forward.

Sudden rain fell, and we dropped to the ground like children, our heads cocked back and mouths open to catch raindrops, but this climate provides rain like a water faucet being turned teasingly on and off.

Just when we mustered strength for the next hike, there came a sudden burst of machine gun fire very nearby. It was random, very much like the combat we encountered the day before, but we weren't being shot at. Somebody else was the target, and that meant friendlies were near. Like a hard wind blown into my lungs, I found new strength. Putnam gained it, and even Hayman emerged from his painful fog. We dug in and crawled in the direction of the noise, and then we heard rustling and the chatter of the enemy. They were heading right toward us. I started shooting when I saw movement coming at me. Putnam fired, and together we downed three NVAs.

We burrowed in, and we waited about fifteen minutes. We grew impatient and were about to move out when a Vietnamese voice lifted through the bush, a most bizarre sound: "GIs? GIs? Number ones?"

"Maje?" I said.

Putnam waved me off. "Shut up!" he frantically whispered. "It could be Arvins, but maybe it's Charlie."

My dulled senses came back to me. Signal codes - it was time to remember why we always had them. Before every mission, we review a coded message to holler out in case we get lost. The little voice danced over the trees again: "Red Planet! Putnam! Red Planet!"

"Yes!" Putnam whispered. He grabbed his .45 and shot a single round into the air - the code of acknowledgement.

Again, we laid in the bush for a dreadfully long time, our eyes sometimes meeting in silent prayer. "Not a move," I recall Putnam whispering.

The silence was broken by the distant thump-thumping of choppers that grew louder by the second. "Thank God," Putnam said, grabbing my arm. "Listen."

"Choppers," I said.

Putnam nodded. "The Arvins probably circled down to sweep a path to them. Let's haul ass, but watch out for Charlie - we aren't out of this yet, Shakes..."

My heart pounded one last reserve of courage into my weary body. We packed up and gingerly moved down to the sound of choppers. They closed in on the base of the mountain, laying a tremendous roar of rockets and M-60 fire. The depleted NVA had doubled back to the tree line, planning to ambush us as we came out. But, unless they were battalion-strong, which seemed unlikely with so many Arvins in the bush, I don't believe even the hard-stoned NVA could see the use in taking on the awesome power of the choppers. We didn't bank on that, however. Our American huey-pilot heads would have made fine trophies for Uncle Ho's wall...

From the ground, I gained new respect for the ferocity of a chopper attack, for the earth literally quaked below those wonderful birds of prey. We worked our way to a clearing and saw two Chinooks setting down with three more coming in. The NVA made its last stand, but this was a Marine ground force assault - Charlie was as good as dead. Under the protection of a gaggle of huey gunships, the Leathernecks poured out of the first four Chinooks and scattered into the grove about two hundred yards away, meeting a still-hot resistance from the NVA. The last transport belched out 40 Green Berets, whose mission in this assault was obvious. They were looking for round eyes!

"Hold here," Putnam said. "Let them secure the LZ. They're assuming we'll track toward them, but let's not take friendly fire now that we're this close."

A burst of fire came from the tree line, but with the swiftness of an eagle descending on its prey, two hueys bolted in and put fire on the guns, exploding the trees into a bright inferno. Hayman cried out. "Eat fire, you bastards!"

The enemy lost strength quickly, and Putnam ordered us to take slow steps through the bush along the perimeter where we could catch someone's attention. We carefully limped from tree to tree, bush to bush. When we reached a large overgrowth, my heart suddenly stopped when I heard the sound of rustling from behind. A black shadow covered me as I tried to turn, and a big hand slammed me down.

A voice. It was God-blessit English: "Don't fuck with me, cowboy!"

He let me turn, and I saw the dark eyes of the largest, blackest Marine I have ever seen! I cried out and thanked God as Hayman bellowed: "Fuckin-A, Bubba! Fuck-ing A!"

With his hand still firmly planted on my chest, the big, ugly jarhead pulled out his radio and barked instructions to the huey commander as several more Marines emerged from the bush. Within seconds, a dust-off chopper (that's a medical evac huey) came in with an escort.

"Fuckin-A, Bubba!" I cried. Another Marine took off with Clairborne's body over his shoulders, and a second Marine hoisted Hayman and took off like a halfback, Hayman yelping in pain the whole way.

Putnam followed them, leaving me still on the ground with the black Marine's hand still planted in my chest. He grinned. "Can you run, gunner?"

"Run?" I said. "I can hardly walk."

"Let's go!" he said.

"Jeeeeesussss!" I cried as he pulled me up and tossed me over his shoulder. He took off, zigzagging through enemy fire with me bouncing on his shoulders. "Easy! The ribs! The ribs!"

He banged me into the chopper and we were airborne before I could suck another breath through my twisted rib cage...

We made it, Rosie. I don't know where we found the strength, but we had a boisterous celebration in that chopper. Putnam and I hugged each other, and Hayman, flat on his back, kept yelling, "Fuckin' A!...Fuckin' A!...F-U-A!..."

But our joy quickly faded as we passed into the clouds and that terrible mountain became a tiny dot on the horizon. An eerie silence came over us, drowned by the thumping of the chopper's rotors. Our eyes fell on Clairborne's lifeless body. We were stunned by confusion as the shock was finally settling in.

"He knew it," Putnam finally hollered over the din. He put his hand on Clairborne's face. "J.C. dreamed he was going to die over here."

Until then, it had slipped my mind that CWO Clairborne, acting very peculiar the night before our ordeal, mentioned something to me about not making it out. Apparently, he told Putnam, too.

We remained silent for the rest of the trip until Soc Trang came into view. Putnam sat with his eyes closed, tears leaking out. Hayman, now overcome by pain, also had his eyes tightly shut. I stared ahead, seeing nothing. It was most remarkable, Rosie. In the heat of our ordeal I had forgotten, but I suddenly reached in my pocket and found the silly Mickey Mouse doll you gave me. He's been with me since he got here. I pulled him out and brushed the blood off his face.

We won our war, Rosie. The politicians will never care, but we won. I'm coming home. I'm going to make it, of that I'm certain; I pray you will hold forgiveness in your heart for what I've had to do to get back. Let's pray God will understand.

We'll be together again, Rosie. I knew it the minute I found that memento from home; I'll see Mother, and Vern, and Jonathan, and little Mary again. As we passed over the clouds, I stared at the sky. I know that sky. It is home. I'm going to make it home...

As Always,
Me

3

Homecoming

1966

"Certainly there is no hunting like the hunting of man; and those who have hunted armed men long enough and liked it, never really care for anything else thereafter."

- Ernest Hemingway

June 23, 1966

Damn, my head hurts! I slept like a tired cadaver, Journal. Why do I drink when it produces such a terrible mess of me? I'm employing the Duke Winslow Bloody Mary Hangover Hanger as I write.

I had a terrible blowout with Steven last night while partying with him and Uncle Vern. It was intended to be a welcome home party. More on that in a moment.

How strange is this feeling to sit here in the downstairs den. Mother kept it exactly as it was when I left two years ago. On the wall are the Yankees pennant and the Broncos poster; on the desk, Rosie's graduation picture. Next to that is a silly Viking helmet fashioned from a 2.75 rocket canister – a trophy every guy gets from the Vikings when he leaves Nam. I also kept my Blue Diamonds of the Delta beret, but I don't wear it these days. The old war horse Mickey Mouse got the best seat by Rosie's picture. He doesn't look bad with a Purple Heart and a Bronze and Silver Star pinned to his chest. You're a real Vietnam hero, Mickey Mouse - don't mind those hippies tossing shit at you.

But, Mickey, now that you've finished defending somebody else's country, don't you think it's time to go look for a job?

Nah...

So, this is Home. I don't feel safe back in The World yet, but that should come back now that I'm finally free of the army. Mother's cooking has been nonstop since I returned, and my bed feels larger than I remember. The cool, dry mountain air feels like angel's breath, and everything here is so serene. Yet, I feel alien and removed as if I don't really belong here. What happened to me the last two years twists and turns inside my colon like a taunting ghost. Even though I sit here in quiet solitude, somewhere in the bush a huey gunship is laying fire on a LZ, a Vietnamese hamlet is being terrorized by the NVA, and an American boy is sucking his last breath.

Now that I've finally reached home - this town, my house

- life is as unfamiliar to me as it was the first day I set foot on Soc Trang.

Six days I've been home, Journal, that's my problem. That's all. Army brainwashing is very thorough. It did keep me alive by making me think like a warrior, but now this edge, razor sharp, is conspicuous within these gentle surroundings. I catch myself looking over my shoulder in fear of shadows. Abrupt noises make me jump. I never really had nightmares over there; hell, I never really slept over there. But I had them regularly when I came back to The World, and I've had three since I got home.

I think writing will help. It's been too long since my last entry. Reading about those last few minutes on the evac chopper brings back more memories than I need, but I'll forge on with a brief review. I spent a month in the Da Nang hospital, recovering from reconstructive surgery on the knee. I then went to Saigon and crippled around as a lousy pogue clerk for sixty days past my DEROS. Orders to go home came just in time to spend Christmas somewhere over the Pacific, and I finished my hitch where the whole nightmare began - Fort Benning. That's where I was given a hero's greeting by some asshole hairheads who hollered "baby killer" at me and tossed dog shit. I guess they weren't particularly impressed with my medals...

I hoped maybe the army might figure I paid my dues and let me out early. Wrong. My leg will never be more than 60% normal, but that was good enough to turn me into a gunnery instructor. Six months of gunfire every day - as if my nerves hadn't been shot up enough in Nam. I think about those recruits - guys my age who were still thinking about their last prom, their last touchdown, their last taste of home cooking. And here I was, crashing the party and trying to convince them to forget The World and concentrate on learning how to waste a gook before he wastes you. No wonder I still have nightmares. I still see their eyes - eyes of boys who will be dead or in pieces by this time next year.

When I think about where I was ten months ago, the mere fact I'm sitting here at my old desk is in itself a miracle.

Jesus, ten months ago...

I was nineteen, going on forty - a terrified kid looking down the muzzle of an AK-47 and considering three options: kill, be killed, or spend perhaps five or ten years in a bamboo cage. I wonder how many more will face similar options before it's over. The war has only just begun. I guess it's going to take some scrubbing to wash the stain of Nam from my brain.

I'm looking at old Mickey Mouse and wondering if he might be better off without the medals. Certainly, he was hurt twice, he dragged Arvins out of the mud, and he carried a buddy out of Hell on his broken shoulder, but maybe he shouldn't be reminded of it every time he looks in the mirror. I think the medals should go in a box for his grandkids to dig out. Maybe it will remind them that people should never go to war unless they plan to win.

Christ, why am I whining? Look at me! Got my legs. Got my arms. I got all my parts, and I'm home. I'm really home…

How happy Mother is, although worry has aged her over these two years. I feel old, too, but one thing's for sure: This is my home, and I'll be damned if anyone takes me away again.

Rosie comes in Saturday. My hands chill at the thought of finally seeing her. At last, the army can't tell us how long we can be together or apart. We'll have the entire summer together. She planned nothing for the next three months, except to be with me.

"Just hold on," she said on the phone last night when I began to choke up with emotion. "I'm going to turn you back into that clumsy teddy bear who used to write me poetry and love notes."

I hope she doesn't run away when she sees the teddy bear is now a Grizzly. God, my hands are cold.

Other subjects: Last night's party with Vern and Steven. What was intended to be a drunken welcome home celebration somehow turned acrimonious. I blame myself, for I have an enormous khaki-green chip on my healed shoulder. We couldn't just be old, reunited friends out for a good time, drinking beer, laughing, telling jokes; no, Steven treated me like I was MacArthur. He kept talking about my medals, and then he pressed me to tell him about the battles and the hueys and the rocket's red goddam glare. Then, he hit me with the news he's going to drop out of college and enlist in the Marines.

"Are you insane?" I said.

"Why?" Steven said. "I want to go and fight for my country like you did."

"I didn't fight for my country! I fought for my life," I said. "My country wasn't over there."

"We have to stop Communism now, before it spreads."

I had to laugh, Journal. "Where did you hear that?" I asked. "ROTC class?"

"How can you talk like that?" Steven said, his back up now. "My country needs me. It needs good Americans like you and me."

"Yeah? Well, my country threw dog shit at me. They said I killed babies. When the caskets came out, they cheered."

"Those are just a few hippie assholes," Steven said.

"Those assholes are your future, Steven," I said. "A hundred and eighty thousand guys like you and me are over there now. They're knee-deep in guts for goddam nothing, fighting a war that Congress denies! Those lucky enough to make it back have shit thrown at them, and others like Mike Golightly come home in a sandwich bag. Take my advice: Stay here, drink your beer, and pray your ass off that this bullshit ends before you graduate. And, something else: If you get drafted after college, lose the John Wayne impersonation and fucking grow up!"

Steven was livid. "You just want that glory all to yourself!"

I don't know what possessed me, Journal, but I suddenly came over the table and got into Steven's face, grabbing him by the scruff of the neck. "Glory?" I cried. "Don't tell me about glory until you look into someone's eyes after you just cut him in half! Don't talk about glory until you find nothing but your buddy's head lying in five inches of guts! Then, if you want to call war glorious, be my fucking guest!"

Thank God Uncle Vern was there to pull me away. I pushed back and sat, my head drowning in a violent swirl. We'd drawn the nervous attention of everyone in the tavern by now. Steven was in shock, I think. In the old days, we never even had an argument. If we'd ever have gotten in a fight, it wouldn't have lasted long. He was a lot bigger than me. But, when I came over that table, I scared the shit out of both him and Vern.

It took a minute, but I finally apologized once I caught my breath.

"Look, I love you, Steven," I said. "We aren't kids anymore, and this is no game; life isn't beer parties on the hill, or a cruise down 16th Street. Look at what Nam has done to me. Have I ever raised a hand to you like that?"

"If you weren't my friend, I'd kick your ass," Steven said without much conviction.

"Is that right?" I sarcastically laughed, my heart raging again. "You wouldn't have a fucking chance, pal! You want to try me? Do you think I'm afraid of you!"

"Hey, take it easy," Uncle Vern said, always the peacemaker. "Listen to that mouth on you. That's not how you talk..."

Vern's words brought me down, and I tried to escape the jungle. "Neither one of you get it, do you?" I said. "Look at me. I have no morality and no self-respect because I found that glory you're looking for, Steven. Those troops are facing an enemy unlike anything they've been trained to fight, and Washington is blind to it." I tried to touch Steven's hand. "Don't let glory come looking for you."

Steven sat silently for a moment, and then he pierced me with dark eyes. "Some fucking American you turned out to be."

"Hold your water, pal," Vern chimed in. "Go wave your flag somewhere else. I'm drinking with the best goddam American in this place..."

I don't care to go on with this, for we jabbed a few more

times until the barkeeper told us to shut up or get out. Steven took off without another word...

I love America, but I loved myself once. Sure, I did my part for God and my country; however, at no time during that horrifying moment I looked down the muzzle of an AK-47 did Charlie and I argue political or religious ideology. When that NVA boy whispered to me, right after I split him in two, I bet he said a prayer to the same God I thanked for giving me a quicker trigger finger.

Ho Chi Minh and Lyndon Johnson aren't out in the bush. A "few good men" are.

But, that's the way it is, so that's okay by me. My country exacted a high price from me, and I received dog shit on my uniform in return. You'll have to pardon me if I'm not overjoyed with the bargain.

Yes, I am alive, and I'm home - for that I'm grateful. That's the trade, so we're square. I won't upset anyone again by telling them I fought in Vietnam. Mum's the fucking word, America; I won't embarrass you anymore. I'll box up my medals and just tell everyone I spent my 18th and 19th years of life on a Caribbean cruise.

Semper Fi, Steven...

Still enraged, I slammed down my beer and tried to give my good old uncle a 'fuck it' shrug. Uncle Vern put his big arm around me and kissed me on the top of my nasty head. He leaned close to my ear. I expected some words of wisdom, but as is fitting of Vern's easy view of life, he just sang "I can't get no satisfaction" with the jukebox.

In a few minutes, he had the whole bar singing...

June 24, 1966

Received a letter from Major Putnam today - actually, Colonel Putnam! He's a full bird now, but he's green with envy at my discharge and reports he's on his way to retirement after this tour. I judge from the tone of his letter that his taste for treetop flying is growing bitter. Although the State

Department denies it, American involvement in the war is expanding to Cambodia and Laos. Putnam's pilot grapevine is full of rumors regarding an escalation of B-52 strikes on the north that began last April. Maje has had enough of it, he says, and he's ready to come home to his family. He's earned a full colonel's pension and figures he had better run with it before his luck runs out. His DEROS is August. Hold on, Maje. Don't screw the pooch now!

He mentioned concern for Hayman, who has not replied to two letters. Hayman isn't much for letters, but his wife wrote me last November and said Dutch was in a stateside hospital for more surgery on his leg. She sent his regards and he promises to kiss me flush on the mouth someday for dragging him out of the bush. I'd love to see Dutch again, but not that much.

To be honest, Journal, I believe my Nam friends will fade into that dark memory of the war. I truthfully doubt that I would have found a Charlie Hayman or Jimmy Moon here in The World. We are very different human beings. In Hell, we had a single purpose, and that was to survive. It brought us together. I intend to continue to write Jack Putnam until he makes it back, because I know how much letters from The World mean. But he, too, will probably fade when he comes home. I do want to stay in touch with Duke Winslow, however, for there might be a place here for our friendship. Only time will tell...

Here on the range I've witnessed a simply gorgeous day. I've never appreciated this climate more! This morning, as usual, I jumped out of bed at dawn, anticipating reveille. Although I've never cared for early mornings, I feel a sadistic joy when I become conscious and realize there will be no reveille, no war and no damned army. I just smile, grab some coffee, and marvel at the sun rising over a peaceful Colorado city instead of a smoky, muddy horizon.

After dawn I began to haunt the quiet house. My first stop was Jonathan's room. I didn't have to go halfway across the planet to be Jon's hero. He treated me as if I'd only been gone a few days. Thank God he's still so young. Perhaps when he's eighteen there will be no war. He's become a handsome little fellow. He was lying uncovered in his little bed; flat on his face, lost in dreams. I can't even remember what it was like to have the dreams of a child.

My next stop was Mary's room. She has certainly grown. She is twelve years old and on the verge of blooming. I left Mary a little child, but came back to find a face that someday will surely launch a thousand ships. And what a surprise Mary had for me when I arrived last week! I sat next to her at the piano and she began playing Mozart with remarkable skill. Mother had written me several times regarding Mary's talent, but I thought the boasts were merely that of a proud mother. But this - it was unbelievable! A year ago, Mary was listening to American Bandstand on television. She sat at the piano and began experimenting when her favorite Beatles song was played. Before the song was over, she was playing it. Mother wandered in, astonished, and encouraged Mary to play every song Bandstand played. Note for note, Mary played along.

Mother took her to the University of Denver's music department and had her musical aptitude tested, discovering she has perfect musical pitch. In fact, Mary's IQ is a remarkable 150 - a true prodigy. She is now training in a special educational program funded by a gifted artist grant from the state. I suggested to Mary she would someday play with a major philharmonic orchestra, but Mary, still my silly television girl, says she wants to play for Dick Clark!

If I didn't think it might endanger my life, I'd throw that blasted TV in the garbage.

Mary has been my shadow ever since I came home. I don't know how much she knows about Vietnam, but she has an unusually mature nature for her age. When I first departed for boot camp, Mary was very quiet, and I wondered if she might be less concerned with my leaving than she was for the fate of the castaways on Gilligan's Island. However, Mother said Mary was deeply disturbed with the war and my departure. She sat glued to the TV when the news reported from southeast Asia, and she cried for hours at a time, Mother said, when they received a letter from me. Mary kept all my letters and my graduation photograph in a little satchel. Often, Mother found her sleeping in my bed, the satchel cradled next to her heart.

As I stood at the open door of her room, I watched Mary take soft, easy breaths. My portrait remains on her night stand. At least I'm her hero. God, I would give anything to shield her from the harshness of life, but the consequential reality is: she is already aware.

I stepped away from her room and quietly walked the back hallway to Mother's closed door, where I could feel the loneliness even before I got there. I stood only a moment and listened to the faint breathing on the other side of the door. There should be two hearts beating in that room instead of one...

There isn't much of Dad remaining in the house. Here and there are photographs that remind us of better days, but for all the years he lived here, there is very little else. I choose not to remember much of him anyway. It's hard to see through the distortion of his bottle.

I do not, however, harbor hatred for him anymore. I'm now very familiar with hate, and that feeling does not apply to Dad.

This afternoon, Uncle Vern came over and joined me for beers in the back yard. Except for Steven, nobody has asked specific questions about Vietnam. It is so painfully obvious they don't want to disturb me, but I feel like a dangerous mental patient at times. After the unpleasant encounter with Steven, however, Vern admitted he was shocked at the things I said.

"If you don't want to talk about it I understand," Vern said.

"I can talk about it," I said. "It was a war, Vern; it was pure horror."

"It was a nightmare for your mom - the whole year you were there."

"One year, one month, and twenty-eight fucking days, Vern."

Vern took a swig and nodded. "Tell you this, Junior, none of us slept a wink when you were missing. Poor Rosie must have called four times a day from California. You may not know this, but she dropped three courses that term because she was failing. The damn thing nearly did her and your mom in."

"Are you trying to make me feel better?" I asked.

"Well, what you should know is this: the important people in your life love the snot out of you; we appreciate what you went through."

"I know, Vern," I said.

"Three weeks, Junior," Vern said. "It took three damned weeks for us to learn what happened to you. We first hear you're missing in action; then they say you were wounded, but they didn't provide any details. Christ, we thought you might be in pieces, but then your letter comes and tells us you twisted your knee."

"I'm sorry you had to worry," I said. "If it makes you feel any better, your concern wasn't wasted. I did a little more than twist my knee."

Vern leaned back and measured me. "I never said anything to the girls, but I thought your letter was watered down a bit..."

I had to smile. "Look, this is between you and me. I left out a lot of details about the crash, because I didn't want Mother to suffer any more than she already had. I wrote to Rosie and told her what really happened, but I don't want Mother to know."

"What do you mean 'what really happened?'"

"It was bad, Vern."

"So tell me," Vern said. "I want to know."

For the first time, I finally verbalized my experience. It's not my wish to become an old war horse with a thousand stories, but having Vern to talk to helped. It took me several hours to tell him about the huey crash and the horror of the jungle. In fact, before I knew it, I gave him a minute-by-minute rundown of my entire tour. He sat in wide-eyed disbelief the whole time.

During the years of Vern's eligibility for service, he was classified 4-F because of a heart murmur he'd developed in childhood. He worked in a stateside munitions factory through the Korean War. He openly admitted his jealousy of Dad, who was in the fight. But I believe his idea of war changed when I told him about Punji stakes, village exterminations, baby bombs, and the nights my buddies and I camped out with the NVA.

"You know," Vern said, "your old man never talked about Korea when he came back. Now I understand why."

We sat and drank; drank and sat. Vern was not his usual happy self. Our conversation hit him hard.

I finally spoke. "Vern, how do you feel about Dad's suicide? You've never said."

Vern took a long drink and sighed. "I'll say this, he picked a worse way to do it than our dad did."

I looked at him with stunned eyes. "Gramps?"

Vern shrugged. "I guess you were too young to figure it out."

"No," I said. "It's something I've always suspected. God, Vern, I have wanted to know for so long, but now that you tell me, it still comes as a shock."

"Your grampa was drunk every day since he was twelve years old," Vern said. "One day, I found him dead as a rock with an empty whiskey bottle in his hand. Most folks said the poor old guy was out of control, but nobody'll ever convince me he didn't know exactly what he was doing."

"Suicide," I whispered.

"Just a little peculiarity that runs in the family," Vern said as he finished his beer. "That, and a taste for firewater."

I began to feel uneasy with the empty beer can in my hand, but Vern has a way of changing the subject when it comes to matters too close to the heart. He slapped me on the knee. "I'm sick of this depressing conversation, Junior. This ain't the way to welcome you home. Why don't you tell me how your loins are tingling with Rosie coming home tomorrow."

"Tingling," I laughed. "But let me tell you something, sir: You keep your hands off her bottom, hear?"

"Oh Christ," Vern said, raising his hands in surrender, "you pinch one butt and you're labeled for life. I told her I was sorry. She slapped me, I bled, we hugged, and we're friends; case closed."

"Case closed!" I said, reaching over and giving Vern a hug.

He hugged me, shook me, and then touched my face. "Thank God you're home, Junior."

"Amen."

Then, as he always likes to do, Vern left me with a tease. "Big dinner tomorrow night, you know that?"

"Do I?" I said. "Mother's cooking already. Rosie's parents and her sister are coming over. You'd better be there."

"Wild horses, Junior, wild horses. But you got something coming, pal. Oh, do I have a surprise for you two."

He didn't elaborate. He just said I'll have to wait. Please, God, don't let Vern embarrass me in front of everybody.

I'm tired, Journal. Ready to sleep. Rosie's due in at 11:30 in the morning. I'll be at the airport by eight. Yes, ready to sleep, but I doubt I'll get much. I can smell Rosie's sweet perfume as if she were here with me. It might be for the best if I don't sleep, for I've had bizarre dreams the last two nights. I woke up several times in the middle of my dark room lost and confused. It's as if there is something in the room with me, but I can't find it.

Get lost, Charlie. Go back to the bush. You're in Hell, and I am home...

June 26, 1966

Such a quiet and peaceful night. Time for reflection.

Journal, I don't comprehend the many subtle nuances of this life back in The World, but one thing on which I relied was the prospect of unshackled time I would spend in Rosie's arms - that the day of our consummation would remain forever etched on my life. I know now I had a reason to survive. Sixteen years did not make me a man, although I thought it had. In fact, my life in the killing fields did not make me a man either. Rosie has made me a man.

How splendid to be another's first love. It is a precious gem that time and circumstance cannot take away. We made love with no intrusion of guilt, for the times in which we live are too severe to disallow us this one gift God gives us.

Marie Rose grew more beautiful with each day I was away, and my heart soared at her countenance as she descended the stairs of the plane. For a moment, I stood motionless, watching her approach. I wanted to take in the sight and savor the moment.

Then, Mother gave me a shove. "Well go!" she said. "Go!"

While Mother clicked her camera, Rosie and I collided in a passionate embrace. God bless Mother; this was such a private moment for Rosie and me, but I would fight to the death for Mother's right to be there. Rosie and I held each other in silence for a long time, perhaps unaware of what next to do, and then the inevitable flow of tears came. This time, however, they were tears of joy mixed with laughter unlike all the tears of the last twenty months. I had almost forgotten such joy existed.

Mother joined in the hugging and kissing, and most remarkable, we managed to squeeze tears from perfect strangers who witnessed this wonderful moment. It took us some time to pull ourselves apart, and we finally began the long walk down the concourse. We were all going home together.

But how I could not help noticing the many military uniforms passing us; boys in uniform, going in the wrong direction...

Mother laid out a dinner spread that rivaled her finest holiday fare. Rosie's parents, Jake and Marie, joined us, along with Angela Robbins (my God, the ugly duckling is suddenly a beautiful woman!), Vern and Aunt Millie, and Jon and Mary. I grew hysterical when Vern came after Rosie and she promptly pinched him on the ass!

And, how Rosie does glow! She is radiant with those

sparkling green eyes, the lovely and long brown hair soft as an angel's, and the smell of her perfume, which I have long since memorized. Every wonderful thing I focused upon while away is enhanced by her maturity.

Talk and laughter abounded at the dinner table, but there was an anxious undercurrent I believe felt by all. It was a kind of desperation for happiness. Mother, knowing Rosie and I longed for privacy, sped the courses around the table like a Chinese waiter. And then dinner was capped off with a huge cake, my late birthday present, I suppose. With the twenty candles was an inscription along with a drawing of a military medal: "Welcome Home Our Hero!"

I wish it would have just said 'Happy Birthday.'

Rosie and I departed around five. We made the flimsy excuse of taking in a movie. I doubt anyone believed we were going to do anything but look for a nice spot to park. But, who would have dreamed that Vern and Jake Robbins would meet us outside as we climbed into Mother's Chrysler. They approached us, wearing Cheshire Cat grins. Vern stood outside Rosie's window and whispered something as he handed her a key. Mr. Robbins came to my side.

"Thank God you're home, son," big Jake said with his distinctive Texas drawl. He handed me a fresh one hundred-dollar bill. "A new civilian on the town needs some spendin' cash."

I couldn't help but laugh. "I just don't know what to say, sir."

"First you cut that 'sir' business, boy - you're a civilian now," Jake said. "Take my little girl on the town and be good to her." He patted me on the shoulder and whispered in my ear. "And if you aren't good, try again..."

Jake let out his infectious laugh and winked. He rounded the car and put his big arm around Vern. They stood together like two cats that just dined on a canary. Jake Robbins was born too late for this time and place. He would have made a good cowboy; maybe a rustler. He's often told me he longs for the days of working the Houston oil rigs when he'd come home black and sweaty with an honest day's work caked on his boots.

So, there they stood, our smiling cats arm in arm, waving as we pulled down the drive. Jake and Vern, seemingly different, are more alike than anyone would know, and something was cooking.

Rosie told me to drive downtown. She was in on the game now. "What's going on?" I asked.

She just smiled and held me close as I drove. "You'll find out soon enough. Drive down to the Center Theater."

We drove past Union Station and into the heart of the city. When I reached the theater, Rosie told me to pull around the corner to the front of the Denver Hilton Hotel, where a doorman stood. I stopped, the doorman blew his whistle, and a big 1966 Cadillac limo drove up! We were quickly whisked to it and welcomed in by a friendly black chauffeur by the name of Jerome.

Within the most elegant confines of the limo, we found what might be mistaken for a hotel suite! There was a small television set, a tape recorder playing Frank Sinatra music, a bucket with champagne on ice, an ice box filled with candies and ice cream bars, and a cooler filled with fresh fruit.

We took a magnificent ride and caught the mountain sunset while sipping champagne from each other's glass. Sitting close, we talked of all the things that occurred while we were separated. We discussed Rosie's college career and the new friends she's made there; we discussed my play and its progress; we hit on my Nam pals, where they are now, how they're doing. It was a wonderful celebration of talk and laughter.

After the ride, we were dropped at a nightclub near the hotel, and we strolled in like Hollywood stars. The Captain seated us down front and snapped his fingers, summoning a platoon of waiters and busboys. I was called 'The Gentleman,' and Rosie, 'Miss Robbins,' making it quite apparent the influence Jake Robbins had in this place. I knew who was behind all of this. I mean no offense to good old Vern, but it would take a month's pay for him to afford this.

After the show, we met Jerome at our chariot. He took us back to the hotel, and Rosie suggested Jerome take the rest of the evening off. She gave me a naughty smile. I wasn't sure what she had up her sleeve, but I wasn't about to argue. I handed Jerome twenty-five dollars for his splendid service, and he thanked me with a sly wink. It seems everyone was winking at me. I suppose that's what happens when you're out with an angel.

Rosie took my hand and we went into the hotel. She gave me a room key, which Vern gave her before we left. This is when I first started to experience a shortness of breath. We went upstairs to a huge penthouse suite with windows overlooking the city. The room was larger than Mother's entire house! There was soft music playing on a hi-fi, and the lights were seductively low in the outer foyer. In the living room was another iced bucket of champagne, and off a large bedroom was a spa, complete with a gigantic sunken tub. By this time I imagine my heart was thumping louder than a huey.

We nervously laughed our way into the big bedroom and sat on the round bed. We were both tipsy enough to feel some comfort in these elegant surroundings, but I know, despite all the times I've dreamed of being with Rosie like this, I was awkward and definitely not in the running for membership in the Don Juan Club of Romance. I kept saying witty things for laughs, when all I wanted was to sweep Rosie in my arms and make love with her. The fact is, however, I didn't know how.

But I was with my best friend. Always my loyal audience, Rosie laughed at every inane wisecrack and hid her nervousness with an occasional touch of my arm or cheek. Finally, from my cavernous mind came the suggestion we open the champagne. I didn't need another drink, but it seemed to quell my apprehension by having something to do. Walking into the living room, I felt a sudden chill at the sound of the water coming on in the spa. I wandered about, finding the bottle and trying to figure out how the corkscrew worked. I found out champagne doesn't need a corkscrew. Come on, Bogey, I thought, you can do better than this.

I brought everything back and found Rosie, now undressed and wrapped in a towel, drawing the bath. I'm glad I didn't faint. She came and put her arms around me.

"Pour us a drink, and come join me in the tub," she delicately whispered.

"Uh huh," I grunted. My mastery of the English language was covered by a pretty good kiss.

Mistaking my clumsiness for charm, Rosie playfully kissed my crooked nose. She smiled, dropped her towel and climbed into the tub.

This simply was nothing like the time I showered with Lyla.

As her soft, white body disappeared into the bubble bath, my nervousness faded. I'm not at all sure why, but I was glad I wasn't going to botch this up by being sixteen all over again. I wasn't scared anymore. This was real. For the first time since I took my army physical, I didn't have an ounce of fear in me. God, it felt good.

Other than spraying myself with champagne when I opened the bottle - and when I slipped on the slick tile floor - I was pretty suave. Rosie laughed anyway, and said, "There's my clumsy teddy bear!"

I climbed into the warm water and moved close to Rosie. I have never felt such incredible tenderness, and I dare say, that night will forever remain in my memory as I recall the first time a woman's body became one with mine. It was the most intimate gift of our hearts. We felt like we saw through each other's eyes and shared our silent thoughts. It was unimaginable joy as the last two years of terror melted into the water.

It did wrinkle us, however.

As I lay there with my head resting on her shoulder, she softly caressed the ugly scar along my arm and shoulder.

"Does that hurt?" she asked.

"It's not as bad as it looks. I had to endure two separate surgeries to prevent me from looking like Quasimodo," I said. Rosie dutifully giggled. "Think that's bad, look at this." I pulled my leg up to expose the Frankenstein zippers on my knee.

She made me drop my leg back in the water.

We laughed a little more, but Rosie was suddenly unhappy. She stroked my shoulder again, mindful of my healed wounds. "It's just not fair," she whispered.

"I was lucky," I said. "Some guys come home without arms and legs."

"You shouldn't have been there in the first place," Rosie said. "It's wrong."

Nam was the last thing I wanted to discuss right then, but I didn't know how to change the subject. And, I sensed Rosie needed to talk about it.

She continued to lightly stroke my shoulder. "When you were shot down, I knew that very instant something was wrong. I remember I had just gone to bed. Suddenly, I sat up, terrified. I knew something happened, but I couldn't get myself to call your mother. I'm sure I would have scared her to death, so I called Angie. She stayed up with me on the phone half the night trying to calm me down."

"No doubt Angie encouraged you for the opportunity to be rid of me," I joked.

"Are you kidding? Angela was in a panic. She knows my sixth sense for these things. When we got word later that you were lost, she fell to pieces right with me. Damn the army; they wouldn't tell us anything."

"I know," I said.

"According to the letter you sent me, I could see they were weeks behind what was happening. By the time we learned you went down, you were already rescued; when they told us you were rescued, you were already writing to me that you were alive; and when they finally told us you were alive, you were in the Da Nang hospital. It was a nightmare."

"I wish I could have let you know sooner," I said.

Rosie laughed. "You should have seen Daddy; he was calling every senator and congressman he knew. I thought he was going to go to the White House and punch Johnson."

"I wish he had."

"I hate them," Rosie said. "I hate them all, them and their stupid war. Do they have any idea how they're devastating families?"

"That's not high on the Pentagon's list right now, Rosie."

We talked about Vietnam a bit further, always a subject that leaves me cold. But I can hardly avoid it right now. Everyone is so curious.

"I try to understand why it's happening," Rosie said. "Johnson talks about stopping Communism, the newspapers talk about our wrongful intervention, the people on campus talk about hate mongers. Meanwhile, you almost get killed while they argue."

"I'm home, Rosie, that's all that matters," I said. "I could try to figure out why I made it when others didn't. I could try to explain the chaos. There are a whole lot of things I could try to understand, but I'd probably lose what's left of my sanity."

"Things on campus are terrible," Rosie said. "It isn't school anymore; it's a political forum. A boy was beaten in front of my dorm for speaking out against the government. Another guy in a ROTC uniform was beaten by some hippies. You can't attend any class that doesn't end up in a political debate about Vietnam. Almost every day, somebody is protesting, and it always ends up in a fight."

"So, why do they take it out on us? Hell, if they want to hang Johnson from a White House tree, I'll buy the rope. But why do they call me a baby killer?"

"I don't know. I got into a bad argument with one of my friends when I told her you were over there. She called you a murderer."

I pulled Rosie close. "Forget it," I said. "She just believes what the newspapers tell her. She's no better than that sow sister of mine who protests violence and then burns down her dorm. I don't deny that babies are dying over there, but I could tell her about a booby-trapped Vietnamese baby who blew up in Jimmy Moon's arms, and she'd call me a liar. Life has no value in a war, no matter the age. The six o'clock news never reports incidents like Jimmy's death. God forbid Dan Rather would let America see what really goes on in that country. God forbid American college students see the truth."

This was not what I wanted, Journal. Here I was on the

most romantic evening of my life, and I was on my soap box.

"I'd love to visit that ex-friend of yours," I said, my blood boiling. "I'd ask what she thinks would happen to those South Vietnamese villagers if we pulled out. If she thinks of anything other than mass genocide, she's wrong. Maybe America isn't handling the situation correctly, but the solution is not peace, love and dope. They think the rest of the world lives like we live. Hippies think Charlie's idea of luxury is a pool in the back yard. Jesus, luxury to Charlie is a chance to cook his rat instead of eating it raw."

"Please..." Rosie said.

"No," I said with a healthy dose of self-righteousness, "the war is run in corporate board rooms, at the world news editor's desk, and in Congress. If those hippies weren't hypocrites, they'd march into D.C. and demand we either get out or deploy enough troops and equipment to finish the job. Instead, they cry for North Vietnam."

My voice was choking. "It isn't fair to throw shit at a twenty-year-old boy who was forced to kill people to survive. It's not fair to call me a baby killer when I let my friend die instead of killing a baby to save him." I began to cry as Rosie held me tightly. "I spent three days lost in a jungle, terrified that I might die like Mike Golightly or be put in a bamboo cage - maybe tied to a tree with my balls cut off. I had to look at a boy whose guts were spilling into the mud, knowing I was the one who killed him. It's not fair, Rosie. All I wanted was to live - to go home. All I wanted was the chance to be with you and my family again..."

I finally broke. I'd shed some tears in Nam. Some were tears of grief, some of loneliness, and some of relief. But in Rosie's arms, my tears were for me - for the young boy inside of me who died the day I stepped on the plane bound for Vietnam. I finally, gratefully, lost control and grieved for what happened to me. But in my rage, I said things that surprised me. The words growled out of me like the grunt of an enraged bull: "I loved killing them...I'm glad they're dead...they can't get me anymore..."

After my tirade, we fell silent for a very long time. I'm afraid my rage frightened Rosie. As the black cloud finally cleared, I felt in my heart both relief and sorrow for carrying on so. I supposed Rosie understood, for she always accepts me for what I am and puts no expectations upon me. She respects my feelings if she agrees with me or not.

"I didn't mean to say those things," I finally whispered. "I don't know why..."

"Stop," Rosie said, putting her hand to my mouth. "You have to let it out. I know you didn't mean it. You need to let go of the person you left back there..."

I shall forever love Rosie for her unconditional friendship, Journal. I pray I don't contaminate her with this bitterness.

It brings further conflict to mind. The World is back under my feet, and it's my responsibility to cherish it. Where do I fit, and how does Rosie figure in? She will return to Berkeley for her final year, and she has strong ambitions to teach school. Rosie's in love with California, and I expect her goals include settling there. It may be divisive as I stand on this shaky plateau, needing a long and arduous repair of my soul. My future still holds hope for a career in writing plays, which will lead me in the opposite direction of California. But, whatever the case, if I can afford the cliché, I need to 'find myself,' and that only I can do – alone.

God, how is it possible I am only twenty? I feel ten times that. In Nam I was treated like a man. Here in The World, I can't even vote. Over there I saw no farther than the next mission, but now I see decades of life ahead with no compass to guide me. Rosie encourages me to chase my dream to New York, but her tone implied resignation. She didn't say it, but her feet are firmly planted in California. She would be chasing a bird in flight if she expected a commitment from me. Two years of my life are gone, and I want them back. Mother invited me to stay home for as long as I wish, but Mary and Jonathan depend on her. I don't wish to take from them.

As I laid so securely in Rosie's arms last night, there were moments of weakness when I almost proposed marriage, but

I believe that was simply an internal cry from the heart without temperance of mind.

I have too many questions for this time and space. I have to reacquaint myself with The World, and I intend to do it at a slow pace. After all, Rosie's only been here a few days now. We need the summer to reacquaint ourselves. We've transcended a new boundary of our relationship and need time to see if we are suited to it. We've had moments of strain between us in the past; times when our attitudes or habits served to annoy each other. I know how stubborn I can become, and I have unusual dark moods that isolate me. And Rosie, too, is hardheaded at times. She has some new ideas regarding this women's liberation business to which I'm not fully accustomed. Good lord, how is it that I would dictate any woman's position or station in life when I can't even define my own? But, it seems many women in this revolution feel that men oppress them, and Rosie agrees.

I shouldn't think I do. I love women. They're by far my favorite sex.

But, this is too much for me to handle any more tonight, Journal, for the time has exhausted me. For now, I know I have never had a better friend than Rosie. She is truly my soul-mate, and we, as she once said long ago, should let love fend for itself. It's just that she excites me so! This summer will be a time of passionate discovery for us.

I need a cold shower.

July 2, 1966

An unexpected letter today from Doug Moon. He wrote from Long Island where he operates his mother's floral shop. Another baby killer loose in The World, this one plants roses and geraniums. Since his discharge last October, he intended to write, but he admits it was very difficult since Jimmy and I were such close friends.

Not long after Jimmy died, I wrote Doug to relate my deep sorrow with a wish for my condolences to be passed on to his family. I never received a reply until now. I didn't feel shunned, but I do admit I was confused by his silence. His letter confirmed my suspicions were true. Recently, the Moon family confronted their pent-up emotions after avoiding the subject of Jimmy's death all this time. Doug's father is suffering from cancer, and they decided it was time to realize that their time on earth was for life, not death.

One afternoon, they pulled out Jimmy's footlocker with all his personal effects from Nam, which had been locked away, unopened in Jimmy's room. They found photographs and other things associated with his stay in Vietnam that allowed them to conjure up the few happy memories of Jimmy's last months of life. Doug says they laughed and cried all afternoon, but it was a thorough spiritual cleansing; they feel they've finally let Jimmy go to God.

This letter, Doug says, is part of his 'therapy.' Thanking me for my friendship with him and his brother is part of Doug's unfinished business, and too, he wished to send me some pictures snapped in Nam. One is a shot of Jimmy, me, Hayman and Colonel Strauss playing poker. From the looks on our faces, Jimmy was winning. Another is one of me, Jimmy and Doug as we walked along a Hong Kong street in our flowered shirts. The other photo was a shot of Jimmy and me sitting in the door of Eagle. I was wearing his Yankees baseball cap, and he was tossing his autographed baseball at the camera. We were smiling. I remember that photo. The Moons probably don't know this, but Jimmy died less than an hour after it was taken.

Doug also sent a gift. He has written similar letters to Hayman, to whom he sent a shirt Jimmy bought in Hong Kong. It had a big ace of spades on the front. I remember when Jimmy strutted into our hotel room with it on. Hayman said: "A spade! Yeah, now he know who he is!" God, how we laughed.

Doug sent Duke Winslow the deck of playing cards Jimmy left on his bunk when he died. I remember Duke once saying he had to quit smoking because he lost all his matches playing poker with Jimmy.

And to me, Doug sent Jimmy's Yankees cap.

I plan to write Doug today. He told me there was an item

missing - his father's pocket watch that Jimmy had carried. I don't look forward to telling of the watch's fate...

July 5, 1966

What a grand holiday we had! What a party!

Rosie's family joined us at our Berkeley Lake picnic. My welcome home parties just never end! I was buried with gifts and a marvelous cake with a wonderfully detailed picture drawn on it: a helicopter with a little man hanging on.

The most shocking surprise of the day was Vern's gift. It's a '58 Corvette, which he bought from a junk heap the day after I left for boot camp. Vern said working on the car was his way of keeping the faith in my survival. This car is gorgeous. It's cherry red with jet-black interior, mag wheels, and an engine that Vern probably stole off a Gemini-Titan rocket.

Among my other gifts: Mother gave me a new stereo hi-fi; Rosie's parents gave me another hundred-dollar bill; Angie gave me a Beatles album; Mary gave me a Mozart record; Jon gave me a plastic decoder ring he got in a cereal box; Rosie gave me another beautiful knitted sweater.

The most hilarious gift of the day came from Mr. Lloyd, my old boss from the drugstore, who popped by to say hello. He gave me a suitcase full of Playboy magazines! He said: "I know you've seen them all, but I thought you ought to have them!"

So much for having Mr. Lloyd fooled!

He also asked me to come to work for him as his assistant manager. He welcomed me to stay as long as I want while I search for the means to reach my loftier goals. It's an attractive offer which requires some serious thought. I don't want to sell Playboys all my life, but the salary would help Mother and the kids.

Another surprise was the appearance of Steven. He was on his way to his family picnic, but he dropped by to apologize for the argument we had. It felt so good to hug that big dummy and erase the ugly moment from our friendship.

Steven also said he was bound for Parris Island on the 10th.

Rosie to sew on my army flight jacket. Under the symbol were the words: "Make Love Not War." Rosie sent it back, and in a moment of her rare but formidable rage, she gave my activist bitch sister a piece of her mind.

Rosie's mom and dad represent an interesting paradox. Jake is a big-time oil executive who would look better in blackened coveralls, but Marie fits the social climber mold. She's a sweet woman with perfect southern manners and a gentle resolve that keeps Jake in line. Jake drank like a sailor yesterday, but he retained his composure and was in constant control.

We were one big family.

We packed up around midnight, and Rosie and I rather clumsily lost control of ourselves in my new car while parked on Inspiration Point.

God, what a day!

July 28, 1966

3:49 a.m.

I have to admit, Journal, I'm drunk.

I'm trying to fend off an unexpected case of the willies that for an obvious reason have me hiding down here in the old den. A bottle of Scotch is doing its best to fight them off, but I'm having some trouble shaking this. You see, it's an anniversary of sorts.

I had no intention of replaying the old jungle camping trip in my head, but two days ago I started remembering where I happened to be just one year ago. Since then, all I have been able to think about are those three horrendous days. I'm finding out no matter how much I try to block out the whole Nam experience, it creeps up on me much like Charlie used to.

I've been pretty sullen the last few days, and Rosie has left me alone - she's better attuned to my moods than I am.

She isn't stupid. She knows the date. In fact, I have to remember that she didn't have much fun this time last year, either.

My celebration of this day was something that leaves me

sitting here now wondering if I may have a damned mental problem. This evening I felt like the house was closing in on me, so I hopped in the Vette and took off for parts unknown. I drove mindlessly into the night for five hours, stopping only twice - once to buy some Scotch, and later to pee it out. I'm not actually sure where I was when the abandoned road I was driving suddenly took on the appearance of the Vietnam bush. If this was a hallucination, it was of a gigantic magnitude. Through my windshield I could see the trees and the downed huey, and I felt the breath of a thousand Charlies on my neck.

I saw Dutch lying there with his splintered femur hideously poking through his leg. I saw Jack Putnam with blood pouring out of his forehead. I saw Jim Clairborne, whose skin was literally bubbled with blisters, his head grotesquely twisted. I heard the voice of that NVA boy who almost captured me, and I saw the faces of each NVA soldier I killed. Everything I saw tonight probably passed my mind in no more than a second, but each image was real enough to touch. And, after it all disappeared, I saw the speedometer of my Vette. I was driving over 120 mph.

Thank God I was out in the middle of nowhere.

Happy first anniversary...

August 12, 1966

I'm feeling blue, Journal. Rosie leaves for school next week. We approach the end of summer with little resolved regarding the future. Every moment we are together, we're lost in a barrage of sexual passion. After she goes, I'm afraid I'll be like some poor alkie without a dime for another sip of wine. Sometimes we just don't communicate very well. I fear it is because we are powerless to control the inevitable changes in our lives. When we're together, we hold on like it will be the last time we'll see each other again. Indeed, I fear we are turning toward opposite shores in more ways than one.

I suspect nothing will ever be again as it has been this summer.

We're changing.

August 27, 1966

Dear Marie Rose,

I miss you.

You truly brought me home. If not for you, I think all the pent-up emotion of the last two years would have festered inside. I don't presume I'm free yet, but you're right when you say I can't change the past - that I have nothing but the future in my control.

The summer is one I shall never forget. I hope this, your final school term will bring you closer to your dreams, and I pray God will help you and me as we face more important decisions down the road. Whatever the result, I love you. I'm already counting the days to your Christmas holiday.

As Always,

Me

"No more be grieved at that which thou hast done:
Roses have thorns, and silver fountains mud;
Clouds and eclipses stain both moon and sun,
And loathsome canker lives in sweetest bud..."

-William Shakespeare

October 28, 1966

What has become of me?

Sat last night, staring at an empty typewriter in search of Strange Potions. It is like a dream that only remains long enough to reach my consciousness, but then flees my memory when I wake. The story can work, but it delves so deeply into the heart that I fear what I might find there. I look in the mirror and see a stranger, just as I look on empty pages and see no play.

Took the Vette for a spin tonight; one which might have been my last. What happened on the road has given me much to ponder, for, like my last highway adventure, this one nearly did me in again.

I took Highway 6 through the canyon into the mountains. It's a favorite ride of mine. With a bottle of Jack Daniels to keep me company, I was set for a long, thoughtful journey. The moon was full, and the air was very warm for this time of year. I rounded past Central City onto 119 to Nederland and down Boulder Canyon. In Boulder, I stopped at a bar near the university to have a few beers. I met a pretty girl who is a student at C.U., and we carried on some empty conversation about her studies, my interest in writing - the usual garbage.

"Funny," she said, "you don't see many guys in Boulder with short hair these days."

"The army doesn't like hippies," I joked.

That was enough for her, Journal. She gave me a strange scowl. "You aren't in the army," she said.

"Not anymore. I got out a few months ago."

She took a drink and mumbled with disdain: "Once a fascist, always a fascist I guess."

I felt a swirl of anger in my head. "What the hell do you mean by that?"

"Please go away. I'm tired of this conversation," she said. "Anyone who murders innocent children for Lyndon Johnson doesn't interest me. Too bad for you, soldier, I was going to invite you to my dorm room."

"Yeah, too bad for me, I guess," I said, standing. I glared at this pig. "It's just as well, you hairhead cunt, because I'm not in the market for a case of screaming clap, anyway." I poured my beer in her lap, and she jumped up with a scream. From behind me, some hippie hero with a pool cue in his hand made an empty-headed threat. I swung and knocked him over the table, and then closed both of his eyes for him. By the time the bouncers tossed me outside, I had a broken beer bottle in one hand, and a handful of the hippie's hair in the other...

I don't know what came over me. I was so full of rage at the woman's remark that I dare say I might have hit her if the hero hadn't stepped in; and never have I ever spoken to a woman that way. Despite her comments, I could have simply walked away, but something inside made me react violently.

Still enraged, I hopped in the Vette and squealed the tires as I ripped out of the parking lot. I slugged down the whiskey to cool my temper, and I headed down the turnpike with a bellyful of Boulder's opinion of me. That woman enraged me, but I was more angry with myself for breaking a promise I made to myself about not telling anyone I went to Nam.

The brisk night air sucked the whiskey to the top of my head, and the anger, still boiling within, made me lay a heavy foot on the accelerator until my eyes twisted down into a cavernous, empty tunnel. The white lines of the highway blurred and then completely disappeared. Eighty, ninety, one hundred miles per hour. The Vette growled as my heart pounded harder and harder. I pressed on the turnpike, thinking I might be able to fly if I got the car going fast enough. My eyes fixed down the small cavern cut by the headlights, but in the surrounding darkness, familiar images reappeared. Again, I saw the black eyes of Charlie. They were wet and wide, his stringy black hair dripping blood on his face. I tried to blink him away, but he just kept staring at me from the road. Dousing my lights, I was flying in complete darkness at more than 120 miles per hour, but Charlie kept looking at me. I stomped on the pedal, but I couldn't run him down. He was moving faster than me.

I turned my lights back on. Suddenly, Charlie was

replaced by flashing red lights reflecting in my mirror. I probably could have outrun the cop, but something told me to slow and wait for him. In another minute, a State Patrol car came into my mirror, and I brought the Vette to earth at the side of the road. I'll never forget the first time I was stopped by a cop. I was sixteen, and I quaked in my shoes when I listened to that inexorable tap-tapping of the cop's boots as he approached my window. I recall pure terror at the sight of the cop's dark uniform and the gun on his hip. But tonight, I felt nothing. Uniforms don't scare me anymore. What is he going to do, I thought, put me in jail? Hey, knock yourself out, pal. I've slept on jungle floors, in mud and blood, and I've faced the devil and kicked his ass. You think some Colorado county lock-up scares me? The state trooper flashed his light in my face, and I rolled down the window.

He gave me a monotonous: "License and registration, sir."

I complied, and he went back to his unit for a few moments before returning.

The cop peered in the window. "In a hurry tonight?"

"Yes sir," I replied.

"Had a few drinks?"

"Oh, yeah. More than a few, sir."

"Step out of your vehicle, please."

That was it. I figured my next move would be to try to remember Vern's phone number so I could request he come and bail me out of jail. I got out of the Vette and stood at attention. The cop first put his light on my flight jacket, down to the boots, and then back on my stubby head.

"You staggered when you got out, son. I think you're drunk."

"Could be, sir," I said. "Or it could be I staggered because my knee isn't worth a shit anymore. Or maybe it's my whole fucking beat-up body that isn't worth shit."

The cop curiously studied me and shook his head. "Somebody's got an attitude tonight."

"I've had better evenings, sir. Course, I've had worse, too. Look, let's just cut the shit. I'm wasted, and I have to take a leak, so why don't you just hook me up and take me in."

The cop didn't flinch. "How long you been home?"

"Sir?"

"Where'd you serve?"

I was drunk, but I finally caught on. "Army," I said. "Delta. Soc Trang. 121st Army Aviation."

"Jesus," the cop said with a disgusted smirk. "Airmobile Light. That explains the flying Corvette."

"Well," I said, almost with a smile, "isn't quite as fast as a huey, but of course I haven't had anybody try to fire a few rounds up my ass along the Boulder Turnpike, so I guess it'll do."

He looked me over, scratched his chin, and walked around my car, inspecting it with begrudging admiration. "Nice ride," he said.

"It was a gift from my uncle. He's one of the few back here who doesn't think I'm a fucking baby-killer."

The cop came back and got directly in my face. "Let me tell you something, son, two hours ago I got punched by a three-hundred-pound woman. An hour ago, I got kicked in the gonads by some hippie asshole on acid. The last thing I need tonight is a wise-ass drunk treetop flyer in a rod like this. How long you been home? Month? Two?"

"Back to The World in December. Got home in June," I said.

"Figures..." He looked at my driver's license. "Twenty years old," he sighed. He flashed his light in my car and found the empty whiskey bottle. My crimes were mounting like sales on a cash register. Speeding, reckless driving, drunk driving, drinking under age…

The cop put the light back on my face. "You're a little young to be a pilot."

"Door gunner," I said.

"Yeah? The suicidal tendencies are evident."

I had to laugh.

"So, you spent your tour peppering LZ's?" he said.

"Actually, sir, I spent most of it ducking and praying."

He nodded without a smile, still looking at my license. "Tell me about it."

"When were you there?" I asked.

"MAAG," he said, "'61 and '62. Spent most of my time near Quang Tri, fencing in Mamma-san and teaching Papa-san how to cut throats." The cop's voice was harsh.

"We just did our jobs, sir," I said.

The cop looked reflectively in the darkness. "I guess we could stay here all night and talk about the good old days, but I have to do something with you. By the way, I got a report that a crazed fool in a red Corvette tore up a hippie hangout in Boulder tonight - seems he kicked the hell out of some poor hairhead. You wouldn't know anything about that, would you?"

"I imagine," I said, "if the poor hairhead got the hell kicked out of him, he must have had it coming, sir."

The cop tried not to laugh. "You put him in the hospital, pal. But, come to think of it, with that bad knee, maybe it wasn't you. And, you know, it's so dark out tonight, I can't really see what color this Corvette is."

"I can't see much, either," I said.

"I still have a problem, door gunner," the cop said. "I clocked you at 132."

I nodded, embarrassed.

"Cowboy," he finally said, "do you remember when you were first in country? You followed the lead of the short-timers, because they knew the way to get out alive, right?"

"Yes, sir."

"Here in The World it's the same gig, so let me give you some advice. When I came back, I found I needed that adrenaline fix I'd been getting on a daily basis in country. I'd go mountain climbing without proper gear, I raced stock, and one time I got juiced up on tequila and started clicking off a .44 next to my head until a round went off about two inches from my ear. I couldn't hear for a week, but that terror fix was like a shot of dope.

"Now, get this straight - this Corvette ain't a huey, and this blacktop ain't the bush. If you don't grab onto reality, you're gonna grease either yourself or somebody else who can't even find Vietnam on a map. You got an edge, son. I see it in your eyes. You laid your ass on the line to get back, only to feel like you don't belong here anymore. You're pissed, confused, and not just a little bit fucking fugazi."

I suddenly felt a ball of acid in my throat. Tears welled in my eyes, and for a second I thought I was going to break down and cry. This cop, who was a stranger just five minutes ago, was suddenly my best friend. He'd been in the shit, and he understood. I swallowed hard and looked at him. Unbelievably, his eyes were wet, too.

"Let it go, man. You're not gonna get a fucking parade. Nobody gives a shit – nobody but your brothers – and your people. You keep that hard-on for The World, you're gonna die here. Then everything you did to get back will be wasted. You're still rocking and rolling at two thousand feet, trying to fix that adrenaline jones. You gotta put an end to it, hear?"

The truth is often like a bucket of ice water down the back. "I copy," I said.

The cop looked me over again. He shook his head. "In a pack of thirty boys, I don't think I'd ever pick you out as a door gunner. College professor, maybe."

"We adapt," I said with a shrug.

"Well, adapt to this, pal - the only reason you aren't in cuffs is because I'm giving you a break nobody else in The World thinks you deserve. You're one fugazi mother right now, but if you don't straighten up, I'm gonna find you out here with four inches of asphalt in your forehead." He gave me a gentle slap on the face. "You look like you got a brain, so put this in it: This Corvette don't suit you, and neither does scrapping in bars. Trade the car for something slower than a chopper, and stop driving like you still have to kill somebody."

He was right, Journal. I'm riding the rails like we did as kids, headed for that bright train light and waiting to jump at the last minute. I'm ashamed of the way I've behaved since coming home. I want to live my life and look to a future. It isn't my war anymore. I want to come home.

I had nothing to say to the cop but "Thank you."

"Thank me by going home - slow. I'll be in deep shit if I come over the next rise and find you splattered."

"Copy," I said.

"Didi mow," he said, and I climbed back into my car as he walked away.

Get lost, he said in Vietnamese. Beat it. Get out of here.

I hope I can...

December 22, 1966

Dear Marie Rose,

Merry Christmas to you in Maui!

It took some careful calculation to work it so this letter would reach the hotel check-in desk before you. Please, if I failed, don't tell me; I spent a whole day figuring this out!

So, how's Christmas in paradise? I'd like you to thank your dad again for his generous offer to take me along on your family holiday. I would love to sing Christmas carols on the beach with you, but I hope you understand how my heart has longed for this Christmas at home with Mother and the family. She scolded me for declining your dad's offer, but I know how much she has looked forward to having me here all to herself.

What I most regret is the very few days you spent here before you departed. It seems we only allow ourselves passion when time is too short. It troubles me. We didn't talk much about the prospect of my leaving for New York this spring, and we hardly broached the subject of your teaching job offer in San Jose. Perhaps we ignored the subjects intentionally? I don't know.

But I must at least tell you I am confident I'm making the right decision to leave and try my hand at the theater. I've stashed enough cash from the sale of the car and the money I've made at the drugstore. I feel like I may finally be chasing my dream!

I hope Christmas is glorious for you and family. I don't know when I'll see you again. I wish you had enough time to come back here before school resumes. Whatever the case, we still have the mail! Merry Christmas, Rosie. I love you.

As Always,
Me

1967

"One of the unhappy necessities of human existence is that we have to find things out for ourselves."

- T.S. Eliot

March 16, 1967

Dear Marie Rose,

I know how difficult writing must have been. I must admit, I am devastated and confounded. I don't know what we should do, but I am coming out there immediately. That you suggest this an imposition is bordering on insult, Rosie, and I will not hear another word about that.

Don't worry about anyone finding out, particularly Mother or your parents, but please understand I had to take Vern into my confidence in order to borrow his van so I can drive out. Vern said to assure you he wants to do anything he can to help, and indeed, he has some ideas I will discuss with you. I share your desperation, but above all, we are in this together. I had to wire this to you rather than phone to avoid the chance someone might overhear, but hold on; I'm planning to leave tonight, and will call when I'm near.

As Always,
Me

March 17, 1967

Needed to stop for an hour or two. My eyes kept closing. It's all I need to roll off the highway asleep at the wheel.

Things have fallen in, Journal. I'm sitting along the road somewhere near Reno. A map beside me tells where I'm headed, but it could not possibly begin to tell me where I'm going. I'm lost and I need some sleep.

Rosie's pregnant...

"You take care of yourself," I said as I walked with him to his car.

"I always do," Steven said. We stood for an awkward moment before he left; then we gave each other another warm embrace. "I'm gonna make you as proud of me as I am of you," Steven said.

"I'm proud now," I said with a hard lump rising in my throat. "You give 'em hell, Steven. And you keep your head low."

He climbed in his car, and as he pulled away, he gave a terrific grin and the thumbs-up.

I felt like I was watching myself two years ago. God, I hate the feeling I have. I don't believe I'll ever see Steven again. But I have no control over that.

On to the party. We ate fried chicken until we clucked. We drank beer and smoked cigarettes, and Mary played her guitar while we sang folk songs. We went to the amusement park across the street and rode the Ferris wheel and the roller coaster. Later, Vern and I crawled into the Vette and took her up north to a long stretch of farm road where I could open her up. That car can fly! I got it up to 120 mph. The rush of blood in my head was terrific. I noticed Vern got a little pale, so I slowed and took him back to the beer. Although he never admitted the ride had been too much, the green around his gills didn't disappear until long after we got back to the party.

That night, we huddled on blankets in the cool summer breeze and watched the fireworks over the lake. How wonderful it was to see rockets without having to dig a hole and bury myself in fear! Some of the louder reports did, however, cause my spine to shiver. I jumped more than once, Rosie and I nervously laughing at my still-raw nerves. A few harmless firecrackers did not ruin this night, for it was Independence Day, and it marked my freedom to go on about the business of life as I originally intended.

All in all, I couldn't have asked for a better time. I'm also glad Lyla wasn't there to spoil it. She's at the University of New York now. Rosie did, however, tell me Lyla sent a gift to be given to me. It was a peace symbol patch that Lyla wanted

4

Directions

1970

"Afoot and lighthearted I take to the open road,
Healthy, free, the world before me,
The long brown path before me leading
wherever I choose."

- Walt Whitman

June 8, 1970

Freedom. I've had enough, Journal. June 8 is my Independence Day.

The time has come to take action. I can't believe I've wasted so much of my life in the drugstore, selling diet aids to fat ladies. I'm outta here!

There, now I feel better.

Hit the road, Jack. I have enough money to journey this country, and I've a half-alive VW bus in which to do it. I'm going to travel the high road and start living my life the way I planned. The dream, so long ago detoured, is going to fly.

I want more than ever to do this right. It's time to banish the rust from my writing - blow the dust off of Strange Potions, too. I resolve to finish it before I reach New York.

Mother took the news well. "You have to do it," she said. "You'll never be happy until you try." Things are going well enough at home, anyway. Mary's scholarship to Juilliard eased the financial burden, so little Jon is Mother's only responsibility. In short, I have no more excuses, Journal. We are taking to the road. New York's my destination, but this may be the only time in my life when I have the chance to point my bus any direction and take off to see what's out there. I'm first going west.

This land is my land, Mr. Guthrie...

June 29, 1970

Yuma, Arizona. An oven. We made the desert crossing alive, Journal, although I sometimes thought Bugbus and I might perish in the hundred-plus heat. I killed an entire case of beer, and I'm sitting under my canopy in a KOA campground, watching the sun set. The swimming pool here felt like a warm swamp, but it was relatively refreshing. Now I'm watching two little urchins splashing around while their parents argue over how to pitch a tent. I'd thought about pressing on to San Diego, but the heat took my energy, leaving me happy just to sit here and watch it grow dark.

I had an interesting taste of cactus justice this morning. An Arizona state trooper pulled me over just west of a smudge on the road called Mescal. It hauntingly reminded me of a night so long ago when I was pulled over in Colorado. That was back when I was still out of my head from the war.

But this confrontation with the law was much different, indeed. The Arizona trooper sauntered up, expecting to find a drugged hippie inside, but he lightened up when he found just a scruffy beard, clean hair, and not a peace sign in sight. I think he saw the beer, but he was looking for pot. Even he could figure out he hadn't bagged Tim Leary. The premise for detaining me was a broken tail light, but upon our close inspection, it worked perfectly. Glory be.

"You know," said Officer Parsons (Corporal Punishment, I later called him after we had fifty miles between us), "you don't look the type to be out here in the middle of nowhere in a hippie bus."

Hippies aren't welcome in this part of Nowhere, Journal.

"My Rolls is in the shop, sir," I said.

Sometimes beer says things I wouldn't normally say. He cocked his brow and breathed a little redneck chuckle. "That right? I ain't sure exactly what you are, but you ain't a hair-head."

This guy had all the markings of a Leatherneck. I can spot them a mile away. "Hairhead?" I said. "Jesus, sir, were you a Marine?" I think my voice squeaked.

"Damn right," he said, and then he gave a cautious eye.

"A Marine pulled my ass outta the shit in the Delta. 1965! He saved my life!"

"You were in Nam?"

"Damn right!" I mockingly said.

He laughed and handed me my license. "I was in Saigon. Got my ass shot up on Tet and had to retire. I'd give a nut to still be there. Damn, I miss it."

I'm glad I didn't vomit on Corporal Punishment.

"Why did you leave?" he asked.

I shrugged. "I got hurt, too," I said. "Guess we were just unlucky."

"Yeah, amen, boy. Assholes here got no respect for a uniform."

"Yeah," I said. "Amen to that."

I apologize for patronizing this person, Journal, but I had no intention of spending a night in Barney Fife's local stir. Corporal Punishment slapped me on the back and sent me on my way. God, it's a shame they had to discharge this mutant. They could march him right in downtown Hanoi and the NVA would run in terror.

"Hey, buddy," he said as he started to get in his car. He gave me a thumbs-up. "We're gonna win it over there!"

Right.

Tell Nixon. That bastard couldn't give a flying fuck about the mothers and fathers whose hearts break every time they think of Over There.

Tell Steven. He left his legs Over There, and now he's wasting away in a VA hospital.

So, we're gonna win it Over There, but what is 'it?' We overpaid the price of victory a long time ago. In the meantime, we have our own war Over Here. Thousands of men are already dead or wounded in Vietnam, and people are getting shot here - Kent State, Jackson State - the real war is on American campuses. Is the price so steep that we have to turn our own country into a kill zone?...

And, why did I get off on this, Journal? I'm the happy vagabond. Until that cop stopped me, I don't think I've given a Nam sermon in more than two years. I've never been to Vietnam; remember?

End of speech.

A couple of hippies just pulled up. They're unpacking for the night. Obviously they didn't meet up with Corporal Punishment. They just waved and gave me the peace sign. Peace, man.

They're lighting up a joint. Jesus. No thanks, I said when they offered. I just drink beer.

"That's cool, man," one said.

Cool? In this blasted heat?

June 30, 1970

Los Angeles! L.A.! Swimmin' pools, movie stars! God, this city stretches out forever. Bugbus will never be the same; I was afraid he'd have a paranoid fit when he first saw these freeways.

I pulled out my map and found Hollywood. That was the first thing I wanted to see - a quick glimpse of Rock Hudson, or maybe Elizabeth Taylor. Boy, was I wrong! No movie stars along Hollywood Boulevard; just more hookers than in a whorehouse on a Saturday night! I made the mistake of asking one for directions to the Chinese theater where the footprints are.

"Oh, honey," she said, "let me put my footprints on you!"

I respectfully declined.

I don't know, but I think I was misled by the travel brochures. I bought a map to the movie stars' homes from a black guy named Ivy. He tried to sell me a watch, but I have one. I drove out to Beverly Hills, carefully reading my map, and I looked at Jimmy Stewart's shrubs, Paul Newman's gate, and Bob Hope's trees. I don't think I'll ever wash my eyes again.

After admiring star shrubbery, I traveled west on Santa Monica. The map suggested I could eventually drive into the sea if I wanted. I love the ocean. I was taken by such a splendid feeling when the Pacific finally came into view. This is the first time I've seen it from the ground, and I can't imagine anything more magnificent. It is vast and untamed - even more than this Los Angeles and all its kooky inhabitants. Now I know where hippies were invented. If there was a brassiere worn, I didn't see it. On second thought, I did see a man wearing one.

I drove along Highway 1, passing beach after beach. I like the amusements on the Santa Monica pier, but the best is Venice Beach, which is more like a faraway planet. I am going to camp here to investigate further.

I've never seen so many skimpy bikinis!

July 2, 1970

Let me out! It's time to move on, Journal. There's an element of weirdness in Los Angeles to which I simply cannot relate, no matter how wide-open my mind. The beaches are a dumpground for rudderless nomads and flower children bent upon turning the entire country into one big Woodstock festival.

The kicker was this: I sat in the sand at Venice Beach, taking in the sun, watching the muscle boys lift weights, and gasping at the jiggling bikinis. A young girl dressed in an ugly, ankle-length dress with flowers on it approached me. In her hair were flowers, and in her eyes was a glaze common to the locals. She asked for a beer from my ice chest. I, of course, said she may, thinking this might turn into a romantic day. My new acquaintance sat her little Bohemian behind in the sand next to me. I'm not much at small talk, but I was Johnny Carson next to this little mouse.

She had an empty smile, and occasionally her eyes shut and she threw her head back and incoherently mumbled. I think she also hummed a Bob Dylan song for a moment. This nonsense went on for about thirty minutes before she emerged from her trance and asked me for another beer.

"You didn't finish the first one," I tried to say as politely as possible, pointing at the full can of hot beer in her hand.

"Oh," she said, "cool..." She closed her eyes and hummed again.

Then, as I was just about to say something, she spoke with her eyes still closed.

"Him?" she said. "The family...he's not family."

I looked around to see what I had missed.

"I can," she said. "I drift. I am the sky. Are you the sky?"

Before I could answer, she continued:

"We are family. I am Sky..."

I felt like Jerry Mahoney.

Then, her eyes opened and she looked at me. "Would you like to screw me?" she asked.

"Excuse me?" I said, stunned. At this juncture, I was certain I'd look around and find Allen Funt lurking behind an umbrella with his camera whirring. (Allen Funt, or, Rod Serling.)

"The vibes are right," she said. "You would like to, wouldn't you?"

"Well," I said, "I hadn't given it much thought..."

Was this bit of insanity enough? No. Behind us, there appeared what I can only describe as a human Yeti. He looked Nordic, standing about six-five, maybe two hundred and fifty pounds. He had long white hair on his head, back and knuckles. Although the temperature was in the nineties, he wore fur, leather pants, and a tire chain for a belt. His arms were the size of tree stumps, and on one shoulder was a tattoo that said: "Born Bad" with a Jolly Roger under it.

He looked me over like a tiger might look over a wounded, bleeding antelope. In the parking lot behind him were about twenty other Yetis on motorcycles.

"Split," he grunted to the girl. "We gotta split."

I prayed he was not referring to my skull. She didn't look at him when she spoke to me. "That's Digger. He's my old man," she said.

"Hello," I squeaked, but I didn't offer my hand. I remembered an old rule Mother taught me when Bob The Dog moved into the neighborhood.

"We're gonna screw," the girl said.

My heart dropped. I couldn't believe what I just heard. She should have just said: "Please kill this little man."

Then, it got really weird.

"No," I tried to protest, "I don't...I didn't...I never..."

"Hurry up, man," Digger said to me. "I ain't got all day..."

He turned and walked back to his motorcycle and popped a beer.

I wish I had a picture of my pale face at that moment. The girl looked at me. Then, she giggled. She started to pull her dress up and spread her legs, but she suddenly stopped. "You want a hit of acid first?"

"I have to leave...sorry," I said. "Maybe some other planet."

"Oh? Shame. Well, later..."

She gave me the two-fingered peace sign. Despite my gimpy leg, I think I broke a land speed record getting out of there...

Peace. Interestingly, the peace sign is also the warrior's sign for victory, but I don't think the hairheads know that.

Journal, I admit this hippie movement is rather clever. The bare feet, dirty jeans and flowers are cute. Even the hand holding sit-ins and the off-key Dylan folk songs are tolerable. But the line between reality and insanity is very thin with them. I wonder where these people are heading. They pump chemicals into their veins and camp in garbage dumps with the world's sewage; yet, they don't understand why they aren't taken seriously. And, the way sex seems to be passed out like hot dogs, the hookers up in Hollywood are going to go out of business.

I can't wait to see what their kids are going to be like twenty years from now.

But, hey, man, it's L.A., you know? Cool.

I'm leaving for San Francisco. Maybe it isn't as strange there...

July 15, 1970

I have to hand it to California. Her insides are askew, but her scenery is beautiful! I've had several days alone to enjoy the majesty of the northern shores. Ventura, Santa Barbara, Arroyo Grande, San Luis Obispo, Morro Bay...

Bugbus blew a tire outside of Carmel, and I've camped here two nights, awaiting an urge to hitch a ride into town to have it fixed. I sincerely contemplated staying here and growing old by the sea, but I don't suppose that would do.

Something unusual: Last night, while I was lying back and listening to the sea serenade the stars, the ground rumbled. A genuine California earthquake! This state is truly a world of its own.

I have to laugh at my last entry. It took less than forty-five minutes for San Francisco to convince me Los Angeles is a monastery by comparison! Even the kooks on Venice Beach would find Haight-Ashbury on the strange side: I sat at a stop light, looking straight up a huge hill and wondering if Bugbus could make it, when I was startled to see a face suddenly pop into my passenger window. It was another hooker, but this one had a five-o'clock shadow.

I remember a day when 'gay' meant 'to be happy.' Yes, that is San Francisco, where the men are men, and so are the women.

So, here I sit, Journal, out in the hills where I'm watching the seals play below in the surf.

But I believe we both know what spell this place holds. I've sidestepped the issue, but I think it's time to own up, because I can't stay here forever...

Going to New York via California really isn't the most direct route. The fact is, I can't move on to my dream until I make a pass through Santa Cruz. I've been unwilling to admit that, but why else would I be sitting here on the edge of a cliff, scolding myself for believing I have any right to come this way? Why, indeed.

I last heard from Marie Rose just before Christmas, '67. A part of me says I should leave here, but another begs me to go find her. I've no concealed intent of romantic reconciliation here. Rosie is my friend, and without that, I feel an unfilled void within. It might be that Santa Cruz is a dead end, but I can't overcome a feeling that she still teaches school there. She's always been as steady as the earth, as predictable and solid as I am unstable and prone to wandering like a sea current. I have her last address, and I imagine I could find a phone number, but I must search the starry sky tonight for a final answer before I leave the cliff.

Would she want to see me? There was bitter sorrow in her conclusion that we were tracing opposite directions. I suspect, however, more to it than just that. She was withdrawn into bleak sadness after we made the painful decision to terminate the pregnancy. She was angry, and I was mad at myself for assuming our passion was easy and unbridled. The whole ugly incident set her back in school and obliterated my plans for New York. Our inexorable lust exacted a high premium. The money I had saved for New York and the bulk of Rosie's nest egg was spent on the illegal abortion. We reduced ourselves to thieves who slink in the night...

It carved a profound chasm between us.

Rosie felt guilt that she stood in the path of my dreams, and I selfishly acted as if her life was no more valuable than the dark and dingy room where the ugly deed was done. She is more important to me than any foolish pipe dream, but there were no words to use. That I was with her throughout the ordeal in support could not rectify the desecration of her body. I don't pretend to know or understand the emotions of a woman who must stand naked to the ravages of a violent and often cruel world. I suspect her resolution to the abortion included far more than my conviction to practicality. We might have married and had the child, but at the same time condemned all three of us to a life of longing for what might have been. I know the river of guilt runs deeper in Rosie, but I feel guilty for not understanding why. Perhaps it is the empty feeling of losing some compassion in my soul, which died in the war.

All that water under the bridge does not, however, amount to more than a deeper ocean that I now blankly stare at like a mindless lemming about to thrust itself in.

This is such folly. Why do I stand in this wilderness, afraid to find the best friend I shall ever have on this earth?

I wonder how she looks; how she is getting on. Is she married? I wonder if romance has been to her as it has to me, God forbid. Since Rosie, women have been to me like house-flies. I finally get annoyed and swat them away. I've hopped from one mild interest to another, pulling away when one demands more than I care to give.

The hour is late. I've sat here watching the sun set and the stars move. I'll muster my courage to head for Santa Cruz.

Tomorrow. There has never been a better day for which one can make a plan...

"Dawn came, and the maiden surrendered herself to Slumber, hoping to find sweeter and more gentle dreams than those she had encountered in her awakeness..."

- Kahlil Gibran

July 16, 1970

Santa Cruz. Thursday. Winds from the northwest. My hands are cold.

I drove by Rosie's address seven times, a coward wandering mindlessly in the wilderness. The building is a very California-ish stucco apartment villa. I almost stopped on the sixth pass, and I opted for a burger on the seventh.

Will she be happy to see me? If I were to wager, I'd bet she'll greet me suspiciously. She has a strong will but a fragile heart. And how will I react? Perhaps I should abandon this and head for the desert and die of exposure - let my bones be picked by vultures.

Jesus, what an idiot. I must get hold of myself.

I'm going to stop this next time around...

-1:30 a.m. –

Silent peace surrounds me.

As I write, I sit on the living room floor in Rosie's apartment. She has gone to bed, and I reflect on all the wonderful hours of conversation we've had. I've often wondered if I would ever see her again, but my heart soared when I laid eyes on her beautiful smile. I must capture this on paper:

After circling the apartment like a hungry buzzard all afternoon, I finally stopped and skulked to the door. A very beautiful woman greeted me, but it was not Rosie. After the last few days of internal gyrations, I was deeply disappointed to think this trip had been in vain. I'm certain it showed on my face. I pardoned myself and stumbled through an unclear explanation. The woman then asked if I was looking for Marie.

"Marie Rose?" I said.

"Yes, she lives here. She's my roommate."

My heart leapt!

The woman perused me and then little Bugbus with the Colorado plates in the parking lot, and she gave a marvelous smile. "Oh, no," she said. "Are you Shakespeare?"

"It's been a long time since I've heard that name," I said.

The woman threw her arms around me. "I can't believe it! I've heard so much about you!"

"Perhaps we can be friends anyway," I said, a little startled.

She laughed and looked me over like a ripe melon. "I'm Linda Fox. Oh, you don't know how much I've wanted to meet you. Marie Rose and I have been friends since college, and I feel like I know you...come in, come in!"

I did.

"My husband is in Vietnam," Linda said. "When you were there, I helped Marie Rose get through it, and now she's doing the same for me. Billy is on a destroyer stationed in Da Nang. He's coming home in three months."

"Thank God for that," I said.

Linda grabbed me again and hugged me. This time I hugged back. "Oh, Marie Rose is going to flip when she sees you!" Linda said.

"That's what I've been afraid of," I said. "It's been years since I've written."

"Don't be silly," Linda said. "She's busy, you're busy, but she loves you to pieces. We often talk about you and wonder what you're up to."

"She isn't in?" I nervously said.

"She's at the beach. You must go and surprise her. She'll be thrilled!"

Linda gave me directions to the beach and walked me to the bus. "I'm so happy to meet you," she said with a tear in her eye. "I'm sorry I'm so emotional, but seeing you makes me think of Billy. We went through hell when you were over there."

"Just keep writing and praying, Linda," I said. "You'll never know how much it means to him."

We hugged again. "Go find Marie Rose," she said, but she pointed a wary finger at me. "Don't you steal her heart again, because she has a boyfriend." She gave me a wink and whispered: "But it's not that serious..."

I followed the road down to the beach. My ever-vigilant

knees were still weak. It was my brain saying she'd be glad I was out of her life, but I've never listened to my brain in twenty-four years; why start now?

The beach was loaded with tourists. I wandered among the cooking bodies for fifteen minutes before I finally found Rosie alone in the distance under an umbrella. There could have been a million people there, but it wouldn't have taken me long to spot this beacon in the darkness. It is Rosie's glow. My pounding heart pushed me forward.

Rosie wore her typical Lauren Bacall look as she sat in a beach chair, her lovely tanned arms resting in her lap as she held a book, and her brown legs daintily stretched out. She wore a wide-brimmed sun hat that dipped sensuously low over her sunglasses. Her wonderful long hair dropped from the hat and over her shoulders. I could smell her sweet scent, which took me precisely back to the first time I ever saw her back in school.

She didn't notice me as I approached from behind, and when I could reach out and touch her, I simply sat in the sand and took in her countenance. She is the most beautiful woman I shall ever know. There may be others as physically stunning, but no one will ever possess the beauty and soul of Marie Rose.

I finally spoke: "I'll bet your daddy's rich and your momma's good lookin'."

At first, she appeared as if she didn't hear. I believe my voice threw her; a familiar sound in unfamiliar surroundings. She then slowly turned and faced me, taking off her sunglasses and revealing her most wonderful eyes. Her mouth opened slightly and her eyes grew moist when she smiled.

"My God," she whispered, and she jumped up.

We gave ourselves a heartfelt embrace.

In fact, it took some time before we let go. We held tightly, both of us laughing and wiping stray tears. Finally, we settled in under the umbrella and talked away the afternoon. We had so much ground to cover...

"The worst of it," I said, "has been Mother's illness. She

had a mastectomy last year, but the doctors are more optimistic with each day. She's working hard at the store, and you wouldn't suspect she's ever had a sick day in her life. As for Vern, he kicked Millie out of the house when he caught her in bed with the pastor from their church. That subject is better left alone. And Mary - she is going to Juilliard this fall."

"I'm not surprised," Rosie said.

"I suppose," I said, "but it's fascinating how she's still addicted to the damned television. At least she watches PBS once in awhile."

"How's Jon and Lyla?" Rosie asked.

"Jonathan turned eight last month. I doubt we'll see a performance like Mary's from him, however. He drives Mary insane when he pounds out 'Chopsticks' on her grand piano. And Lyla, pardon my language..."

"Oh, stop," Rosie said with a laugh. "Are you two still enemies?"

"Enemies? With Jane Fonda's ugly twin? Why should I despise her? No, she's doing just what I would expect. She's in law school now. She's an immoral pig, so law will make a perfect profession for her."

"You shouldn't be so hateful."

"That's my choice, Rosie. But enough of me. How are you?"

Rosie then gave me some disturbing news. Last year her doctor discovered an irregular heartbeat. "I take medication for it, and they say it's no reason to be worried." After I went through several paternal admonitions, Rosie told me to stop. "I'm fine."

"But -"

"I'm fine. Leave it alone."

Damn, that woman is stubborn.

"Daddy is still with Mobil," she continued, "and Mom is still the social bug. They're both well."

"I haven't seen your parents in a long time," I said. "I miss going with Jake to the union hall for poker, and I miss the spats we had over his Oilers and my Broncos."

"He misses that, too, you know..."

For an uncomfortable moment, we sat in awkward silence.

"I thought he might hold some contempt for me," I finally said.

"You're wrong," Rosie flatly said. "You're wrong on several counts if you assume anyone close to me has anything but love for you."

I took a deep breath and gathered myself before saying anything stupid. "I'd wager Angie doesn't miss me."

"Wrong again," Rosie said. "She asks about you now and then. She lives in Dallas now. She's a successful model."

"My God," I said, "I can't help but remember such a sadly awkward little goose back in high school. I can't believe how she got so beautiful in such a short time."

"She's still my cynical big sister, though," Rosie said. "She won't let anyone get close to her. She spent all of high school waiting for a boy to like her, and now that she has them on a waiting list, she cuts them up, one by one."

"Revenge is sweet," I said.

"Perhaps," Rosie said. "What about you? Has there been anyone special?"

I shrugged. "I think I'm doomed to the eternal stag line, Rosie. You know how I enjoy my solitude. In my own way, I, too, have trouble letting anyone in."

"Amen, Shakespeare," Rosie said, touching my hand.

"I understand you keep regular company?"

"Yes."

Rosie told me the man with whom she shares her time is kind and thoughtful, and they have much in common. (Hardly any reason to want to have a relationship if you ask me.) Rosie did not, however, imply this wonderful, thoughtful, kind, goddam Superman holds any particular spell upon her...

Listen to me.

There I go again. I'd give my life for Rosie's happiness, and I have no right to sit here in a jealous muck. If it had been anyone but me who caused Rosie so much pain long ago, I'd have taken his head and squashed it like a grape. But, it was me, and I don't want to squash my head. This man who makes Rosie happy deserves her.

And I am lying like a bad Jell-o. Nobody is good enough for her!

"His name is Niles Meesters," Rosie said. "He's an industrial arts teacher at my school."

(A 'shop' teacher, Journal. A 'shop' teacher.)

Rosie showed me a picture of her shop teacher. He's thirty-one, blond, and he makes Adonis look like Don Knotts. His forehead looks made of stone, and his eyebrow is one long bush that runs along the cliff.

"He's a vegetarian," Rosie continued, "and he doesn't take drugs or drink."

"A Communist," I mumbled.

"He grew up in Encino and has a brother who is an executive at Disney Studios; and a sister who is a resident at UCLA Medical Center..."

Rosie went on: A USC All American linebacker, a surfer, rides motorcycles, jogs...

I didn't ask her any of this shit, she just told me. I imagine, although Rosie didn't mention it, if he potties on your shoes, it wouldn't stink either. How wonderful for Rosie. She has a boyfriend who can get a discount on surgery, drinks carrot juice instead of Budweiser, and probably is a personal friend of Donald Duck.

Damn, I feel such jealousy!

It isn't right for me to do this, Journal. The romantic bridge between Rosie and me was dismantled years ago. It would be wise if we simply enjoy the sturdy ground of our unbreakable friendship rather than cross over dangerous rapids of love.

Besides, I tried surfing when I was in Santa Monica and I dented the pier with my head.

To hell with my petty jealousy. I have Marie Rose back, and I celebrate it. Tonight was filled with more conversation and reflections. Linda was kind enough to depart for Oakland to dine with her parents and spend the night, leaving us some privacy for our reunion. I felt a burning desire to take Rosie into my arms, but this is not the reason I came here. She has a new life, a new man, and I don't intend to complicate it with old business. We simply talked, laughed, and drank from the cup of our love until this late hour, which is nearing two-thirty. Rosie went to bed, and I enjoy the warmth of my sleeping bag on her floor.

Rosie has promised a busy day tomorrow as she intends to show me the better half of San Francisco. We're going to see Chinatown, Alcatraz, the bridges, trolley cars; and we'll cap off the night with dinner at Fisherman's Wharf. I truly believe Rosie is excited to see me, and I cannot say how grand I feel at this reconciliation.

I've thought several times tonight about the abortion, but haven't had the courage to mention it. I don't allow myself to dwell on it, and I don't want to hurt Rosie by bringing up the subject. Back then, she was embarking on a career, and I pursued a dream. For the times we were in, it was the right thing to do, even though the process was unfortunate. I'd just as soon leave it at that. I can only pray it did not hurt her terribly, although I wonder how it could not. We fell apart so quickly afterward - it must have been a profound rejection.

I hear her moving in her room. She's coming out. I suppose there are always more things to talk about...

July 17, 1970

Am sitting in a cafe in San Jose.

The coffee is black and strong, and I'm sneaking whiskey in-between. I believe I'll head for the mountains. Somewhere barren.

I honestly believed I would never again feel Rosie's body next to mine, but it happened last night.

And now, as usual, I'm alone.

She came to me as I wrote the final passage of the last entry:

"I'm lonely," she said. "Ever since we met, we've only had select moments together, but they've filled my life like nothing else. We'll never have forever, but we have tonight."

I shared her resignation, which is painfully true. She reached for my hand, and I stood, taking it. "Is this right?" I asked.

"When will we see each other again?" she said…

We made love, Journal. It made me feel as if the hardened world relented if for only a few precious minutes. The smell of her skin penetrated me like a pure diamond point, and her gentle touch carefully pieced together the brittle framework of my heart. We held each other all night without speaking, but I believe I know we were thinking the same thing: Nothing, not even love can overcome the restraints of time.

When the sun crept into our imperfect space, it served to remind us there has never been synchrony in our physical world together, despite the perfect rhythm of our hearts. I could only offer these words as compensation, words I have often written but have had difficulty saying. "I love you."

The last words Dad ever spoke to me were the same. It was the first and last time he ever said it, and it was too late then, too.

To further remind us of that cold fate of dawn, there came a loud rapping at Rosie's door. Rosie bolted from our solitude in panic, covering herself with a robe and running to close our open door as a man appeared in the front room.

It was Niles Meesters coming to pick her up this morning to drive to Salinas for a teacher's seminar. We were so lost in our past that Rosie had entirely forgotten to change her original plans for the day. Rosie was awkward as she tried to slip out of her room, but I'm certain Niles saw me lying petrified in her bed. I cowered in that silent room, praying I was not about to be pulverized by an All American linebacker/shop teacher.

There came muffled voices outside - Rosie's apologies, followed by a shattering silence. Then, it sounded as if he apologized for the intrusion, and a moment later the door outside shut. Rosie came back in. Her robe fell to the floor as she sat on the bed. She was visibly upset as she sighed and put her arms around me. I wanted to speak, but she hushed me.

"Not very long ago," Rosie said, "he told me he wanted to make love to me. I told him I couldn't - that people make huge mistakes when they let passion outweigh their judgment. I said I wasn't going to bed with anyone again until it was completely right, and after I'm married." She looked at me with sad eyes. "Do you imagine what he must think? He comes here to find a beat-up bus outside, and you in my bed."

I put my hand to her cheek and tried to apologize.

"No," she said. "We're here. That's all. There's always been a price for happiness when it comes to you." She stood and walked to her closet to dress. "Frankly, I've been fooling both Niles and myself, thinking he and I could have something as strong as what you and I had. I'm not in love with him, but this was a bad way to show it. I don't like hurting anybody."

"I'm sorry," was all I could say.

Rosie stopped and sat by me. She took my hand and looked at me with those most remarkable eyes. "I'm the one who's sorry. I didn't mean to imply you're to blame. It just seems, for some reason, we've always been a perfect fit at the wrong time and place. Something has always stood in our way; my ambitions, your ambitions, the army, the damned war..." She stopped and stared at the floor. Standing, she silently cursed and walked out of the room, saying, "You better just go before we both end up hating ourselves..."

Rosie is right. It was a dream, but now we're awake. We didn't say much after that. I packed my things and loaded them into Bugbus. We ate breakfast in silence, but when I headed for the door I felt her grab my arm, and she pulled me into her. For one final moment, we held each other. "It better not be another three years before I hear from you again," she said.

"I love you, Rosie," I said, my voice choked with sadness. She is my rock. She is my beacon. We shared a final kiss, and then I turned to leave.

"You're my best friend, Shakespeare," she said. "I'll always love you for that. Now go out there and be somebody."

I couldn't speak. I left without looking back. The woman I can never have is the woman I'll love forever.

July 21, 1970

Dear Marie Rose,

Unlike Hemingway, I am not a fisherman. Never have been.

I am a camper in the Pacific Mountain System and am contemplating following in the footsteps of the infamous Alferd Packer if I don't find a cheeseburger soon. In fact, I did see a tasty looking little fellow with a fishing pole just a few moments ago.

I remain here in the wilderness, however, to be alone with my thoughts and my hunger. You're reading the fifth draft of this letter. Each has contained words that have not expressed what I want to convey. They feed my campfire as I write.

It was upon my sixteenth birthday, May 8, 1962, when I first laid eyes on you. I knew, at that very moment, it was the beginning of something extraordinary. But even in that starry-eyed moment when my knees were weak and the words of Byron lilted through my head, I didn't realize the magnitude of what would transpire during my journey into you. Indeed, you are the stars in the sky and the sun on my face, and you have been a companion through both my darkest hours and brightest days. Through everything, we've loved each other, and we have more importantly traversed life as friends. It is now within that spectrum we reside. Without you, there would be an intolerable void in this circle of life, and it's my wish we shall never lose what we have. But I fear I will always be lost in the river that separates us, unable to find either shore.

I regret what happened the morning I left you, but I cannot help the feeling our bonding has given me. No matter the passage of time, when we touch in body or spirit, my life moves forward.

On friendship, Gibran says: "If he must know the ebb of your tide, let him know its flood also."

You have always accepted me not for what you want, but

simply for who I am. No one else may ever again give me such a gift, so I am grateful. I pray I will always give you the same in return.

I am sorry for what happened, and I hope you will forgive me and yourself as well. You and I have never been very graceful together as we trip across this earth, but you are a part of my life so sweetly held with love; forever a part of my soul. Some things never change.

As Always,
Me

July 23, 1970
Journal, no matter that she's gone; she is always here...

5

Arbitration

1971

"...I slept, and dreamed that life was Beauty,
I woke and found that life was Duty..."

- Ellen Sturgis Hooper

April 9, 1971

Dear Marie Rose,

A marvelous surprise to hear from you! I received your letter via Mother's address; however, it need not be forwarded as I am back in Colorado! I arrived just one week ago, so your timing could not have been better. It's time to catch up, since what few words you've heard from me have been through picturesque postcards from garden spots; Des Moines, Duluth, Texarkana - you must wonder what became of my wanderlust. In short, it has died. It passed on just before the death of Bugbus. Yes, I am sad to report my four-wheeled Aryan friend threw a rod on a stretch of road just outside of Denton, Texas. After a proper memorial service behind a filling station, me 'n Joe-Bob Walker, the Happy Trails Conoco attendant who towed me in, negotiated a twenty-five-dollar transaction for Bugbus' corpse. I then hitched a ride into Dallas, where I boarded a slow-moving northbound train for Denver. (Had a chance to call Angie, but her roommate tells me she's on a photo assignment in London...wow!)

I've finally returned to Colorado with a new perspective on my goals, Rosie. The vagabond dream-chaser in me is satisfied, and I've found that Dorothy was right: 'There's no place like Home...'

The news of your tennis team's championship is wonderful! Congratulations! Your coaching has made the difference, I am certain. It's lucky, however, you don't coach the boy's team because they'd have trouble concentrating with someone like you hanging around in a short dress!

Happy to hear your parents are well, and yes, I plan to look them up now that I'm home. Sorry, however, to hear about Angela's troubles, and I hope your fears will be unrealized. Perhaps she is merely experimenting with drugs and will soon outgrow the problem. She lives on a fast track, and it is considered high status to use designer drugs in certain social circles. I doubt if there is much you can do to stop her from so far away.

Now, to honor your request for the family progress

report, I'll begin with Lyla. She is as deceitful as ever, and is progressing well in law school. She'll be perfect. Her last letter to Mother, the one letter she writes per year, told us she decided to devote her practice in the area of social issues. She hopes to work for the Civil Liberties Union. She has also joined Allen Ginsberg's pals, the Hare Krishna. Christ, what a slut. After reading her letter, I told Mother I planned from now on to slap her flush across the face every year on Lyla's birthday.

On the subject of Mother, she is well and sends her love. She's now a buyer for the store and loves it. Jonathan is in his pudgy stage, which makes Mother's raise timely. He is an interesting little guy. We call him Johnny Jekyll because of his dual personality that moves him in a moment's notice from cherub to demon. One moment he is holding the ladder, and the next he's pulled it out from under you. He'll make a good adult someday.

Vern is now selling insurance. I'm sorry to have done it, but he asked me to enclose some pamphlets. He said to tell you it isn't too early to plan ahead. There are two kinds of people in the world, Rosie: Those who...wait I've forgotten this already. Let me ask him. (He's under the sink right now fixing Mother's pipes.)

Okay, I have it. There are two types, Miss Robbins: Those who plan to fail by failing to plan, and those who plan their work by working their plan. And what's the plan, you ask? Glad you asked, ma'am. One word: Mutual Funds. (I must remind Vern that Mutual Funds are two words.)

That's that. I have now kept my word to Vern that I'd pitch you. He just broke a pipe and water is running all over the kitchen floor. This is a good opportunity for me to sneak in the advice to trash his pamphlets if you want. He's driving everyone in the neighborhood crazy with his cold calling.

I kept a nest egg at home, but I left it in Vern's suspect care, which proved unwise: As Vern's obsession in the financial world grew intense, he saw fit to invest one hundred of my savings dollars in a 'sure thing' stock based on a suspect tip. At three cents per share, Vern was assured this company would make us rich, for it was projected to take off to the seven or eight-dollar range. Today, we cannot even get a quote. Its price is somewhere around 1/16th of one cent. I'm afraid that if we wait for this ship to come in we'll drown. I told Vern I'll kill him if he doesn't keep his grubby hands off my money in the future.

What a pain in the patoot.

As for my terrific year on the road, I don't know where to start. Perhaps I'll begin on the day after I popped in to see you, screw up your life, then leave. I put old Mickey Mouse on the dash to watch for traffic, and we forged eastward. I didn't hurry, and often stopped for a week at a time to search out temporary labor to replenish my gas and beer money.

I traveled most of the summer, working my way east, until the spectacular Manhattan skyline appeared on the horizon. With Mary now living there, I had accommodations. She shares an apartment with two other girls, and I must say that was a memorable experience! Like Mary, these girls are wonderfully gifted musicians and every bit as precocious as Mary. When I think of Mary living in this jungle, it makes my belly button pucker, but she seems to have taken to it quite well. She took me to see the sights for several days, the Empire State Building, Statue of Liberty, Guggenheim Museum, Times Square, Wall Street - God, Manhattan is a combination of lunacy and class all rolling down the rails of an underground train network at light speed.

Mary invited me to stay as long as I wished so I might explore the jungle and find if this was truly what I wanted for myself. But I believe, Rosie, I had made up my mind long before I set foot in this city. I had the entire summer to search myself for answers to the question of my destiny as a writer.

The idea for a novel has spun in my mind for some time, and subsequently I've been questioning my abilities as a playwright. With this in mind, I have written some experimental fiction based upon Strange Potions. Mary introduced me to her many new acquaintances in school, and to those who are closely tied to the search of new talent emerging from Juilliard. Most of them, too, are chasing dreams - directors, writers, and actors who toil away off-Broadway, waiting for that big break. One man, and I use the term 'man' questionably, took an interest in Strange Potions and said he would like to read it. I lied that it was nearly complete, but I would send it the minute it is finished. The arts are full of promises, but I cannot allow too much hope in this world when I see those who make the promises.

After a delightful stay with Mary, I felt like I was imposing, and those three girls were beginning to drive me mad with their incessant practicing, giggling, practicing, giggling.

It made sense that I leave since Mary was straining her time to be with me. I wanted to move on to Connecticut to see Duke Winslow, who mentioned a job at his son's newspaper. It was hard to say good-bye to Mary, for I cherish my little sister and marvel how that sweet, talented flower could have come from the same loins that produced Lyla.

Seeing Duke again after all this time brought unspeakable joy to my heart, and how vital and healthy he looks! Duke stayed in Vietnam until late 1969 when he retired and came home to fully devote his time to writing his Nam textbook. We've kept in touch, however. Duke's son, Malcolm, edits a local newspaper and needed a fill-in columnist to write book and movie reviews while the regular reviewer took maternity leave; so, I became Westport, Connecticut's answer to Rex Reed!

Duke also writes an occasional article for Malcolm's paper whenever he feels cantankerous, and he freelances for Newsweek and several East Coast papers, but his life has grown calmer as he gets a little older. I can't think of anyone more deserving of a bit less calamity in his life. The majority of his time is spent sailing and working on his book about Vietnam. Duke has a beautiful three-story home in the country, and he offered me lodging at no expense other than keeping the icebox full of beer.

Working for the newspaper was a joy. I was paid to watch television (Mary was jealous), movies, attend theater, and read books. Malcolm was pleased with my work, and knowing I was just a temporary wanderer, he gave me much latitude. Although I did enjoy most aspects of the job, my inborn distaste for the media and reporters did create some tension in editorial meetings. Being an arts critic apparently invalidated my opinion on current issues in the eyes of the more self-righteous reporters. We more than once butted heads on world issues, specifically you-know-where. The swill they mandate as the truth regarding Southeast Asia is unbelievable, specifically at that time their discussions of the My Lai massacre. I found it difficult tolerating these self-appointed historians, whose closest encounter with that part of the world is trying to open a can of Chun King chow mein.

On the upside, I had the opportunity to see several Broadway plays and attend the Metropolitan Opera. It was this exposure to the medium that led me to the ultimate conclusion that I may not, in fact, be as suited to writing plays as I first imagined. During my stay in Connecticut, I composed a half-dozen or more short stories. Some were destined for the wastebasket before completion, but several were received well by Duke. He tells me my head is "brimming with literary imagination." And I just thought I was neurotic.

At Duke's urging, I have outlined two novels originally haunting my head as plays, and I am eager to pursue them in this interesting new framework of the novel.

I believe a new side of myself awoke during my journey, but that, too, created in me a desire for life in Colorado. New York is wonderful, and I marvel at its splendor, but something there seemed to grate upon me. I am a mole, suited to the more serene calling of this place rather than the bizarre world of New York theater. The privacy and isolation of the mountains is more compatible with my new and mysterious interest. I truly believe my muse lives here and not in the east as I once believed.

But, while I was in Rome...

One afternoon, I came home and found Duke staring at his typewriter, helplessly cemented in writer's block. He was writing a portion of a chapter on the 1964-era Delta struggle, and he was having trouble remembering a few details. We set out to break Duke's brainlock, but instead of filling holes in his book, we found ourselves laughing about one of the few happy times we spent on R&R in Hong Kong.

We fired up a half-dozen boilermakers, and we lost ourselves in conversation about the no-good old days. A wonderful thought came: In all the years Duke had been back, he had not looked up Doug Moon, whose New York floral shop was just a short distance away. So, we decided to surprise him!

It was all Doug could do to keep from crying when we casually walked into the shop. The reunion was raucous, and Doug's mother was a bit overwhelmed by it all until she learned who we were. Then, her tears flowed, too. We met Doug's wife, Georgia; his little daughter, who easily is the cutest little cherub in Manhattan; and their brand new baby boy, James. They call him 'Little Jimmy.'

Doug insisted a reunion was in order, and we promised Georgia we would have him home by dawn. He took us to a great restaurant on Long Island, and then on a bar tour to end them all. God, did we tell stories! At three a.m., we staggered into Doug's house. Poor Georgia got up and happily brewed coffee and cooked breakfast, all the time laughing and shaking her head at us. We then attended to some important business that had been one of the primary topics of the night's conversation. We got on the telephone and called Charlie Hayman in Mississippi. It took Dutch five minutes of sleep-drunk confusion before he finally comprehended who we were, but after he realized it was us, he stopped cussing and started adding stories of his own.

We took turns on the phone as we hollered insults over the line, and then introduced ourselves to his wife, Charlotte, who did a nice job of hiding her irritation. What a treat to hear the Dutchman again. He is a sheriff's deputy in a small town near Biloxi, and he has two sons and a daughter. I can only imagine in my worst nightmare being a northerner zipping down some old deserted road in Mississippi and being pulled over by this cigar-chewing fireplug!

A few days later, Doug's mother invited us over for dinner, where we spent a bittersweet evening in fond remembrance of Jimmy. The scar of a broken heart is still evident in his mother, but it is tempered with pride. On her wall, flanked by military pictures of Doug and his late father, is a beautiful portrait of Jimmy in dress uniform, and his Congressional Medal of Honor framed next to it. At the end of the evening, Mrs. Moon held me close and gave me a soft kiss on the cheek.

"Jimmy said in his letters that you and Dutch were the best friends he ever had," she said. "Thank you for being with my baby when he went to God."

I confusedly hugged her and caught a wink from Doug. Mrs. Moon never knew just how badly Jimmy's body had been ravaged, Doug later told me. She didn't know they buried virtually an empty coffin. Doug simply left that horror out of his mother's life and let her believe Jimmy died in one piece with me and Hayman by his side. I cannot fathom the pain this family has endured along with the families of thousands of others lost in this damned war.

The reunion was easily the highlight of my journey, but I knew in my heart that it was time to come home. Shortly before I departed, Duke came to me with the completed draft of his book. He honored me with the first reading. I began, believing the huge manuscript would take me weeks to read. However, this nonfiction, historical account of Vietnam and its warriors so riveted me that I read straight through for two days. My obsession far exceeded the fact that I wanted to give a friend's work my full attention. In fact, the book was brilliant. It is a stunning account, its pages possessed by every ounce of the terror, devastation, and horror over there. Duke captured the pure tragedy that exceeds the physical wounds and loss of life, and he brutally indicts the war machine that has produced a horrendous body count in return for little or nothing. Duke's revelations will shock the country. His agent has an interested publisher, but I cannot help but wonder; while the war continues to drag on and families continue to live out its horror, is the world ready for this kind of truth?

Afterwards, Duke made an interesting proposal to me regarding an idea he has for a novel based upon our experiences over there. He has never pursued fiction, but has a rather compelling plot idea based on a three-month stint he spent with one of the first American platoons to go into the bush. He wants me to write a story.

I confessed, however, I would have to look at the project with a wary eye. Vietnam does not exist inside of me anymore, and I'm a little bit frightened of unearthing demons. As you remember, Rosie, locking that beast away wasn't easy. Duke understands my reservations, but he asked that I let the idea simmer for now.

I don't know, Rosie, I think my opinions are still too biased to objectively try to write an extended work on the subject. If you have a suggestion, tell me what to do.

It was a sad farewell when Duke and I said good-bye, but I know our paths will cross again...

It feels good to be home, for I stand on more secure ground here. I have a desire to get on about the business of writing while I secure some kind of work that will pay the rent.

Immediately upon arriving home, I tried to renew some old acquaintances, but the experience has been less than gratifying, to say the least. I called Marc Komac and discovered he and Kathy have a second child and live in a large home. Marc must be doing well in the commercial real estate business, but I couldn't help but notice how married life has made them listless. They've put on weight and look ten years older than you and me. I guess everyone can't be gorgeous!

I visited Steven yesterday and am sorry to report his attitude has worsened. He is still lost in a profound depression, and his father confided in me that Steven attempted suicide last Christmas. When I saw him at the VA hospital, he was belligerent to the nurses and doctors. He looks very old, his hair is greasy and draped down his back, and his beard is untrimmed and dirty. I'm told he still shuns the idea of being fitted for artificial legs, and he belligerently rejects the apparatus needed to eliminate waste and must be diapered.

He's simply unwilling to adjust to his handicap. He wallows in self-pity and revels in taking it out on the hospital personnel. When I visited with him, I could not deter the conversation from Vietnam. I realize it is a subject that forces itself upon us no matter how we try to push it away, but for anyone to move on, there requires self-motivation and desire. I tried to take his mind from it, talking about baseball, music, even the damned weather. I mentioned you, and he said, "Tell Rosie I'm dead."

He is deranged, Rosie. He calls everyone 'gooks' because he considers everyone the enemy. It's as if he cannot come out of the bush. He even cursed his parents, whom he accuses of not caring. "How can they think I can adjust to being a castrated stump?" he said. And he vented his rage on his brother Chris, who successfully obtained a Conscientious Objector classification in the Selective Service.

The end of this visit came abruptly when I leveled with him and said he should try to behave like a civilized human being.

"You, more than anyone, should know how it is," he said.

How can I know, Rosie? I cannot relate to his plight. Certainly, I took some lumps over there, and I deeply resented it, but I didn't have my body so violated that it would permanently alter my entire life. So how can I know?

"You couldn't wait to go over there," I said. "You must take responsibility for what happened and get on with life as it exists now. Other handicapped soldiers are making that adjustment."

I only agitated Steven, and he ranted at me until I finally walked out in disgust.

The whole thing makes me sad and angry. His parents stay by him despite his contempt. When I spoke with them they seemed to me like amputees themselves. We visited right after I saw Steven. His mom is pale and drawn, and his dad is without his old fire. The only remnant of their son is the high school graduation portrait of him on the television set.

Christ, Rosie, when I think of that pathetic, smelly lump of flesh sitting in its wheelchair, regurgitating life all over itself, I can hardly remember the handsome boy in that picture with whom I shared the portal to manhood. Our summers of swimming, beer parties, and elaborate practical joking are just blank memories with a faceless boy who might as well be dead. Steven worshiped his parents and was his brother's best friend, but now he abuses them with obscenities and filth. You remember how politely he treated you and all the other girls, but now in that hospital he reduces nurses with lewd remarks and crass sexual fondling when they are caught unaware. I wish I could help him, but what can be done?

His therapist cornered me in the hall when I left the hospital. Steven has spoken of me, the doctor said, and he wanted to know what I thought. I could say nothing positive. He then asked if I might be interested in sitting in on a group session he conducts with Steven and several other handicapped vets. He suggests my input might be valuable since I am a Nam vet.

I couldn't help but remember my discussion with Duke about buried demons. The doctor's suggestion intrigues me, but I expressed my lack of optimism.

"They have to help themselves," I said. "I might serve only to antagonize them with my good fortune of getting out of Nam with all my parts."

"It isn't about handicapped soldiers," the doctor said. "It is about the war; about self-pity; about cold terror. Here, they are secure because no one expects anything from them. Pity, they have. Confrontation might be what some of them need, but it isn't effective unless it comes from someone who's been where they've been."

I was nothing but lucky to have come out of that mess alive. I might just have easily been sitting in that wheelchair if it wasn't for pure, dumb luck; and if it had been me, I ask myself if I would be any better off than Steven is now. I pray I would have the courage to go on, but that is something I cannot know.

Do you teach psychology, Rosie? If so, please forward some advice.

I can't tell you how your letter brightened my day, and I dare say I had better conclude this since postal rates are as high as this epic letter is long. You can reach me through Mother's address for now, and I will forward a new address just as soon as I have one. Mother sends her love. Mary, Duke, Hayman, and Doug said to do the same when the opportunity arose. Jon says: "Rosie Who?"; and Vern, who just finished mopping up the mess he made of Mother's kitchen, says: "Hubba hubba, lets you 'n me rubba!" Oh, he concludes with: "Remember, Rosie, when you fail to plan your financial future, you'll financially fail your future plan." Jesus, what a putz...

As Always,
Me

September 8, 1971

Is it you or me, Journal? Happiness makes me nervous. Contentment is contemptuous. I have adapted to my new job, the new apartment, and new clothes. Writing advertising copy gives me no aesthetic satisfaction, but it keeps my mind nimble. I seemed to wow the head of KWBY Radio with the tag "Your Rodeo Radio Dial!" Keep the customer satisfied...

In fact, advertising is ideal for me, for it is feeble and mindless work that does not tap creative energy reserved for my fiction. Strange Potions is as complete as it shall ever be. I'm sure it is my first, and last play. I'm boxing it up and sending it to Rye Ellery, Mary's director friend who wanted to read it. Hope he remembers me.

'Rye Ellery' indeed. I'd bet my patoot his real name is probably Morty Wingneeesky.

I've rewritten the play as many times as I care to, and have decided it must sink or swim on its own. I believe in it, but is it truly good? I'm now expanding it into a novel outline, and I hope to begin writing soon. Yes, I'm happy. I am.

So, what's the problem?

I'm dating. Enjoy it, in fact. I'm making money, not a fortune, but it keeps me hip-deep in Premium Saltines. I even caught myself admiring my reflection in the bathroom mirror the other morning.

Maybe it is this: Steven has been on my mind of late. Got a call from his therapist, Dr. Carter, and he again pitched his idea of me joining in on Steven's therapy sessions. I've put him off twice and was comfortable with the decision, but my last visit with Steven was terribly unsettling. He's changing again. Now it seems the vulgar spite has boiled down to black resolve. The doctor agrees that Steven is retreating further. Steven has the same hollow look in his eyes that Dad had when he walked in and blew his head off in front of me.

I must try to do something, because I can't allow any more of that in my life. This all makes me remember back to a long time ago when a scared boy in a Corvette, driving at the speed of light with the war raging in his eyes, got some sound advice from a nameless friend. I suppose, in my own way, I was then as self-destructive as Steven is now. That cop put a light in my head. Perhaps it's time I return the favor for someone else...

September 13, 1971

Dead tired, but I want to write. Just got home from the hospital. As I feared, this first session was brutal. I found myself sitting with mere fragments of human beings, not one of them whole, and all of their vile madness splashing about like water in a rocking tub. It was a shock to go from writing radio jingles at work this afternoon to this VA hospital horror house.

There are four in the group. Steven is called 'Stumps' by his peers. The second man is 'Pogo,' an ex-Navy F-4E Phantom pilot who was shot down near Hanoi. He lost a foot and eight fingers to torture in a POW camp. Pogo was released last spring in a prisoner exchange after four years in captivity, and he is diagnosed as a paranoid schizophrenic. They gave him his nickname after the cartoon character he likes to loosely quote: "The enemy is us," he likes to say. He's batty as a cave.

The third member of the band is a Marine grunt from Colorado Springs. His spine was shattered in the house-to-house battle for Hue during the '68 Tet Offensive. He hasn't been able to move anything but his head since, and he's hooked to machines. They call him 'Robby,' after the robot. Robby is a cynical bastard who tries to goad a fight all the time, but in fairness, I don't know that I'd be any more pleasant in his circumstances.

The fourth man is an enigma. They found him pink and healthy, living with some Montagnards near Cambodia in 1970. He was wearing four sets of dog tags, all belonging to dead soldiers who were found floating in the Mekong River six months earlier. The military hasn't a clue who this boy is, and neither has he. He at various times has claimed to be Jesus Christ, Adolf Hitler, Douglas MacArthur, Twiggy, and Citation, the '48 Triple Crown winner. For simplicity's sake, the fellows call him 'Casper the Ghost.' The search goes on for Casper's identity as the war department occasionally troops in an MIA family to see if they can identify him.

Actually, Casper is the only happy person in this group. He is articulate and witty, but he rarely joined tonight's conversation. He did, however, give me a most exciting hoof-by-hoof account of his victory over "Better Self" at the Belmont Stakes. He told me Eddie Arcaro was the greatest jockey in history, while I sat, nodding in agreement.

God, what a stupid world.

Tonight's session was tense, more than usual I'm sure because of the presence of a stranger. When Dr. Carter asked me to introduce myself and tell the group a bit about my history in Nam, I tightened up and gave only sketchy details. However, Steven, suddenly fueled with my long-awaited acknowledgment of Nam, jumped in with unexpected fervor and expounded upon my experiences, portraying me as some lunatic fringe chopper jockey who destroyed the NVA and came home with "an assfull of medals, one of them a Silver Fucking Star." Steven's tales produced little reaction from the group, except for a comment from Casper:

"You must have had a wonderful view of the countryside in your helicopter," he said.

The session began with a round-table discussion of current feelings and events. It isn't necessary or encouraged to talk about the war, although Dr. Carter warned me it is always the topic of discussion. Before long, Vietnam was broached. Steven is obsessed with it, and Robby followed his lead. Pogo seems less concerned with the war, and Casper simply banters on about nothing. Dr. Carter later told me that Steven hadn't been speaking up in weeks. He was certain my presence had evoked something positive despite the fact everything Steven talked about was soaked in bitterness and self-pity.

I'm beginning to wonder if he is not simply displaying symptoms of something deeper that might have existed in him even if he'd come home in one piece. He was a Marine, and he was wounded in one of the fiercest battles of the war. Steven has an edge that most grunts had when they came back to the world, but he hasn't lost it like most of us eventually did. He and Robby both have it. Pogo and Mister Ed have nothing.

I pray I haven't made a terrible mistake.

September 14, 1971

Dear Marie Rose,

God, I am embarrassed.

You must think I am raving mad after my late-night phone call. I am now of a more sound disposition, and am writing to apologize for frightening you.

Last night when I called, I was whiskey-soaked, but I assure you I was still the fellow in love with your toes.

I had a most terrible nightmare, no doubt manifested by my participation in a therapy session with Steven. Having noted a touch of skepticism in your voice during our good-night, I thought a follow-up letter from a clear head might belay your worries.

To clarify the rattled explanation I gave last night, I was so horrified by my dream that I simply had to hear your voice. I had to be absolutely certain of your well-being. It was simply an old haunt of the past, a chapter of life I thought I had neatly closed, but it unfortunately crept into the sanctity of my sleep and wreaked havoc. I'm sure it was brought on by the anxiety I'm feeling for these sessions at the hospital; that, mixed with my fatigue and one too many cocktails before bed.

I'm sorry if I scared you, Rosie. I cannot assure you any more of my good health. I am not a candidate for the House of Ha Ha, I promise you. Really. I'm fine. Love to you.

As Always,
Me, Napoleon

September 23, 1971

Tonight was another piece of unsavory pie, Journal. I wish I was out of this disaster. These pitiful excuses for men are dragging me into their quicksand. Tonight, Dr. Carter brought up the subject of how to cope in The World.

Pogo: "Fuck the outside! Fuck getting a job! Who's gonna hire any of us geeks? What's Stumps gonna do? Be third base at a ball park? Is Casper gonna get a job pulling the Budweiser wagon? The fucking door to this place says 'In' on both sides..."

I haven't said much in any of these sessions, and I wasn't going to start now. Pogo was right. These guys are terminal. They're bound for Nowhere. Dr. Carter - they call him 'Jewboss' - just let the storm rage, asking dynamite-packed questions, one after another, and sitting back to watch each explosion. He lives in his textbooks, and he loves applying salt to the wounds of these rodents. The only one of these men with potential for living on the outside is Steven, and he's happy to stay and wallow in his own shit. Pogo's homicidal, Casper's on cloud nine, and Robby is flat on his back the rest of his life.

Robby: "You may think there's no outside, but I sure as hell ain't gonna die here."

Pogo chilled the air with a hideous growl. "Push it, Robot," he said with someone else's voice. "You'd love for me to come over there and waste you, and you know it. You'll still be rotting in that bed fifty years from now." Pogo's eyes are hollow, and deep inside of them twists a psychotic whirlwind.

There was silence. There always is after an outburst like this.

Then, Jewboss lit another fuse. "Is it important to get out, Robby?"

Silence.

Jewboss looks at me and calls me 'Hero,' the tag they gave me. "What's it like outside?"

At this point, I had been contemplating a quick exit out the window. He caught me off-guard. When I realized I was still a part of this flock of loons, I said: "Outside? It's life. Freedom. I wouldn't want to live here."

"Why?" Casper asked. His eyes aren't holes like Pogo's; his are mirrors.

"Why?" I said. I laughed for no reason. "If you were out there, you would know."

This brought on another one of Pogo's icy chuckles. When I looked at him, I could swear he hadn't opened his mouth. "You're sliced fuck, Hero," he said.

My intestines twisted, but I kept my composure. "Is that right, Pogo? Then what are you?"

"I'm a fucking war casualty!" Pogo screamed at the top of his throat. "They ought to sell fucking tickets to me! Nobody would pay to see a nigger like you!"

That's the second time I've been called a nigger in my life. Jimmy did it once when he was kidding with me, but I'll wager Pogo wasn't kidding. I was stupid enough to wonder if Pogo actually thought I was black, but what I'm understanding a little bit at a time is that I shouldn't resort to logic when it comes to Pogo. It was too late to ask, anyway. His holes covered up. Often during a session, he suddenly turns off like that. He closes his eyes and simply sits there the rest of the time no matter what is said to him. Dr. Carter says he'll sit there for an hour or more after everyone leaves the room.

These guys don't need a therapist. They need a zookeeper.

The remainder of the night was spent with Jewboss lighting fuses, but the conversation was dull with Pogo off in a trance. Jewboss might do better with a whip and chair. I tried to throw in an occasional "I was there and I know how bad it was" and some other bullshit, but I didn't even believe myself. Vietnam seems like another life to me - one I can hardly recall.

Steven didn't say a word all night. He's dead. He could make a living out of pulling off our old mortuary gag.

I don't know what to do...

September 30, 1971

- 4:02 a.m. - I have to go to work in four hours, ahead of me a day's load of brochure copy to write for the ad agency's most important client. I'm putting down drinks to stop my hands from shaking, and now I need some coffee to keep me from staggering around the job all day.

What's happening to me? I sit here naked, clinging to the typewriter. My clothes and bed sheets are in the wash because I peed on myself when Charlie struck my dreams. God damn, this had to be the nightmare of nightmares. It began in Nam. Charlie was there, but we somehow ended up here - in my damned bedroom! My bed was churning and thumping. I was on my knees, clinging to my pillow and aiming at the closet where Charlie was hiding inside. He was there; I know it. I saw his black eyes and heard his gibberish. The bed pulled up and we circled him twice while I drew a bead. No need to check windage in the old bedroom, I was too close to miss. We put down as the rotors chopped through my head, and I screamed at him to come out. He suddenly jumped out, but he was holding Rosie as a shield in front of him. He yowled his hideous laughter, and I held my fire. Charlie suddenly ripped Rosie's head off and waved it at me.

Jesus Christ, it was too real. I'm going mad. I can't stop crying...

- 4:30 now - I think I'll stay up. If I do manage to finally fall asleep, I'll never wake up in time for work. I've been drinking so much coffee that I'm floating. The night's almost over and the apartment is getting friendly again.

God, what a terrible nightmare.

A banging at my apartment door finally made the dream disappear. Still dazed, I stumbled out, opened the door, and saw the final remnants of the dream standing outside: A snakelike Chinese girl. But the sight suddenly changed, and the girl's hair turned to gold, her black eyes to blue, and the silk of her dress to flannel. I recognized her to be my upstairs neighbor; Sara is her name. What a sight must have greeted her! The anger on her face extinguished like a light bulb when she looked at me. Earlier, I had gone to bed exhausted, having no strength to pull off my clothes. Now I stood before Sara, totally disheveled with my best slacks soaked to the knees.

She realized all the commotion that awakened her was not the inconsiderate revelry of some unthinking bastard, but simply her neighbor in a firefight with the NVA in his bedroom. I searched for a word or two, and she asked me if I was all right. I felt like such an imbecile, but I finally spattered out an apology for the noise and confessed my actions were the result of a terrible dream. I almost asked her to come in and check my closet for a North Vietnamese soldier carrying my friend's head around, but thank God I bit my tongue instead.

The poor girl must think I am insane, but she didn't let on. In fact, she asked if there was anything she could do to help. From somewhere in a box of hidden charm, I suggested she might hold me and burp me, and that broke the tension. She said if I wanted to talk about it, she'd brew some coffee and listen. I thanked her, longing for the company, but I was standing there, stinking in my own juices. The whole thing was terribly embarrassing.

Besides, Journal, I have you. I'm now going to turn on the television and see what nocturnal mindlessness it might hold for me. I'm going to fix a bowl of hot chili to assure me I won't again sleep this night. Charlie's in there somewhere.

October 4, 1971

Mind Movie strikes again. Another vivid nightmare. It was not as spectacular as last Thursday's, but a whopper in its own right. I'm certain this problem is a result of the therapy sessions, for the dreams coincide on or around the day I go there. Terrific. I stopped having these damned dreams less than a year after I came home to The World, but now I'm having them as a result of therapy. I'm going to need my own therapy to recover from the therapy I'm going through.

Tonight's session was the same old thing. I think I'm doing no good, but Dr. Carter insists I am.

"Give it time," he says. "Things are going to come out for the fellows because of your intervention." Great. How about a little help for me, Sigmund. Things are coming out for me, too. They're creeping out of my closet every night.

Tonight, Steven was particularly active, relating every conversation subject to the war. Robby followed the lead while the others dodged in and out of the conversation. At one point, Dr. Carter asked Steven about his schooling prior to joining the service. Steven was strong in mathematics throughout school.

"Perhaps," Dr. Carter said, "this is the area where you might return when you're discharged from here."

"Numbers, man," Steven said, "they suck. They're not important."

"What is important?" Jewboss asked.

"Nam," Steven said. "Nothing else." He vacantly stared at the floor while I tried to suppress a deep sigh.

"Why does that supersede everything else?" Jewboss said.

"Winning," Steven said. "It's what all us geeks in here paid for. That's what's important. Winning, politics, terror, the fucking pain - there's gotta be a reason for it."

"They won't let us win," Robby said.

From over by the window where Casper had wandered, he spoke: "The bush..." The room fell silent. Casper has never said a word about the war. He stared out the window, his mirrors reflecting the night sky.

Pogo jumped in. "What the hell do you know about it? You're a fucking horse!"

I closed my eyes and chuckled as Jewboss chimed in. "Go with that, Casper. What about the bush?"

"Probably's pissed on his share!" Pogo said.

"Shut up!" Steven said. "Go on, Casper. Forget the Section Eight shit and tell us something about the bush. You were there, so why don't you be a man for a fucking change and tell us who you are."

We waited for some profound declaration like: I'm so-and-so, and I have a mom and a wife and a house in the country, and I want to go home and be normal again.

Bullshit.

Casper turned and looked with his mirrors at us zoo animals. "I'm Lainie Kazan, and I have to sing in an hour..."

"Oh, fucking Christ!" Pogo cried. He burst into laughter.

"Fuck you!" Steven hollered. I looked at Jewboss and saw unexpected frustration in his eyes. I think for one fleeting second he really thought he was Nobel Prize-bound for thinking he was going to spread the crack Casper had inadvertently allowed.

After the room settled, Jewboss continued. "Go on, Steven, you were talking about winning."

"All we ever do is talk," Steven said. "I lost my legs and my nuts to a mortar shell in Khe Sanh, but by-fucking-God, we greased the gooks."

Steven forever dwells on Khe Sanh. I can't imagine what he and the Marines went through there. The battle went for 77 days with some of the most vicious fighting of the war. Steven had just re-upped for a second tour. He could have come home, but he'd gone through his first tour without injury and thought he was bulletproof. In February of '68, his luck ran out.

"Thirty fucking thousand gooks against fifty-six-hundred Marines," Steven said, "and we kicked their slope asses. They had us surrounded, but we stood our ground and took them out. That's what the fucking Marines are all about."

"Semper fuck you," Pogo said. "Who cares? Where's your

Jarhead friends now?"

"They're kicking ass," Steven said with hatred in his eyes. "I'll leave this place if you want. I'll leave right now as long as you let me go back. I'll fucking crawl if I got a chance to waste gooks."

"Can't do that, Stumps," Pogo said. "Marines don't want nobody without balls!" He laughed again.

Steven bellowed and flailed about in his chair, trying to get at Pogo, but Pogo teasingly stayed out of reach.

"Stop!" I said. My gut churned as I shoved Pogo back in his chair.

"Fuck you, Hero," Steven said. "I want him!"

Pogo glared at me with his holes. It put a chill in my ass. "Big hero," Pogo growled. "Someday I'm gonna find you. Yeah, do you hear me? You see the enemy? The enemy is me. I'll waste you when I'm on the outside..."

God, why did I get in this mess? I'm seeing myself the way I used to be a million years ago when hate rotted my brain.

As usual, Pogo backed off. "Hero," he said in disgust. "Big man. Tough guy. Silver Star. He-fucking-ro!"

"Give it a rest," I said. I slumped back in my chair.

Meanwhile, this idiot Dr. Carter sat through the entire confrontation taking notes. "Tell us more about winning," he said to Steven in that uncaring tone of his.

"Aw, Jewboss, we do this bullshit day after day," Steven said. "How do we find a place to live? - Where can we find work? - How do you piss in a public latrine? Instead, we ought to be organizing a march on Nixon to demand he get down to goddam business - make him and Congress put a nuclear warhead up Charlie's ass and turn Hanoi into a piece of toast. He owes us, man."

"Amen," Robby said.

Jewboss turned to me. "What do you think, Hero? Should America bomb Vietnam with nuclear weapons?"

"It doesn't matter what I think," I said. "It'll never happen. It's 1971 - not 1946 - and this enemy isn't Japan."

"What the hell does that mean?" Steven said. "Ain't it typical of you to stand clear of an opinion - Jewboss asked if you think we oughta' toast Hanoi."

"You don't get it do you, Steven?" I said. "We have nothing to do with the political machinery that runs the war. Maybe you and I fought the North Vietnamese, but the machine has been fighting Moscow the whole time."

"Fuck them!" Steven said.

"Is that right?" I said. "You'd better remember one thing, Steven: When you fuck somebody, you're getting fucked, too. Read the papers! You talk about marching on Nixon with the demand that he risk a nuclear war with Russia? When you were lying here in '69 bound up in stitches, a quarter of a million people marched on D.C., demanding Nixon get out of Vietnam. Last April, half a million protesters did the same thing. Next time it will be a million. They're tired of watching Americans get killed in a war against an enemy that has no limit to the number of lives it will sacrifice. Hell, there are even traitorous Nam vets testifying and lying before Congress, saying that we are baby killers - just so they can join the political brotherhood and get on the right side of the goddam left! We were in a no-win situation from the start, because politicians are running this machine, not warriors."

"Bullshit!" Steven barked. "We can win! Just let Nixon use the bomb!"

"Christ, Steven," I sighed. "Nixon inherited a war so distorted over the years that there exists no option but retreat; otherwise, he'll be run out of office just like Johnson was. The voters want America out at any cost - even defeat. Hell, Nixon's been promising a reduction of troops for two years so he won't lose his bid for reelection. Do you seriously think he's going to be returned to office if he suddenly drops an atom bomb on Hanoi? Jesus, come out of the dark, Steven!"

I definitely had the floor now. Pogo's lights went out sometime during my speech, but the others were still interested.

"If you guys were out there in The World," I said, "you'd know what I'm talking about. We are tiny cogs in a huge machine. You sacrificed your lives for their war, and you want someone to feel an obligation to you; but I have news, guys: Nobody does." I clicked my fingers, "Cogs in the machine; click, click, click; pawns in a chess game, click, click, click. We're not at war with Vietnam, boys, we're playing chess with Russia, and Nam is the chessboard. Nixon's trying to make voters think he's at least playing for the draw Ike got in Korea, but he's just playing for a second term. What's his move? He'll keep killing American teenagers until election day. Click, click, click - Nixon and Russia playing chess - and neither gives a flying shit how many pawns go down, just as long as nobody lays fire to the board..."

Click, click, click, Journal. I was a lost pawn early in the game, and I decided to live with that. Just let me put Charlie back in the closet and lock the door behind him. I don't share common ground with these poor fools at the VA. I only did this because I thought it might keep Steven from cutting his wrists. But it's too late for that. The Steven I once knew died the day I watched him drive off to boot camp.

Jesus, I have to get out of this thing...

I just answered a knock at my door and found Sara with a banana cream pie and a six-pack of beer. She's flirted with me ever since she found me jammed up the other night. She is beautiful, and introverts like me get very little opportunities like this. In fact, she's damned sexy. How can I turn down food and beer? I told her to come in and have a seat while I finish this entry, which is going to end right now. I might get lucky tonight if I'm any judge of the way Sara's looking at me!

This is what life is all about, Journal. I should be enjoying the company of a nice woman, rather than wasting time worrying about Steven, or Pogo, or Charlie, or Tricky Dicky. I resolve to get out of this therapy business before I die in the bush. If I'm going to lose my mind, let me do it in the arms of this nice girl.

Click, click, click...

October 7, 1971

Am I drunk!

I'm liberated from those damned sessions at the VA! To hell with the whole thing! But, as in any fight for freedom, it was bloody. God, it was bloody...

I had it nicely planned: I'd simply announce all of my misgivings about being a part of the group. I'd make a nice apology and blame myself for assuming I could help. I would gracefully bow and leave quietly. In fact, I thought everyone would say 'good riddance,' but instead, they ambushed me.

"You don't give a damn about your brother veterans," they said.

I couldn't believe what I was hearing! I have contributed nothing, sitting endlessly like a dried-up potato with little to say other than my soapbox speech the other night. Now, when I decide to leave, they jumped me:

"You don't give a fuck, Hero!" Steven said. "You come in here with your hotshot medals and run down America like you think we're stupid to be proud we fought for our country!"

Steven's words stung like a bolt of white lightning. "That's ridiculous, Steven," I said. "I'm just saying it's time you learn to let go of the things you can't change."

"Yeah, it's easy to move on when you got two legs and medals on your chest," Steven said. "You didn't even appreciate that you got out not only in one piece, but a goddam hero, too. Instead, you came back and told me to be a chicken draft dodger."

"You're wrong," I said. "I warned you because you thought that war is Gary Cooper sipping wine with French girls; that it's Teddy Roosevelt charging up San Juan Hill. But you had to go ahead and find that war is catching mortar fire in your gut and coming home in a basket." I regretted that shot at the moment I said it. I don't like Steven anymore, but I didn't mean to attack him.

"Fuck you!" Steven said. "Fuck you and your goddam medals! All you ever talk about is how scared you were over there."

"Hell yes, I was scared. Only a damn fool wouldn't be. I got a Silver Star for carrying my buddy out of the jungle when I could hardly walk myself. I got it for killing a pack of Charlies on the way. The army called me a hero for that, but I was just luckier than Charlie - and maybe just more afraid to die than him. Being scared of losing The World made me faster on the draw. That's why it doesn't matter that America threw shit on me, because I got exactly what I fought for. Maybe you did face thirty thousand Charlies without fear, but the fact is, you're more frightened of facing a country that doesn't care that you left half your body scattered over Khe Sanh."

"Oh, that's good, Hero," Pogo said. "You try facing life without your balls while The World says you lost 'em for nothing. You is the enemy. You is we! We is us!"

I was seething. "Piss off, Pogo," I said. "Your sudden compassion doesn't wash with me. You don't give a rat's ass about Steven." I looked at Jewboss for help, but he simply sat and took it in, all the time scribbling on his damned pad. Perhaps I'm just slow, but suddenly it hit me. This was all part of his plan. This was his idea of therapy. He wanted me to push Steven to the very confrontation that was unfolding. These pathetic morons are his little white mice running through a labyrinth, and I was the cheese.

"I saw plenty of balls cut off in Nam," Pogo growled. "Maybe I ought to cut yours off right now."

Pogo's insanity is so profound that I almost felt pity for his childish provocations. I simply ignored him and turned to Steven. "Look, Steven, I'm sick of trying to spoon-feed a life into you. If you can't get yourself together until somebody thanks you, you're going to die in here. America decided a long time ago to forsake us. Maybe to you and me those medals they pinned on my chest represent something important, but to America, they're badges of shame. That leaves you two choices: Rot in this place while waiting for something to change, or let it go and get on with your life the best you can. But whatever you do, you better realize it may take more than a lifetime to convince anybody out there that you sacrificed yourself for any rightful purpose."

Steven shook with anger. Pogo's eyes suddenly closed - goodnight sweet prince. Casper stared off into space. The only ones left besides Steven and me were Jewboss, who continued to scribble, and Robby, who avoided the altercation until now.

"I'm on my back forever, Hero," Robby hatefully said. "Don't you tell me it was for nothing."

"I'm not the one telling you, Robby," I said. "Can you honestly say you were fighting for the hippies and the newspaper reporters the day you crept into Hue, waiting for Charlie to snap your spine in two? You went in there with nothing else on your mind but survival. And when they wheeled you off the plane, did anybody wave the flag? Robby, there are people walking in front of the hospital this very minute who would take one look at you and say that you got what you deserve."

"Bullshit!" Steven said. "This country won't give up on me! You're just part of those minority faggots who tear America down every chance you get! Nixon isn't gonna let me down! He's gonna win!"

"The only thing he's gonna win is the election!" I heard myself holler. "After that, he's bugging out! If you have any sense, you'll bug out with him - turn with the skid, for God's sake, and pray nobody else has to come home in the same shape as you and me!"

Steven wheeled over to me, his eyes on fire. "Go on! Leave! Go join the faggots and burn the flag; go throw your medals into the river...you probably already did!"

"Oh, Christ," I said with a moan. "When are you going to play the cards you have in your hand? Stop waiting for a pat on the ass. As far as America is concerned, we've lost the war already. They don't hold parades for losers!"

"It ain't lost!" Steven said.

"It's over," I said. "They can't keep bringing body bags home to heartbroken mothers without an acceptable explanation. Meanwhile, the Communists keep coming, click, click, click, their machine keeps turning out soldiers, except they have more spare parts than us. If all the Vietnamese die, send in the Cambodians, the Laotians - if they die, send the Chinese. They have more pawns, and they're willing to lose them for as long as it takes! We can't afford the price, Steven! People are going to war right here because of this thing! But what's more important to you is how long you're going to wallow there in your own shit...you're pathetic!"

Everything was a blur from this point, Journal. I lost myself in my anger with Steven. We drew up nose-to-nose as my final words literally bounced off his face.

Steven suddenly lashed out and hit me with his fist. My head rattled, and I was sucked into an uncontrollable rage - a black hole I thought I had filled up years ago. I unbelievably pounced on him, consumed by violence, and hit him twice as his wheelchair crashed over. He screamed out and flailed at me as we rolled on the floor. I was utterly blind with anger.

I shoved Dr. Carter away when he tried to pull me off, and I took Steven by his long hair and lifted him up, ready to pummel him again. But suddenly, my own sword pierced me. I drowned in the cold realization that, although on my knees, I held Steven so high that his torso was completely suspended off the floor. His body was no more a burden than if I was holding a sack of beans. He pitifully squirmed, still with the spirit of the warrior he once was, but looking more like a poor cockroach with its legs plucked. A ball of acid rose in my throat as I dropped him and fell back.

"God almighty," I whispered as I scampered back on my ass, suddenly aware of Casper's confused eyes upon me.

"Fight me, motherfucker!" Steven cried as he futilely swung his arms and banged them against the floor. "Come on, Hero! You won't get no fucking medal from me! Fight me! Fight meeeeee!"

Dr. Carter tried to calm Steven as I pulled myself up and gasped for air that had grown the thickness of mud. Pogo never opened his eyes, while Casper continued to look at me with a frozen stare. Behind me, I heard Robby curse under his breath.

"I'm sorry," I whispered. I backed to the wall.

"I'm...sorry."

Steven spewed obscenities as Jewboss poked a needle in his arm. An orderly ran in and helped Carter right the wheelchair and lift Steven's weakening body back in. The orderly strapped Steven's hands down and glared at me. I can only imagine what he thought. Jewboss, on the other hand, threw me a more sympathetic glance as he instructed the orderly to take Steven back to the ward.

I finally had enough. I turned and staggered to the latrine where my stomach purged, exploding dinner and a beer all over the toilet and my shoes. By the time it was over, I was on my knees in my own mess, my head still spinning. Thank God I relented on a sudden urge to jump out the window.

God doesn't give cowards a break.

I finally collected myself at the sink, and I washed the blood and vomit from my face. I didn't want to go back outside, but I already overruled the window. After toweling myself, I sat on the sink counter and took several long breaths. This was not exactly how I had planned to tactfully bow out of the session.

I needed a drink. Thankfully, I had a flask in the pocket of my jacket, and I wasted little time skulking out of the rest room to retrieve it. The only people left in the room were Robby, who was forgotten in the excitement, and Casper, who faced the window. My eyes were still wet and my forehead hot as I took a long and deserved drink from the flask. My anger subsided, and I tried to reassure myself I wasn't someone who might enjoy kicking a dog. But the image of Steven's pitiful body flailing about while I held him at bay will remain with me for a long time; of that I am sure. It was a surreal vision, like a cartoon. No one was laughing, however.

"Screwed the pooch, Hero," Robby said from his bed as he watched me drink.

"Shut up," I said. "I don't have to be nice to you anymore."

"Just who the hell do you think you are?" he said.

"I don't want to hear it, Robby."

"What do I care what you want to hear? That's your problem, Hero; just because you got a grip on the stick, you think every goddam vet is as smart as you." The air spewed from Robby's worthless lungs.

Resigned, I sat and took a long drink. "Okay, you want a shot at me? Take it."

"You're some piece of work, you know that, Hero?" Robby gasped. "You must have been hell-on-wheels in that chopper."

"Yes, Robby," I said, my hands still trembling so badly that I needed both of them to hold the flask to my lips. "I was a regular killing machine. If the VC would have just sent a division of guerrillas in wheelchairs at me, this war would have been over five years ago."

"You're a fucking smartass too," Robby said with a breathy chuckle. "But tonight, you were stupid."

"No," I sarcastically said. "What could possibly be stupid about beating the hell out of a legless man?"

"What's stupid, Hero, is that you didn't do him right."

I exhaled smoke from my cigarette. "Do him?"

"Kicked the holy crap outta him, dipshit - mopped the floor with his sorry half-ass."

I couldn't help but laugh. Whenever I expect someone to say 'black' around this place, they say 'white.' "Thanks, Robby, I'll keep that in mind; tomorrow, I'm going to cruise for trouble at an old folks home. Maybe you'd like me to come and tip over your bed?"

"It doesn't sink in, does it?" Robby said. "You came in here thinking you were gonna shake Stumps out of his hard-on for the world by telling him to forget the parades and get on with his life. Hero, if he came outta Nam without a scratch, he'd still have his attitude - and some attitudes need adjusting with a fist, not logic. Dudes like him need more than words, Hero, and for the first time, you did something to shake him up; to shake me up. Maybe him and me don't have any use for your opinion, but at least you finally gave one instead of sitting over there with that sorrowful look on your face. You want to apologize for not getting your legs blown off."

I sighed. "You want to get to your point?"

"We got a load of pity around here. We get it from the nurses, the doctors, our families - we don't need it from somebody who waded in the same shit we did. You hung your ass on the line; you got nobody to apologize to, and tonight you finally made us feel like you were one of us."

"I didn't tell you what you want to hear," I said.

"Oh, you're so smart that you know what we want to hear? Look at Casper over there. You got any idea what he wants to hear? You want to tell me he don't have a mom out in the night somewhere, dying from grief for not knowing where her son is? What the hell do you care what we want to hear? I think your opinion sucks, but I'd rather hear it than listen to you talk down to me."

"I beat up my friend," I sadly said.

"So what?" Robby said. "He threw the first punch!"

"I have a baby brother who throws the first punch now and again, but I don't kick hell out of him."

"Jesus Jiminy, Hero, it's no wonder the slopes didn't waste you. Nobody could put a round through that granite skull of yours. Stumps ain't a baby. He's a man. I can't tell you how many times since I got cemented in this coffin I wanted somebody to treat me like I ain't some circus geek. It ain't got nothing to do with Nam. You pissed him off and he reacted like a human being. You beating up on him was a damn sight better than him doing it all these years. Christ, you know what I'd give for somebody to plant a haymaker on me cause he thinks I'm a prick? I got a right to be pissed for what's happened, but when I bitch about it, I get a pat on the head. Maybe a bust in the chops would work better."

Robby's eyes were moist, and his voice quivered from fatigue. "He punched you, and you retaliated like he was a whole man who deserved an ass-kicking. But you screwed the pooch when you stopped and apologized. You would have busted his beak and closed his eyes, but he would have come to in the morning feeling like a man who picked shit with the wrong guy; instead, he'll just remember you looking at him like he's a freak."

I could only sit in silence and stare at my hands. Click, click, click. I took another long drag from my cigarette and crushed it on the floor. Finally, I put the flask to my lips and had a final bracer before I pulled on my jacket. Robby still looked right through me as I headed for the door.

"Hey, Hero," he said, "where you going?"

"To finish what I started," I said.

"Yeah? Before you go - you know, I ain't had a drink since the day I got capped."

I looked at the flask in my hand and then at Robby. He watched me come over and examine the machines connected to him. "You can drink booze with all this hooked to you?" I asked.

"What's it gonna do that ain't already been done to me?"

I shrugged and reached down to pull his head up. He gratefully gulped the booze down. He choked and his eyes filled with tears. All I needed right then was to drown Robby. He belched with satisfaction. "Damn, that was good."

We shared a smile, and then, although I'm not sure why I did it, I reached over and gave him a swift whack across the face with my open hand. The shock in his eyes was evident.

"You are a prick, Robby," I said.

His face curled into a smile. "Peace," he finally said.

I turned and headed for the door, but Casper, who still stood at the window with his back to me, caught my attention. He was crying. I walked over and touched his shoulder and he looked at me. "Find her," I whispered to him. "She misses you."

Casper turned back to the window without a word, and I walked to the door.

"Hero?" Robby said. "That hooch hit the spot. One for the road?"

I waved the flask so he could see it. "Fuck you, Robby," I said. "If you want some, come get it..."

I passed down the hall as the sound of Robby's laughter trailed behind me.

Steven's ward is at the end of the building. When I

walked in, I was greeted with the familiar odor of rotting flesh. Quite a few of the men were already asleep as I walked the long corridor down to Steven's bed. He laid quietly, his eyes half-opened and his breathing regular. I came up over him and reached down, taking him by the collar and raising him so he could see me. Although he was drugged, he recognized me.

I got in his face and spoke with decided finality. "I'm never coming back here, you bastard," I said. "You and I were once friends. That's why I didn't finish you tonight. But if you take a shot at me like that again, I'm gonna have a short memory, understand?" My stomach wrenched at my lies. I shoved him back down in the bed. "You ever want a piece of me, you know where to find me." I walked out without looking back. I pray I mended what I damaged.

Click, click, click, Journal. The closet door is locked...

December 15, 1971

Dear Marie Rose,

Merry Christmas, Rosie! Once again, you beat me to the punch, but at least my greeting comes before the holiday. I enjoyed your card and all the news from your end.

Where to start? The last you heard from me, I babbled about ghosts under my bed. I appreciated your kind letter that followed, and I took your advice, although giving up on the psychiatry business was not an easy task. You were right that I have no business picking at scars. Indeed, the combat in my bedroom was evidence I'm not good at reminiscing. I gave up on the sessions shortly after you wrote, but not without an ugly grand finale. I don't wish to go over the details of my departure, but believe me, I went out with a considerable bang. I marvel at your insight for these things. You are correct that my sensitive nature leaves me vulnerable to what the doctor later told me is common in many vets who have apparently adjusted to life in The World. These flashback events are more than just a simple bad dream. I fanned the flame by dredging the war up with Steven and the other fellows.

Dr. Carter, although at the time appearing a sadistic tyrant, assured me he feels Steven made some positive progress. He emphatically apologized for the twist it put in my colon. He even offered me some free time on the couch, but I declined. I resolved the conflict with my ghosts, and I will leave Steven to his own devices. I'm not convinced he made much progress, but I suppose all we can do is pray he can find his place on earth.

My friendship with him is dead. That saddens me, but as Mr. Vonnegut says: "So it goes."

Onward: My professional life at the ad agency is less than fulfilling, but it pays my rent, feeds my belly, and leaves a dime or two for typewriter ribbon and beer. Writing pitches for pizza, soap, furniture, and denture cream is mindless, but it does not intrude upon my creative efforts to write fiction.

Rosie, I hope someday I will be able to laugh at all of this when my ship comes in. As the fat lady says before digging into her spaghetti: "Someday, this all will be behind me..."

I recently had a wonderful visit with your mom and dad. I brought them a holiday basket full of those frightfully delicious fat things Mother bakes for the occasion. Angela was home. I'm sorry to have to bring up a troubling observation: You may already be aware of the situation, but I simply cannot go without mentioning how startled I was at Angie's appearance. Your father also privately expressed his concern to me. I would wager she does not weigh an ounce over eighty pounds. When we embraced, she felt like a frail bird in my arms.

I wasn't thinking when I exclaimed how thin she is, but she seemed genuinely flattered by my observation. I assure you, I was not complimenting her. She attributes it to an excruciatingly competitive market in her line of business where a model must remain thin, but it does not strike me as a particularly healthy attitude. Throughout my visit, your parents and I gulped down the good food and drink, but Angie didn't eat. Later, she excused herself to go to the basement for her daily workout. Perhaps you'll have the chance to visit with her more when they meet you in California next week. Just keep her away from the edge of any piers, for one stiff gust of wind might blow her into the sea!

On this end, I suppose it would be best to dispose of Lyla first. She plans to grace us with her presence this year, accompanied by a boyfriend she met at a peace rally in New York. Bully for her. Mary is due tomorrow and plans an extended visit through New Year's. She continues her studies at Juilliard and performs with a small symphony orchestra that will be performing three of her compositions this spring. There is no boundary to the height of her future in music, and I can hardly wait to hear her play for us! I love her so.

Jonathan gave us a scare last October when he took a swan dive from the old elm in Mother's back yard. Fortunately he only suffered a cracked wrist and a bump on the nose (just like him to want to be like his big brother).

Vern's insurance career was short-lived, and he now has a job at a savings and loan. Something unusual is happening to him. I am afraid he's becoming a Republican, and I see no possible way to stop him. Vern goes through stages like Liz Taylor goes through husbands. This ugly political phase appeared after he took an interest in the financial world. I should have seen the warning signs - the gray pinstripe suit, the haircuts every other week - but I don't think I began to worry about him until he started taking an interest in conservative politics. If I'd had any sense at all, I would have intervened then and demanded he seek help. However, the final straw came when I went over to his trailer to watch football and caught him putting a "Nixon's the One" bumper sticker on his Oldsmobile. I can't tell you the shame I felt.

My heart ached, Rosie. My uncle wants that pencil-nosed liar in the White House four more years. It seems it was only yesterday when he picked up a twenty-year-old hippie at a transcendental meditation class, ate drugged mushrooms with her, and stood naked atop Mount Evans until they were arrested for indecent exposure in front of a tourist bus full of nuns. I long for the uncle who later explained the only thing he remembers of that day was something about thinking he was attacked by a flock of screaming penguins.

I'm relieved that was his only experiment with hallucinogens, but this new blight of conservatism in Vern has me worried. Discussing politics with him is about as stimulating as talking to paint. And, this 'Nixon's the One' business...well, to illustrate my point:

"He's the best man for the job," he said. "He has vision. He's making friends with the Chinese. In fact, there's only one other man better qualified for the job."

"Who?" I asked.

"Ronald Reagan," he said.

Reagan? Yeeks! I wanted to go home and cry.

There's simply too much gonzo on my poor uncle's scratched brain, but I love him nonetheless. I love you, too, Rosie. I wish you great things for '72. It's ten years we've known each other. How is it possible we are going to be twenty-six? Growing up...what a bummer!

As Always,
Me

6

Collisions

1973

June 19, 1973

Dear Marie Rose,

So what does he have that I do not? I mean, besides maturity, money, a Fiat, three kids, and a good job, that is. So what if he's a school principal; has five acres near Monterey; is president of the Santa Cruz Rotary. What kind of future do you have with this rogue who is ten years older and very stable? He's a widower? You've been dating for over a year now? Sounds like a whirlwind romance to me. And what? He flew to Denver just to ask for your father's approval to marry you? Sounds like a shallow character.

You love him?

And I thought I had heard all the stupid reasons to get married.

But nonetheless, I wish to express my delight at your news! And, don't be silly feeling apprehensive telling that 'someone' with whom you have shared some past romantic history. You're my best friend, and I cannot be happier for you! I am honored that you care enough to include me in this, your very special time. It's wonderful that you've found the love you so richly deserve, but I'm concerned that you intend to wait another year or two before you take the big plunge.

What are you, responsible or something?

Yuk yuk.

Again, my congratulations, and please express the same to Gary for me. He is the luckiest man in the cosmos. Inform this rogue, Mr. Wonderful Gary Tobias, that he had better realize this, otherwise he will incur the wrath of my typewriter!

I am very excited for you and wish you the greatest joy, and just as soon as the fireman coaxes me off the window ledge, I plan to mail this letter to let you know...

But, while I am here enjoying the sight of the city skyline, contemplating a leap, I might as well catch you up on news. Since you ask, I, too, have maintained a somewhat stable romantic relationship that has progressed beyond the hand-holding stage. In fact, I first met Sara two years ago around the time I called to tell you about a little oriental man who jumped out of my closet and tried to shoot me...

Sara lives upstairs, and she came down that night to complain that the war in my closet interfered with her sleep. I believe finding a cold and wet puppy shivering at the door unleashed some parental instinct in her. Either that, or she simply has a love for dumb animals, but whatever the attraction was, she found some reason to like me. As time wore on, my apartment slowly began filling up with more of her belongings; a toothbrush here, a slipper there, and some truly exotic cooking utensils in the kitchen. Even the Campbell's Soup cans and the single blue tomato in the refrigerator were banished and replaced by things like roast beef, pasta, and chocolate chip pies. After my little head movies began to disappear, Sara found other reasons to hold me, and we've kept steady company since.

I wouldn't say we live together since my wee-hour typing keeps her awake, but if the gossip columnists kept track of nobodies, we'd make a few headlines. Yes, I care for her, and since she stuck around after I stopped getting into arguments in my closet, I think she is able to tolerate me. We share certain interests like literature, film, chocolate covered peanuts...

Yes, I like her.

And, I lie like stagnant water!

She incessantly whines that I spend more time with my writing than I spend with her. Even as I write, she's in a huff because I'm writing a letter to my best friend. She's angry because I am depressed at the news of your damned engagement. She drones insufferably about my drinking, and lays guilt on me whenever I'd like to be alone once in a while.

Other than that, yes, I'm happy, and I'm glad you are, too. Best of luck...

As Always,
Me

June 20, 1973

Please, Journal, tell me I didn't do it. If there is a God, he would not have allowed me to mail it. I know I wrote it. So, where is it? If it was just a bad dream, maybe I didn't write it at all. But, if that is so, why is my last envelope missing? And, why was I driving to a mailbox last night in a rain storm at three in the morning?

Now I've really done it. I can't believe I mailed that letter to Rosie! If there was a prize for the biggest boob in the world, I'd beat Raquel Welch in a landslide. That letter was just written to blow off steam, but the moron drunk in me mailed the damned thing! Rosie has suffered so many of my ridiculous drunken stunts over the years - how many times can I do this before she finally has enough and dispatches me from her life forever?

God dammit. When am I going to finally escape this terminal adolescence? I'm pushing thirty, for God's sake! Jesus, I'm such an idiot!

And, on the topic of alienating the women in my life: I got to work late this morning with a head the size of New Jersey. Sara stomped into the office around noon and instead of suggesting lunch as she usually does, she threw my apartment keys at me, saying she cleared everything out. She cried, too, and told me I could be alone. "Just as fucking much as you want..."

I think she was upset.

I don't remember much, to be honest, Journal. After reading Rosie's letter, I remember a cocktail or two - just a toast to her happiness. Then I started to write, and something happened; something like a '58 Cadillac coming through the place. I think I'm dead...

As I sit here in my apartment, I hear a great deal of banging around upstairs right now. Sara might be mounting an attack, or, it's a sign from God, who, just for his own amusement, allowed me to create a little mischief for myself. What I better do is call Rosie and warn her to ignore any letter that might arrive in the next day or so. Then, I should go upstairs and apologize to Sara.

Or, perhaps I'll just have a drink and forget the whole damned thing.

December 29, 1973

Dear Marie Rose,

What a pleasure it was to see you this holiday season! It was a novel idea someone had to have a premature Class Of '64 reunion during Christmas when more of the old clan might be near home. I'm only sorry the rush of the season and the madness of the party prevented us from spending more time together.

I was shocked to see how bad so many of our old classmates look in just ten years when you and I have not aged a day! It's sad to find how many we have lost; how many boys without arms or legs, etc. There but for the grace of God, I guess. I was disappointed that Steven didn't show up, but that is asking too much. I haven't heard a word from him since he left the VA hospital.

I enjoyed meeting your Prince Valiant, and was delighted to find him everything you said he is. He certainly made me feel at ease. Sara, however, might have shown the same maturity and not behaved so coolly toward you. I apologize and hope you are not offended. All the way home from the dinner dance, she went on about how charming and wonderful you are, and when I agreed, the tension mounted all the more. She's been rather chilly ever since. I suppose we'll have our monthly breakup as a result.

Girl and boyfriends should avoid school reunions. It either bores those of Gary's mature nature, or rubs raw those of Sara's when school pals try to behave like they didn't do anything crazy with each other when they were kids. I wonder how many divorces are the result of high school reunions.

Nevertheless, I'm sure Sara will get over her snit. She always does. We have grand plans for New Year's as Vern is going to have a party. Pray for us.

I'm not unhappy that 1973 is leaving. In fact, I'm glad. It has been a strange year, one that sealed me in mediocrity from the very beginning. I'm making a resolution to rejuvenate my writing habit, which has waned since the odd disappearance of Strange Potions at the hands of Mary's queer friend. Mary assures me this Mr. Ellery character can be trusted, but he gave the script to his boyfriend who took it to London to show it to some unknown director over there. I suppose I just don't trust boys who like boys who like boys...

But onward I plan to go with my novels. Discipline. That's my word for '74. Vern called as I was writing this. Says 'Hello, sorry I didn't see you while you were here.' Vern's snapping out of his political ignominy since Nixon started erasing tapes. I'm trying to convince Unc to make his New Year's party an impeachment rally.

My best to Gary. Let me know the minute you set the big date. I plan to shoot out his tail lights on that terrible day! It was wonderful seeing you again. Although I said it several hundred times at the reunion, thanks for ignoring that brainless letter I sent last summer. I'm a goof sometimes.

As Always,
Me

December 30, 1973

It was Bogey who said it, Journal: "Of all the gin joints in all the towns in all the world, she walks into mine..."

1975

December 16, 1975

Dear Marie Rose,

I can't believe it's been two years! Time is fleeting these days. We move at such a maddening pace, sometimes we lose track. Don't concern yourself with missing last year's Christmas card. The truest joy of our friendship is the lack of need for gestures of reassurance that we care. Receiving your long letter today was as if the last time we corresponded was yesterday. It reassures me that some ties are timeless, for greetings from you always warm my heart.

So, not married yet? You two must have great patience. Not to worry, however. You are not 'getting old.' Of course, Gary is, so you had better get him off the pot before he dries up and blows away.

Yuk yuk.

You must have had a wonderful holiday last year in Europe, but I am concerned, however, hearing of your father's surgery. How his granite heart could have become ill is a mystery to me, but it is no surprise he bounced back so quickly. I intend to get in touch with your parents soon. I am sorry to say it has been the same two years since I have seen them. The passage of time evokes changes. People often pass through each other's lives for only a short time, but I do not wish to lose touch with your family. I care for them.

I was so glad you enclosed a picture of Angela so I might believe for myself how she has changed! Her illness must have been trying on all of you, but thank God she recovered. It is hard to imagine a nervous disorder associated with starvation. We are simply a nervous generation. Her picture reveals she looks human again, and it appears marriage is good to her. I'm happy for her contentment, and also, congratulations to you for becoming an aunt!

Now for the news on my side. Mother is pink and sassy,

although there is a patch of gray here, a new wrinkle there. Her job continues to be a success, and she finally gave up the old homestead and moved herself and Jonathan into a small townhouse. Jon, on the downside, has reached his fourteen-year-old 'worthless' stage. I'm not sure how, but this transformation took place on his birthday. What was once a happy and helpful little tyke who used to fall out of trees is now a rude, cigarette-smoking, foul-mouthed rascal with dirty hair clear down his back. I recently discovered he squandered a month's allowance on a bag of pot.

"Big deal," he said when I challenged him. "You gonna do something about it?"

I'll say this for my little brother - when he makes a mistake, he doesn't do it halfway.

His drugs are now with the wind, and his smart lip is swollen. I doubt he'll ever lay the gauntlet before this old door gunner again. I suggested to Mother that she play her old trick of leaving military school brochures out as an exercise in terror. In fact, Mother still considers it for me in light of the way I handled Johnny Jekyll's pot problem. I simply am tired of his attitude, his poor school grades, his constant bullying of the neighborhood, and his general distaste for anything decent around him. Mother defends him, saying he has had a difficult time growing up without a father. I think he is a piece of walking feces and intend to give him a few more fat lips when he needs them.

And, speaking of feces...

We heard from Lyla recently. She claims she's enjoying great success with a law firm in Philadelphia, and she is adamantly dedicated to the single life, that is, single without men. She casually told us she lives with a woman and has discovered her latent homosexuality. She blames her home life with a drunken tyrant and a "co-dependent mother" as the reason she could never unleash her true self until now.

What a sow.

Lyla deliberately tries to send shock waves through this family, yet, Mother takes it without letting on her despair. If Lyla was within my reach, I'd employ the same manner of persuasion I used on Jon, but with her I'd use a baseball bat. Her radical feminist garbage mixed with her hatred of men combines to make a sour soup indeed. I detest her.

On the other side of this circus tent, however, is Mary. She brought the good news of a new job with the Buffalo Philharmonic Orchestra. As usual, she always returns home on holidays and brings such happiness and joy with her. Unlike Lyla, Mary has always sent monetary support to Mother and writes to us religiously. Mary and I often spend hours on rather expensive long distance phone calls. We lose track of time as we cajole and share intimate thoughts, or, we simply laugh at whatever latest scheme Vern has concocted. Mary retains her wide-eyed precocity, unaffected by her success, yet she is possessed of such charm and maturity for someone so young. It does embarrass me that I'm supposed to be the older brother. I'm always the one asking for advice on how to cope with this stupid world!

As for Vern, he spent a short time in jail for mail fraud last summer. I warned him that his 'Mail Order Business' smelled illegal, but he insisted he knew what he was doing. Vern ran an ad in the papers: "Make money in your spare time addressing envelopes." I don't care to elaborate on the messy details, but what Vern was doing was an old shell game that federal laws forbade a million years ago. He got caught when he solicited a county judge, but they went easy on him. If he reimbursed everyone, they would reduce the charges to a misdemeanor, making the amount of time he was actually in jail only a little more than a week.

It wasn't a complete loss, for, while in jail, Vern sold three life insurance policies to other inmates in the county stir.

Millie showed up briefly just before Vern's run-in with the law. That was back when he was working at the fireworks factory. She was pregnant by an Arab, who hopped on his carpet back for Saudi after he found out he had just made a new towelhead. Vern was truly upset at Millie's reappearance and he considered taking her back. He thought he could become an instant father and a forgiving husband, but I finally got through to him. I reminded him of the day he found Millie in bed with the preacher, and that seemed to snap him out of his turmoil. He pointed Millie and Abdul Jr. toward the door, and off they went.

Vern is now working for a parking meter manufacturer. He gets to park downtown for half price.

So much for the clan. As for me, I continue to do nothing. Strange Potions reappeared after Mary threatened Rye Ellery bodily harm. It came back from London without success. I've corresponded with Duke Winslow several times. He passed on a few names of people who might like to read the script, but no takers. I have finally roughed out a novel of Potions, which Duke's literary agent, as a favor to Duke I'm sure, agreed to read when it is completed. The play, however, seems dead in the water as is my imagination. It's not that I don't write. I just don't ever seem to finish anything.

You asked about Sara. I must report our affair ended. In fact, she married not long ago. We parted company shortly after the Christmas of our class reunion. Her quiet evenings at home of watching the blasted television, bantering on in mindless conversations, ad nauseam, seemed to alienate us. We simply lost interest. I just do not fit in her mainstream, for when I sit and simply do nothing, I feel myself aging as if life is sneaking by me. Romantic endeavors of the nature Sara and I pursued are not for me. It's entirely possible that falling in love may have been a solitary experience for me.

Enough whining. Please keep those cards and letters coming. I look forward to hearing of the big day. Tell Gary he isn't getting any younger! Love you.

As Always,
Me

December 16, 1975

Feel low tonight, Journal. 'Tis the season, despicable as it is. Returned a letter to Rosie. I hope I masked my depression. As I wrote, my heart ached. I hope she is well. This booze is making me shake.

1977

"The only absolute knowledge attainable by man Is that life is meaningless"

-Leo Tolstoy

"How sweet it is!"

-Jackie Gleason

May 8, 1977

Happy birthday to meee. Happy birthday to meeeee. Happy...

Oh, to hell with it.

I haven't had a pleasant birthday since the day I turned sixteen, and even that one was spent alone. Thirty was traumatic. Thirty-one simply makes me numb.

What happened to the plan? I figured to have a bestseller, perhaps a Tony Award, and a mountain chalet by now. Instead, I have a dusty script on the shelf in a two-bedroom tract house in the suburbs, and a rocky marriage.

Meeting publisher deadlines remains a fantasy replaced by sitting in the same old office, writing underarm deodorant commercials.

Happy birthday...

December 20, 1977

Dear Marie Rose,

Merry Christmas to you, my Rose!

A merry one indeed as we celebrate your nuptials at long last! Congratulations, Mrs. Tobias!

This season shall be a happy one, I trust, as you celebrate for the first time as a family. Please relay my best wishes to Gary and his three: James, Tommy, and Cynthia. Talk about instant motherhood!

And so, as it has been the custom for me to report on the clan and related affairs, let me break tradition this year and begin with me, for I believe I have something of note to pass on.

I, too, am married.

Rosie? Are you there? Should I summon a doctor?

They said it could not - would not - be done in this lifetime, but I stand in defiance. Someone does put up with me! It came about rather suddenly last February when my heart was assaulted and swept from solid ground by Elizabeth. We were acquainted for several years, both of us working at the ad agency while I was still on the writing staff. I was then promoted to sales, and we spent time preparing presentations and attending social events. It created something less platonic. In reality, I believe the cocktail parties clouded her eyes and made her see what charm and wit I possess. Whatever the attraction, we took the vow.

But, enough of that. With regard to Strange Potions, I received a small ray of hope from Duke's literary agent, Walter Sachs, who in passing mentioned my play to a director in New York. It interested this fellow enough to request a reading, so off it went. In the meantime, I have polished the novel and am preparing to send it to Sachs. If for nothing else but a penchant for enjoying the humiliation of rejection, I suppose I at least persevere. I simply see no goal other than to communicate what words fall from my head. Writing is a disease, Rosie.

The family is well. Mother is healthy, Jon's a future criminal, Mary labors away in Buffalo, Vern's a shoemaker, and I am Me. Congratulations again. I love you.

As Always,
Me

December 20, 1977

No urge to say much other than 'hello,' Journal. I'm in a cave with no light. Strange Potions. Strange indeed...

1980

May 18, 1980

It was a rather loud bang, I suppose. Mt. Saint Helens blew her top. Mother Nature and her tantrums. How fitting. It was just a bit louder than the bang Beth made as her final farewell. Just like the mountain, I suppose it had been building and I simply did not notice. I never do, she said.

God is such a symbolist.

It's a laughable coincidence that she removed the last of her belongings from the house today. She thanked me for nothing in this marriage while I watched the wrath of that incredible mountain explosion on the news. As she angrily crashed around, I was mesmerized, lost in the wake.

"You're writing another story, aren't you?" she said, confronting me at the television. "That empty look is in your eyes. You pour down the Scotch and out comes another ridiculous idea of what you suppose is good literature."

Beth's idea of good literature is either a quick glance through Erica Jong, or the latest headline in The National Observer.

"When are you gonna grow up?" she asked when she left. "I'm not waiting anymore. You can hide inside that head of yours the rest of your life for all I care."

Oh yes, her parting shot was, "You drink too much."

What a laugh. If not for that last line, you could have put a moustache on her, flattened her breasts, and she would have made a good impersonation of my father. She is the one who drinks too much, not me.

It's for the best. In my head I'll gladly hide in favor of facing Beth's idea of reality. I don't fit in the real world; I have no taste for it. Because she's a part of it I dare say I won't miss her.

May 19, 1980

Jesus, I detest this depression. I detest the Valium and the booze.

What are the roots of this blackness? This nonsense has gone on for over a year now. It simply cannot be a passing lull, for it has endured too long. Perhaps I'm becoming my own character in Strange Potions, or, more aptly, "Strange Potions and One Night Stands." My work is much like my marriage; fleeting in its success. How could just Beth's rejection strike such a brutal blow? It must run deeper than this divorce coming on the heels of my play's death.

Drink up. Last call...

May 20, 1980

Couldn't find a reason to leave the house today. My unemployment runs out next week. I should look for work.

Beth called. As a generous favor to me she plans to pay this month's bills but not a penny more. Charitable. It leaves me with enough money to make next month's rent and a quart of Scotch. After that...I don't know...

Maybe I do drink too much. Do I? Does it cloud my mind? Or...

"I love the child who steers this riverboat
But lately he's crazy for the deep;
And the river seems dreamlike in the daytime
And someone keeps thinking in my sleep..."

- David Crosby

June 9, 1980

I came home and found a twenty-dollar bill and a note from Beth on the table. "Good luck, it's for the best," she wrote. "Please spend this money on food, not liquor. I still love you enough to beg you to get help..."

For the best.

As I sit in this silent house, it is as if she had never been here at all. What the hell does she mean, 'get help?' Some help my 'wife' was, constantly berating my fiction, my muse. The only help I need is getting her out of the house. Help, indeed. I can take care of myself, thank you.

A lone light burns dimly above, watching me. Hey, light bulb, I need help. Jesus...

Beth wants nothing more than what she has taken. No money, no property, as if I had any; just damned near everything in the house that she bought - after she, my 'wife,' fired me from my job. It was decent of her to leave a card table for my typewriter, and of course, my light bulb. Oh, yes, she left the guest room bed, two chipped coffee cups and plate. Such is the legacy of the artist writer. What else does a bachelor need, anyway? Yes, in all, it will be a clean divorce.

I try not to resent her leaving a few dollars for me, but it does tread on a flattened ego nonetheless. When times were good, she was happy to accommodate my muse, but during the curves, she was gone. I must believe that I do not need that which I do not need.

The only thing to flourish through all of this is the novel. Fiction is indeed my home. I finished ten pages tonight as the words poured out like hot honey. Like Hank Williams said: "Bad times make good songs..."

June 28, 1980

Bad day today. I was turned down for employment by six agencies. No work available. They say I have too much experience to start over, and a bad track record in sales. Pounding the streets in search of a job sickens me. I fit in this three-piece suit world like a bird in the company of fishes. I find it ironic as I walk downtown - I'm certain I see many of these corporate 'suits' as old 1960s hippies who worked against the very system they now worship. Today, I ran into an old high school friend, Marc Komac, who is of this new breed.

I remember our days at Jefferson High when our blood matched and our spirits communed. But today, I found myself in the company of a stranger who looks no different from the other clones on that busy street of dreams.

"Things can't be better," he said. "I'm into penny stock brokerage. This is where it's at. There's unbelievable money to make in domestic exploration, options and futures. It's the fast lane, pal."

He claims to be making a fortune in gas and oil futures. I couldn't grasp his language, but I know it is spoken in this city. Marc made sure to check his Rolex a dozen times during the conversation, and he adjusted his diamond stickpin so the sparkle burned my eyes. Then, he boldly pulled out a gold coke spoon.

"Want a toot?" he asked me with a wink. I declined and then watched him snort cocaine like a pig in shit right there on the busy street. It's as much a symbol of his success as the watch and stickpin, I would guess. He inhaled, sniffed, and rubbed his eyes. "Ought to try it," he said. "Helps you keep your balance, and you look like you could use it."

I couldn't believe his audacity, but I guess I didn't look much like the company he is accustomed to keeping.

"What are you doing these days?" he said, looking through his stupid eyes. "Last time I saw you, you just got back from the Big Apple and decided it was time to get a real job."

I told him I was doing well in freelance. I lied, all the time embarrassed that I did not have a Rolex. I hate myself for my lies, but my pride prevented me from telling the truth - that I've failed as a writer, in my job, as a husband...

"What do you hear from old Steven?" he asked. "He still in the hospital?"

"No," I said. "He's out. He left town, but I don't know where he went. His mother said he was out west somewhere - Arizona, New Mexico - I don't know."

"Too bad about him," Marc said. "What a waste..."

Marc doesn't care about Steven. To my knowledge, he never visited him in the VA hospital. Marc's father was a personal friend of a state senator back in the sixties, who arranged for Marc to serve in the National Guard instead of Nam. How incredibly fine is the line fate draws for us. One time long ago, I suggested he go with me to visit Steven, but he declined, saying hospitals just aren't for him. Marc wouldn't have wanted to step on that hospital ward floor. Rolex watches don't work in a vacuum.

We said our good-byes after lying about how good it was to see each other, but not until he suffered me with pictures of his family. Kathy is fat, and their children looked spoiled, judging from the amount of expensive toys surrounding them. We then parted and I watched the former Homecoming King strut down the street all covered with high finance and gluttony in which he so happily wallows.

I stood, with the booze in me boiling, looking not much better than a hobo as I cursed myself for being thirty-four with no stickpin of achievement other than a drawer full of publisher's rejection slips and a theater script lying somewhere in a New York trash bin. Even my vices are passé. Booze on the breath makes me the subject of disgust while Marc sucks cocaine up his nose before his admiring public. Perhaps I'm a drunk destined for a cardboard box shelter by the rail yards, but in some ways, I don't see much difference in him wobbling toward an uptown gutter.

But, he does have a wallet full of pictures...

June 29, 1980

This morning I lay in my bed as the sound of a distant church bell created in my mind an image of longing. It was cool and dark in the room, and my ears were sharply attentive to the bell's invasion of a soft dream of the past. In that darkness, there were faces, familiar but younger than they are now, and there were places that were as I remember them from long ago. In my dream was Dad as I recall him from my childhood. There was no gaping hole in his head. There, too, was Steven Joel, still in one healthy piece. He was full of good mischief, and his smile reflected the innocence of his youth.

Time shifted. There stood Marie Rose Robbins, my first and best love, and around her were bells; the church bells that eventually woke me. But in my dream, the bells were the laughter of Rosie. As I awoke, the bells were so real that I imagined Rosie was in the room with me. My eyes finally learned the truth that I was alone...

June 30, 1980

I stayed inside all day with the blinds down, my best intentions dashed by reality. Sunday's help-wanted ads glared at me, all dutifully marked, but I ignored them all of this day. I've resolved myself to accept any job for the sake of survival, but something called me back to the reaches of my muse. I could not face the world. Instead, I wrote.

It was to my advantage to not face a prospective employer with my head hurting like this anyway. Tomorrow. I'll try tomorrow.

The novel has not suffered. I created eleven pages of which I am proud, but the words bleed from me as I go over and over the pain of Strange Potions. Look at this place. Scattered about are empty beer cans and dead whiskey bottles. The cigarette tray overflows, and the house looks like an experimental breeding ground for bacteria. It's the home of drunks who write about drunks.

"Top of the world, Ma..."

July 1, 1980

God, it is hot. Summer...

Did not sleep well in this oven. I was disturbed by peculiar dreams. There are ghosts in my mind...

Went out and sold Mother's bureau to a dealer for four hundred dollars. Put the money into rent, some food, gas for the car, and booze.

Easy Street...

July 2, 1980

Took a lengthy walk through the city today. I sold my wedding ring for thirty dollars to a pawn just a block off the financial district. Considering how much I paid for it brand new, I'd say the event was poetic.

Love on the secondary market sells at a deep discount.

The city sparkles with glistening hope for wealth and happiness, but on its underbelly are the homeless who wallow in shattered lives. I'll join them soon if I don't find some means of supporting myself. I have the urge to seek out Vern for help, but his times are not much better than mine.

I reflected upon the best and worst times. Took a walk to breathe the air. I imagined a world resting upon a plane much higher than exists within the conscious mind. Rise above the city sounds and sights of those who live upon life's cutting edge as they move to and fro, frantically waving for balance and living or dying with each passing moment. There are those at each end of the spectrum; one of despair, the other of glory. The suited executive will cross the street to avoid the bum for fear he might look down and see his own face.

I'm on the middle of the board. Something hovers overhead, fraught with accusations and guilt, but I don't know what it is. It threatens to push me over before I can find a place where I might be secure. My dreams are leaving cryptic hints, but they don't reveal the dark demon at work on my heart. Perhaps writing about my father and his 'Strange Potions' is causing this depression.

Scientists say there are black holes in the universe into which entire stars and planets can be drawn. I wonder if Eternity may be in those holes. Something is drawing me into a black cavern of my own, and I am powerless to resist. I get closer every day. I have never before thought of death in such a way. In fact, death never frightened me until now. We step closer to the hole with every passing minute. What dwells inside is determined by the route we take. If a soul does not reconcile with its own imperfections before the body dies, it might be similar to entering a dark cave without light or direction. Something in my life is unresolved, superseding my need to move ahead. I can neither attain my goals nor complete my tasks if I do not distinguish what it is that so tears away at me. At the same time, I am alive because I don't know. This morning I almost took my own life to free myself of my misery; but I relented. I must first satisfy my curiosity in what ghost hides in my head and torments me this way; otherwise, I'll enter the cave without a light.

I am no longer of sound, logical thought. I fear I am going mad.

This demon eats away at my health and devours my heart, and yet, I am able to do one thing. I write. My work has never been better, but will it be complete?

What is this ghost? I've tried to absolve myself of guilt for my past - the war, my selfishness, my blind disregard for anything but my muse. But, there is something else.

The devil is in me, but he revels in his disguise...

July 3, 1980

Vern plans a party tomorrow. I am running dry. Losing words for you, Journal. Everything went to the book. Such irony to write about a father's self-destruction by booze as I sit here drunk. Who is who?

Strange Potions.

The art and artist are becoming one, and that should never be. In a dream last night, Dad told me from a cold grave: "I love you." There he laid in the ground, declaring his love. I awoke in an icy sweat.

I need money. Haven't eaten in two days...

July 9, 1980

Click, click, click. The world grows smaller as the cogs turn and close in like a vice. I'm at the bottom of my pockets. I may have to turn to Vern again to pay my rent. It pains me, but I have nothing of value to pawn. I hesitate to think of Mary, but she did offer some help. I cannot bear for her to see me like this. Perhaps my luck is in for a needed turn and a job will break soon. I did manage to submit my name at three different positions today, all of them menial in nature, but honest work nonetheless.

I've stayed away from the bottle for two days, and my head is a bit more clear, but God, what I wouldn't give for a drink right now.

The formless demon still stalks me. I'm a wounded animal waiting for the end, yet, bound to live on to remain unspoiled so I may be slowly eaten alive. I am my father's son, but I cannot suffer his fate. No longer will I allow any thoughts of suicide. I am not a coward. There is much unfinished business, and too many souls would suffer in my blood. I will not do to my family what Dad did to me. If only I could grasp what pushes me to these temporary moments of self-destruction. I sit here, afraid to live and afraid to die while I cling to my bottle and my muse. My art serves my consciousness while the drugs and booze allow me respite from my mind. Often, I manage a dreamless sleep where I may rest inside my dulled darkness, but I have such vivid recollections of those dreams that do occur: Looking in a mirror and seeing Dad's reflection, I scrub at my face until I bleed...

With each passing day, I take on more of his countenance until at times we seem of a single mind. When I push, he pulls. He draws me in. Could it be this is what is killing me?

I must keep writing, for that appears the only means by which I may banish his image. I must write and create his horrors - embellish them and pray they remain apart from me. It is his legacy, but I refuse to accept it as my fate. This demon inside only masquerades as my father. It can't be him. That would be too easy...

July 26, 1980

Emotions are numb. The novel is finished; my best work to date. The deep cavern inside widens as my soul spills in. It is difficult to deal with this state of mind, as I'm let down with both relief and apprehension at the completion of the work. I'm frightened that I might not have anything more to write. My hands shake.

Mary sent me a check for a thousand dollars. It is a godsend but a burden at the same time. It is not my baby sister's duty to support me. There may only be one person on this earth whom I adore as much as my little Mary. I vow to God I'll someday repay her kindness.

I looked to Vern for companionship today. Jon joined us at Vern's to drink and watch baseball. Three peas in a pod. Jon is too much like me. He is rebellious and lost within. Mother's death made him grow up faster than he might have wanted, and now he bounces from one scrape to another. He would have no part of my suggestion that he consider joining the service.

"Look at the shit you went through. Look at your gimpy leg. The army crippled you for a war that meant nothing," he argued.

Indeed. It seems ludicrous that I give advice to him when I wander through this depression like a lost dog. But, I had to try.

"There was a war then," I said. "Soldiering is different today. You get education and discipline. The army isn't in the business of carnage anymore."

"What about the Middle East?" Jon said. "What about Iran? I could end up fighting ragheads. There's always an enemy..."

He might be right. But I see nothing but trouble for Jon if he continues down the road he's chosen. In fact, by looking at what sailing the waters of life without a rudder has done to me, one might think he would heed my words. But, when you're eighteen, no one is smarter than you...

Received a letter from Duke yesterday. He is going to California to meet a movie producer next month and wants to know if he could stop here on the way. I'm torn between wanting to see my old friend and wishing to hide so he does not see my destitution. He made distinct overtures about discussing the Vietnam story he suggested we collaborate on years ago. In fact, the film producer he is meeting is interested in the idea. That is all I need right now. Daily, I struggle with the ghosts of Strange Potions, and now Duke wants me to open the war closet again.

Duke has suffered the indignation of many publisher rejections of his Nam textbook. However, he said after years of being told that no one wants to read about such a dark and unpopular subject, there seems to be a birth of sudden interest. A publisher is now seriously considering taking a chance on his book because of the construction of a Vietnam memorial in Washington. It seems the country is finally beginning to assume some of the blame for letting almost sixty thousand Americans perish in a war it badly botched.

Perhaps Duke's book was premature for its time. He sincerely thinks he may have a chance now, and that is why he is reviving his idea of our writing a story. There have been several successful films about Vietnam in recent years; Coppola's surreal Apocalypse Now, and the terrifying Deer Hunter, but those films distorted many truths by making us look like drugged-out murderers and rapists. I just don't know if The World is ready to see what Duke envisions as a film complete with actual news footage and real battle scenes to which he has access. His idea of creating a fiction-based-on-fact story about real grunts is compelling, but I am not sure America, even in its new enlightenment, is quite ready for that much horror dropped in its lap.

I'm not sure I want it either...

The devil came back last night.

He was in my dreams again, although, as usual, I did not see him. It only leaves an aftertaste in my wakefulness that implies it was there. It is peculiar. Lately, Rosie has been appearing in these images every third night or so. It's been so long since I have thought of my dear Rose, but there she is. In the dream, I stand in full view of her, but she can't see me. Then, the nightmare strikes. I'm suddenly caught in some violent concussion. My body feels devastating pain. I usually awake with a terrible cry. Never, even in all the time I was in the war, have I ever dreamed of my own death like this. It troubles me.

I have other Rosie dreams that follow a more recognizable pattern. Again, I see her but she does not see me. There is sometimes a partition or window that separates us, and often there is a child either near her, or in her arms. He is a boy, and the love between them is apparent.

The boy reminds me of me. God, like me…

Freud might have a field day with me. Perhaps Rosie represents Mother, whom I miss so terribly. I know sometimes I reach for the phone to call her, or I'll unconsciously plan to take Mother on a Sunday drive, forgetting she is gone.

But, why do the dreams lead to my death? Until I reached the thirty-year milestone, age and death had no tangible significance in my life. I am not old by any means, but I feel within me an unseen demon of guilt that makes me fear for the death of my soul. When Charlie leveled his weapon at my teeth I did not feel such fear as I do now. I have odd components in the search for what ails me: Rosie, Dad, death, and this small boy. Is he me?

Or, does he know?

August 8, 1980

Another whopper.

These damned nightmares are coming every night. Rosie and the child. I can never reach them or speak to them, but I hear them laugh and talk and love. I believe I am dead and am looking in. God, the fear that I'm losing my mind grows stronger every day. I detest myself. I drink to get drunk, and I take pills to sleep. I drink to face the morning. I take pills to stay awake. And, all the time I write to flee from the cumulative effect.

Rewrites of Strange Potions strengthen the work with every new word, but I fear my blood is staining the pages.

Dad, what is it like to be dead?...

August 12, 1980

I didn't leave my room all day. It is dark in here. Last night, my dream was more real than reality itself.

Is the child me?

Yes...

August 14, 1980

Slept the entire day, exhausted. I watched the walls close in on me until I could scarcely breathe. The booze made me pass out, but it did not protect me from my nightmares. First I see Rosie, the child, and then I die. The child is me; or, he is my ghost. I was dead. I may be dead now.

It's too hot outside...

August 16, 1980

Mary sent another check. She keeps me alive.

Jon's in jail. He was drunk and wrapped his car around a pole last night. He called and pleaded with me to come bail him out, but I had no cash; and I, too, was too drunk to find my own car. Vern is out of town, so Jon stayed in jail until he finally sobered up and found a friend to get him out.

Welcome to the real world, little brother.

Had another dream. Why do they haunt me? I feel so much pain when I see Rosie and the child. Why did I die?

Perhaps I didn't.

Something did...

"I grieve that grief can teach me nothing."

- Ralph Waldo Emerson

September 5, 1980

It has been weeks, Journal. I'm bound together with weak string, but I'm still functioning. Strange Potions is packaged and mailed to Walter Sachs, Duke's agent.

Duke visited for three days, and we bid farewell this morning. He stayed up for two nights reading my book, and he gave me a needed boost when he said he loves it. Duke is not an easy mark, making his critique all the more encouraging. He bombarded me with his Vietnam collaboration idea, for he has completed a synopsis and an outline, and he has developed several principal characters in whom I see great potential. The producer he is meeting is John Handley, of all people, one of Hollywood's 'bad boys' who took the film world by storm in the last few years. Duke says Handley is looking for a strong Nam screenplay right now. As much as I hate to admit it, this might be what I need to replace my completed project. Duke's masterful plot deserves a lengthy treatment.

"Get to work, Shakes," Duke said, "this is going to be a boo koo success...I know it..."

I suppose it is time to dust off my scripting technique. This would be much easier if I were sane.

By the way, Journal, I have a job. Today is pay day, in fact. Imagine, a drunk working in a liquor store!

Might as well leave Mickey Mouse in charge of the sharp cheddar...

September 6, 1980

Stayed up all night formulating dialogue for Duke's action sequences and reading his endless notes and research. His ideas are stunning. The ideas flow sometimes faster than I can retain and record them. I wake at night with three pages spilling from my head!

My only criticism, that which I discussed with Duke on the phone today, is his single, central character around whom the vivid images of war revolve. It's a worn war picture cliché to portray a common grunt as John Wayne instead of John Doe. In Vietnam, there were just too many players involved, and too many questions that had no rational answers.

"War is waged by kings but fought with pawns," I told Duke. "The grunts, the VC in the bush, the farmer in his rice paddy – we had one common bond: we all were trapped in a cage of circumstance with no escape. There was no control – no purpose, so why not portray the story as such? The secret to a Nam story is that there should be no plot. Our script should be a metaphor for a complex machine driven by one simple cog – survival."

Duke exploded with joy. "Jesus, Shakes," he said. "You just said in one minute what I've been trying to write for fifteen goddam years! You gotta go with it!"

Click, click, click...

I opened the closet, Journal, there are gooks on the wire, but this time I'm locked and loaded. I have to call Duke right now. He'd be getting up in another three hours anyway...

September 7, 1980

I tried to sleep this afternoon, but I awoke, soaked in sweat from images like tornadoes, Nam, a '58 Cadillac...

God, my mind loves to torture me.

Was on the phone with Duke for over two hours this morning. I can barely make my bills with the small salary I draw from the liquor store, yet I'm on long distance to California where Duke's meeting with John Handley went well.

Duke applauded my latest ideas for the script. The heat over the line could have melted our phones. What is more, Handley told Duke he wants a more extensive treatment and some sample scenes immediately. Walter Sachs sent Handley excerpts of Strange Potions and explained that I was an ex-gunner on a huey crew. Sachs phoned me and said Handley, after reading my work, agreed that I should be the person to write the Nam screenplay. He told Sachs he was impressed with my 'talent.'

I need a drink.

My stomach is a ball of twine. These nightmares keep

intruding on me when, for the first time in my life, I see a horizon of promise.

God, Rosie, what are these dreams? Why don't you see me?

September 15, 1980

A roller coaster. I'm up and down, up and down. Have heard not a word from Duke or Sachs, but I forge on with blind faith.

I've perused the archives of this journal and dug out the days of Soc Trang to refresh my memory of those black days. Hayman, Duke, Jimmy, Putnam, Colonel Strauss, Doug. The names and faces are clear now. Many of the characters Duke and I created mirror these people. I also turned the pages of my time with Steven and those boys in the VA. Duke's story is set at the beginning of America's offensive in Nam, focusing on the birth of the Air Cavalry (formerly the 11th test AAD with whom I trained). It culminates in the historic battle at LZ X-ray in the Ia Drang valley - the army's first deadly clash with the NVA.

I had almost forgotten the language of the bush: LZ, Kill Zones, Charlie, gook, slope, dink, zipperhead, firefights, Zippo Raids; and the nicknames: Blackjack, Dutch, Cowboy, Fury, Rage, Shakespeare...

Despite this new lease on life, I still can't shake this damned depression. I'm still ridden with dreams about death. Although I have turned thirty-four times around the sun, I am without a legacy. There is a theory regarding eternity: that human existence is perpetual, evolving to a final judgment. Previous lives stack upon each other, building on the former life's achievement. Patton believed he was a warrior in every life. Would that elevate or damn him?

Purity is judged by the heart, which is Matthew's concept of the dwelling place of the Holy Ghost. Sins committed by man, Matthew says, can be forgiven; but to sin against the heart is damning. To quote a lesser-known sage, Me: "When you fuck somebody, you're getting fucked, too!" (Forgive the French, Journal, just a nostalgic trip to the VA hospital.)

This demon still has me. I'm sinning against my own heart, but I know not what it is I am doing. These dreams of Rosie and the child still lie unresolved in my head. Is that child me?

Or, my legacy?

Pogo once said it: "the enemy is you, Hero. You is we, and we is us..."

My legacy. In my dreams, I die. In my dreams, a child rests in the arms of Rosie, who - is the child's mother.

Dear God. The child in her arms is ours...

Is there any greater grief suffered in this world than grief suffered in the death of one's own child?...

September 16, 1980

I've been awake over twenty-three hours. I read again and again my war diary and keep returning to the day Jimmy was killed. Going over it in my mind, I see that little boy running toward the troop carrier. I knew in my heart that child was a walking bomb, and I knew Jimmy would die if he reached the kid before I shot. It was my choice. They called us 'baby killers' back then...

September 17, 1980

I live in total darkness, and yet, I reside in life's most revealing light. I finally know who the enemy is, Pogo.

Even my father, during his blind and murderous self-destruction, would not have taken that which he created. He proclaimed his love for me instead.

I have prayed I am not my father's son. Now I know I am not. In Nam, I didn't even consider shooting that little boy in the bush, but with my child in Rosie's womb, I pulled the trigger and never looked back...

In all this time, I've looked for the demon to reveal himself when he was standing in plain sight. I simply did not recognize him, for when he gazed at me from the mirror, he looked too much like me.

Last night for the first time in recent memory I slept a dreamless sleep. Perhaps it was a mourner's slumber. I don't know when I have been so clearly awake...

September 29, 1980

Dear Marie Rose,

It's Me.

Too many years have gone by since our last letters; therefore, I am compelled to reach out and write an overdue epic, for I am consumed by thoughts of you as of late.

I've much to write, but need a warm-up with the tidbits of news from the clan. The first item is of a sad nature. We lost Mother in late summer of '79. Her fight against cancer was valiant in the years following her mastectomy, but she lost the battle to the inexorable march of time. Her spirit was unfailing, but her body simply wore out. We'll never know the pain she must have suffered, for she remained bravely quiet to the end. I miss her dearly and find myself expecting to hear her voice on the other end of the phone, or to pull up and find her sitting in her favorite chair on the veranda. Time allows these expectations to fade, however. She was a good person who deserved all the love we could give. God bless her.

Her funeral reunited the family with the exception of Lyla, who had no time in her busy schedule to come home and bury the woman who gave her life. I don't know why I continually allow myself to be disappointed by Lyla.

Mary, of course, got home before Mother passed. To see Mary's face again gave Mother much joy. Mary is with the Philadelphia Philharmonic, and she tours as a guest performer in orchestras all over the country. I don't suppose I should be amazed at how she has developed such a reputation, for Mary has always been the jewel of this family.

Jonathan graduated from Jefferson High last spring, I believe out of the kindness of the county's heart more than by any academic achievement. Perhaps they simply wanted him out of the system. His grades were dreadful throughout, and he spent more time in trouble than he did in his classes. With his portion of the inheritance, he bought a Camaro, which he promptly slammed into a telephone pole last month. Jon is destined for hard times, I fear, but there is yet a soft sensitivity about him that he chooses to hide. Living in a glass house myself, I hesitate to try to stand before him as an example, but I nonetheless badger him about responsibility and such. Do as I say, not as I do...

Vern is out of work right now, after being laid off from his summer job of picking asparagus. He recently invested five thousand dollars with some fellow who convinced Vern the world is ready for the comeback of the hula hoop. The deal looked bad from the start, but Vern didn't heed my reminder about our oil stock, which still trades for less than a penny. He's a dreamer. It runs in the family.

He now has two thousand hula hoops stacked in his shed. He still awaits word from his 'partner,' who went to Hawaii eight months ago on the pretense of meeting a Japanese toy promoter. Aloha, Money. Vern still thinks he'll hear something from this guy, but I'm not holding my breath. If you ever have the urge to hula hoop, I know where you can pick one up dirt cheap.

As for myself, I've struggled down a long and arduous road as of late. The slide began last year, when my play, Strange Potions, caught the attention of a New York director referred by Duke Winslow's agent. This fellow decided to obtain backing to produce it in a small off-Broadway theater. This all came about right at the time of Mother's illness, and the strain was terrific while I tried to care for her, hold down my job at the agency, and maintain connections with New York. I was spending energy and buckets of money, traveling to New York several times to secure the deal and trying to involve myself in the production.

Duke Winslow advised I should take the money (which was very little) and run with it, for my input was unwelcome from the outset. I learned very quickly that directors equate writers with sewer water. But I labored with blood and guts to write the play, and I wasn't about to let it go.

Unfortunately, Duke was right. I was interfering with property that I no longer owned. Finally, the director unkindly asked (called the police) me to leave the set when my frayed temper and constant badgering finally pushed him over the edge. I couldn't refrain from protesting his incompetent interpretation, structuring and staging. The

Manhattan Police, however, didn't care about staging anything other than my immediate evacuation of the theater. It will suffice to say I made a scene of my own. After cooling down, I apologized and went home.

Meanwhile, back at the ranch, my job was 'terminated' while I was on my little hiatus. I was told that I neglected and lost clients due to my persistent drinking and my numerous trips to New York. Furthermore, my boss said I was taking advantage of her position by expecting her to cover for me, since she happened to be my wife. Yes, Beth moved up in the world while I continued to move sideways. I wonder if this is the first time, in this yuppie world, that someone has fired an employee and then went to bed with him that night.

I tolerated it. I was, after all, about to become a famous playwright. I didn't bother to find a new job, since fame and fortune were imminent. A month later, Beth, Vern, Mary, Duke and I journeyed to New York for opening night. At last, my ship was about to land in port.

Strange Potions opened and closed the same night.

The critics rightfully shredded it, for it was an abominable production. They blasted the director, and they crucified me, despite the fact that the script was virtually rewritten.

I came home, leaving my spirit in a New York dumpster. Beth, of course was working, so we had money, but I was inconsolable. Mother passed away shortly afterwards.

Beth was patient while I laid around the house in a puddle of self-pity. Soon thereafter, however, she justifiably began to question my plans. She wanted me to get on with my life, but unfortunately expressed it with words like, "Forget this nonsense about writing and get a job."

You can guess my reaction. I told her I planned to complete the novel version of Strange Potions; that writing was my job, and she should respect me for that.

Suffice it to say, we were on the Road to Trouble.

Our marriage crumbled. Beth couldn't understand why I would continue writing after a New York critic declared me inept. I angrily fought back, unable, however, to convince her of my resolve to learn from the experience and try to improve my work. She is not an artist, and I had no patience for her inability to empathize. It got very ugly.

To conclude, our final divorce decree is due in days.

So much for the good news.

Rosie, I must admit this letter is not a product of impulse, nor is it intended to be a simple correspondence to let you know what new job Vern has. Long before my theater career and my marriage crashed and burned, I've wandered through a strange and dark forest of uncertainty. Lost in the throes of depression, I've experienced most disturbing dreams and visions. I thought it was simply the mental amplification of my failures in the past few years, but it ran deeper than that. I dare say that even if my play had been a success, I would still be lost in this.

My mind has been dominated by memories of you. I first thought it was a simple unconscious longing for better times when our childish eyes were blinded by innocence and idealism. As youngsters, we believed all we had to do to find happiness was to expect it to happen. As children of the '60s, we inherited an unlimited supply of hope no previous generation enjoyed. But that era was just a passing breeze that died with the crack of a bullet in Dallas and prematurely terminated our innocence.

The world became a forbidding place, but the transformation went unnoticed by our naive eyes. We still believed success is obtained by the simple turn of a dial, push of a button, or drop of a quarter. We perceived problems to be just as instantly solvable. What a rude awakening to find this is not true; that hard work is not always rewarded; that wishes don't always come true; that an instant cure often feeds a larger illness. I've been blind to my destitution, blaming failure for my depression.

Recent events served to fuel my enlightenment. I can no longer deceive by thinking these dreams amplify my subconscious longing for the youthful idealist.

If it was that simple, the latest ray of hope in my life would be the perfect salve, but it instead energized the light of my dark awakening:

Duke finally convinced me to collaborate on his long-suffering Vietnam story, which was recently given new life by John Handley, who wants to make a film about the war. Handley purchased an option from us, which gives him temporary rights to the script while he explores the possibility of obtaining funding for the project. The option buys him time to decide if the movie would in fact ever fly. Never before has the outlook been better...

And yet, I've remained mired in this depression, which only now revealed its evil roots. This revelation, however, does not simply chase from the darkness the guilt that has diminished me. I can't move on unless I share this with you and release the demon from my heart.

I cling to many wonderful memories of times we shared, but there is a dark one I would change if it were in my power. Ironically, it has taken me all of these years to finally find tears for a fear that we may have destroyed the very essence of our souls. Putting my life ahead of all else, I did it freely and selfishly, without regard for these terrible consequences I now suffer. I never considered the more important nature of what it did to you.

I do not know how I can express the sorrow and guilt I feel.

Rosie, I desperately grieve for the life of the child that together we created and then willfully chose to end. It may take the remainder of my lifetime, but I must find a way to rectify this wrong for which I feel responsible, and for the pain I know it caused you. Words alone may never allow me to adequately apologize to you, but for now it is all I can do.

As Always,
Me

October 2, 1980

The phone rang. I answered, and Rosie's voice filled my heart.

"You never told me how you felt," she said.

"I never faced it, Rosie," I said. "Until now, it's been just another ghost creeping inside my head."

"Your apology means much to me, but don't forget, we both made a mistake. Now that you know, you'll have to find a way to forgive yourself. That's how I live with it. We did many things back then that I regret, but I can't change it; nor can you. You said it yourself: We grew up in a time that forced us to become adults before we had the chance to be kids. But don't let that excuse be your false cure for the larger illness. Now that we both understand what we did, maybe now we'll find an answer."

I could not find much to say, but just having Rosie share this was comforting to me.

"It makes it easier to know I'm not the only one who feels the same way," she said...

> *"Those friends thou hast, and their adoption tried,*
> *Grapple them to thy soul with hoops of steel."*
>
> - William Shakespeare

December 20, 1980

Dear Marie Rose,

Merry Christmas, my Rose.

I don't know how long it will take me to learn to stand in this light. The enemy is easier to deal with when it is not in the shadows. Thank you. I believe I can change, for even the complex earth has its seasons.

Whatever the changes, one thing does remain constant. You are my friend...

As Always,
Me

1981

"And then the windows failed - and then I could not see to see."

- Emily Dickinson

January 20, 1981

An actor in the White House is better than the hayseed we had before. He gives a good speech, too. President Reagan took office today, and there I sat, for a brief moment optimistic about the future. Of course, no amount of Reagan's strength as a leader could overcome the influence of my old friend, Jack Daniels. The country may be heading in the right direction now, but I'm still buried in the old black hole of depression.

I actually voted for Ronald Reagan - probably the first thing I've done right in twenty years. I may be a drunk, but at least I'm at long last free of that self righteous, disease-ridden Democratic Party. God, how times have changed.

Minutes turn to hours, hours to days, to weeks, months...Click, click, click.

Liquor and pills. My pals.

The Children of Duty script goes slowly. I can write very few pages in one sitting, for the images frighten me. They exhaust me. The gore, the terror; smoke and grass and sticks, human entrails soaking into the mud...

Charlie doesn't attack from my closet, thank God.

Why do we war? How do mothers endure it? Their children died unspeakably...

February 7, 1981

Finished the first act of the Duty script. It surged through me despite the agony each word caused. My only reservation is the question of America's readiness for a story like this. The wounds from this war did not heal, but the truth about Vietnam resides in these pages. We can't forget the men who put their lives in the bush. We can't forget the sight of the last American chopper pitching into the smoky Saigon sky, later to be dumped into the sea like a disgraced, dead eagle.

I will not let this work die in futility. The World will see, if I have to cram it down its throat...

March 30, 1981

A dark reminder of history today. The unthinkable. It's a sight that should not be endured in a lifetime, but there it was again. John Kennedy, Robert Kennedy, Martin Luther King, Malcolm X, George Wallace, Gerald Ford.

Today, someone shot Ronald Reagan. Reports are the President will survive, but he is yet another victim of assassins in the bush. This day conjured the unforgettable memory of my father's death. It was the day Kennedy was murdered in Dallas. I can almost see Dad standing before me right now. Friday night, November 22, 1963:

I was writing in my journal when my attention was drawn to the door. I stopped when Dad appeared. He looked at me with someone else's face. His eyes were so striking that I did not notice the revolver in his hand.

"I love you, son," he softly said. His words were spoken with such pure clarity. It was the first time he had ever said these words to me, so I did not understand.

Dad's smooth hand reached for his mouth, and my mind told me he was about to bite into an apple. Then, with swift resolve, my father loved me for the first and last time in his life when his head exploded. His eyes remained on me as if he did not yet know he was dead; just like Charlie in the bush, they all die the same...

His knees finally buckled as I watched in horror.

Kennedy, King, Malcolm X...Dad.

They died at the hands of assassins in the bush...

April 14, 1981

This morning, I awoke in the closet.

It was dark and cool in there. It was Dad's voice that woke me. Other voices were in there, too. There was the voice of Marie Rose. There was the voice of my mother. There was the voice of my sister Mary. There was the voice of an unseen child...

They all said, "I love you..."

I awoke in my closet today. I cannot remember the passage of time between last Thursday and today, Tuesday. A vacation from my mind.

My home is a wreck, and my clothes are foul and damp. My demolished car is in the drive. Vern tells me I didn't make it home Saturday night in one piece, but somehow I managed to call him and he came and got me before the police did. I've lost myself.

I'm Vonnegut's Billy Pilgrim: Unstuck in time.

In my memory, I cannot find the last five days. All I find are tiny remnants of me spilling from the lip of an empty bottle here, a spent pill box there. It must end, Journal. My head feels like it is stuffed with barbed wire, and my stomach feels like it is shredded in pieces. When I try to concentrate upon the moment, my mind falls into the black hole. I'm going mad. Vern is here. Mary is here. Vern told her he can't control me anymore. He even struck me across the face and cursed me. Mary cried.

I'm sick. I don't want my Mary to see me like this...

What is happening to me?

May 8, 1981

Thirty-five years ago today I popped out.

Perhaps I should pop out. I'm dry for twenty-four days now. Surrounded by hospital walls Mary paid for, they tell me I can stay dry on the outside, too, if I take it one day at a time. A lonesome drunk in the confined care of this fine institution, I feel I'm just another nut in the jar.

James Taylor sang about his days under lock and key:

"Just knockin' around the zoo
on a Thursday afternoon
there's bars on all the windows
and they're countin' up the spoons..."

I long for sleep. I don't want to be bothered by my pathetic existence. They let me write all day in here, but my words cover the horror and death of my past. A noble gladiator of the twenty-first century will never care about these words. He will be too busy warring to read ancient history.

I'm not a teacher. I can't change things...

"And if I'm feelin' edgy
There's a chick who's paid to be my slave;
but she'll hit me with a needle
if she thinks I'm tryin' to misbehave..."

Click, click, click...

I'm going home tomorrow. I can't breathe in this place...

August 14, 1981

Walter Sachs called from New York today. He had a major publisher nibble on Strange Potions but lost it. I admire his persistence, but I count ten rejections now. He won't leave me alone about the Duty script either. I fight my growing disenchantment with the entire project, as it is making a shambles of my health.

"Keep working," Sachs said, "and leave the driving to us." Then, he adds: "Keep your lips off that bottle, schmuck." Somewhere inside of Sachs is a Jewish mother.

Even Vern hasn't had a drink in three months, thinking his example might influence me. However, it just makes drinking all the more lonely for me. I nearly bit his head off the other day when he came over and badgered me about the beer in the refrigerator. Mary calls every day, too, but I'd die before I vented my anger at her.

I'll quit drinking. I can do it. But I'll do it when Duty is finished. I'll do it when my brain decides to stop scolding me. I'll relent when my heart decides I've paid the bill for killing my only child...

I'll quit.

Until then, drink up...

August 22, 1981

Visited with Duke this morning. His call woke me from a death-sleep. He said the phone rang ten times before I answered, the impatient bastard.

Duke is blue despite the news that Handley still considers the Duty project a high priority. He told Duke he loves the advances we sent, and he looks forward to meeting me. Good lord, is he in for a surprise.

So why the blues, Duke? He's hit more snags getting his historical manuscript published. His editor asks for rewrites Duke refuses to make, and it threatens to be a deal-breaker if no accord can be reached. Duke is stubborn about his craft, and he resents the suggestions he lessen the gore and reality of Vietnam for readers of feeble heart.

"Fuck that," Duke says.

Give 'em hell, Duke.

He then suggested we shorten the full title of our script from Children of Duty, to the working title, Duty. No changes, I told him. Duke doesn't hold the patent on stubbornness. I only hope Handley won't rock the boat. It is just a name, isn't it?

I wonder if I can write science fiction...

December 19, 1981

Dear Marie Rose,

Humbug.

Have you no mercy? A Christmas card from Maui? Does your father ever get a notion to spend the holidays in the snow? I envy you all, but wish you a happy season nonetheless.

It sounds like everyone is well, and how about that

Angie! Three kids now? Someone should inform her and Ted that the country is indeed suffering from terrible inflation, but that does not pertain to her belly! And congratulations to Gary for his City Council election. Perhaps someday I will be able to say I know the First Lady! Send him and the kids my love.

What a Christmas for me. Vern is out of town, Mary is in Europe, and Jon is in Germany. Can you fathom that Jon is now a Marine? To spare the gory details, Jon enlisted after another scrape with the law. I think boot camp and a slick uniform has made a positive change in my hoodlum brother.

Vern has a girlfriend. He met her in Tijuana in November when he was there on business (he's still looking for a hula hoop buyer). He's secretive about this romance, but he says his little 'jalapeno' did something special to capture his heart. Olé, Vern!

And so, here I am, alone for the holidays. I'll miss the company of the family, but I will finally spend a Christmas the way I'd like: in church where this whole thing was supposed to be in the first place.

The only better way would be if the church were in Maui! My love to you, Rosie.

As Always,
Me

1982

March 9, 1982

Received an unusual letter today. A twenty-year-old boy named Emory Ruson got my address from Doug Moon. He wrote to me with the startling news that he is the son of Jimmy Moon.

What odd circumstances. Emory was born shortly after Jimmy went to Vietnam. Jimmy never knew Emory's mother was pregnant, for the relationship faltered just before he left. The girl went home to North Carolina, where she raised Emory with the help of her grandmother. The girl was only sixteen at the time. She never told Emory about Jimmy because of the shame she endured, but the boy recently began asking questions. He received some rather tilted information about his father. The girl told Emory that Jimmy was no good and he deserved to die in Vietnam.

Emory did not accept his mother's bitterness, and he ventured out to find Jimmy's family. It was an emotional reunion, and Emory learned the more truthful history about his father. Doug referred Emory to Dutch Hayman and me, so he could learn more about the circumstances surrounding Jimmy's death. It pains me to write to Emory, but I must:

Dear Emory,

Your uncle is accurate in his description of my friendship with your father, Jimmy Moon. I do not suppose he was closer to anyone outside of his family than he was to Mr. Hayman and me.

Although your mother painted an unfavorable picture of your dad, I must disagree with her. Jimmy Moon was the kindest and bravest man I shall ever know. I'm sorry your mother does not feel the same way. She may see Jimmy in a false light because of the burden left upon her at such a tender age. I do not pretend to speak for her, but I suspect she is bitter and hurt. You must understand, Emory, we all were children back then, prone to mistakes, and victims of a terrible and uncertain time in our history. Jimmy was barely older than you are now when his life ended. I pray the truth will evoke from you the same love I have for him. I was close enough to your father to assure you, if he had known of your birth and had lived to see you, you would have known no greater love than that he would have given you.

I served with Jimmy Moon in the 121st army Aviation Company, a decorative name for a group of hardworking, dedicated men who valiantly served their country before America officially involved itself in the Vietnam War. We flew helicopters out of a little village in South Vietnam called Soc Trang, our mission to transport South Vietnamese soldiers to strategic areas where the Viet Cong - Communist guerrillas - engaged in terrorist attacks on the villagers who resisted them. During those early years, we tried to help the free south fight against Communist insurgence, unlike the direct American combat involvement in the years that followed.

It is not my intent, however, to try to explain the war. I cannot, even with so many years behind me, yet understand it myself. I venture to say it will take decades of reflection to dissect our involvement in Vietnam. But America called your father to serve, and he answered. Try to imagine yourself right now being thrown into a war in which you have no defined purpose; you are ordered to defend yourself from terrorists, but you have no authority to directly involve yourself in attempts to stop them from killing innocent people. If that sounds confusing, perhaps you'll understand what your father faced. We saw the evil brutality of the Communists, but we were not empowered to do anything to stop it.

This is what your father faced every day for almost two years before he died. We saw terrible atrocities - entire villages vanquished, mass graves full of children and old people, and deaths of American boys, many of whom were our friends. But, in all of this insanity and terror, your father retained his decency and compassion. During my darkest moments of fear, Jimmy was always there for me, sharing my fear and often calming me with his great smile and delightful sense of humor.

Jimmy was quite a poker player. His nickname was 'Blackjack' because of his prowess at card playing. He had the richest cache of match sticks, cigarettes, nickels, dimes and quarters on the base. I will never forget one evening when your father played poker with some South Vietnamese soldiers, none of whom could speak English very well. He taught them how to play poker; however, Jimmy taught them the progression of hands in reverse order, making a pair the highest obtainable hand, a royal flush the lowest. Jimmy knew that two American pilots were going to join the game later, and when they did, the resulting confusion was hilarious. The Vietnamese boys were betting the pot on pairs and then accusing the pilots of cheating when they lost.

But I'm sure your uncle and grandmother supplied you with hundreds of humorous anecdotes about your father and his wonderful spirit for mischief. You wrote me to learn how he lost his life, and unfortunately, I witnessed his death.

The day was March 13, 1965. Your father, like myself, was a gunner aboard a huey gunship on a mission near a tiny hamlet called Can Tho where Communist forces had overrun the area. I was aboard one helicopter with Mr. Hayman, and your dad was on another, our job to escort large troop carrier choppers and protect them as they landed to deploy the South Vietnamese soldiers. The landing zone was a scene of utter chaos as the enemy fired upon us from thick jungle cover. We were in a hot battle as we circled again and again, driving the enemy away from the deploying soldiers.

Our people suffered many casualties that day, and we were ordered to land and help medical teams evacuate the wounded soldiers. During this evac, there suddenly appeared near the trees a North Vietnamese soldier with a small boy in his arms. He put the boy down and pointed him in the direction of one of the landing troop carriers. Unknown to the rest of us, although your father suspected it, the soldier had strapped explosives to the boy. They were rigged with a timer to go off when the boy reached the helicopter.

Emory, this innocent child was an unwitting human time bomb, destined to run to that helicopter where the explosives would kill him and countless American Marines aboard. These were the wicked tactics of our enemy, something which rarely made the front page of any newspaper. Stories like this were often passed off by some as American propaganda used to unite anti-Communist opinion in this country.

But this was real, Emory. This wasn't some lie made up by an army propagandist. This was a child, frightened by the horror and destruction, who was sent running to "safety" by someone he trusted. Because your father was a tried veteran, he knew what would happen when that boy made it to the chopper. But, rather than shooting the child to save the men, Jimmy ran to catch the little fellow and maybe prevent the bomb from going off. Jimmy knew that, in his act of heroism, he risked death. On that gamble, Jimmy's luck finally ran out. The bomb went off and your father and the little boy died, but he saved the lives of everyone aboard the helicopter. For his extraordinary bravery, he was posthumously awarded the Congressional Medal of Honor, the highest honor for bravery bestowed upon an American soldier.

There will never be any means by which we'll understand why Jimmy and the child had to die that day, Emory. All we can do is remember him as a man who sacrificed himself in an unparalleled act of human decency. Despite your mother's unfortunate feeling about your father, please don't let it deter from the fact that he was a true hero. Jimmy Moon was gentle, compassionate, and always with a good word. Above all, he was a moral and decent man in a most immoral and indecent world. Your grandmother gave you his medal for you to keep. It shall never replace Jimmy, but I hope you cherish it as a reminder of who he was, and who you are, for his blood flows through you, and that is reason to be proud.

I love Jimmy Moon, and I hope you do, too. Though the years have eased my pain, his honorable spirit will be something I'll never forget. I am proud to have called him my friend...

* * *

Journal, I hope these words will help Emory. I think of Jimmy's name among the fifty-eight thousand etched in the memorial they are building, and I wonder if America really cares...

Reflecting upon this letter, I am haunted by the question - did Jimmy feel his death? I wonder what thought passed through him before falling into darkness. How quiet it must have been to be suddenly swept away from all of that deafening terror. There was no body left, and I never saw a soul rise from the smoke. I recall a day long ago when I watched a boy drown in the reservoir. There appeared no eternal soul rising above the body, but I cannot help but believe in a powerful energy within us that can never die. Jimmy's body is gone, but his energy manifested itself in this letter, and his spirit lives in Emory Ruson. It serves to remind me of the child Rosie and I created together. I must find some way to atone for its loss. I simply must.

In life, should a man somehow become disembodied from his eternal soul so that it became visible to him, would he recognize it as his own?

I believe I would recognize mine.

That might be fearsome...

June 15, 1982

Black. The walls are closed. My stomach is knotted in agony, and I waver in drink. I am lonely. Damn, I am lonely.

My mistress blankly stares back at me with high expectations. Words, she demands words. I must finish this script, but I am blank. I depend on these tranquilizers, but I hate them at the same time.

I often awake in my own juices, disgusted and appalled. I looked at the cracked image of my father in the mirror, but I refuse to suffer his fate. I grieve over the unchangeable, and I peck away at myself, leaving shards of my flesh on the floor. The nerves are shattered. I hate myself for my own destruction, but feel powerless to stop it. If I do not stop, I will die. I must hang on. The bill has not yet been paid.

Mary called this evening. When we said good-bye, she cried.

My Mary. When we were young, she was a little baby on my lap. Dad's funeral was over, and in her innocence, she could only understand that I was with him when he died. "Did you kill Daddy?" she asked.

I didn't answer. Daddy killed me.

July 9, 1982

The ninth day of July. I have, for the final time, sacrificed myself to liquor and pills. It is over. I win.

It came to me as a pure, clean ray of light. I will compose a novel to replace my dependency on artificial life. The lives I've taken may be resurrected by this book, if I achieve my goal.

I declare this day the final darkness of longing. The specter of my father, my unborn child, and all the self-incrimination is kindly invited to leave my head. I am free.

The Duty script is finished, and I allow it to signify this day as the last time I will awaken in a drunken haze, beaten by drugs, and rotting inside from guilt and self-pity. I've lost jobs, my home, my dignity, but I refuse to lose Me.

In my mind, the words of Jake Robbins echo through me: "It's done from the inside out. You can't finish something if it ain't been started..."

I promise you, Journal, I will never take another drink, nor rely upon a drug. I owe too many debts. There are too many ends to tie. Excerpts of my life must be bound together before I complete the circle of life...

7

Excerpts

1983

"I'd like to think I can still think about
the things I used to sing about
when I was spending all my time alone;
by myself and on my own
seldom seen and quite unknown..."

- James Taylor

December 20, 1983

Dear Marie Rose,

When the sun cast its warming light upon this cold December morning, I knew, in my heart, why this abnormally frigid and bleak holiday season would brighten. Indeed, there came to my door your Christmas card, and with it, your sunshine! This year's letter was so very special with the family portrait, and how the report of everyone's well-being brought me joy.

I hasten to mention since you asked, to get this over with early on, I am not yet rich and famous, but there remains hope which I will later mention.

Life here at the old banana plantation remains steady and remarkably uneventful. Last year, I remained silent from you for a purpose only now that I am willing to address. But I am also happy to include a certain amount of success I've enjoyed in literally cleaning out the very harmful cobwebs that muddled my poor brain.

I have won a battle, Rosie. My weakness for the drink was never a secret, but I have finally come to acknowledge that I for years have been powerless to avoid its trappings. Embracing liquor was yet another temporary 'cure' for symptoms of a larger and more deadly nature. But, I have won. I am free of my dependency, and am sober now for sixteen months! Because I never made an honest attempt to quit before, I am not sure I fully understand how or why I stopped so abruptly. I simply awoke one morning and knew. Something inside of me decided it was time. I could never bring myself to share with you the darkest moments of my dependency, but I wish to say if it were not for my beloved Mary and Vern's patience, I might not be alive today.

I don't mean to go on so, but I must say that my life without booze is more intact. I had no earthly idea how avenues of thought are more easily traversed when they're not wet with alcohol! One of my more positive characteristics is the ability to eventually adapt to perpetual changes in this stupid world. Regarding my propensity for inebriation, I have finally learned to commune with, rather than defy the spirits in my head. This rendered the spirits in the bottle much less interesting. My thoughts, for the first time in decades, are clear and clean, and what bizarre and wonderful imps they truly are!

On to the family. I haven't mentioned the black sheep for several years, so I might start by reporting that sobriety has not changed my feelings about Lyla, with whom I remain alienated. It does not concern me, however, for I'm resigned to some inescapable inevitability in life of which my dislike for her is one. That I have not heard a single word from her in years is certainly fine with me.

On the brighter side of my crew, Mary recently taped an appearance with the Boston Pops to be aired next month on PBS. You will want to watch for her third album of classical music to be released this spring, too. However, the best news is she is in love! She lives with a wonderful fellow by the name of Justin Michael, who is a cellist with the Philadelphia Philharmonic. I took an instant liking to him when we met, and he obviously adores Mary. They both work very hard at their art, and they share a dream of building an arts center someday. I imagine we will hear wedding bells in the near future. Mary has never glowed so brightly as when Justin's name is broached. There is no one on earth that deserves more happiness than my little girl.

Other happy news includes Jonathan's discharge from the Marine Corps. It is remarkable the positive change that has come over Jon. He and I launched a new friendship into calmer waters as we share old service stories, discuss sports and politics, and generally tease each other for what sorry sacks we both were in past times. He was overjoyed to learn I gave up liquor, for he too has abstained for six months and feels quite well. In all, we've never enjoyed each other's company more. I'm certainly glad that the armed forces at least went one-for-two in its effect on our father's military sons. I may have come out slightly neurotic, but Jon came out a decent man. Unbelievably, he now has dreams of becoming a police officer! At last, the grass is greener...

On the Vern side of my clan, I'm apprehensive to report

he is missing. I have no idea where he is. Last July, I stopped by his mobile home and found it empty with a simple note on the front door: "Gone fishing, will call."

Although I'm slightly concerned, I trust he is safe out there somewhere in the universe. We speculated he might have headed for Mexico in search of lost love. (His hot tamale girlfriend jilted him for a border patrol officer.) However, we received a card from him in September from Alaska. "Rubbing nose with the Eskimos," he wrote. "Love, Vern." The picture on the front of the card was a naked woman on a sled…

Other news includes one note of sadness. Marc Komac's eldest daughter took her own life last summer. She was found with two of her junior high school friends in Marc's Mercedes locked in the garage. One of the other girls also died, and one survived. Apparently, it was a suicide pact. I met Marc on the street several years ago, and he appeared to be successful, but he was clearly addicted to cocaine and all the trappings of the lifestyle he was leading. At the time I felt I was the only one lost in such madness. Now that I more fully understand addiction, I regret that indeed Marc is yet another victim - his vice was power generated by chemicals. Unfortunately, his daughter suffered his neglect of anything else. The local newspaper ran a photograph of the family at the funeral, and I was shocked to see how badly he looks. Marc, I fear, is the victim of his own undoing.

And, about this weary time traveler: I work at a menial warehouse job, but I am thankful for employment in this depressed city. Children of Duty, our Vietnam screenplay, remains with John Handley, who just renewed a second option. I was taken by surprise last fall when he called me from London, where he is filming some kind of outer space epic. He flattered me with the desire to send his regards. He was reading the script for the third time, and he had several suggestions for rewrites to suit a particular brainstorm of his own. This came just at a time when I was considering calling Wally Sachs to suggest he tell the ambivalent Mr. Handley to perform an unnatural sex act upon himself for stringing us along. I confessed this to John, humbly of course. He was amused at my candor, and he bolstered my faith with the reassurance that my script is the subject of his obsession despite his current preoccupation with space creatures. The problem is financing. He has encountered endless negative responses from his best sources because of the film's volatile content. He hinted he may bankroll the film himself if his space movie is successful. He bid me farewell with a most touching compliment:

"Your soul rises out of this script, Shakes." (I can't seem to lose that nickname.) "I sometimes have to put the damned thing down because your work literally flies off the pages. I find myself either crying, or absolutely terrified. What you and every boy and girl endured over there will not pass without honor. Keep working with me on some refinements, and trust a feeling I have in my gut that someday we're going to shock the world with this script..."

Rosie, I know I'm a simple artist with simple needs. I know that I am happy to enjoy the tilted ghouls my odd mind unleashes without any desire to become a famous Hollywood scriptwriter. But after receiving a call like that from one of the best-known movie producers in the world, I'll be danged if I slept a wink that night! It soars so far above a night so long ago when I stood nose-to-nose with a pipsqueak New York director who called me a drunken halfwit boob. He was lucky he wasn't running through a jungle as I hovered at two hundred feet with an M-60 in my hands!

Meanwhile, Strange Potions, the novel, is still alive as Sachs keeps pushing it at skeptical publishers. I moved on to a new novel, its contents a secret I can't share with you yet. I also pounded out a science-fiction fantasy called Lido, which is a story of a man who is born fully-grown at the age of thirty-one in 1967 America. The country has been ravaged by nuclear war and overthrown by radical hippies who don't know what to do with the government once in power. The child-man, who has no knowledge of world history, rises to power by building a new world in the fashion of a French nightclub.

I assure you, it may lose something in this description, but it's good. It's brilliant, actually. Sachs was overwhelmed when he read it, calling it 'a bizarre literary masterpiece - absolutely unsellable - but I'll show it around anyway.'

Another story I plan to undertake is a tale of a man who endlessly gains weight although he eats nothing but health foods. It's a parody, you might have guessed.

Jesus, I'm amazed how friendly those little ghosts in my head have become since they sobered up!

I am renewed every time I hear from you, My Rose. I dearly love you, and I wish you and your family happiness in the upcoming year. By the way, Duke sold his book! He finally ironed out all the wrinkles and reached a very lucrative deal with his publisher. The text, Insurrection: The Vietnam War, will be released this coming year! He and I raised a glass of Dr. Pepper over the telephone lines, and he promised an autographed copy for you, me, and all the guys from Soc Trang. I am elated for him. There's hope! Here's to us!

As Always,
Me

1985

May 8, 1985

Dear Jack Benny,

How are things in Heaven? Are you still fighting with Fred Allen? Is playing the Firmament as tough as the Palace? At least you have a captive audience.

Ha ha.

(You can use that one if you want.)

I'm writing to you because today is my birthday, and I'm thirty-nine. If you aren't too busy cracking up God, I wonder if you could take a minute to write back and tell me how you managed to stay my age all of your life. Don't worry, I included return postage...

Sincerely,

Me

P.S. Say hello to Dad for me.

June 3, 1985

Brace yourself, Journal. Sachs called this morning. We're going to Los Angeles!

December 14, 1985

Dear Marie Rose,

Christmas again!

It's hard to fathom, Rosie, but I'm in the Philippines! I haven't returned your letter of last month because I saved this surprise until I could share with you my good fortune here in the armpit of the world.

We're shooting! Not guns, but film! Last June, John Handley announced to Variety, God, and everybody else his intention of filming the Vietnam War film to end them all, and here we now are on location!

I moved in with Duke this summer, where we spent the

time in rewrites while John scouted locations and finalized the financing. Duke is on Cloud Nine with this, his second big score in the year! And me: I paid off every debt with just a fraction of the advance I got. If that's not enough, Sachs immediately sold the book rights, which means I have to get busy expanding the Children of Duty script to novel form. Most of the future location shots will be done in Mexico, but I'm here as a script consultant and adviser on the helicopter scenes. Just like Vietnam, it's muggy and hot here, but what a change from the old days to be able to sleep in an air-conditioned mobile home with Coke and Perrier in the fridge. I'm even going to be a movie star! Handley gave me a bit part of a Marine officer who calls a grunt a 'pussy' in my big scene.

"Don't be a pussy, Marine!" I say.

I've been rehearsing for two weeks.

All my old pals are here, too. We hired Jack Putnam and a bunch of his old pilot cronies to do the flying. Doug Moon and Dutch Hayman are here for technical advising, and Eddie Strauss is choreographing the flight stunts. Colonel Strauss so mesmerized Handley with his pirate persona that he was given a screen test and cast as a tough one-eyed Marine colonel with several lines. Duke will also be on the silver screen with a short appearance as an old war-scarred general. Our schedule is brutal, but we feel like children turned loose at the Hershey factory. We're considering membership in the Screen Actors Guild. Watch out, Eastwood and Hoffman!

Our free time is one big nostalgia party as we all sit around and trade war stories and enjoy the peace, unlike the last time we were in a jungle. The shooting is scheduled to wrap up in two weeks, and we'll go back to being nobodies, but this has been the highlight of my life. The actors are all kids, and they complain endlessly about the Spartan lifestyle of the bush, but we old codgers have a party every night!

Handley will be calling upon Duke and me from time to time after we leave here, but he expects we won't be needed to any great degree through the remainder of the shoot. He expects to finish sometime next summer. This breakthrough has opened a world of possibilities for me because Sachs is getting publishers interested in my work now. He wired me three days ago to inform me he has an offer for Lido, and has packaged Strange Potions into the deal. He wants me to stick with work like Lido because he says I have more potential with light satire than the dark tragedies. It's ironic that publishers enjoy my fantasies more than the reality of poor Dad and Me.

Sachs encourages me to finish Mr. Chunks, my tale about the fat health nut, and is pushing me for new proposals. In a way, I'm overwhelmed by all the sudden attention. I've spent thirty-nine years laboring for no one but my typewriter, and now there's a sudden onslaught of exposure stripping me bare before the public.

Yeeks!

Sachs is holding my hand, as always, and I am glad to give him his cut to do so. He tells me this film is the breaker. If it's good, we're going to sell other projects quickly; if not, back to the drawing board. It makes my bellybutton pucker.

Let me go on to other subjects before I get worried. Mary and I spent Thanksgiving together in New York. She and Justin married last October at Justin's family home in Vermont. I had the honor of giving away the bride. I had a great deal of time available to spend with them, giving me the opportunity to become better acquainted with Justin. He is perfect for Mary, and he loves her almost as much as I do. I have great expectations for their lives together. They still have plans for an arts center, and now I hope I may be able to back them if this ship comes in. Mary saved my life, and I will forever try to repay her.

Jon was unable to join us for the holiday, for he is completing his training at the Denver Police Academy. We laugh at Jon when we remember him in his fast cars, his rock and roll, and his life in prison. He has also fallen in love and plans to get married to a wonderful girl next spring.

Enigmatic Vern is still on the loose, however. We get post cards now and then. Jon tracked Vern down to a metaphysics ranch near Big Sur where he pops in occasionally and takes up residence with a woman who has written several books about karma and such. Vern pitches a tent in the mountains for a week or two, and they meditate in search of past lives. Now, here's the weird part: Vern believes there is a new dawning of man emerging where mankind will evolve into one single religion, one universal government. This new age shall usher in the visitation of beings from another planet who have lived for thousands of years and are waiting to guide us in this new life. They will teach us how to contact our individual spirit guides who live in another dimension, and I suppose everyone will ultimately look like hippies. Vern has communicated already with his spirit guide; a chap who lives on a star called Arcturus.

Rosie, Vern swears to me he isn't drinking anymore, but I think he's fibbing.

He's sixty-nine, but he won't grow up. He has searched his entire life for a cause, and now, finding none around Denver, he's perusing the universe. What a shlemp.

I hope and pray you all are well. Last year's Christmas card photo is certainly testimony to how quickly your kids are growing up. I trust you have made the transition into adopted motherhood without difficulty. I am impressed with Tommy's performance at UCLA and his ambition to go to medical school. Has James decided to attend Oklahoma? From the sounds of his football success, you may have another John Elway on your hands. I am also impressed at his ambition to become a writer, but please suggest he not do it the way I did!

As for Cynthia, I implore you to refrain from killing her! Fifteen years old is a disease from which she will recover. I would not recommend locking her in her room for the next five years as you suggest. You must resign yourself to her opinion that you and Gary are the most ignorant humans on the face of the earth. I promise she will someday outgrow this monstrous age, become an adult, and have smart-aleck children of her own. Then she'll finally suffer the indignities she is now creating for you. The world has a way of working itself out this way. It's God's perfect, circular universe!

As for Yours Truly, my health is good, but my knee seems to be getting worse. I take to a cane now and then, and my doctor suggests I consider surgery to replace the joint. It's funny how they suggest those things after they find out you're making money!

Keep your fingers crossed with the wish these movie moguls know what they are doing. I pray Handley's pockets are deep. I haven't reached my goals yet, but this might be the catalyst to make it all work. For the first time since long ago when I first laid eyes on you, I am happy! I'm not sure I trust the feeling, but I'm willing to live with it for as long as it chooses to stay.

Merry Christmas, Rosie, and send my love to Gary, the kids, and to your wonderful family in Denver.

As Always,
Me

1986

January 4, 1986

Dear Marie Rose,

Jon has been tending to my personal affairs at home, and he inadvertently opened your Christmas card. He extends his apologies for intruding upon our private correspondence; however, it is good he did, for he immediately wired me of your father's passing. I am not sure how long it will take for this letter to reach you, but I hope it will quickly follow the Christmas card I sent last week, which was full of joyous meandering I now regret. It is so very hard to absorb such an unexpected loss, especially at Christmas. Please accept my sincere sympathy.

Your father was such a wonderful man that it pains me to see his passing at such a young age. If there is a blessing to this, it is that he at least did not suffer long to the swift heart attack.

I would like to share with you a moment I had with Jake not long ago; something which meant a great deal to me. During the final and terrible dark days of my life within the deathlike grip of alcoholism, I reached a point where I was beginning to question my will to fight the seemingly endless futility of grief that blackened my every moment. I was drifting farther and farther away from myself, lost in a rolling and dark sea, existing in a bottle that provided only empty promises. I was eating Valium, which allowed me to sleep without nightmares, and I was drinking all day to keep myself from fearing the next night. All the time, I was falling deeper into a hole from which there might be no escape. With every passing day, I was taking on the countenance of my father, who succumbed to the same vices that were now eating me whole. Dad solved his problem with a gun, and I admit I contemplated a similar resolution.

Whenever those dreary thoughts began to get the best of me, I took endless walks through parks, along empty country roads, or down city streets. One day, I chance met your father downtown. I detected the shock in his eyes, for we had not seen each other in years. I was pale, underweight, and the booze made me look and walk like a man of ninety. Jake took the time to talk to me that day as we walked the streets together. He kept prodding at me in his aggressive way, questioning me relentlessly as to why I was in such dreadful shape until I finally confided in him our deep secret, Rosie. I could not help but confess to him how it was persecuting me for putting such a terrible burden upon you, and how it had left a dark void in my life.

Rosie, I know you did not want anyone to know the truth, but please understand I was desperate and honestly unsure if I could go on without confiding in someone. What I said hurt him, but he treated me much like he would have treated you: with simple love and understanding. The hurt in his eyes was evident. He was disappointed in our failure to believe we could not come to him for help.

"Don't you know we would have stood by you?" he said. "We could have helped you raise that child while you took the time to grow up yourselves. I love my little Rosie with all my heart. I wish I could have helped you and my baby girl..."

Jake went on to remind me that, if I truly wished to atone for what I felt was a wrongful act, drinking myself to death wasn't the answer. He assured me that you and he expected better than that from me. I felt ashamed, but I believe it was a pivotal moment in my recovery.

He vowed to never tell you he knew our secret, Rosie, but I somehow regret not revealing this until now. Your father was a very dear man, and I shall miss him very much.

If there is anything I can do for you, Angie or your mother, don't hesitate. The boundary of time and space will never separate me from any of you. We're family.

As Always,
Me

September 29, 1986

Memo to Sachs:

You think you're so damned smart? I told you Strange Potions would sell faster than Lido. I didn't, however, expect Book Of The Month! Have a cigar on me. Please forward the enclosed dedication of SP.

To wit: For my father, and for Me.

1987

"If a man sitting alone, cannot dream strange things and make them look like the truth, he need never try to write romances."

- Nathaniel Hawthorne

March 13, 1987

Memo to Sachs:

Stop being so pissy. Perhaps you are insulted by these memos from my secretary, but don't forget I am now a yuppie just like you. Telephoning you consumes too much time of your endless advice. You're the one, after all, who secured a two-million-dollar advance for Excerpts, and now I'm the one facing not only the damned tax collector, but the twelve-month completion deadline as well.

As for your tirade over my lunch with Haddy Glover last week (how the hell do you find out these things?), she flew me out to New York and bought me filet mignon and Dom Perignon. (I didn't drink any – honest.) She believed she could woo and screw me into dropping you. Although she didn't remember, several years ago she sent Strange Potions back to me with a note saying, "We don't handle inexperienced writers."

After she pitched me and picked up the lunch tab, I returned her the note and said, "I'm sorry, Haddy, I can't be represented by an inexperienced agent. Wally Sachs believes in nobodies."

I've waited a long God damned time to do something like that! Jesus, it felt good!

So stop being mad at me. You are my agent forever. I love you. I want to have your children. You stayed with me even when my unsolicited manuscripts smelled of bad whiskey. I wouldn't stiff you now even if I did have lunch with a pooh-pooh from the largest literary agency in the solar system!

Please, do not have me killed as you promised.

Now, be a good boy and forward the dedication we forgot for the first edition of Lido:

To wit:
For The Chicago Seven: anarchists, liars and murderers, but otherwise a lot of laughs...

P.S. You never bought me filet mignon.

December 18, 1987

Dear Marie Rose,

Gad, it's Christmas again...

You were certainly nimble in passing along your Christmas card this year. I loved the picture of the family! How do you manage to stay so young and beautiful while I grow paunchy and wrinkled? You are as gorgeous as the first day we met. Gary is the luckiest man on earth.

Pass on my congratulations to James. Shame on you to report his accomplishments as if I know nothing about college football. In fact, I follow his every move at Oklahoma. If I survive my neurosis over the premiere of Children of Duty next week, I plan to jet to Miami and join you in cheering him on at the Orange Bowl! He flatters me with his kind words about my books, and I ask that you thank him for me. I'm astonished he read Lido as a required assignment for his English Literature class. In fact, I'm told it is served up in a dozen or so university courses around the country. The ink is barely dry, for God's sake...

Perhaps James can find time after football season to write to me and let me know what the reaction is in the scholarly community. The critics are dissecting the work and claiming it to be something I never imagined. I don't wish to complain, for the response has been flattering; however, I had no idea I was so brilliant! I had always fancied myself a bit of a goof.

As for the advice that James, the budding author, requested (asking me for career advice is somewhat like asking Rambo how to be charming). I can tell him this: Writing is a lonely lot in life. We're like Limburger cheese - few people like us, and even they think we stink. Writers tend to skulk through life, haunted by characters that brutally scratch and pound inside their brains. They find little right with the world, and are most happy when they're sitting alone in a room, immersed in a world that does not exist. In short, if James is neurotic, selfish, aloof, ignorant of the needs of those closest to him, an egotist, and he can type, he should make a fine writer of fiction. Above all else, he must lie.

As for Tommy, it sounds like he is doing well in medical school. I admire his persistence. If you will permit my opinion, however, with regard to Cynthia's pondering a career in law, I think it is quite irresponsible of you, Rosie, to allow such a notion. Nice human beings like Cynthia simply do not become lawyers. Tell her I have a sister who is a lawyer, and she is a vile and emotionless soul who stalks the world upon all fours. Tell young Cynthia that attorneys fall, in stature, just a cut above newspaper reporters, and a full step below child molesters. If she does not believe me, I shall introduce her to my lawyer. Please, My Rose, convince her to become a doctor, an astronaut, perhaps a fry cook, but do not encourage her to become a member of the Despicable Brethren. End of speech.

I'm sorry about Gary's gall bladder. He can do without it anyway. And congratulate him for me on becoming a scout master. Jesus, what's next? Sainthood?

And, I'm glad to hear for once that Angela is not pregnant.

In my brood, Mary and Justin continue planning their arts center. They moved to Toronto, where the city fathers greeted them with open arms. I'm able to devote most of my Lido royalties to their efforts, and they've been securing many wealthy patrons to get the ball rolling up there. Mary insists she is going to put my name on the building devoted to budding writers and poets, but I suggested that she might name one of the neighborhood pubs after me instead.

They envision the facility to be accessible to artists of all financial and ethnic classes. We patrons will offer sponsorship to anyone in need. It never ceases to amaze me how such a wonderful and philanthropic person like Mary came from the same womb as Lyla. It may baffle geneticists for the next century.

Jonathan is also, again, pregnant. It is a good thing he never knew Angela! He and Jennifer seem to be a human production line. I thought twins would have tempered their passions, but they hope for a second set! He continues to toil away as a police officer, scraping human debris off the streets and putting them before judges who promptly let them go. I say a prayer for him every night.

As for Vern, he became disillusioned with the New Age movement when he found out he had to pay a thousand dollars to hear Shirley MacLaine speak on how to talk to the dead. He retired from universe traveling, deciding his new religion is just a scam constructed by a washed-up actress in need of a gig.

He came back from California with a bad taste for all the metaphysical hocus-pocus and resolved to get back to his roots. I insisted that he quit looking for another career and retire, giving him an attractive checking account and access to a tax-free cash drawer. In return, he kissed me flush on the mouth. Finally able to enjoy some financial security, he started hanging out in bars where naked women dance on tables. It was at one of these places where he met Valerie, the girl of his dreams. I get this image of Vern's eyes full of stars, as Valerie is bent over and looking back at him between her legs.

Perhaps it isn't love made in Heaven, but Valerie quit her job and moved in with Vern. She is thirty-one and cusses a lot, but there's no doubt in my mind she loves Vern more than his money. Once I get past Valerie's vocabulary, and her gigantic silicone breasts, I find a very nice and caring girl who thinks Vern hung the moon.

As for your devoted pal, my new life allows me no time

to sit and feel sorry for myself. My nerves frayed months ago when the countdown to the Christmas premiere of Duty became a reality. After facing a mountain of production nightmares, budget overruns, and many other disasters Handley doesn't care to discuss, I'm told it is time to do, or die.

I didn't like the way John put that.

I had confidence in him all the way up to last week when he called and asked if I would be too disappointed if he trashed the entire project and tried something easier like a Japanese version of Gone With the Wind. He was joking, but I was not amused.

I, too, have mixed emotions about the premiere being held in Denver. John honors me with the choice, but the papers here are hyping the film and its 'native son' screen-writer as if this was the Second Coming. I haven't seen one second of the film and cannot even guess how good or bad it might be. I keep remembering the night we watched my play die in New York. At least back then no one knew me and I was able to sneak out of town without anyone giving a diddly. If this thing crumples, I picture my shocked face on the front page of the Denver Post.

The whole thing is puckering my navel.

Did I mention that?

Variety has not been able to find another subject to hype since Handley announced the premiere, and he's been appearing on morning shows, afternoon shows, Johnny (genuflect) Carson, and even Letterman. His damned face is on TV all the time. He planned the premiere early, so the movie would open all over the country on Christmas Day. However, last minute snags have pushed the premier to the evening of the 25th.

Today, I called him, but his secretary said he was in editing and could not be disturbed. Editing? Yeeks!

And this premiere thing. Never in my wildest dreams did I picture myself someday strutting into a theater in a tuxedo and rubbing elbows with Hollywood's Beautiful People. Gad, Handley's invited Coppola, Spielberg, Kubrick, and they're all planning to attend. Even Barbara Walters is coming.

I can't take this!

And, amidst all this insanity, my publisher wanted a rewrite of an entire chapter of the book version of Children of Duty. The damned thing is supposed to be packed and mailed to bookstores by now! I've spent hours at my word processor, restructuring the chapter. If that isn't enough, we're getting a titanic winter storm here, and my phones could die at any minute.

And I thought success would have found me sitting in a hot tub with Playboy bunnies by now.

Thank God for Duke, who arrived Tuesday. In fact, as I write this letter, he and my secretary are cursing me for taking a moment to breathe and send my Christmas greeting to you. We're going to take the rewrites to New York in a few hours. We'll pick up Mary, Justin, Doug Moon and Doug's wife there to bring them back with us for the premiere. Sometime during all of this, I hope I can get some sleep.

Jon, Jenny, Vern, and Valerie came up here to my buried mountain retreat and are awaiting our departure so they can bulldoze this place and make it livable for company. Mary and Justin will stay here this week while Duke and his sons, Hayman, Jack Putnam, Eddie Strauss, Doug, Wally, and all their respective families are staying downtown at a hotel. The whole family is going to be here!

Pray for me, Rosie. I'm sorry that you and your clan cannot make it for the big show, but don't think for one moment that I don't understand your important Christmas plans. This is a big week for James, and he will need all of you to cheer him on in Miami next week. Your attendance in spirit means more than I will be able to convey in this letter.

Pray, too, for Children of Duty. Its success along with the two bestsellers may finally give me a glimmer of hope for that time in the hot tub! (I was just kidding about the bunnies.) As I wrinkle in the water, perhaps I'll have a moment to wonder if this just isn't a rare good dream. Time will not allow too much wondering, however, for I'm facing another deadline next month for final rewrites of a novel which I believe is my best work yet.

More on that later, for Duke is insulting my mother and pulling me away from this letter. We have two hours to plow down the interstate and make a plane. Grab the snowshoes!

Merry Christmas, Rosie!

As Always,
Me

December 18, 1987

Editors: Please find enclosed Children of Duty rewrites; note attached dedication.

To wit:

For Jimmy, Emory, and all the children...

1988

"He who has never failed somewhere, that man cannot be great. Failure is the true test of greatness"

- Herman Melville

January 4, 1988

Got in from Miami last night. Slept for eighteen hours. When I woke up, I wanted to go to bed. Sorry to ignore you, Journal, but that bed simply felt too good. I'll fill you in now. It's nice to have some peace and quiet in the house.

Rest assured, there's no turning back now. I only hope becoming a part of the public domain won't take from us the privacy we've enjoyed for all these years. Journal, I love you. I don't suppose I've ever told you, and I apologize for assuming you'd simply know. I love Me.

Good times can make good songs, sometimes.

I've basked in glory for several weeks now. But, I'm a bit glum.

Must be withdrawal. The house is so empty now that everyone has gone home. This hollow feeling cannot be due to the film. Children of Duty has gone into orbit; the novel sold out its first printing before it ever left the press, and there are back-orders for the second printing.

America is demanding us now. Twenty years ago, she spat on us. Times do change.

Time to relax, Journal, that's what we need. The phones are unplugged, and Sachs thinks I'm busily into Excerpts rewrites, which should keep him from dispatching the mounties when I don't answer the phone. Let's rest.

The Duty manuscript drained more from me than the screenplay, but it was a necessary labor to take advantage of the commercial appeal the film generated. This crapshoot will hit a major jackpot, thanks to the brilliance of John Handley.

Good God. I just opened a notice from my publisher. Another two-million royalty from Duty just deposited in my account. The studio deposited five yesterday. I never really thought about making this kind of money from my ghosts...

It isn't that I oppose making a dollar; God knows I spent enough years in need of one or two, but it isn't my wish to create lesser work that has mass appeal at the expense of compromising my art. The screenplay was a necessity, but I wish to be a novelist, and the Duty novel seemed to be old news for me. I found myself trying to win a war that I won long ago, and writing the book was work, not my obsession. I resolve, from this day forward I will create work of my own choosing; I long for the spirit of Lido and Mr. Chunks. I long for the heart of Excerpts. This year, I'll let out more ghosts and see who they might be. If they're rich too, I guess that's alright.

For now, however, I must feel proud of Duke and Me. We created a script from which John was able to paint a masterpiece. His stunning images left the critics breathless in the wake of the harsh and often devastating portrayal of the Vietnam War. The work of the young cast was simply staggering. Most of those young boys were not even alive when the real men were fighting that war. One of them approached me after the premiere with tears in his eyes, and said, "I knew I was acting, but I felt the terror. Seeing it in context on the screen horrified me. How did you ever survive it?"

"I'm not certain I did," I said. "I hope it's something you remember to tell your children..."

The film had a similar effect on everyone. Handley told a story about a war, humanity, insurrection, violence, and conflict without a moral to the tale. He condemned no man; he simply told the truth. I found it amazing to watch cold film critics emerge from the theater with swollen eyes. They trembled at the chest-pounding huey scenes, laughed only when the boys could laugh, and cried for them when they died. My only reservation is the stark realism Handley created, which might bring too close the memory for the veterans who will see this film. I hope they see the truth in this story about what

Coppola first called The Apocalypse - a war of the soul.

I was moved when a crusty old critic from the New York Times approached me at the post-premiere party. He took me by the shoulders and said with wet eyes: "How wrong we all were to condemn the warrior instead of war..."

Indeed, you liberal bastard. Better late than never, I guess, but media hypocrites nauseate me no matter how well presented...

I'm spent, Journal, but inside of me remains the spark to finish Excerpts, which calls with promise and hope.

But, what a time this has been! I don't know when I ever enjoyed a Christmas more. What a joy to reunite with my best friends, some of whom I expected, and several I did not.

Of course, sharing all of this time with Duke has been terrific. I have such great admiration for him, my real father. How often I forget the man is in his seventies now. He is so energetic. He indeed has lived such an exciting life. And yet, he found time somewhere along the road to raise two fine sons who stood with great pride at the premiere.

When the movie ended, Duke took my hand and smiled. "We finally let it go, kiddo," he said, "we finally let it go..." I always smile when I think of Duke Winslow, and I know I always will.

Then, there is Doug Moon with his ghost-like Jimmy smile. He has such warmth and charm, and there is so much of his little brother in him. He wrapped his big arms around me and whispered in my ear: "Jimmy would have loved it, Shakes..."

Doug and Georgia brought Emory Ruson along. He looks so much like Jimmy that I couldn't help shedding a tear when we met. He proudly wore Jimmy's Medal of Honor around his neck. Imagine, he said it was an honor to meet Dutch and me. He hugged us both...

And, good old Dutch 'Don't Call Me Charlie' Hayman. He is much more refined in The World. He's a gentle family man. The only reminder of his war days is the chewed-up cigar and that old switchblade 'Betsy,' which he now uses just to dig under his fingernails. I love him even more now, with his potbelly stomach wriggling from laughter at stories about treetop flyers: "Then Shakes takes a round in the foot," Dutch said, laughing so hard that the beer resting on his belly toppled, "and out he goes! Out the door just when Maje lifts off! 'Hep!' he hollers, 'Hep me!' - and I look over and all I see is these two legs kickin' in the air!"

I never thought I could laugh about that day, but I was in tears with everyone else.

Hayman cried at the movie. When it ended, he sobbed in my arms and kissed me flush on the mouth.

"All these years we ain't been together, but I still love you like my brother," he wept. "I never thanked you for saving my life, Shakes."

"The kiss was a bit over the top, Dutch,'" I said. Our tears turned to laughter...

Then there was Major Jack Putnam, my life-saver. He hasn't aged a day since Soc Trang, except for perhaps a gray hair here or there. He doesn't fly six inches above the trees anymore, but he says he occasionally has the desire to fly his 747 ass-above-nose into O'Hare. I asked him if United needed any door gunners just in case the critics panned our film...

Eddie Strauss, the cowboy-pirate, and now movie star. After the movie, he came up and nearly squeezed all the air out of me.

"You remember I once told you to tell the truth, Shakes?"

"I never forgot it, sir," I said.

He just smiled.

Strauss stood out at the premiere in his black velvet tuxedo, accented by a purple eye patch tied to his shaved head. In the film, his Marine colonel dominated the scenes in which he appeared. As an actor, the old colonel was quite competent, and he confessed he is seriously considering an offer from Handley to appear in his next outer space adventure.

"You look like something from Mars," I told him. "Why

not let Handley make you famous?..."

Those friends share with me one common link in a long chain of life, but I'll cherish the bond that at one time held the key to my survival. It was wonderful for all of us to be together for perhaps one last time.

And the magic of the day was not limited to just the reunion of old war friends: When we all arrived at the theater, I was taken aback by the sight of a man sitting in a wheelchair. He deliberately wheeled up to me and smiled while waiting for me to recognize him.

It was Steven Joel. My friend, Steven.

In that chair sat a whole man. His hair was cropped short, the beard was gone, and his smelly, unwashed clothes were replaced by a splendid tuxedo. On his lapel was his Purple Heart medal.

For a moment, we simply looked at each other, both of us trying to contain our tears. Then, he reached for my hand and he pulled me down to hug me.

"I don't have tickets for the movie," he said, "but I told them I know the big shot hero who wrote this thing. You mind if we crash the party?"

Accompanying Steven were his mother and father, his brother Chris, and a very lovely lady who introduced herself as Steven's wife.

"I'd be honored," I said.

Damn, I was in tears and the movie hadn't even started yet.

When his family went in, Steven and I hesitated. "You know," Steven said, "the night you left me in that hospital, I promised myself I was going to get out of there and kick your ass. But somewhere along the way I realized I can't punch a guy who makes a living of saving lives." He reached for my hand and I took it. "You're a good hero, old buddy..."

I'm not the hero, Journal. Steven is.

But that wasn't the height of this night, if that can be believed, Journal. I must digress back to the morning of the premier:

Christmas morning, we gathered at my home early and exchanged gifts under the tree. Everyone was here, and the place looked more like a hotel than the quiet mountain retreat of a reclusive writer. I had engaged a catering company for the week. They set up a huge brunch complete with a crew to clean up the mess so we could all get down to the important business of preparing for the premiere. By the afternoon, utter chaos prevailed as we all scurried about, pinning our gowns, doing our hair, straightening our cummerbunds, plucking our nose hair, and generally trying to prepare to hobnob with The Beautiful People. At the same time, we dodged in and out of the menagerie of children who were destroying my house with new Christmas toys. As I barked final instructions to the frustrated baby sitter, Mary called for me to come upstairs. She needed to be zipped up.

"Use your husband!" I hollered. "That's why you married him!"

"He's in the shower! Come on, help me!"

Annoyed, I limped up the stairs, mumbling, "A famous Hollywood screenwriter, and I have to rescue my baby sister from a zipper..."

When I came in her room, Mary was already zipped.

"Thanks," she said. "But I got it." No apology. She just smiled, gave me a big kiss on the cheek, and told me to get out.

"Wench," I grumbled as I turned to go back downstairs. But, when I reached the top of the stairs, I stopped as if run flat by the old '58 Cadillac. Looking down the staircase, my eyes perceived my memory's most wonderful vision.

Marie Rose.

She stood at the foot of the stairs next to Vern, dressed in a white gown that would humble the angels. I was speechless.

Vern laughed at me. "We got you a date," he said.

Journal, I would trade all of this success for just another look at my Rosie, my dearest friend. It is as if my heart resumes its beat every time I see her again. I let out an undignified yowl and nearly fell down the stairs before giving her a backbreaking hug.

"I can't believe you're here!" I said. "I thought you were in Miami."

"James had to be in Miami today," Rosie said, "and everyone went down with him. But they dropped me off so I could go to the movies with you."

Rosie was then buried in hugs from the family as they explained to me how the surprise had come about. She cooked it up with Duke, Vern and Mary. Vern had conveniently forgotten his tuxedo, no surprise to anyone, and left the house for Denver that morning. Instead, he met Rosie at the plane and brought her up.

Indeed, this triumph would not have been complete if I could not have shared it with her. So much has been sacrificed, and I know I might not even be here if not for Rosie's belief in me.

And what a grand evening we had! As if we were truly important people, we rode up in pretentious limos. This was my family: Duke, Malcolm and Doris, Carl and Linda; Wally Sachs and his wife, Ruth; Mary, Justin, Jon, Jenny, Vern, Valerie (side note: Valerie's peek-a-boo gown made the pages of People Magazine!); Doug and Georgia Moon; Emory Ruson; Dutch and Charlotte Hayman; Jack and Carol Putnam; and Eddie and Cora Strauss.

The reviews of the movie were quite flattering - in fact, the critics unanimously predict an Academy Award. But I imagine the only criticism may come from Barbara Walters. Perhaps she'll label me as one of the year's ten worst dressed, for I emerged from our limo in my tuxedo, wearing a beat-up New York Yankees baseball cap turned backwards.

It was our triumph. My only regret: There wasn't one more limo for Mother, Dad, and Jimmy...

Is it any wonder, Journal, why I now sit here drained of emotion? Here I sit in my lovely kingdom alone. The clock struck midnight and I'm back to being a rather well-known nobody.

Buyer's remorse perhaps? By most standards of success, I've made it. I turned my dreams to reality, but to accomplish this much, I made a trade. I'm alone.

To only you, Journal, I admit I'm still helplessly in love with Marie Rose Robbins. Did the ignorance of my youth prevent me from finding a way to have it all? I traded a life with her for this life I have. I pray what I've given The World is of equal value, for the cost to me has been very dear. At least, thank God, if I could not traverse this life with Rosie by my side, I could at least live it with her in my heart.

First love was best; and last...

January 5, 1988

Dear Marie Rose,

What a joy it was to have seen you after all of these years! Thank you for sharing a special time with me here, and thank you and Gary for allowing me to share in your family's fun in Miami. But most importantly, Rosie, thank you for being my friend.

You've believed in me; and you gave me reason to believe in myself. God bless you.

As Always,
Me

June 4, 1988

Memo to Sachs:

Elvis gave Cadillacs. I've never cared for them. The fact that The King is dead is proof he had bad taste in cars. A Ferrari does not fit your image because you are too stuffy. A Rolls, however, is perfect for you, so please accept it with my love.

Don't thank me, for I'm thanking you. I hope it will replace my having your children. I'm going to stay funny because maudlin makes me cry.

Nobody, not even Duke, could have persuaded you to stay with me if you didn't believe in my work. You've tolerated my whining, my bizarre proposals, my abhorrent alcoholism, and worst of all, my memos. Of those four, you must still suffer three.

Recently, I stood frozen with terror before the Almighty Academy and forty million TV viewers as Duke and I accepted little Oscar for best screenplay. Because I was overwhelmed with nervousness, I don't remember if I publicly thanked you for helping to make it all happen. If I remembered, it might not have cost me a Rolls Royce, but to be safe, I hope you like it.

There is no way to express how much I appreciate you, but one thing is for sure, you can't have my Oscar. He's standing next to Mickey Mouse on my desk and that's where he's going to stay.

Now, before you and Ruth take a joy ride, please earn your points and forward the following dedication of Excerpts to my editor.

To wit:
For Rosie, forever.

P.S. Keep those hands at ten and two!

December 13, 1988

Dear Marie Rose,

Beat you to the punch this year, My Rose! The reason I'm so efficient is that I'm vacationing, well deserved I might add. I'm sitting on the beach at the Breakers Hotel in West Palm Beach with nothing to do but write Christmas cards. That's right, I left my stories at home and don't care to write anything for the next four weeks. I did, however, wake up at three this morning with a delicious idea for a new tale and simply had to jot it down. Let's call this a busman's holiday anyway.

So here I am on the sand with a bunch of delightful old and fat New York Jews. They call me their token goy. I'm entrenched here, sipping pineapple juice and drooling over the near-naked prostitutes who wiggle by. I'm not their catch, but I believe I've uncovered the secret of attracting the attention of near-naked young women. To think it took me forty-three years to find all you have to do is be rich and hang out on the beach with a bunch of fat old men!

Rather than hiring someone to give me the perfect fatal disease, however, I'll just be content to drool while I sunburn myself and write a card to my favorite human.

Actually, I'm not alone on this holiday, for I brought Jon and the 'Jon-Squad,' and Vern and Valerie (they're married now!). I sent Jon and Jenny with the troops to Disney World for the rest of the week because I was losing my sanity with those little twits running around. They kept asking old Uncle Me to piggyback them into the ocean in search of the Great White Shark. Fat chance.

Vern and Valerie spent a few days with me on the beach, but Vern was getting tired of the endless stream of lifeguards parading past his bride. Her bathing suit is more of a Band-Aid than anything else. I gave them an early Christmas present by making reservations for them at a nude beach not far from here. Well, it was something they've always wanted...

So, alas, here be Me in the sand by the sea...

And now for the news: Vern and Val are moving to the mountains. I got a great deal on a beautiful little place near Estes Park and surprised them for Christmas. Vern broke down and cried, and Valerie knocked the wind out of me with a big hug. They're an odd couple, but they are deliriously happy in each other's company. I believe they were meant for each other in an odd, demented sort of way. I put them on a nine-week Scandinavian cruise for their honeymoon last summer, and next February they're going to tour the Orient for two months. It warms my heart to see Vern so happy, in love, and not communicating with aliens anymore!

Mary and Justin are happily in the red with the arts center in Toronto. The first phase of construction was completed in August, and they began auditioning students for the center's maiden voyage, scheduled to launch this spring semester. They anticipate the entire project will be completed in five years. Mary insists that I drop by to lecture once in awhile, although that would seem foreign to me. But, anything for my little girl! The remainder of this vacation will be spent up there as we wing to Canada for Christmas and New

Year's.

Jon and Jennifer are again pregnant. Someone needs to plug them both. This is number six, for God's sake! He resigned from the police last June to our collective relief. It was a difficult decision for him, but he based it on two factors: After three successive close calls with little gun-toting gang members, he feared he was losing his nerve - perhaps a premonition that he might leave that huge family by themselves. Secondly, the stress from those incidents was taxing him and he was sneaking away for a drink now and then to 'relax.' We've decided that sneaking off 'to relax' in this family is a no-no. Luckily, Jon realized he was playing with fire(water).

I think Jon was star-struck by the premiere last year. He has a serious interest in film-making and writing, and he's taking classes at the community college. I'm encouraging him, and we've set up a trust for the family so he can explore these new avenues in financial comfort. Unfortunately, they spoil their children, and I'm certain they train them to torment me.

Duke, by the way, said to be certain to send his regards. Before I left for Florida, I spoke with him on the phone and casually said I was pondering a cruise to Tahiti next year sometime; he, in turn, mentioned he was going to Cairo to see the pyramids for the first time in his life. The next morning, I awoke to the sound of steel drums as an entourage of dancing girls and a calypso band pounded into my house and treated me to a huge luau. They handed me a card: "Merry Christmas, Duke." Not to be outdone, I had a live camel delivered to his front yard.

So, 1988 comes to a close, and what a year it was! I pray you've enjoyed a good one, and wish your family happy holidays. I have not been terribly humble in enjoying the success of Children of Duty, Lido, and Strange Potions making the bestseller list in a short span. Since most of my life has been spent trying to kill myself, I figure I have the right to gloat for a time. The Duty novel did not persevere as a bestseller after the movie ran its course, but I have great pride in the work and was happy for the Academy Awards bestowed upon it. We have received thousands of letters from veterans who appreciated the film's empathy and its rightful portrayal of those true heroes.

But, onward we go. Handley has returned to making movies about little green men, and he recently tantalized me with a proposal for a script about some real-life fellow who has 'documented proof' of his abduction by little people in a UFO. It's all rather frivolous, but it might be fun to work with John again on something less taxing.

Until that happens, I am now anxiously awaiting the release of my latest, and my best work to date, and it is now that I wish to tell you about it. The book has been my secret passion, and I am greatly encouraged by the reaction of several critics who previewed the manuscript last month. Critical review is a sorry nature of the business of art, a necessary evil that can kill a novel before it ever sees the light of day. I dare say, by the present-day standard of literary success as viewed by today's critics, some of the world's greatest writers might have never found their way onto a publisher's production schedule if there appeared no mass appeal to the average reader's questionable intellect. Fortunately, I haven't been executed by the critics so far. Perhaps some of my work is simply so bizarre that no one considers it anything but bad luck to pan a koo-koo like me, but I believe this new work may again pass that commercial test.

However, even though I've garnered my publisher's trust by cultivating an audience that reads literary works like Lido and Strange Potions, I would not be disappointed if this work of the same ilk, entitled Excerpts, fell off the Safeway shelf the first day. It is by far my most substantive work because it was written not for the public, but for you, and for Me. (If, however, Wally Sachs gets wind of this confession, I'll deny it.)

In fact, if it had not been for the not-so gentle prodding of my dear pal, Sachs, I might not have shown it to him. I cautioned him at the time that this manuscript was final and not open to the brutal swipe of an editor's pen. Fortunately, my publisher agreed the work was suitable as is, despite the risk of it appealing to a narrow scope of readers.

Indeed, I wrote this for you, Rosie, and I wrote it for Me. When we last were together, I was touched when you mentioned you were involved in your community's unwed mother shelter. That you feel you are helping yourself through helping those young girls is a similar feeling I have derived from writing this novel. By writing Excerpts, I've been able to experience a certain degree of atonement for our mistake of long ago.

The story is a fictional piece, but it was written to say that love between certain souls inevitably survives regardless of where their lives lead - either together or apart. It is dedicated to your understanding of how I truly value the meaning of your existence in my life as friend and inspiration. Secondly, it serves as penitence - to right a wrong that caused me to live many years apart from myself. I believe, to ensure eternal strength with my God, He and I must get along. By writing Excerpts, I now feel fully anchored to those whose lives to me are so dear.

There are others to whom I've owed similar debts, but to you, Rosie, there can be no minor consideration less than this work. Excerpts is our life, not our history; it's what our friendship stands for, but it is also the essence of what we are. I hope you'll honor me by accepting the first copy with my respect for you and your lovely, decent family. It shall have wings when the ink dries!

As Always,
Me

8

Passage

1992

"He made the stars also."

- Genesis 1:16

April 14, 1992

I shall miss him, Journal. He never in his life hesitated to say "I love you," and those were his passing words as his fading hand weakened in Valerie's. Vern's dark eyes turned to me, and there was the faintest smile. Then, he was gone.

Vern was born near the railroad yards in the blustery cold northern Colorado winter back in the days when Edison and Ford were pushing man into the future. Vernon Hill was the second son born to Alder and May. He was brought screaming into a world destined for miraculous change. Vern accepted every new shift, while his brother - my father - rejected them. They were sons of a hard-drinking railroad engineer and a 19th-century woman who stood perplexed by the swirl of emerging technology. Dad and Vern searched for their lives through the black-gray haze of coal smoke. Vern found peace within the possession of himself. Dad was owned by the bottle that killed him and his father and father before.

Vern was more my father than was my real dad. He was my friend, and my mentor. When my days were darkest, he was the sunshine. He found peace as a traveler, an experimenter and a lover of all that touched him, despite the difficult times he himself faced. Vern was a loner, seldom with close companions, yet, many were honored to be called his friend. In his final years on this earth, when time slowed his gait, he found love most unusual. That was Vern.

Despite his eccentricities and faults, my uncle was a giver and never a taker. He was happy to be just another face in the crowd, and although his memory will never live beyond the handful of those he left in this world, his smile, his spirit, and his heart shall live forever. A good man, Vern.

Shortly after his stroke and the inevitable dawning of his numbered days, Vern raised his cool hand to mine in a private moment and spoke to me with weak, labored breath. Though his words were slurred and soft, his meaning was clear. "Care for my Val," he whispered.

I touched his dry face, and I promised. Vern and Valerie wanted for nothing as far as material goods were concerned.

My only regret is they did not have more time together to enjoy each other and our successes. I'll keep my promise to be certain Valerie will be comfortable, and that she'll share in our legacy. But I have a sad feeling that Val, who is certainly a much prettier version of Vern himself, shall eventually pull up stakes and move on. If that is so, I will see that she remains subsidized by the trust intended for both of them.

Au revoir, Vern; Je t'aime

1993

December 19, 1993

Dear Marie Rose,

I remember a day when it seemed an eternity between sunsets; and now, years swiftly pass at the blink of an eye! The only bright light that shines upon my body's slow demise is Christmas time, because it means I shall hear from you.

The family photo did you all justice, as usual. It is unfair, however, that my body is not governed by the more merciful canons of age that command you. How is it that you retain your teenage beauty while I resemble a prune? With each gray hair you fraudulently claim invades your frock, your radiant glow takes a silvery countenance, while my gray frosting looks more like someone has been smoking my head.

What a long and enjoyable letter you wrote! I wonder just what sum of money we have spent in correspondence over the years. For our legacy of words alone, I have hundreds of volumes stored in my safe. Your latest edition brought me such great joy and pride in your achievements and those of Gary and the children. First, let me congratulate Gary on his retirement. He has an exciting plan to write a textbook, and by all means, when the work takes shape and is ready for a critique, I would certainly persuade Wally Sachs to give it his attention and consideration. I am not well-versed in Gary's field and the potential of publishers for his work, but dear Walter is a chameleon within the hideous jungle of publishing. He would know where to turn over the right rocks. For a writer, there is no better friend in this world than Wally.

Now, for your congratulations! Doctor Rosie! San Jose State could not have made a better choice in appointing you to their faculty. Must I now address all upcoming letters to Marie Rose Tobias Ph.D.?

I can't believe Tommy will be entering private medical practice next summer! It simply does not seem that long ago you were writing of his exploits in high school. As for James,

I believe the support you give him is admirable and correct as he searches for his path in life. He mustn't allow his unfortunate failure in athletics to discourage him. He is not the first man to dream of a professional football career only to have it dashed by the realities of a hard business in which to succeed. I wish him well and would be happy to refer him to Malcolm Winslow, Duke's son, if he is serious about pursuing a sports-writing career. And, as for Cynthia, what a lovely young woman she has turned into. How can it be she is now teaching History at a high school? Damn that clock!

Now, for my report: This year's chronicle will contain a rare appearance by someone who had been exiled from my traditional Christmas greetings, except for an occasional slur from Yours Truly.

Several months ago, I was taken by surprise when I received a letter from my long-forgotten sister Lyla, who, for some unrevealed purpose, has found reason to offer a truce with me. Her letter was strangely emotional, even sorrowful, which is quite uncharacteristic. She requested that I search myself for some reason to accept her offering of peace, and she apologized for boring the deep chasm separating us all these years. She confessed pride in my recent success, and concluded that she wished for no conditions to this reconciliation; just a wish for peace with no other agenda.

You can imagine my astonishment. I might have first expected the earth to spin backwards before I would hear such words from Lyla. But, rather than casting her letter aside, I simply sat and wept. I am now weighted with guilt, blast it all! Over these years, I developed a certain joy in my hatred for her, and now she flings me into this morass. She left nothing but a post box number for my reply to ensure her sincerity. After all, I'm certain she'd think I'd suspect she might just want to make peace with me perhaps for a later financial favor.

I could not have written my reply with any more haste. In years past it would have been my pleasure to lock and load my pen to ambush my elder sister in this, her apparent moment of truth. But that was before I could recognize my image in the mirror. I may not yet completely trust her motives, but I have no right to question her apparent sincerity. I wrote that I honored the truce and shunned her request for forgiveness, deeming it unnecessary. The shots were fired from both sides, I said, and perhaps we are better suited to move forward. What relief I experienced when I mailed the letter! Peace, Lyla.

Onward: Christmas without Vern is as empty this year as the last. I'm sad to report I hear very little from Valerie with the exception of Christmas cards. The latest was sent with the love and affection she's always shown for us. She moved to Maine so she could care for her grandmother, and she works for the telephone company. That along with her trust makes her life comfortable, but I detected a lingering pain she has at the loss of Vern. It was a remarkable change in her when Vern entered her life. I only wish they had found each other sooner.

Mary and Justin's life is secure and happy. Their enterprise is growing rapidly and both of them have a busy schedule running the arts center and performing when they can. But something is missing from their lives in my opinion. Last Thanksgiving in Toronto, we were sharing one of our traditional midnight conversations when it happened again. Shortly after the release of Excerpts, Mary called to give her usual can-do-no-wrong review, but in the course of her sisterly accolades, she began to cry. The story touched in her something much deeper than simple sibling pride. Nothing further was said at the time, but in our conversation last month, Mary confided she had been quite moved by the work. She has never exhibited a matronly side, for her career has always taken precedence over her personal life. Mary tearfully confided, however, that she and Justin would like to start a family, but they are having difficulty. I had not thought of it until then, but it now saddens me to see how Mary and Justin make over Jon and Jenny's children with such longing...

Alas, because I'm retired from the psychiatric profession, I should steer clear. But, while still on the subject, I have it on good authority that Jon and Jennifer have stopped their baby assembly line with the birth of number seven, Vernon, last January. Another Vern, God help us! Unfortunately, Jon's fatherly success lies in contrast with his professional writing aspirations. For a short and unnerving interval last spring, Jon stumbled over frustrations, and he slipped into the bottle, which threatened the sanctity of his family, and incurred my wrath. The fall was brought on by continued failure in his creative endeavors. Jon's screenplay has suffered endless rejections, complete with harsh criticism of his skills. I'm afraid I have not been able to refute them because, as a beginner, Jon simply has not yet developed into a consistent craftsman. Understandably, the rejection hurt.

He began with occasional binges, but those quickly turned into all-nighters as he started disappearing into the black void of booze that has hovered over our family like a plague. I simply could not stand by and watch him destroy himself and his family. I intervened and sat Jon down, pointing out the reality of this disease we all have and how it has literally killed so many of us. Thank God he listened. Jon has the capacity to see many sides of himself. Once I calmed him in his fit of insecurity, he turned away from the booze and looked instead to his family for support. I'm greatly relieved as you can imagine.

For Me, I'm tired, My Rose. Exhausted. John Handley managed to squeeze every creative drop from me in last year's completion of Sky Lights. I could barely muster any enthusiasm for the film's success due to the deadlines imposed upon me for two new novels. Since October, even my journal entries are unimaginative, and I'm beginning to suspect I'm suffering the infamous writer's block no doubt brought on by such an intense schedule. My publisher is asking for new proposals, but my mind is blank. I've been trying to fire my creativity, hiding away in my mountain abode and searching for something new and unusual. Unfortunately, I find myself fascinated simply watching the snow fly. My usually prolific head is filled with concrete!

In the meantime, I have accepted a few lecture offers, but I have never been comfortable at the podium, especially when it engages me with university masters and doctoral candidates. Some boob once published a paper defending my 'genius;' that I'm a 'modern master,' for Christ's sake. I frustrate audiences with my flippant attitude, but I honestly don't understand some of this symbolism they see in my work. The scholarly praise is flattering, but I don't perceive myself in the company of the masters. They just refuse to believe the fact that I'm just a lucky fool who's made eighty million off my ghosts. I recently sat with these stuffy idlers for three hours, my face growing pale in light of their cerebral praise of Moonpie. They declared it a 'metaphysical journey into the New Age.' But, Rosie, Moonpie is just a tale about a clumsy time traveler who takes a wrong turn in the cosmos and lands in a 1968 Queens bakery, which he mistakes for the White House. It was two hundred and thirty-six pages of silly satire, but now it's called a literary masterpiece? Please!

Why am I misunderstood, Rosie? I don't believe the money they give me for sitting in front of my computer and giggling at my own stuff!

I wonder sometimes if Picasso simply took his brush and said: "I believe I'll put this gal's nose where her navel should be, and I'll put her boob by her ear just for grins!"

He probably sat back and laughed when everyone then looked at the painting and said, "Well, I suppose if it is Picasso, it must be art."

What I need is inspiration, something with sex and sizzle. All I see right now are snow-covered pine trees. It's the world, I believe; the world has grown boring and more stupid than at any time in the history of mankind. It leaves me with nothing formidable to lampoon. Bill Clinton is too much a moron to be believed, and Jay Leno, too ugly. What am I to do?

Alas, My Rose, I'll come up with something. For now, I'll say Merry Christmas and convey my wishes for a happy new year to you and family. Peace.

As Always,
Me

1994

November 29, 1994

Memo to Sachs: Attached dedication for Fixing Trees.

To wit:

For my cat, Macbeth. In most every case, I like him better than humans.

P.S. Glad you blew out the kidney stone, Walter.
Wondered why you were so grumpy.

1996

May 30, 1996

Memo to Sachs: So sorry I forgot to forward the dedications. Am sending them ship-to-shore from somewhere in the Caribbean. Jealous? Your wire sounded frantic, and I believe you may have broken some law transmitting the obscenities, but never fear, Me is here. I'll have you know I had to leave an icy ginger ale and a beautiful, stuffed bikini-clad shuffleboard partner to come and send this. Here goes:

For *Clobberhead,* to wit:
For Vern, the biggest one.

For *Woman's Tear,* to wit:
For Mary.

P.S. That wasn't so hard, was it? Now you can straighten your colon.

1998

June 19, 1998

Journal, whose idea was it to go on a safari? Do you really think this bounty of four hundred or so photos of snakes, spiders and one blurry tiger some two hundred yards away might ever replace the splendor of vacationing by the ocean? Africa is horrid. I know not when I have ever been happier to get back to Casa Me. Gad, I'm a walking one hundred and eighty-five-pound mosquito bite!

Ah, to be home. There must be a hundred letters to open, but one is from Marie Rose. Drop everything!

June 19, 1998

Dear Marie Rose,

I called and spoke with Tommy. He told me you are spending time in Avalon and cannot be reached there by phone, but he gave me your address. I have only read your letter of May 17 today, for I have been out of the country since April.

My Rose, how could I ever adequately express my shock and sorrow at the news of Gary's passing? Tommy told me he had been suffering from cancer for over a year. Why did you keep this from me? I don't suppose my knowing would have made matters easier, but I love you both so dearly and wish I might have been able to provide some comfort. I am so terribly sorry and want you to know I am at your call should you need anything.

As Always,
Me

June 20, 1998

I came to know him well, Journal. Such a loss; my heart aches for Rosie. Gary was a noble man who loved her dearly and gave her all she deserved in their life together. God bless him for being the man she loved and needed, and for unselfishly sharing her with me.

I am indeed the selfish one, Journal. My grief encompasses more than Rosie's loss. I grieve for me because I am alone. Here I sit in my kingdom in my beloved mountains possessed of more than everything I ever wanted, save one thing. Who may I share all of this with except for a scruffy cat who might be just as happy dining in trash bins than here at the palace?

I have turned around the sun fifty-two times in this solo flight, and it grows more apparent with every pass that I shall complete the journey alone. I cannot count the number of women I have encountered through the years; some are quite alluring and some downright provocative - every one enjoyable for brief companionship, but I have simply felt no spark of interest beyond the occasional, albeit weak, cry from my aging loins. It leaves me quite damned alone. Welcome, self-pity. My old pal.

I grieve for Gary, but am jealous that he had a good life within the love of one wonderful woman. If I would die tonight, how long might I lie here before anyone missed me? Certainly, I have Jon, Jenny, and Mary and Justin - I had a long romance, and I had a marriage, but there is no one with whom I have fully shared my heart other than my first teenage love; my Rosie. And it has been decades since I had that. I'm an emotional cripple, married to my muse. I have made my bed.

And I'm alone.

Is the compensation of health, wealth, and the discretion of a king enough? Perhaps. I've not suffered a life in exile, and I cannot say I've been unhappy. My successes have outweighed the struggle.

And so, how does one measure happiness? Is it dispensed from a can? I have truly given little thought to what it is that creates fulfillment of mind and heart other than to strive to do and be what I want. It's not unreasonable to believe my achievements might never have been realized if it had not been for the many unsavory moments of my earlier years. Depression's ugly blade scarred me, but motivated me as well. I might have never given to my work as I did if not for the severity of my times in the black hole. It, too, has now given me reason to greet each new day with the enthusiasm of my teens when I envisioned the world as a land to conquer. I've learned not to fear the ghosts in my head, but rather, to love them. They now live with me in harmony as I turn them into enterprise rather than sorrow. Since coming to grips with them, I have never written so clearly, as their stories jump from my head to the paper, delighting readers, and making publishers richer. I now collect a bounty for the head of every ghost and nightmare that ever haunted me.

They have created all that now surrounds me. Even with my twisted mind I never could have imagined such material wealth.

Had it taken another direction, had I married Rosie and had a family, life might have been different, but at what cost?

God bless Gary Tobias, and thank you for loving Rosie.

1999

June 22, 1999

Memo to Sachs: Wally, thank you for wiring me about Duke. God, how I wish I could be there. Please extend my condolences to Malcolm and Carl, and please let them know I am dreadfully sorry I could not attend Duke's funeral. This strikes at an unbelievably terrible time. We are in the throes of a disaster, and now my mind is shot with grief for Duke. God damn, I knew he was ill; I suspected this was coming, and yet, I'm devastated now that it has happened.

Do not, repeat, do not ask how the film is going. It isn't. I hate Brazil, and I'm beginning to hate my little brother, too. Jon is impossible. I am losing money by the barrel and am about to pull the plug on the entire production. Jon simply has no talent for this business.

Why, you schmuck, did you not tie me up and shoot me when you had the chance? I know you told me Jon had no talent, but why didn't you make me listen? You know how I am when it comes to family. Jon and I are at each other's throats. Wally, I implore you: If my brother ever speaks to me again, and his words are: "I have a great idea for a film, and I need your help," please, Wally, I beg you...shoot me.

God, I'll miss Duke. It seems everyone close to me is dying. Please don't forget to send the boys my love.

2002

December 15, 2002

Dear Marie Rose,

Merry Christmas! I was dropping into my traditional funk when your card arrived, and as usual, you brought me from the depths! I don't know how I'd survive Christmas without you. But first, let me say I am concerned about your heart illness. Do not think for one moment that you comfort me with your doctor's reassurance that the situation is controlled and you feel fine. We're not kids anymore! We are fifty-six, missy, and we're not at liberty to gorge at hamburger stands these days! I've developed this damned emphysema from all the cigarettes I've sucked down over the years. You know your father had a heart ailment, too, and you should be particularly attentive to your prescribed diet and exercise programs.

End of sermon. I'll stop badgering you now.

Oh, how often I think of you, my Rose, and hope you are happily situated. It sounds like your career at State continues to flourish, and it eases my mind knowing your wonderful kids look after you. But, I'm concerned that they have all moved so far from you. From the sounds of it, however, you are not without good friends to keep you company.

You must plan a trip to Colorado for a visit, or, as you suggest, perhaps I can come to California. It seems, however, that our lives are burdened with demands. It's only with my unfettered devotion and love for you that I've managed to devote these few moments to write. My bags are packed and I must move quickly to make a flight for Barbados, where I am to sail on a National Geographic expedition. Avast, lubber! I'm all a-tingle at the prospect of writing a four-month series for NG, more because I'll be free of deadlines and Wally Sachs phone calls. I'm going to have plenty of sea time to sit and watch the water flow by.

But, since airplanes wait for no man, I must press on with the more important business at hand. First, it is with mixed emotions that I must report the death of my sister Lyla. I learned of her passing last summer in New York to an overdose of tranquilizers and alcohol. The news reached me via Mary. She heard from one of Lyla's colleagues, who recalled Lyla once mentioning her relationship to the well-known pianist. It was like Lyla to have so disembodied herself from her family that it took the concern of a complete stranger to get word to us.

Mary could only find out that Lyla suffered chemical addiction for many years, and was despondent over a recent series of career and business failures, coupled with the deaths of several friends in the World Trade Center disaster. God, Rosie, we are all cut from the same cloth of this terrible disease. I only wonder now, if Lyla had been closer to us, might we have helped her?

If this news had come years ago, it would have barely warranted my attention; but if you remember, she once contacted me with an odd and moving truce. Because of that, I was sincerely overcome with sadness. Perhaps if Lyla and I could have further regained some form of contact, I might have recognized this demon that brutally stalks my family. My conscience rests, but it does not lessen my grief. Our paths were clearly defined. I truly hope Lyla is with God.

Brother Jonathan has not had an easy go either, but I am happy to say he is at last finding his niche. I fear my shadow darkened Jon's path over the years, for he recently confided in a personal conversation his frustration and self-imposed feeling of inferiority dwelling in the wake of a brother who has enjoyed considerable good fortune. This revelation astonished me. I thought my own strife and indiscretion didn't create an image that anyone might care to emulate. With a yardstick anyone might measure the gross disparity between my successes and failures, but Jon failed to realize that my success did not come without a price. He fancied himself a writer, yet he was critically measured by the standard set for me. If that wasn't enough, the sad fact is that Jon has no propensity for writing.

I was no help, for I blindly encouraged him, when in fact I knew he was not built for the same road. The sad revelation came during an aborted film project in Brazil, which nearly cost us our love and friendship. But I believe that experience, painful as it was, was the tonic for Jon to realize he has other stars to chase. When the dust settled, we kissed and made up.

Jon is a businessman, not an artist, and his negotiating skills are formidable. He is molding a career in the same light as Wally Sachs. Jon represents several local actors and writers, and is considering a partnership with Wally. Sachs is looking for someone to pamper his substantial clientele when he retires, and Jon just might fit the bill. If he can sell my ideas, he can sell anything. Even as late as yesterday, I watched Jon blanch when I told him about my latest epic; a story about a woman who overthrows a small African government and imposes a law which requires all the third-world natives to dye their hair red.

On to the only sane member of the family: Mary. She and Justin continue to do well in Toronto. She accosts me several times a year to instruct on a full-time basis, but I simply have no desire to teach. I do visit the academy once per semester and dazzle her young writing students with my insanity, but I don't want to tie myself to an academic schedule.

Mary insists I consider a current proposal from my publisher to gather all of my short stories and notebooks for publication in a single text. I'm conducting a formidable self-debate regarding what purpose anyone might have in peeping into my private thoughts, however. For biographical purposes, I'm told my journal notes and short tales would make for an interesting anthology, but I shudder at the thought of serious English students perusing the embarrassing entries I've written over the years. But, while digging through these archives, I've had a good laugh at my youthful innocence; back to the days when I first fell in love with you; when I discovered my penis; and the days I haunted mortuaries...

I just don't understand what a scholar would find interesting about a batty drunk who wanders the pages of his tired old journal. They would ultimately discover that there is no genius lurking there; just a fellow who found his fantasies more interesting than reality. Lies are more fascinating than the truth.

But I do not lie when it comes to you, Rosie, and I feel a fresh breath of life whenever I hear from you. Perhaps we can visit sometime this year. I hope to find more leisure time since I've decided to retire from screenwriting. Sachs inundates me with hundreds of lucrative film offers, but this fifty-plus year life is beginning to tax my health. I want to write novels, and I want to scribble at a less frantic pace. The screenplays have always been to me a lark, but they are more a burden as of late. Hollywood was never truly for me. It's a nasty web of spiders who trap and sting you until dead.

But, listen to me. It is time I stop this ego-stroking so I might wish you a merry holiday. I love you, Rosie. That never changes. Obey your doctors!

As Always,
Me

2003

July 22, 2003

I slept on the veranda last night in the cool, crisp air. The silence was clean, save the gentle rustling of the wind through the mountain pines. Far away from the city lights, the dark summer sky is a magnificent symphony of diamonds. On the wave of smooth breezes, the entire sphere of time was at my command, each sight and sound belonging entirely to me. Sometimes it is purely a pleasure to be alive.

I spent the morning reading an old book I dug from the shelf of my library, and I came across the words of Thomas Fuller. I never fail to be awed when reaching into the cosmos and pulling from it the thoughts of someone who has long since left the earth. It's man's only shot at immortality.

Fuller was a charming man, a religious soul with a delightful sense of humor, but these words touched me with his deep insight to the heart:

> *"It is best to be with those in time*
> we hope to be with in eternity."

Indeed. The old Englishman's spirit must have guided me to his words on this day when my thoughts are on Marie Rose. It so moved me that I was compelled to telephone Rosie, but alas, there was no answer.

I depart for the Florida Keys tomorrow. Did I pack my snorkel? I may have the urge to write underwater. If I had reached Rosie, I would have invited her to join me. Thoughts of her dominate me as of late. I feel her presence in my heart, and am teased by strange thoughts of how the future might hold reason to reunite us.

No matter where she goes, she is never gone...

December 22, 2003

Dear Marie Rose,

Damn! Again, Damn!

You heard those words over the phone, I know, but I must say them again: Damn! I simply did not vent all of my anger with you when I called moments ago, so bear with me. You know my feelings for you! I realize I could not be reached at home last summer when you fell ill, but I am never out of touch with Jonathan and Wally Sachs. They would have immediately informed me you were in the hospital, and I would have been by your side in hours. I guess Mary is right, as she has forever badgered me to get a cell phone, but you know me and electronics . . . I just never could get used to carrying one of those damned things around, receiving production updates and book-signing reminders from Sachs while sitting on the toilet.

But, god dammit, it pains me to think you spent that time alone.

I might be on a plane right now if you hadn't sounded well on the phone. Some Christmas greeting you gave me: "I had a 'little heart attack' last summer." This was not a hangnail, you know! Or, do I have to remind you of a time back in the dark ages when I was in a hospital and you were six thousand miles away?

I promise you haven't yet heard the last of this. I'm still considering cancellation of plans for Toronto so I might come out there to really let you have it.

You know what I meant...

As Always,
Me
P.S. Merry Damned Christmas

2004

February 8, 2004

How good I am at self-inflicted wounds, Journal. I sit here high over the Pacific en route to paradise, but a one-day stop in San Francisco just upended my heart.

There's no excuse for my masochism. This damned schedule Jon has me running left me with little time to realize I'd be stopping in California on my way to Hawaii. Making due with a one-day stop to speak at USF, I at least had some time to see Marie Rose. I had to see for myself if she is feeling as well as she claims. But this has consequently left me in a quandary. If I had paid attention to my schedule, I could have called ahead; instead, I dropped in and surprised her. Her marvelous eyes were aglow when I wandered into her office. She was disappointed that I did not give her some advance notice when I suggested she drop everything and go with me to this blasted lecture at the University of Hawaii. She would have gone, but she had commitments impossible to cancel this late.

Instead, we just dined together, and I hobbled on my arthritic knee back to my hotel to pace the floor all night, occasionally dousing my stupidity in a cold shower! Blast my hormones for not having the courtesy of growing old with the rest of me!

May 14, 2004

Dear Marie Rose,

It is all arranged! I don't know how I can stand these next two weeks awaiting your visit! It has turned me into a scatterbrain and made me miss a deadline, which gave my publisher and Jonathan reason to want me dead...

But, your airline reservation is confirmed! I so look forward to the day you and I will dance together at our high school reunion; we shall feel like we're seventeen again! Forty years, can you imagine? Our old friends will be so terribly decrepit, and I cannot wait to see a floor full of sixty-year-olds wriggling around to The Beach Boys, The Animals, The Rolling Stones...

I don't walk well anymore, but on that night I will toss my cane aside and boogie down, I assure you! (I'm told there will be ambulances standing by.)

Thank God that you and I won't look any different, for I'll again be the fellow with the most beautiful girl in school! Don't forget to pack your smile, Rosie.

As Always,
Me

June 21, 2004

Loneliness. It is gone.

I'm looking upon a Sunday sky and remembering the most wonderful time of my life. The house is empty, but the sweet smell of Rosie remains. We shared this home, and our hearts. How wonderful it was to have her in this place where we shared five days remembering all the compassion and love that traversed forty-two years of true friendship.

Together we journeyed back into time at our school reunion, where we communed with old hearts and minds. It was a lovely party, but a bittersweet one indeed. Time has treated us unequally, and yet, within the souls of those people - children of the '60s - there remains the naive heart of gold, the quietly neurotic dedication to change whatever is deemed wrong, and the bold urge to be different. What a strange generation we are - we Baby Boomers...

As if entering a time warp, I found my two best friends, Marc Komac and Steven Joel, whose life paths strangely crossed and landed at opposite ends of the spectrum. Steven, who wasn't expected to live to see a forty-year reunion, is a whole man. He was a successful chemical engineer by trade, retired now, and still happily in love with the woman who brought him back to The World. He's still in his wheelchair, and his health is growing frail, but his mind is complete. Marc, on the other hand, looked physically and mentally beaten and drawn from family tragedies and a frantic life in the corporate fast lane. Poor Kathy is in a psychiatric hospital, having never recovered from the death of their daughter.

Indeed, we were the 'Me Generation' of change, but instead of changing an immovable world, we only changed ourselves. In our lust for independence of thought, we blindly followed each passing fad without anchoring ourselves to the ground. As a generation, we've made a shambles of the institution of marriage, created a world of gun-toting children, given rise to an uncontrollable drug culture, and padded the pockets of the psychiatric profession...

We've always demanded everything without expecting to pay for it, and when some of us finally attained our goals, we realized there was very little difference between the darkness and the light.

Indeed. I discovered the true value of my accomplishments when one classmate, once she finally remembered who I was, said: "My God, I thought you were dead!"

She almost sounded disappointed.

I must confess I have physically wilted to time, but Rosie is unchanged. One might have never known she belonged to this crowd of wrinkled ex-hippies, yippies, yuppies et al. Her loving sparkle remains.

I sound like a schoolboy in love. Was I ever not?

And now for the big news. Journal, I asked Rosie to be my wife.

I hope I am not premature with my proposal in light of Gary's death, but Rosie has been alone for six years now. Is it not our right to seek happiness? We still have many years ahead. I don't wish to conclude this life by myself, and I know, in my heart, only Rosie can fill the void. Am I wrong to assume she might care to spend the remainder of her years in my company? She hasn't been well in the last few years, and perhaps it's time I take care of her for a change.

"Yes," was her answer. "But I need some time to help me separate myself from my grieving for Gary."

We parted in love. She asked that we not correspond this summer while she ponders our new life. Roads don't often follow the same path to mutually arrive at the same destination. I've yet another endless summer to long for Rosie, as it seems my life is turning its full circle. But, I have a new novel to write, and with it new hope.

I love her, Journal, and would sacrifice all I have now just to spend another moment with her. God bless her. God bless Me...

September 4, 2004

Dear Marie Rose,

A long summer without you. This is to let you know I'm back in Colorado.

I spent the summer at Mary and Justin's cabin by Lake Ontario, where I hammered out the first draft of my new work. I thought I'd feel rested after spending time in such serene environs, but my mind put in a great deal of overtime on other subjects. Perhaps we should talk?

October 7, 2004

Dear Marie Rose,

Good lord, it's October! How the time flies. Received a handsome advance for my latest project. It's begging to be spent on a Christmas honeymoon. Interested?

November 12, 2004

Dear Marie Rose,

I cannot help my confusion over your continued silence, Rosie. Might you phone? I confess I've tried to call several times without success. If it is more time you need, I understand, but may I have a word from you?

November 22, 2004

Dear Sir,

This is a very difficult letter to write to you, but I must inform you of the death of my stepmother, Marie Tobias. I'm sorry to send word in this way, and I'm equally saddened to be so late in finally reaching you with the news. Naturally, we were shocked at Mom's passing, and we were lost in the endless legal and emotional crisis that followed. Mom wasn't the best at keeping records, and I couldn't find your address or phone number. I finally tracked you down after several frustrating attempts to find you through publishers, who gave no information, and your former agent, who retired and left no forwarding address. The New York Times literary critic finally gave me your box number, and it is through this that I hope my letter reaches you.

Mom passed away in her sleep on July 18. Because my brother, sister, and myself all live outside of California now, it was several days before she was discovered. But her doctor assured us that the end was swift. Her heart simply gave out.

Mom spoke of you often, and the entire family looked forward to your holiday greetings from far away places. I myself have always admired your work, and I know Mom was quite proud of you and loved you very much. She always referred to you as her dearest friend. She was a wonderful and loving mother, and she and my father spent the best years of their lives together. I don't think my dad was ever any happier in his life than when he met Marie. He also thought of you as an important extension of Marie, who obviously was an inspiration for many of your novels.

I've enclosed three unopened letters from you, which were found among the stacks of mail that came after she died. They unfortunately were misplaced in the shuffle during this difficult time of sorting out her personal effects. I also included an old piece of paper that was in her hand when she was found. As you can see, it is dated 1962, and I suspect, because you knew her then, you might know what it is. I recognize Mom's handwriting at the bottom, which says:

"Byron, your John Alden, and you, my Shakespeare." We think she may have written it just before she died. I thought you might know its significance and would like to have it.

Again, I'm sorry for being so slow in reaching you. Please accept my condolences. We all loved her very much and will miss her.

Sincerely,
James Tobias

"...if we go anywhere we'll go together
to meet what happens, maybe we'll be better off
and blither, and learn something,
May-be it is yourself now
really ushering me
to the true songs (who knows?)..."

- Walt Whitman

December 16, 2004

Dear Marie Rose,

Once upon a time...

A young man saw in the spring of life a vision so lovely that his eyes would never know the sight of anything more pristine. He loved her 'till the very end of time.

I still smell your fragrance, Rosie. I still see your eyes sparkling in the night sky. I still feel your heart beating next to mine, as it did a million years ago when we pursued the dreams that would never come true. The world was ours then, but we changed; we were nothing more than specks of sand on a vast beach.

We'll not be remembered.

Eventually, we'll be mere words on a yellowed page, ravaged by the passage of time. But you will remain with me, My Rose. For, in this wasteland, there forever springs hope for love, the only true essence of humanity. And in love, none is the same twice over. The first and last love, for me, was sweetest of all.

If you are somewhere beyond, I'll see you again. It's the bitterest, but sweetest taste of life to not know what lies beyond the physical cord to which we cling. To live forever, or to sleep, it is the wonderful tragedy of existence.

You are my truest mate, my breath, my heart and soul. Although worlds apart, you were always in me. I am grateful.

Where do we end? Who knows? Who, indeed. For some, life ends unexpectedly, and for others, it passes precisely. I love you, My Rose. God, how I do...

As Always...

PREFACE

When honored by the request to preface this anthology of my beloved brother's notebooks, letters, short stories, and his last unfinished novel, I at first felt compelled to attempt an all-inclusive definition of his genius. Certainly, it's not unreasonable for an outsider to expect that I could, but to fully diagnose the layers of cognition in my brother's work is impossible without him here to explain. His fiction was enigmatic until he chose to define it, but his life was easily understood, because its definition was clear. As close as we were, I suspect I actually know very little about the writer, but I was on very intimate terms with the person.

As he insisted, he was merely human - an artist, a sad and lonely wanderer bedeviled by the 'ghosts' who took residence in his imaginative and fertile mind. The only difference from him and Everyman is that he embraced rather than feared those ghosts, and he gave them life in his perplexing stories. The fine line separating fact from fiction for my brother was as thin as a telescope's cross hair. His focus was frighteningly precise, and his writing a haunting and satiric reflection of reality that we as readers could only understand when he wanted us to.

He never thought himself a literary man, and was never commercially motivated to write his eccentric tales. But at the same time he enjoyed the financial success of his craft and generously shared it with those who believed in him. He did not concern himself with the few critics who considered him an unworthy hybrid: a philosopher of telling insight perched over the world upon a lonely fence post, and a commercially popular author/humorist, who often exploited the very art he created. He left his favorable critics frustrated, shrugging off their vision of a deep-seated genius toiling to define the human character. He himself viewed his work as simple storytelling laced with fantasy and folly. Who's to know if his work was written to flippantly point at the world with a laugh, or to sadly acknowledge it with a tear?

Once, in a letter to me, he expressed his confusion over a

pointed critical essay in Atlantic Monthly, which claimed he had little empathy for the symbolic tragedy of Orsen, the esoteric character in his bestseller Mr. Chunks:

"Explain it to me if you can, Mary," he said. "They infer a sterile, philosophical edge to a man I thought was someone who merely couldn't control his own appetite for the world. I feel very much like Orsen - if it's lust for carrot sticks, or lust for happiness, we are still gluttons with little conscience. Higher consciousness means nothing to the beaten man in the gutter with an empty belly; the loveless woman in her room with an empty heart; or the unborn child in the womb with an empty soul..."

His life was his work, and his work, his life. He was the product of a unique generation of change; a people dedicated to revolution that never came. They were caught between their passion for independence and the history of proven conventionality. He walked a tightrope and precariously teetered between the two. His work reflected the paradox. Evidence of this is the long list of best-selling, commercially oriented works such as African Hairline, Fixing Trees, and the powerful Vietnam War epic, Children of Duty. In stark contrast are the more literary pieces that left English scholars in a quandary: Strange Potions, Lido, Mr. Chunks, Moonpie, Woman's Tear, and the highly acclaimed Excerpts.

Literary critics disagree where the life given to these tales originated, and arguments persist that most of his fiction was a manifestation of his often troubled life. Too much has been made, however, of his terrible and dark depressive years. He was never comfortable with the theory that his Vietnam post-stress illness and his battle with alcoholism and drug addiction served as the catalyst that colored his work. He never believed his human weaknesses were the seeds of his art, and he deeply resented speculation that he discovered his muse while institutionalized for his addictions.

He once said, "Magic is the only thing that is real. The magician is the illusion." Or, to quote his favorite line during literary seminars when students pressed him to relate his life to his fiction, he jokingly chided: "Pay no attention to the man behind the curtain..."

Indeed, in my judgment, my brother wrote not to appease his legal obligations or the demands of his public - he wrote entirely to suit himself. The rest of us just looked over his shoulder. This was displayed by his dramatic cessation of writing in November 2004, after he learned of the death the previous July of his lifetime friend Marie Rose Robbins-Tobias. Her death had a profound effect on him both physically and spiritually, and his health plummeted in the months to come. His own untimely death eighteen months later will undoubtedly be the subject of endless speculation as to cause. Persistent critics insist it was suicide, but there is no corroborating pathological evidence; in fact, the cause of his death remains a mystery. Those who maintain he died of a broken heart say it was love that breathed life into him, and when it passed, he followed. Certainly, however, time will embellish the legend of the discovery of his body in a mountain meadow, in his hand the Byron passage first found in the hands of Marie Rose when she passed away.

We are grateful to the executors of the estate of Marie Rose Tobias for providing us with a lifetime of my brother's letters to her, and for giving us permission to include them in this anthology. His mind was dedicated to his muse, but his passion was a product of his unbridled heart.

If only to serve my loving memory of him, I declare he shall indeed live forever with 'Rosie,' and all the 'ghosts' who wandered his mind. He conquered his greatest fear of dying in obscurity, his eternalness forever rising from the words he wrote. He was a solitary man on this earth, but I am left to wonder in his passing if he found the eternity he sought.

I, for one, believe his infectious laugh will forever haunt the halls of scholars, and his words will perplex many generations to come as he playfully ducks behind the curtain.

He was, as always...

Mary Michael
Toronto, Ontario 2007

Letters to a Rose

Consider These
Book Club Discussion Points for *Letters to a Rose*

> *Letters to a Rose* has numerous thematic elements that slowly tie together as the story progresses. Identify and discuss how these elements relate to each other.

> Rosie and the Narrator are members of the baby boomer "Me Generation," who grow up in the turbulent 1960's. How do the times relate to their basic ambitions and need to grow as individuals?

> Discuss and suggest reasons why the author chooses not to give the Narrator a name, other than his army nickname, 'Shakespeare'.

> Discuss the reasons why the majority of *Letters to a Rose* covers the Narrator's struggles to succeed as a writer, while devoting a much smaller portion to his phenomenal success.

> *Letters to a Rose* is written from the first-person narrative point of view. Discuss how much the reader can trust what the Narrator is saying is factual and not self indulgent fiction, and why you believe he can or cannot be relied upon to give you a true account of his life.

> Discuss the merits of first-person narration versus third-person narration and how these distinctions apply to *Letters to a Rose*.

> Regarding their Vietnam War experiences, discuss the Narrator and the men in the VA hospital, and compare and contrast their differences and similarities.

Book Club Discussion Points for *Letters to a Rose*

> Discuss the many changes that take place over the years in the Narrator's personality and general world view.

> Some characters in the story tend to come and go, while others, primarily Rosie, remain a constant throughout the Narrator's life. Discuss some of the characters who have a significant influence on the Narrator.

> *Letters to a Rose* treads carefully into the controversial subject of abortion, and how it affected Rosie and the Narrator. Discuss why the author chooses to focus primarily on the Narrator's point of view regarding the abortion, while only briefly touching on Rosie's experience.

> The Narrator seemingly passes through the abortion experience quickly with little regard to the consequences he later suffers. Discuss the Narrator's numerous experiences that eventually lead him to a crisis regarding the abortion, and how he eventually reconciles his grief and guilt.

> At a few points in the Narrator's life, he has an obvious short window of opportunity to move to California and reunite with Rosie, but he doesn't act. Explore the basic nature of his personality and speculate why he resists.

> Suggest reasons why the author makes the unusual choice to end the story on a sad note, rather than allowing the Narrator and Rosie to 'ride off into the sunset' together.

www.ingramcontent.com/pod-product-compliance
Lightning Source LLC
LaVergne TN
LVHW020653110826
845149LV00012B/1976